THE
SEVENTH
SISTER

THE SEVENTH SISTER

EYE OF PANDORA PUBLISHING
139 Randolph Circle
Troy, VA 22974

Dedicated to Caitlin, Lily and David

THE SEVENTH SISTER
Table of Contents

CHAPTER I
YURAH

Her feet were bare in the cold water. The fish beneath her studied her pale toes. The girl held still, not daring to breathe, waiting for him to come. But she had forgotten the bright one who silently rose in the pale sky and as its brilliant face burst over the trees a shaft of light caught the creature's eye. With an arrogant flip of the tail, the fish flowed downward with the current. Stepping carefully upon the shifting rock the girl moved to follow. The river caught the hem of her skirt in his cold fingers and teased her with his freedom. This was time that drew her to him.

It was in these first fragile rays of morning that minute lights would rise above the rushing riverbed. The girl anxiously studied the exquisite globes as distant lands began to take shape. Still ponds and moors glided by her. Ordered fields of corn and wheat lie alongside thick woods. Lush meadows, filled with birds, hummed in faraway realms. All that was great and small surged along the Riverman's rolling path. Contained within the delicate spheres were kingdoms and cottages, plain homesteads and gleaming fortresses. Bright cities streamed with banners and lights. Narrow streets were crowded with mothers and children, fathers and sons, but what delighted her most was the parade of creatures. Fur and claw, skin and scale, wing and fin, all followed the path of the churning river. The girl reached out to touch the transparent images, but the lights passed through her fingers as if she did not exist at all. Above her the sky was growing brighter and soon the glowing lights had faded away, leaving her alone with the rushing river. Thrashing and complaining the Riverman ran through the glen, down the stony bed, and between the gray cliffs. Willow wands, with their golden tips, kissed his icy run and just beyond the giant oaks rustled in the clean breeze. The coloring leaves were changing the morning light as the enchanted bargain between sun and leaf went about its silent affairs. An elder oak called out in his quiet way. Often, he had seen the girl who wandered with her feet in the water. Yurah gasped aloud when the sending was suddenly before her.

1

His gray legs were shapely and the sun fell from his shoulders making his garment a living cloak of light.   He wanted her attention and he spoke clearly,

"Take what is given child.
And drink of streams, unseen,
Yours is the fate to listen,
To the heart of visions dreams.
Through every spiraling heaven
A voice does tremble down
In bone, in sea, in leaf, in land,
The living song surrounds,
By the passing of the moments,
Through the passing of the days
The light is meant for growing
So it is to know the way.

The gentle words were carried off by the wind as the sending returned to the soil and sun. She stood amidst the racing river, allowing his message to fill her like a draught of cool water. The sun above bathed the land in its autumn glow. Mosses cast off their dampness while the last of the Riverman's lights moved downstream. She looked after them and wondered.

"Yurah!" Like a breaking glass the sound spilled into her thoughts, "Yurah! Ho, sister! Where are you?"

Yurah's cloak was speckled with glistening bits of the water and her hair hung wet about her shoulders. She was chilled by the river's rough caress. He was calling her name, filling her with the burden of his never-ending flight, but she pulled herself away from his jealous voice and answered her sister.

"I am here, Raeyn." she called, looking back toward the gray cliffs. "Here with the Riverman." She felt his current quicken. The river had intentions of his own. Raeyn stood upon the edge of the forest path. Her face stretched into a smile when she realized the water teased her sister. She laughed aloud, breaking the spell the Riverman had woven through the glade.

"He calls to you to him only because you grow." Raeyn answered the question that was forming in her mind. "You are coming into your own, Yurah."

It appeared to Yurah that Raeyn kept a secret and she found herself vexed with her sister who stood dry upon the shore. Raeyn was wearing her hunting gear. Her tunic and boots shared the colors of the pale river froth. A bow hung over her shoulder and an anlace rested at her side. Around her golden hair she wore a circlet of silver and under it her dark brown eyes danced with mischief. Raeyn was the fourth daughter of Iao, while Yurah was the seventh child. It seemed however long her life might be she would never attain the skills of her elder sister. Years before Raeyn had journeyed into the wilderlands of Raldabon and, in that time of solitude, she learned the voice of the forest. It was her wisdom of wood that gave Raeyn her uniqueness among the seven sisters and Yurah knew the Riverman would never take such liberties with her. The river's breath brushed against her cheek. Faintly, the unseen voice lured her with a fragment of a tale, a bit of story she must complete and as she fretted his mood grew sullen. His force surrounded her like a fresh skin, and an unknown fear moved through her gut. The jolt made her shudder.

"Be aware of the Riverman, Yurah." her sister called. "He is harsh for he only understands the most ancient of laws. But remember little sister, there is no reason to fear him. No water can oppose your will." then she smiled widely. "Come now. Our father has called us home."

Yurah gathered her wet skirts and as she walked the river's cold hands pulled at her hem. He spoke of what lie beyond the boundaries of her father's house. She heard him complain as she moved against his voice and, when she stepped from the water's edge, she was agitated.

For many long moments they watched the river tumble by. Fish jumped from his white caps. Birds dived to capture insects that walked upon his quivering surface. Snakes slithered from his banks and the trees drank freely. Yurah's frustrations left her as she listened to the roar of the water.

"I knew I would find you here Yurah." said Raeyn finally.

"He was in my dreams again this morning, insisting I meet him at sunrise," she sighed, "But I do not understand it Raeyn. Why does he call to me in the night? And what are these lights he carries within him under the new dawn? "

"They are sparks of life moving from one place to another." Raeyn said.

"Where do they go?" asked Yurah, confused by the answer.

"They go with the Riverman as he makes his way to the Endless Sea."

Yurah knit her brow. "The Endless Sea? What sort of place is this?"

"It is the Riverman's destination. There he empties what he has gathered back into arms of his Four Fathers. It is from this place the lights move ever onward and outward."

"Into the sea?"

"In a sense. The Endless Sea is a place of many layers. Time there is not as we know it. The waters of the Cosmic Dark hold all possibilities. "

"Have you ever been there Raeyn, the Endless Sea?"

"When I returned home from my years in the wilderlands, Father and I journeyed to the edge of the Riverman's realm. It is most peculiar, the border of earth and sky."

"The Riverman's lights are most peculiar as well." Yurah nodded thoughtfully. "They are filled with beasts and cities, mountains and seas, but when I try to touch them they pass through my fingers as if I do not exist at all. How is it that all these things are contained in so fragile a shell?"

"It is light that holds all things." came the gentle reply.

"But how are they there and where do they dwell, the lives within the lights?"

"They are here, held within the flowing waters, and they are at the place that they are fated to be."

"Where they are fated to be?" Yurah asked, but her questions had begun to sound clumsy. Instead of perfect realms of lovely things, images of empty dark and vast spaces touched her. "Is it their fate to dwell within in the Endless Sea?" she said, her fear seeking refuge in her sister's eyes. "Is this why he calls me to him? Is this what shall happen to me, Raeyn?"

The sounds of the forest filled the air. Insects buzzed in distant trees, birds quarreled and the Riverman whispered her name. The wind stirred the drying leaves and, behind every sound, the river waited.

Raeyn chose her words carefully, "Creation grows each moment. The path from our father's house may lead anywhere."

"Anywhere? Anywhere within the Endless Sea?"

Raeyn did not answer but gazed up into the silent sun shining over the edges of the gray cliffs.

"Do you know that star Yurah?"

"Yes. Of course I know it. That star is our brother sun. Taygeth is its name. It is the twin of our realm."

"As we speak, it is watching every motion upon our world. Yes and Taygeth can be quite persuasive this time of year for now is the season which brings forth the fruit of the years toil. The wizard, Doxomedon stewards the sun." Raeyn replied.

"I have met him, Doxomedon visits father each year during the midsummer moon." Yurah answered thoughtfully, remembering the long stern face of the wizard.

"Doxomedon cares for the lives of those that dwell upon Taygeth just as father cares for the lives of Raldabon." continued Raeyn. "Did

4

you know that Doxomedon is aided by a consort?"

"I know her name is Derdekea. And I know she is a Star-Gazer," Yurah nodded, "but I have yet to meet her. And I do not understand why." Yurah answered looking to the sky.

"There are none more skillful in reading the pathways of the far heavens than Derdekea but the realm of Doxomedon and Derdekea is quite different from our world." then Raeyn replied as she stared into the sun. "It is a difficult thing to understand. It is difficult because expressions of Life are as infinite as the space between the endless stars. In other words, the beings of Taygeth are quite unlike ourselves. They are rarely solid, little upon Taygeth is at all like the Raldabon. Its trees, nor creatures, nor firm ground exist in the same moments of time as do we. In fact, most often the lives of Taygeth exist as waves of heat. The Muses of Doxomedon's realm are such beings."

Yurah nodded her head. "Ah yes, the Muses, Sothis has told me a little of them in our lessons together. She has said they are able to travel upon the beams of star-light."

"And upon waves of breath, such is the nature of Doxomedon's realm." Raeyn added.

"Sothis also said the Muses bring gifts to those they favor but she would not tell me how and she would not tell me why."

"The Muses have many gifts to give Yurah?"

"Then please tell me Raeyn. It appears to me that this day is ripe for me to finally know it."

Raeyn laughed, as she began to explain. "They are five in number and, if they are so inclined, they will inspire those who ask. It is said; that happy is the one that the Muses love."

"Inspire? What do you mean?" Yurah said, her eyes growing a bit wider. "What do they do and how do they do it? Have you ever seen them?"

"One question at a time, please Yurah."

Yurah wrinkled her brow, "All right then, the most important one first. Have you ever seen them?"

"No, but I know they are there." Raeyn smiled, "The Muses are as mysterious as the heart of the wind."

"But if you have never seen them then how do you know if they are real?"

"Every poet and every artist comes to know them."

"But where would you know to look for them?"

"I suppose you might look for them anywhere."

"But how would I know where to look?' Yurah insisted.

Well I suppose that the gentle touch of a starry night might be a good place to begin."

"But then how would I know if it were really the Muses? "What are their names, or do they even have names?"

"Oh course they have names Yurah. All things have a name, a name that makes all what they are."

"Then please tell me. If I am to understand the Muses, it seems this something that I must know."

Raeyn paused and then smiled at her little sister. "The first weaves the chorus of life." she explained patiently. "She is called Euterpe."

"Euterpe, so you say Raeyn, but how would I know if it were really her if she chanced to come to me?"

"You would understand her voice in the quiet of your thoughts. Her rhythms are the heartbeat of all things. String and pipe are her voice. She can be found on the calling wind."

"Euterpe." Yurah repeated slowly, remembering the countless songs the wind could carry.

"I would expect someday you will hear her call your name."

Yurah grew quiet, turning the Muse's name over in her mind, wondering what her voice might truly sound like and she imagined herself standing in the sun with a soft wind whispering secrets all around her and after a long moment she asked, "What is the name of the second muse Raeyn?"

"Calliope. She is a storyteller, a spinner of tales upon the warm summer nights and the keeper of secrets in deep winter dreams. She is beauty as she is sadness. Calliope is the giver of words to Euterpe's songs."

"She is a poet then?"

"It is said she whispers what lies in the heart."

"And there are so many things which lie in the heart," Yurah replied and the leaves above them rustled in answer. The morning light danced over her hands and she could hear the old oak whispering softly.

"Please tell me of the others." she said as the sound faded away. "What of the third?"

'Tersicyre is the third muse," replied Raeyn, brushing a strand of wet hair away from Yurah's clear face, "Hers is the realm of dance. In her, the breaking and rejoining becomes a seamless motion. She is all, and she is separate. This is why Tersicyre is ever moving with the fourth muse, Thalia Melpome."

"Thalia Melpome. That is a beautiful name."

"Aye, and so is she. The fourth muse is the comfort of laughter and the grimness of tragedy. She will touch all with her whispers of joy and shards of pain.'

'Each in their way, the Muses inspire all they touch. But it is the last muse, the fifth, who holds all things. All song, all motion, all grief and joy are under her domain. The gifts she carries are tempered by the knowledge of what has gone before. The Fifth Muse holds the lyre and stands with the Sun. She goes by many names and not the least of which is Mnymosyne."

"Mnymosyne, such an odd name."

"There are many meanings held in a name. Mnymosyne is the memory of what has come before and the knowing of what will come be."

"Then she must be a Fate Reader." Yurah replied.

'Oh not exactly, what Mnymosyne brings is quite different from fate. The far memory is her realm. The Muses are beauty, the art of creation, and the reason for toil. They seek to inspire the life that struggles to understand." Then Raeyn fell silent looking steadily to the glowing sun and when spoke again she asked her sister an odd question. "Do you know how our world, Raldabon, appears to those who dwell upon the star of Derdekea and Doxomedon?"

"Father has often called Taygeth, the Twin."

"And it is so. We are two forces forever bound and, while alike, we upon Raldabon are not the same as our perfect imagining, Taygeth."

Yurah looked to the bright light hanging the heaven. "I suppose I had considered Taygeth as just another star-sun, like all the thousands of other twinkling lights that glitter in the black sky."

"And it is true Yurah, our starry home, and our twin, Taygeth, and all the other twinkling lights are but passing grounds to other worlds." replied Raeyn. "It is the intelligent light that makes it so."

"Intelligent light?"

"Yes. The light is a conscience force. It is the means by which time passes and the essence of all that exists is contained within it."

"Even the light within the Riverman's glowing orbs?"

"Light is the true substance of all that is," she answered, "be it the flesh of beasts, or the souls of men, the inspirations of a muse, or the song of the elementals which flow through our father's land.   The light is the connection between the nature and fate."

Yurah pulled her brow into a knot of concern. "Nature is what is seen and what is touched. But fate," she continued broodingly, "that is a different thing entirely. Fate I can not hold in my hand and some part of it frightens me terribly."

Raeyn smiled, "I know you have heard the tale of the three Fates who live within core of every burning star."

"Of course I have. All children know it. The story goes that it is the youngest which spins the life into being as the middle sister weaves the path ahead and so it goes, until the eldest cuts the bond between body and time."

"And what happens then, little sister?"

Yurah did not answer straight away and so her sister explained.

"When the connection between body and time is severed, the point when corporeal death does come, the clear memory of any lifetime is lost but that is not the end Yurah. The substance the sisters have created has not been undone. The stuff of Fate can move beyond and between lives. Fate can be more likened to a door, a gate that stands between one life and the next. It has one side and it has another."

The Riverman roared in agreement and a blustery wind blew through Yurah's damp clothes.

'The Riverman feels the rhythms of the fate-filled stars." Raeyn said, sensing his fickle mood turn. "It is their force which thickens and thins him. He remembers their voices and soon he will not be contained." and as her voice trailed away, a thick wind surrounded them. Yurah took her sister's hand.

A cold mist was spreading quickly over the hillsides. Yurah shuddered as the heavy breeze swept through the forest. Suddenly the tempest was full upon them, whipping their clothes and stinging their skin, and the Riverman threw his wild arms upward to join her. He called out Yurah's name as he joined the wind and the jealous motion pulled her breath away. She saw herself as a heavy stone, an unwilling bearer of burdens unseen, and around her the wild airs whirled.

"I am afraid, Raeyn." she gasped as the storm thrashed around them, "The river grows too wild. He has spoken my name and I fear him. I am small and he is ancient and cruel. He is pulling me away from here. Surely I shall be crushed by such a force."

"Do not fear Yurah." her sister gently replied. "It is true what the oak told you. The day is new and its light is meant for growing. And do not forget Yurah, no water can oppose your will." and as Raeyn spoke, the sound of the wailing wind and screaming river faded. The torrent moved through the gray cliffs, pulling the damp fog onward to the sea. Her uncertainties vanished as the light of Taygeth broke through the clouds once more. The sisters turned away from the wild Riverman and began to walk along the path to their father's house.

CHAPTER II
THE HOUSE OF IAO

The shadows were telling secrets to the trees as the girls made their way home. The storm had passed. Its wind and water now toiled far away. Raeyn kept a quick pace and Yurah hurried to keep up. Graying leaves covered the faint path. Along their tattered edges fern and fungus thrived. Ahead a group of noisy blackbirds were settling in the branches of an old cypress. Yurah slipped her thoughts behind their dark eyes to sense the forest through the minds of the fidgety creatures. Unfamiliar and odd, the shadows were suddenly sharpened by the colorless world. The shifting light carried with it the hints of danger and promises of hidden harbors. A breath of air swept through the branches. The wind was calling them together. Their thoughts had turned toward other concerns and the sight of a gray wood swirled beneath her. She caught her breath remembering she looked through the eyes of the birds. Colors returned and she realized that Raeyn was leaving her behind.

"I must hurry," she told herself as another sound caught her attention. A she-badger was lumbering through the bracken but the beast had no interest in the girl as pressing thoughts of winter clouded her mind. Yurah watched until the thick tail slipped behind a tangled briar. Then lifting her skirts she ran up the last bit of hill, calling for her sister to wait. The crest held a long view of their father's lands. Weathered peaks framed the far horizon. Leaf tips, dressed in reds and yellow-golds, speckled the glade. The broad hill sloped sharply into a glistening lake and from the north the sound of its feeding falls spilled over the valley.

The path grew wider as they drew nearer to the falls. The waters poured from ridge to ledge, filling the glen with a damp mist. Patches of watercress grew along the edges. Silvery fish swam through their roots and large insects rested upon the water. Yurah left the path to climb the stones. She cupped her hands to drink.

"We shall never get home if you must stop and stare at every creature and loiter at every turn."

"Oh, Raeyn, it only takes a moment to drink." but as the words left her she recalled her father's summons. "Do you know what father wants?"

"When I saw him last he was saddling his horse to go on an errand to the village. He asked if we could gather by the mid-morning." she answered. "And whatever it is I have the notion that it concerns you more than the rest of us."

"Your notions are likely in your mind, Raeyn." quipped Yurah. "Father will have business with one or the other of you. It is always so. He treats me like a child."

Raeyn shook her head, "Yurah, do not misunderstand what is meant for your good."

"I wish I knew what was for my good." sighed Yurah looking down at her hands, "Things that once would have pleased me, now give me no comfort at all. My nights come and go in waking dreams. and I find myself walking in colorless halls. When the morning finally comes and I rise from my bed, I am not refreshed but troubled. It is as if I am a dancer, without a dance; or a bit of music, without a song."

"Such notions could lead to strange places." answered Raeyn.

"Such notions are strange places."

"Perhaps." her sister yielded, "We can speak more of it later. We must hurry now. Father will be waiting."

They hurried down the slope and crossed the bridge that lead through the oaks. A fast stream flowed from the west and the white water churned down the long hill to meet the lake. Iao's house rested upon a slow rise along the northern slope of the valley. It was grown from the ancient stones of Raldabon and it had stood upon the spot for eons. The silver gray walls were covered with vine. Gabled porches were set to every side and its garret roofs faced each of the four directions. The seven sisters dwelled there with their father but this had not always been so. Many long years before this lovely place had been home to one other. Though centuries had come and gone since the Lady of Raldabon had walked in the oak groves her mark upon the place was forever present. It was during those days long passed by, she had been the one who had tarried under the fierce light of Taygeth and she had been the one to sing her song to the Riverman. She was the woman who had brought to Raldabon each of its seven lovely daughters and she was the warmth that had filled its clear air with her heart's joy. But as all is destined to change, it came to pass the Fates extended their hands to her and Yurah's mother was lost to a fearsome storm, never to be heard from again.

There was no one waiting when they opened the door. A fire was burning in the hearth and all was clean and swept. In a far corner a few books lie scattered upon a desk. A dim lantern burned within an inglenook and a large gray cat lie upon the window ledge. He flicked his tail when he saw them, but aside from the lazy creature, the long room was empty.

"Where do you think they are?" said Yurah looking down the hall.

"The kitchens I suppose." answered Raeyn.

"But it is long past breakfast, I think we have arrived too late." she said worriedly.

"First you care not then you worry. Stop your fretting Yurah. All is well."

The sounds of the crackling fire were lost as they headed to the kitchen. The cat stared at the door, looking upon the remains of a phantom light that lingered in the room. Yurah ran her finger along the window sashes of the hall, gazing out to the ribbon of road that lead to the village. A lane passed through a stand of rowan trees. A flock of finches were stirring in the dry leaves, scattering messy berries onto the ground. Along the other side of the hall there were rooms of different sizes and sorts. Some were filled with books, while others held measuring devices and instruments to capture light and sound. They passed a narrow chamber, stacked high with shelves. Its door was standing open. Along the ledges were amber colored jars filled with potions. Root powders and bits of leaf were sealed in clear urns. Dried herbs hung from the ceiling rafters, while paints and papers littered a long, low desk beneath. The room held the work of their eldest sister, Sothis. An oil lamp hung upon a moving arm. Under the glow of the lantern were scattered piles of parchment. Yurah placed her hand upon the threshold. She wanted to see what Sothis had left undone.

"Yurah, what is it?"

"Oh, I just wanted to look." she answered turning from the door. "But I can see later." and she stepped up quickly beside her.

"Yes, later." said Raeyn, shaking her head. They rounded the corner of the hall and the sound of their sister's voices met them.

A curved dais looked over a deep ravine. The stone floor was patterned with shaded river rock and formed the image of a great tree. Its gnarled roots rested upon a slow curving arc and its delicate branches reached to the stone rail which bordered the yard. A table, set with flowers, sat under the shade of a locust tree. The morning wind was chilly and Yurah's sisters stood in the warmth of the sun. Sothis was in the kitchen. She called to them as they opened the door.

"Raeyn! Would you mind picking up these loaves and that bowl of butter. And Yurah, I have forgotten the honey. Could you fetch it from the pantry? My hands are full."

In a moment Raeyn's arms were filled baskets of bread and a platter of spiced apples. Yurah hurried to the pantry. She selected a waxy comb and ladled a generous portion of honey into a covered bowl. Sothis carried a clay pot, holding its bottom with a thick cloth as wisps of steam escaped from its edge. As she set the pot upon the table, the sounds of hoof-beats were clear.

Yurah wondered why her father had called them together as she followed them to the table. Standing among her sisters she noticed, ever again, how unlike they were. Sothis' eyes were black as ink. Working side by side, the stern scholar and the pale huntress appeared as different as the night does to the day. Lyli and Tyla sat together upon the edge of the wall. The far drop to the stream below did not concern them, their laughter rose and fell through the roar of the rushing run. Born in the same day, Lyli was a few moments the elder of Tyla. The twins were as the dusk and the dawn. Lyli's hair was the golden light of a bright morning, flamed in red and Tyla's long curls burned like a red sunset, burnished in gold. Their radiant blue eyes glowed with warmth.

Anath was the second born. Black lashes wreathed her green eyes and her hair was the color of rich earth. She was a beast speaker and a shape-shifter. She was a shepherdess that wandered through the valleys and waded through clear streams. From cold hillsides Anath watched the stars as they rose and fell in the skies.

Eide was the third born. Her skin was like moonlight and her gentle eyes were the color of a faded summer sky. Eide's love was music and though she could play any instrument laid before her, her favorite was the flute. She spoke rarely but when she did her voice was a musical thing, like a song that is played from one heart to another.

Yurah felt plain and unimportant. Her skirt was muddy from the river. She touched the matted strands of auburn hair and knew they had become a tangled knot of hapless curls. Her hands fumbled with the bowl. Placing the honey on the table she walked to the edge of the veranda. Her father was rounding the stand of rowan trees. He left his pony to wander along the grassy lawn and shortly his footsteps could be heard coming through the hall. Sothis held his hand as they walked into the sun.

"Hullo, daughters." he smiled winking at Yurah "It is a beautiful day." he said looking up to the sky.

"What was your business in the village, father?" Lyli asked smugly.

"My business was with the metal wrights," he answered and the twins laughed aloud. "A change of season is upon us and Yurah's birthing day is not the least of which."

Yurah eyes grew wide at the mention of her name, though her birthing day did lie at the turn of the moon, its approach had not concerned her.

"What sort of thing father?" she asked.

"It is the sort of thing not much intended for words child, though it will take many to understand it." he smiled and Yurah caught a hint of sadness about his eyes. "I have had news from Doxomedon."

"What sort of news?" said Raeyn.

Iao looked to each of them and slowly he replied. "As always, Derdekea has been watching the turning of the Great Wheel and again the Bull and the Greater Bear draw close." he said looking to the skies once again. "This is particularly important to you Yurah. It was under this very same conjunction that you came to us and, when the moons grow full, you will come of age. The time has come that you must be made aware of birthright and the heirloom passed on."

"Birthright? Heirloom? Please father, I do not understand."

"It is difficult to know where to begin." he said, thoughtfully pushing back the folds of his cloak. "and it seems that some things are better understood by seeing rather than by saying." Yurah gasped aloud, for along her father's side hung a long sheath. It was black as ebony and edged with delicate silver threads. A long, slender sword gleamed within its cover. Iao pulled the blade from its scabbard and brandished it under the morning sky.

"Father! What need have I of a sword?" she cried, bewildered by the gift.

"This blade is your birthright. The Fates have laid it in your hands and you will learn to wield it. You are growing Yurah, coming into your own."

"My birthright," she answered wonderingly. "to wield a sword?"

"Yes Yurah, and I am sure it will come quite naturally." Iao replied placing the hilt into her hand. Clasping her fingers around its handle, the metal blazed under the mid-morning sun.

"See it Yurah, the living fire? The glow within that blade shall never dim."

His words confused her as she ran her finger gently along its sharp edge. The magic tingled.

"This blade once belonged to your mother." he said to her softly. "And it was her folk who forged it, molding it within the inner heat of Benetnaugb." he explained thoughtfully, "And your mother's kin are skilled in more than metal craft. The Annyd have endowed the sword with the unseen force of Endless Sea. It is a magical device, a talisman, able to bridge the waters of life with the inner fire of all that exists." And as he spoke a curious voice rustled through the leaves. Iao smiled and acknowledge the sound with a nod of his head. He pushed back his cape and removed the sheath that hung from his belt. "And now Yurah, the time has come when all shall be put back as it was before. This is not the first time the metal wrights of Raldabon have crafted a sheath for the Sword of the Annyd. It is a perfect replica of the gift I presented to your mother on our Bonding Day. Enlayed within the scabbard are the mystical chantings of the Eldest Ones. Its voice is called Senzar." Then Iao kneeled and clasped the gift around his daughter's waist. "May it serve to guide you when no other voice shall suffice."

She wondered what he meant as she touched the delicate patterns. "What do the runes tell me, father?"

"They are an oath. Their words I shall give you, but it is your heart that must truly understand their meaning."

The wind stilled and the air grew bright as the verse filtered into her mind.

There is a voice that calls to rouse the sleeper
Restless, she shall come.
A breathless flame to fill the dark spaces
And that which is, shall be as One.
And that which is not, shall be cleaved asunder
Through the daring will.
Through the silence the echoes sacrificed,
The cup forever filled"

The rhyme had a shape and color. The vibrations moved under her skin and suddenly the world was torn into pieces. Iao was before her, wearing a robe of the morning sun and she realized she was at two places at once. Her mother's sword was no longer in her hand and, as she knelt upon an ice covered lake, someone standing above her was speaking words she had never heard before.

"Cuimnech. O traod annrach, Cuimnech. Cuimnech an." was the shape of the sound and somewhere in her heart their meaning stirred.

"The sword has been in my keeping for many years." Iao was saying, his voice faraway as he spoke from another place. "I have had it since your mother disappeared."

"I remember little of my mother." she answered and the blade blurred into a silvery mist.

"But you do remember her name." he said tenderly.

"Cuimnech. O traoad annrach, Cuimnech. Cuimnech an." The Senzar repeated and a misty vision of a gray-eyed woman appeared in her mind's eye. "Sro." Yurah replied softly, " Sro was my mother's name."

"Yes. Sro, was her name. The moment is upon us that you must know her story." he said touching the hilt of the shining sword. "Sheath your blade. We shall sit together and I shall share the tale."

The mountain shadows slipped between the walls of stone. They sat upon the dais and the twins brought each a steaming cup of soup. It warmed Yurah's chill hands. The black scabbard, with its whispering magic, murmured at her side.

"Some of you know part of the story but none among you know all in full. So I shall begin at the birthing bed." he said putting his arms behind his back. His boots made little sound as he paced against the backdrop of the ravine. "Names are powerful things my daughters. A name contains within it what is nature and what is fate. It is the birthing name, the Ainm, that is able to touch the realm of soul, the Anim." he explained. "A name can be for good or for ill. When one's true name is spoken it becomes possible to call upon the spirit that dwells within the form. The magic of a name can be used in knowledge or in ignorance. Such is its nature." he said, pausing a moment to listen to the wind and water.

"I am Iao." he said finally. "I am the father of bone and leaf upon this land and it is only those things that I have named. It is the way of the Ren, the mother source, to bestow the Ainm to the newborn life. It is the birthing name that grounds the essence of life to any realm."

Iao then looked upward to Taygeth, "Long years have passed since Sro moved into the Endless Sea." He said leaning against the stone wall. The fine lines drawn about his eyes made it difficult to tell if he were young or old. Black brows framed his shining eyes. The pale grays appeared transparent in the morning light. She felt his thoughts burn inside her head.

"She disappeared just a season after she gave to you your birthing name. It is a sad thing that you hold so few close memories of her, Yurah."

"There is one thing I do remember father." Yurah said gently, "I remember her eyes."

"And when you look into the mirror I hope one day you shall remember much more. For you share not only your mother's eyes but her grace as well. "

Yurah's hand moved upon its own accord to brush against her face. The dark sword pressed against her and its weight made her uncomfortable.

"I recall the time before Sro came to me," Iao continued. "In those years I dwelled alone upon Raldabon with only the beasts and trees as company."

His daughters were stunned. They had never considered that Iao was once without a companion. They had thought, but wrongly so, that the two were set to dwell together upon Raldabon by the hand of the Oldest One. In that moment, they knew had never asked the proper questions and uncertainty filled them. He read their thoughts and he calmly continued.

"I spent slow eons walking upon this land with no-one else. I helped the forming lives of Raldabon as they grew and in this I was content. But things change, as all things must. The stars turn in their spiraling dance just as they did when Sro was borne away."

Yurah's senses swirled. Suddenly a wall of water was crushing her. The Riverman was pushing her under its weight. Her breath was gone as his force flooded through her every part. His untamed voice called her name and she was filled with icy dread.

Iao leaned down and touched her brow. "Be at peace, little daughter. There is no need to reproach the circling stars. There is no need to fear the hidden Fates and, most of all, do not condemn the Riverman. He is but a servant to the most ancient of cycles. I owe him a great debt for it was he that brought her to me."

Lyli and Tyla fidgeted with their teacups and spoons. Sothis sat quietly, her dark eyes taking in each subtle gesture and every unsaid thought as Iao continued.

"In the time before Sro, I walked alone with only the comfort of stars and moons. That was until the day came when I found myself standing with the Riverman. I heard him laugh and I wondered what his laughter could mean. Then my eyes were drawn up to the western sky and I saw her there. Sro had journeyed across the Endless Sea and she held her hand the sword you now hold. With the Fire of newborn sun she tamed his wild Waters. Sro brought to me the parts that I lacked. I am Iao. I hold dominion over the Wind and the Earth and together we made each other complete.

Raldabon was forever altered by our bonding. In those early years, the naiads and dryads came to dwell within the streams and valleys. Soon after, Oiolosse, and his kin, came with their harps and flutes and magical verse and settled in the mountains of the north. The land was happy and as Raldabon changed, so did Taygeth. Alike and different we are, but in truth we are each but a mirror of one another's light."

A flash of doubt passed through her and Yurah wondered if she were the only one of the sisters who had never heard any of this before. She glanced to Raeyn but no answer came to the unspoken doubts. Her sister was preoccupied with questions of her own. Iao read the troubled thoughts.

"Do not worry." he assured them all. "It is only now that the time is ripe for telling. Change comes. That is nature, and bound tightly within its core dwells the far-memory of all lives that have come before. But alas my precious daughters, not all memories are sweet and we are not the only ones who grieve for what has been lost. Derdekea and Doxomedon know that pain well," He looked into his empty cup and set it gently upon the ground. "Grief and joy are but some of parallels we share. Sothis was our first-born child and on her birthing day the muses of Taygeth sang and Raldabon thrived. We rejoiced again in the presence of Anath of the Earth and then Eide of the Air, and years passed by until all our daughters grew into masteries of their own. Eide would spend her winters in the cold mountains, playing the music of Oiolosse's people and uniting in their living thoughts. Anath would linger in the valleys and has her consorts there. More time did pass and Raeyn came to us and, in less than four seasons, and on the birthing day of our own twins, Derdekea and Doxomedon were also blessed with a child.   Our young daughters and their young son spent happy days together until Raeyn was drawn to learn the secrets of the forest and Lyli and Tyla came to know the true purposes of the flame. But the boy, the son of Doxomedon and Derdekea, did not understand his purposes and though he carried the gifts of the Muses he became restless. When he came of age he began to wander from the light of Taygeth. Further and further, he traveled from our realms and even as he was loved completely by all, still the boy could not be satisfied. The Muses' songs and laughter; tears and tales; were not enough and the day came that he stole from each of them a bit of their hearts. He took these precious things in secret and he slipped away. He left Taygeth without a word and he faded into the Endless Sea. The boy's name was Kiel, the lost son of Derdekea and Doxomedon."

"And no word of him has ever come?" asked Yurah.

Iao shook his head. "We have searched and we have called, and if he has heard us, he has never answered."

"I remember Kiel." said Raeyn. "He was fair, with eyes like a seastorm. But it is his voice I recall most clearly. It was mellow as summer wine for the Muses had shared with him all their secrets. When Kiel was happy he would send his joy upon the wings of song. But as he grew older he was not often content. Sadness would cling to him and he would want no companion near. The last time I saw him he was standing upon the cliffs, looking over the River, throwing stones and calling to the clouds. I went to him to see if I could ease his mind but he would say no more than he could find no comfort. It was the last time that I spoke with him. I have often wished I had pressed him further but I did not know what he had planned."

"But Raeyn, is it not awful and wrong to have cast away what was given and to steal that what was not yours to have." asked Yurah, for such notions had never crossed into her mind before. "Harm will only follow such things."

"The greater aim of any life may lie hid away from the world. None of us know the true purposes of Kiel." Iao answered her gently, "And this made it all the more urgent that we find him. Derdekea mourned long after his disappearance. In those years Sro visited her often and would use her powers to search for Kiel. In the early morning she would go to the Riverman and call his name. Years passed and then Yurah, you were born to us and though we still grieved with Derdekea and Doxomedon our joy was perfect. There was not a morning that Sro did not go to the River and call for the lost boy. Finally the day arrived when everything changed. A great storm covered the skies of Raldabon. The Riverman broke through his bonds and swallowed the land. That was the day Sro did not return to out house. We searched the valleys and finally we found her Sword. It was buried deep in the fens that separate the River from the Endless Sea." and then he paused a moment, watching a single cloud as passed over the sun. "I have often wondered what circumstance forced her sacrifice."

All the while Iao spoke, Yurah's fingers played absentmindedly along the hilt of the blade and the scabbard murmured words she did not understand.

"Since that time, we have searched the stars for both Sro and for Kiel." he was saying, "Doxomedon nor Derdekea have not rested, nor faltered, nor have they grown weary of the task. For all the years of your life Yurah they have cast their eyes far from our familiar skies and now at last, they are finally aware of her presence."

"She is found!" Lyli cried and Tyla rose up beside her. Raeyn leaned forward to touch her father's knee. "Is she well, Iao? Is she safe?" she asked in disbelief.

"We are only certain that her intent has passed through the seven lamps of the Greater Bear." he answered, sadly he shaking his head, "Since that time, Derdekea has searched the milky skies for signs of where Sro might be and she believes she has caught a glimpse of her dilemma. She has found a small satellite that circles a yellow sun. She has said it is a dark place that can make no light of its own. And more disturbing still, my children, though we are sure that Sro lives, we also sure that your mother does not live free."

A shudder ran through the wind and Eide hung her head. Raeyn drew a ragged breath and spoke the thoughts of all. "And what is life without freedom?"

The blade and its bindings stirred along side her. Yurah pulled the sword from its cover and laid it across her knees. The voice of Senzar rang in her thoughts.

"The force approaches.
The rejoining and reparting all that binds.
The undoing and remaking of all things that fall apart.
May the wanderer know what that sleeps within every heart.

To remember what was lost.
To understand that which is,
And to know that which is not. "

Iao placed his hand upon Yurah's shoulder. "That is your path my little one. That is the narrow way of those who are born to wander."

Yurah looked into the reflection of the blade and, to her surprise, she realized it did not mirror the light of day. Instead its clear face held an unfamiliar night sky and its stars fell backward before her.

CHAPTER III
THE BIRTHING DAY

To her right were windows and to her left were doors. The halls seemed without end. She ran her finger along the dark glass. It was cold and bit like fire. A turn lay up ahead and she hurried toward it but, when she arrived, she found only another endless hall. The long windows and closed doors threaded their way through the dismal tunnels. She shook each handle, leaving the echo to rattle through the corridors. She pressed her weight against the door but the locks were sealed tight. On and on she walked through the gray light but morning never came. The shadows around her deepened and the colorless halls slowly ebbed to black. The windows grew taller as the dark crawled through her. After a time she could no longer see her feet but even as the light failed, the silence was breaking. Distant at first and then soft but definite was the sound of running waters. She stopped to listen. The air was thick and fear crept close. She looked behind her but there was nothing to be seen. The sound changed as she moved toward the source and soon she found herself wading through thin pools. Groping along the gritty hall she found an opening which led steeply down. Her heart beat quickly as she began to feel her way along the damp walls. She walked more slowly for all light was now gone and she knew the hall had ended. Moving her hands in the wet dark she felt a closed door before her. She groped along and found its handle. Gently she touched it and the handle moved.

Drawing a deep breath she pressed all her weight against the wood but the door was not a door at all, it had become nothing more than a sheet of falling water. The deluge flooded her, moving like a wall it passed through her skin. Her breath was gone but that did not matter, motion was effortless. A light glowed through the liquid sea. She heard her name. She moved toward the sound.

Raeyn was holding a candle at the edge of the bedstead and behind her the moons of Raldabon were shining full. The gray cat sat at the window sill and blinked its green eyes.

"Yurah, wake." Raeyn was saying. "Wake now to be with me."

Yurah blinked. "I am awake, Raeyn."

"I saw your dream," she said, brushing her hair from her face. "I saw the waters come. There will be no rest for either of us this night. Come downstairs. There is a fire."

Wrapping her blankets around her, Yurah rose from her bed. The back stairwell was cold. She ran her hands along the twisting hall, following her sister down the narrow steps to the kitchen below. The cupboards and shelves were filled with moonlight which lit their way to the hall. Yurah was grateful when she pressed her chilled feet into the deep carpets. They needed no other lamp when they reached the hearth. Her chill began to fade as Raeyn tended the flames. Its red glow shadowed her stern face and when she was satisfied with its progress, she told Yurah to stay near the fire, saying she would be back shortly. The salamanders danced cheerfully along the broad logs, changing from white to blue, and from yellow to red. Calmness grew and the cold faded. It was not long before Raeyn returned holding a board of bread, jam and tea. They ate by the fire and spoke softly of quiet things.

"Look Yurah." said Raeyn, taking a sip of tea. "It is snowing."

Along the wide lawn white specks were floating through the air. The meadow was fast turning from dark to light as the clouds shrouded the moons. Yurah went to window and touched the glass. Bits of her dream filtered back into her memory as the white frost climbed upon the panes. The ice fingers caught the firelight and Yurah traced it with her finger. She was trying to remember something.

"Today is your birthing day, Yurah." said Raeyn, stepping beside her.

"I had forgotten." she said as a shudder of uncertainty passed through her. "It does not often snow upon my birthing day." she sighed looking through the window glass, "and though the Lady is lovely, in her blanket of white, today her chill leaves me troubled. There is little that means to me what it once did, not even the lovely trees and their icy crowns." then Yurah looked to the floor to say softly. "I am changing Raeyn. Nothing is sure anymore I do not know how to go. I am the dancer without the dance."

"the bit of music without a song." answered Raeyn.

"Aye, without a song, am I." she answered sweetly. "And my dream this night is troubling. A door is now pushed wide apart and I have become the water."

Raeyn stared out the window. The snow outside had begun to fall more quickly. Black trees were set against a gray sky and the pale moons were hid behind the clouds.

"Autumn will not linger much longer." Raeyn mused. "And though winter will keep its secrets well, the dryads and naiads wait patiently for the sun. Watching and alive they will move unseen though the short days and the long nights. How I long to be with them, Yurah. How I wish to share their breath and walk in the white forest and gaze with them through the sparkling night. But that is my way. That is the nature of my song. What is waiting for you lies far away from this land I know so well. Your road leads instead along the endless paths of the spiraling stars."

"But I am frightened now Raeyn and my heart knows no joy when I look upon them." she answered, shaking her head.

"Your heart will be what guides you," she said kindly. "and, when the time is right, you will know its work."

"And there you go Raeyn, saying things that I cannot believe. Now that I am more than a child, the world I once knew as peaceful and perfect, I find is flawed beyond all measure. I do not think I can face the awfulness of our mother's fate. How can I be one to follow in those footsteps? I will tell you Raeyn, I am not ready for such a task. I am the least in courage and the least in skill. I am clumsy. I am unsure. I walk best in dreams, sister. Lovely though they may be, they are nonetheless dreams."

"Such is the beginning. It is always so. Follow your heart and you shall know the way."

"You are more certain than I." she shuddered.

"The cold creeps through the glass." Raeyn told her gently, "We must go back to the fire. If we warm ourselves for a bit we can go make breakfast for the others. Busy hands can ease the worried mind."

"Yes," Yurah smiled a little. "Yes, that they do, and the smell of spice and coffee can drive the chill from the heart."

So they tended the fire until the flames roared and soon after they were about the kitchen, starting the cooking stoves and kneading the loaves. The windows were covered in mist and outside the gray sky lightened. The smell of coffee and spice layered the air and soon feet and voices found their way to the table. The blanket of snow covered the dais. Heavy drifts spilled over the stone rail to fall into the gorge beneath. The snow had all but stopped as the sun rose in the cloudy sky. A raven waited in the black locust tree. Its call rang against the freezing glass. Yurah reached her thoughts into its mind as she pulled a hot loaf from the upper oven. Laying the bread carefully upon a wooden board to cool she began to stir more spice into the bowl of baked apples. Her whispery thought touched the bird and to her surprise the bird returned a word of greeting. It was a message was from the Riverman. The watery language stirred her mind and her thoughts formed around the shape of it.

"Forget me not, O daughter of the Master. Forget me not, for I wait for you." Her hands trembled and she gripped the spoon more tightly.

"You shall choke that spoon to death, Yurah." said Lyli picking a bit of apple from the bowl and popping it into her mouth. "Surely it has done you no harm."

"Of course not, Lyli." she sputtered, "I just had something else on my mind."

"And what thing might that be? You know it is your birthing day, Yurah." answered Tyla, "and I know you cannot wait to see the gift we have prepared."

"Ours will surely be your favorite. It is the best gift among them all, we made it from the. ."

"Stop, Lyli! Now is not the time to give our surprise away! We must wait for the others to come downstairs."

Raeyn came from the pantry with a basket of dried pears and a half wheel of cheese. "Good to see you up, sleepyheads! It is almost time to make the eggs."

"The eggs! I will make them. I make them best of anyone." chimed Tyla already reaching for a frying pan. "Lyli, fetch me some onions from the pantry. And Yurah, where have you put the butter? Oh and Raeyn, cut me a slab of that cheese there and I think it would be best if I had a bit of potato to fry along side them. Yurah, would you mind? Run to the cellar and grab me an armful."

"I had less work when I doing it all myself." said Yurah.

"That is right, Yurah! It is your birthing day. Do not be her hands and feet!" exclaimed Lyli. "Get them yourself, Tyla. I make eggs better than you at any rate. And here, here is the butter, right next to the board there, and we shall need the larger pan. Hand me that one. I must use that one, instead! And I do not like onions in my eggs so we shall not be needing any of those, Raeyn."

"But I love onions." cried Tyla. "Must you always have your way, and what about the potatoes?"

"Well the potatoes, that is something that should be done. I am surprised it has not been started already," said her twin, cocking an eye toward Raeyn. But she brightened as she saw Anath enter the room behind her. "And Anath is here now. She will not mind going down to fetch the potatoes, would you now, Anath?"

"I will go Lyli and I hope between the two of you we shall end up with some eggs upon our plates this morning." then she bent down to kiss Yurah's head. "Happy Day, Yurah. Cast aside your worries. You see, it is an early snow and that is a fortunate sign." And lighting the lamp, she went down to fetch the potatoes. Yurah took her apples to the table to finish stirring the bowl. Lyli and Tyla were happily consumed in the buttering of bread and the tasting of jam. Raeyn poured a mug of coffee and leaned against the window to watch the gentle snow fall.

"We shall let them finish this, Yurah. And besides, we can get no word in between them."

Yurah was not listening. Her eye rested in the locust tree. The raven was worrying her and she wished it would go away until a mist of swirling snow blew across the dais. The wind caught up the icy crystals just as a bit of sun split through the sky. An illumined whirlwind glided under the locust tree and in its shining wake appeared her sister, Eide. She seemed clothed in frost and at her side, was another. Yurah recognized him immediately. He was the eldest son of Oiolosse, the keeper of the Cold Mountain. His garments were gray as a thundercloud and his cloak a faint green. He was pale as fog and he carried upon his shoulder an ashwood harp. His name was Driin. The raven cried out once more and Driin cast to it a hard glance. The crystal eyes met the black. The bird rose from the branches and flew south. Iao opened the doors and Yurah quickly set another place upon the table. Soon the board was spread thick with fare and yellow candles burned happily.

They ate slowly and talked softly while the platters were passed from one to another. Iao was pleased to see Oiolosse's son and communicated with him in the silent way common to his people. Yurah caught bits of the thoughts that passed between them. Most was of simple things, such as the state of birds, or beasts, the paths of wind, or the swiftness of water. After a time they began to discuss the qualities of the upper airs and the nature of the new children born within his Kingdom. It seemed to Yurah that all was well. The children of the Cold Mountain were strong and the air in his realm was bright with music. She wondered if some time Eide might take her there. She took a bite of potato and was glad that Anath had gone to fetch them. The candles were dripping when Lyli filled her cup for her for a third time. The meal was finishing and they sipped upon their mugs. Again she heard Iao and Driin in silent conversations and it seemed the tone had become more serious. Driin's thoughts begin to form in her mind. He was telling Iao of an ill wind that blew from across the Greater Bear into the skies of Raldabon. She struggled to listen and found herself in a dream realm, moving in shapes and blending into colored streams. She saw a wasteland, with dying trees and barren hills. A bird cried out and she startled. Driin was watching her from across the table. His message was plain as it was soundless.

"Happy Day child. I have come to celebrate with you. The folk of Oiolosse's mountain have long awaited the moment you would take up the ancient sword. Our good will is with you, Sro's child."

Yurah trembled at the intrusion of his thought. Eide touched her arm. "Worry not, sister." the touch said, "His speech seems strange, for more than words does it bring. It is the voice of the heart. Be still. You will become accustom to it."

Driin smiled but said no more. Lyli and Tyla made quick work of the washing and all the other busy hands left the kitchen neat. The cloths were hung to dry and the teapot was filled and ready, on the warm stove. Yurah fed the cat.

Soon all had gathered before Iao's long hearth. The windows were uncovered. Snowy patches huddled under the shadows while the warm sun dazzled the coloring leaves. Yurah's sword now rested upon the mantle and Iao smiled at her as he fastened it about her waist. "Happy Day, child." he whispered.

The crackling of the apple wood blended with their laughter. Soon the sound of the flute and string filled the room. When the song faded it was the time to share their gifts.

Lyli and Tyla were waiting as patiently as they were able beside the fire. Their bright eyes were fixed upon her.

"We must go first Yurah." cried Lyli.

"Yes! We always do." exclaimed Tyla.

Yurah laughed at their expectant faces and the twins laughed with her. Tyla drew a crystal flask from her pocket. Raising it above her head the room became bright like the sun. The light spread from the windows and rainbow prisms sparkled over the lawn. Yurah covered her eyes as Lyli threw a heavy cloth over the flask.

"Do you what to blind us all?" Lyli giggled, handing the covered flask to Yurah.

It was usually heavy and Yurah placed her other hand beneath it. The crystal was warm through the dark cloth.

"It is the breath of the fire star that crystal holds." said Lyli. "It brings all gifts that come of the flame."

"It is warmth and life." whispered Tyla as if she were sharing a grave secret. "Its cloven tongues bring inspiration."

"It will purify but you must take care," said Lyli. "It is a restless glow. It might consume the form."

"Though it will bring hope."

"And inspire courage."

"And reveal the way to the within." Tyla said.

Yurah turned the glass around in her hands. Lyli handed her a supple strap. "It is heavy, eh sister. That is the nature of its substance. We made this for you, so it will be no burden."

Lyli adjusted the strap. "There. That should do fine."

"It is no burden at all." Yurah replied, her eyes wide with wonder. "How did you come by such a marvelous thing?"

"Now she wishes to know all our secrets, Lyli." said Tyla.

"And we will be hard pressed to keep her from finding them out. But even if we did tell her, she would not likely believe the strange things that must be done to keep a speck of sun held within a bottle."

"A speck of sun?"

"The smallest bit we could glean." grinned Tyla widely. "But take care Yurah and handle it gently. It is a restless light."

"A restless light." she wondered again at the words.

"The starry light has its own clear intentions, Yurah." answered Iao to the unasked question.

Yurah placed her hand around the flask. She knew an end was coming and a beginning was soon to be.

Raeyn gently interrupted her thought, "I have left my gift upon the mantle." she said. "But please understand it is not from me alone. It has been shaped as slowly as the earth does form around itself. It is blessed by the Elder Oak and by all the children that will ever come of that seed. It is there." she said pointing to the hearth. An egg-shaped stone rested upon the mantle. Yurah ran her fingers along its edge until she found a hidden catch. The top opened slowly to reveal a glowing amber seed that rested within it. Yurah held it up to the flame and it began to hum. Quiet at first but, as the warmth of her hand spread to it, the sound grew louder. The tall oaks at the edge of the lawn began to sway. The pitch of the stone altered ever so slightly and the evergreens reached their long arms closer to the house.

"Still the stone Yurah or you shall wake them all." Raeyn warned. The trees were drawing close as the stone began to lift from her hand and float into the air. Raeyn handed her the stone box. "Keep it here. Let it sleep until there is reason."

Yurah settled seed back in its case and clicked it shut. Slowly the hum diminished and the trees outside grew still. "What is this, Raeyn?"

"It is a Tree Summoner, made from the amber of the eldest Oak upon Raldabon. The wise trees forget little of what has gone before. They know the hearts of every life that has lingered under their sheltering leaves. They will guide you with their old wisdom. And Yurah, if there be great need, they will come to your aid."

"Thank you Raeyn." she said, turning the stone over in hand, wondering shat words might suffice to tell her all she wished to say, then she notice that Eide had drawn near. She did not speak but her eyes shared a secret. Driin was close at her side and she noticed that Oiolosse's son held a silver reed. Its metal seemed spun from the light of the moon as Driin handed the delicate instrument to her and gently Yurah placed it to her lips. Eide took her own flute and joined her and soon Driin took his harp and a cold, wandering melody danced upon the breath of the reed. The song moved through the window glass and out into the sunny day. The melting snow began to run in rivulets along the edge of the wood. Iao joined the song, and then Raeyn, and through the restless wind the Riverman whispered his own sounds of freedom. Ever so slowly the song ended. The day had passed. Twilight was upon them and the setting Taygeth glimmered through the trees. Yurah wished to thank them but words were not enough to let them know. And yet, know they did, though not sound was uttered between them. Eide gave to Yurah a soft casing. Gently she took the silver reed and showed her how it rested within the folds. Yurah bowed her head and was glad.

The gray cat sat on the window sill, flinching his tail. Anath came to her, bearing the gift she had prepared. It was wrapped in a square of black cloth and tied with a black ribbon. Yurah undid the bow. It was a circle of silver, a bit more than a hand's width across. It was plain except for the black stones that marked the four directions. The middle of the circle seemed void of any substance.

"It is a scrying device. Though the center seems empty, the middle place holds a seed of the greater dark." explained Anath. "The dark will mirror many things so great care is needed. True meanings can be difficult to understand."

A mist swirled within the void of the silver ring and the far distance a light burst into view. A liquid fire filled the center of the circle. Something new was beginning. But what happened then did not go right. In the midst of the new creation, a disturbing force was wandering close to a spinning globe. The thing was without a solid design. It desired to possess the new world, wishing to fashion the infant sphere after its own intent. The burning will bent its desire upon the forming orb. And what was meant to be whole and lovely was instead malformed and cruel. Soon the little world's cry of torment was heard across the far havens. A concerned ear was turned toward the Little Kingdom and a cold wind answered from the deep of time. The cry rose higher and was met with rain. The sky poured forth and the waters of life quenched the flames. The upper winds brought a new order to the wallowing seas. The maleficent force was unseated from the newborn realm and left to fret in the outer dark. The land was cleansed and the Rainbringers sowed seeds and soon a great tree began to grow. The seed twisted and the seed bent, until many things lived upon the land and moved within the seas. A blue twilight graced the above and a green garden spread over the ground. But within the deep core of that world a dark root slept uneasily. Centuries passed and still centuries more, and Yurah watched as the dark grew in the center of the mirror. A great sucking mouth formed before her eyes. The teeth spiraled down the endless throat and tore asunder all that had ever been. She watched in horror as the first designs were ruined and could not be put back as they were. Much of what had been beautiful was undone. In the distance, the mother of the land, wailed as all was brought to bits and the distraught father stood upon a mountain. His eyes poured the blood of all things that had once lived and as Yurah's tears fell in the center of the circle and the vision passed. Anath took the mirror and wrapped it in the cloth.

"You have seen what once was." Anath said handing the gift back to her sister. "But you have yet to see what will come to pass. New strength rises with every dawn, little sister. Blessed Be, Seventh Daughter of the Seventh House. I will watching from afar."

And though Yurah was filled with grief, something was growing within her. Perhaps it was the warmth of the flame held within the crystal flask; or perhaps the sweet music her heart would never forget, or maybe it was the wind that whispered within the box of stone. She touched the sword that hung at her side and its scabbard hummed.

Through the long of the day Sothis had silently watched all that had been exchanged. She drew close to Yurah and from her pocket she pulled a small book. The imprint upon it was of two twisting snakes pressed deep into the black of its leather.

"It is a Book of Secrets, little sister." she said pressing it into her hand. "It is the heart and bone and blood and seed of all that is. It holds within it every knowable thing. Speak your need and, within the leaves, the answer will form. And when you read what is written, take heed for the heart can only understand what is truly real. Use it wisely and be not afraid. Keep it pure for its knowledge is of the two worlds. The Book is yours to use as thou wilt." With those words, Sothis bowed her head and moved quietly away.

"The moons are rising, Yurah." her father said softly, "The stars are calling for us to act. Under the cold sky we must speak the words that can only be uttered under their domain."

They carried no candle with them for the stars and moons were light enough. Their foggy breath hung under the night and bits of wind blew drifts around the trees. The cat waited at the door. The icy cold burned her cheeks as Iao spoke to the stars.

"Gone is the gloom under the everlasting sky.
The work begins anew.
The Word succeeds.
For what was Past can no longer hold sway.
And what is Present is all that remains.
Behold Children, the chord sounds
Its mystery ever in motion.
The Future is upon us
Calling from above

We may embrace all where peace resides."

The starry light whispered back and Iao answered with a word unsaid. He pulled a plain leather pouch from under his cloak.

"This, my dear, is my gift to you. It holds within it the Wind of Raldabon. Do not open it until need arises. But understand you are never far from my heart and you may always return to me. The Wind of Raldabon shall ever bring you home."

And though the pain of parting hung about her, under it all there was a rising joy. The cold autumn night was shattered by the brilliance of a thousand, thousand stars. They looked to the above as the light of a new beginning touched the face of Raldabon.

CHAPTER IV
THE LONGEST NIGHT

The light of Taygeth wrapped around the icy trees. The embers were fading in the hearth and Yurah hurried across the chill floor to tend it. The cat brushed against her long gown.

"What are you doing here, Hathor? Where is Anath?" she asked, scratching his head. The cat rubbed against her again. "So she has not fed you.' The cat almost winked, then he turned and went to wait at the door. "In a moment." she laughed and Hathor scampered down the hall.

Yurah slipped on her blouse and leggings and then began to brush the snarls from her long hair.

"This will take far too long." she thought impatiently, pulling at the knot of curls. She sat down on the wide windowsill and began to untangle the knots. Across the frozen snow she could see the path that led to the barn. A lantern's glow spilled from the crack in the door and she knew her father must be tending the mangers. Steadily she pulled apart the matted hair and when she was almost satisfied, she put on her old cloak and fastened her sword about her waist. She forgot about Hathor and left by the front door. The stable was nestled in a patch of thick firs. Yurah pushed the door open and slipped inside. The horses greeted her with stamping feet. The barn was comfortably warm. Iao looked up from his work and smiled.

"Did you sleep well, daughter? We kept a late night."

Yurah nodded, remembering how the stars had kept them company as they shared a midnight supper. The cheerfulness of the food and the comfort of song had lingered for many hours. The uncertainness of what lie ahead had not seemed quite as frightening as she took to her bed. But now the sword at her side was restless and the runes upon its scabbard were chanting words she did not know.

"You have brought your blade," he said setting down the pitching fork aside. "Are you ready for another lesson?"

"Yes father, I was hoping we could." she answered pulling the sword from its cover and holding it out before her. He walked around her to study at the slope of her shoulder and the bend of knee. She stood in a ready position; both hands upon its hilt, her right foot to the forward.

"That is good, Yurah." he said, adjusting her left foot to a slight angle. "Relax a bit more, I need to see it." he said clearing a pail from the aisle. "Let the tip drop. A bit more. Closer now, closer to the ground. That is good! Now step forward and begin the first habit."

Yurah began to trace the steps he had taught her. Gracefully she followed the path of the ancient Dance of Blades. Moving along the dusty aisle, her shadow rose and fell along the stable walls. Her front foot slid forward as the sword arced overhead. Her back foot followed, the point snapped upward, and she was ready to begin once more. Four times more forward and five more back. The sword cut through the empty air. Forward and back again; she moved in the dance, from the left arm came the strength, from the right the fineness of motion.

"Pull the sword. Do not push." Iao reminded her.

"Relax the shoulders." she thought. The sound of the blade was smooth. She moved away and toward the silhouette upon the wall. Forward and back, the scores were balanced as the breath of the blade rushed by her.

"One cut decides the battle." cried Iao. "Let it come!"

She raised the sword and twisted sharply. Her shoulder followed perfectly and the strike swung to the side. Swiftly, she pulled the blade back to her, its aim to cleave the breast. The air sung as her shadow glided along the wall.

"Good! That would have ended it." her father replied.

"Yes, that was very good, Yurah." said Raeyn who had been standing against the door. "You have learned quickly."

"I have had an excellent teacher." Yurah answered bringing the sword to a resting position.

"The sword is part of you, Yurah. I only had to remind you of it."

"Be that as it may father, I have only begun to learn the art of the blade. As yet I have done but empty cutting and I must wonder what a real opponent would feel like. The true press of battle would be different thing entirely."

"Different indeed." agreed Iao. "In those moments of struggle, it is the grace of the dance that will hold the razor's edge. It is more than metal you wield, Yurah. The ancient sword is able to wield the fire that comes of rain. Its voice will call through the storm and such a sound shall never go unanswered."

"That is the way of things, Yurah." continued Raeyn, her eyes bright. "When one part of life is disturbed, the greater life does know it."

"But when shall I know it Raeyn? Here I am, waiting for something to happen and all the while worrying that it might."

"There is virtue in waiting." laughed Raeyn. "Wiser folk than I have said, it is in the excessive practice of patience there lays the greatest good."

"But is it not possible to wait to long and to miss what is there to be had?"

"The true practice of waiting is always to be ready. But I agree daughter. We have had too much talk. Are you ready for an opponent?"

"Who will stand opposite to me?"

"I shall little sister." answered Raeyn pulling an anlace from her belt. "The steps of the dance are known to me." The blade of her knife was far shorter than Yurah's own long sword. It was broad at the hilt, ending in a fine taper and the handle was set with amethyst. The fine metal gleamed an icy blue as Raeyn stood ready.

"That little more than a dagger!" she cried. "The match is not even. I cannot! I will not, not even in play."

Raeyn laughed, "There are times you will have the advantage and times that you will not. Step out and I will show you what I mean." she held dagger out before her. "Come! I am ready."

Yurah took her place in the aisle. She bent her knee and steadied her weight. Raeyn's breath came easy, her bright knife relaxed in her hand. But suddenly, and without warning, she thrust swiftly forward. Yurah slid towards her, raising the sword over her head, preparing the strike. Raeyn's free arm blocked the motion along the bone and Yurah stumbled. Yurah reversed quickly, raising the sword over her head once again and swinging as she moved away. Raeyn pressed her sharply. Her breath was close enough to feel. Abruptly Raeyn stepped aside and reached her hand forward grabbing Yurah's sword arm with her strong arm. She held it tightly and twisted the wrist. Yurah was trapped. Her sword, still in her fighting arm hung useless and the tip of Raeyn's dagger was upon her throat.

"Nowhere to go?" Raeyn smiled coyly.

"How did you do it?" she cried out in amazement.

"I used your will against you. You were trapped by your own blade. It is a simple counter. " she answered dropping back with a smile.

"She has shown you well, Yurah." said Iao. "Do not fix the all of your attention on any one thing, not even your own weapon. The Dance of Blades is a living motion, changing in each breath. You cannot think each step. The dance is the battle and the battle is the dance."

"Yes, father." she answered, looking down upon the symbols etched into the scabbard. She heard their soft murmuring but did not understand the words they spoke.

"All things follow in their turn." said Raeyn, interrupting her thoughts. "It is the blade's destiny that will hold you to the course. But I had more than sword play on my mind this morning. Sothis sent me with a message. Breakfast is almost ready."

"Breakfast, yes I could do with that." said Iao, nodding. "Cold brings hunger with it. And these creatures feel the same. There are a few things left to do before I can sit at the morning table."

They helped him finish and when all the troughs were filled the smell of grain hung sweet in the still air.

Iao left his stained boots outside the kitchen door. Sothis was pouring the last bit of batter into flat pan. The table was all ready laid. Cheese and cold meat sat alongside the stacks of griddle cakes. There was a bowl of honey and jars of jam scattered amidst platters. A kettle whistled. Yurah took it up and filled the teapot that waited on the sideboard. The scent of sweet clover drifted by her as Lyli and Tyla came clattering down the stairs.

"Where is Hathor?" cried Tyla.

The cat was in the window, ignoring Tyla as she called his name.

"There he is!" said Lyli pointing toward the window. Hathor rolled a green eye idly towards them, giving a wide yawn. "What have you done with it, Hathor?" she commanded. Hathor rose leisurely and stretched his long legs .

"Is this what you want, sister?" said Sothis, holding up a pouch, embroidered with thin silvery threads.

"Yes, that is it." she exclaimed, taking the bag. Carefully she let the crystal runes fall into her hand counting and complaining as she went. "He snatched them from my stand. He put in his mouth and left, right smart down the hall."

"He carried it to the kitchen." explained Sothis.

"He wanted to be fed.' laughed Yurah, "He had come to me earlier, but I had forgotten him."

"Then where is Anath? She tends to him best." said Tyla, glaring hotly at the cat. "Though he is a cat and he could tend to himself!"

"Do not worry. I gave him what he wanted and he is content for now in his bit of sun," she said, raising a brow at Hathor. "It does not seem that your wrath much worries him."

"Well it should worry him. He filched the Firestones from beside my bed as I lay right there upon it and he knew I would not take it lightly."

"He knows far more than he shows." agreed Sothis. "And with Anath not here to see too him, I suppose he felt he must make his own arrangements."

"Where has she gone?" asked Yurah, glancing out to the frozen trees.

"It was after midnight when Garan and the others came for her. They were traveling in the form of deer. They gathered at the edge of the wood and called from the bridge." said Raeyn.

"So she has gone to the hillsides." nodded Yurah looking over the frost.

"Yes, but that was likely to be Yurah. Winter's blanket has again come early. They are the shepherds of the woodlands and there is much to do on the night of the first deep snow. The spring born creatures do not understand the coming of the cold. The Amadryades have many ears in which they must whisper and many safe harbors to seek."

Hathor jumped from the sill, ignoring Lyli's fierce gaze as it followed him across the tiles. He trotted directly to Yurah he began to rub against her, purring loudly. She picked him up and he pushed his head against her chin. His green eyes flashed and within their depths another image grew. Yurah saw a shadowy glade filled with white snow. Among the trees there walked a gathering of fair does and silvery harts. They moved in the hushed forest, speaking to the creatures that shivered in the white cold. The palest among the herd she knew was Anath. The gentle face looked through the eyes of Hathor and her message formed in her thoughts. "Greetings Yurah! All is well on this winter morn. I travel now with Garan and the Amadryades. But I promise you, little sister, that before the shortest day shall end I will return to the House of Iao and know, until that day comes, I will watching all from afar."

Yurah blinked and the vision was gone. Hathor arranged himself comfortably as she set him back upon the sunny ledge. Complacently he looked over to Tyla but Tyla shot back to him a glance which seemed to sting him like a bite. He leaped from the ledge, running along the cupboards he knocked a saucer to the floor before scampering up the stairs.

"Tyla!" cried Yurah. "Why did you do that?"

"Anath could have chosen a less maddening familiar." answered her sister. "When she is away he makes it his business to bother us."

"Poor Hathor. Such a sting." laughed Raeyn.

"He is not innocent." replied Sothis, "He enjoys the chase as well as the hunt."

"Aye. That he does." agreed Lyli, placing the pouch within the pocket of her vest. "He is filled with trouble today and I think he has not had the last word."

"The last word, indeed! The last straw, I say!" cried Tyla as she cleared the broken saucer from the floor. She placed it a bowl and put it near the fire exclaiming, "I shall put this back right later. And when I do I will make these bits into a new bowl that will bear his name and he shall taste his own mischief each time he drinks from it!"

"Oh calm down Tyla. The cat enjoys your wrath almost as much as you do!" said Sothis. "Here take the salt and put it back upon the table."

"Oh very well but I shall be watching him. He does not behave well at all when Anath runs with the Amadryades."

The Amadryades were the shapeshifters that roamed among the hills of Raldabon. Anath had long been the partial to the group and Garan was her favorite. It was only rarely would she not heed his call for companionship, and always she ran with the band in times of necessity. The Amadryades spent much of the winter traveling in the frozen forest; for while some lives slept, others struggled, needing hints and whispers to lead onward to the coming of spring.

"She will return before the shortest day shall end." said Yurah. "At least that was the message he held before you sent him on his way."

"Hmm, well he is good for something then." groused Tyla.

"The food is growing cold." said Raeyn, pulling the bench closer to the table. "Leave to the cat to tend to himself. He should be no more trouble today."

"I could only dream of such a sweet thing," Tyla answered looking up the stairwell.

"Have Eide and Driin arrived?" asked Iao, who had been watching from the corner sink, washing his hands much longer than necessity demanded.

"Yes. They are there now." said Lyli, pointing to the path that led to the village. "They are coming home"

"Where have they been?" asked Yurah as the pair swept lightly across the deep snow.

Sothis answered. "It is the custom of Driin's people to walk under the sky as the year changes from season to the other. They have spent the night wandering under the turning stars."

Bits of ice flew into the hall when the door opened. They sparkled for an instant before casting their dampness into the warmth of the room. Their faces were pink with cold as they hung their cloaks along the hooks in the hall. Driin did not speak as they joined them at the kitchen table so it was Eide who told them of their walk under the skies. So rare it was to hear her voice Yurah was drawn into each word. Her words rose and fell like echoes of a faraway song casting its magical hand over the forest. The images poured into her mind, but afterwards only a small portion of the tale did Yurah ever after recall;

"It was the Wind that carried the white hand from the upper Airs drawing us close into her cloudless mind. So much and ever greater than we who stood within the shadows of his forest was the touch of

autumn's hand. We gazed upon the rushing waters and walked within the living wood. Unrelentingly she came. The change pressed him until the will of the forest yielded. His sap fell from the tips of the trees and his power seeped into the simple ground. Gently she turned her face from the sun. And as the world sighed multitudes of stars broke through the dark. Their hopeful voices blessed the frozen ground. We could hear them as we walked on under this waking dream. We wandered far under his rustling branches, tasting the night and drinking the chill.. We knew not weariness only the motion of the thinning golden leaves, the turning of the ice and the rending of the long summer days to the long winter nights. And when the break of morning spread across the sky our joy was complete. The night had left all shrouded in white, and so we turned our faces from the sleeping glen and looked into the bright sun for the new dawn was upon us."

All had fallen silent listening to the tale. The sun spread down the gorge and the snowy drifts began to loose from the black arms of the trees. Thick patches of snow were melting upon the diaz. White cascades slid from the sharp angles of the gabled roofs. Lyli and Tyla looked out into the warming day and delight filled their faces. They rose from the benches, kissing Iao upon his brow before they left the kitchen. Standing under the glow of Taygeth, they cupped their hands and trapped the warmth, turning the frozen white into flowing water and then on to steam. The hazy plumes spiraled into the blue morning. Their laugher traveled with the mists to catch in the snags of trees. Yurah pressed her face against the glass, watching the twins in their work and when all was complete they walked out under the low autumn sun. They spoke some of simple things but mainly they listened as the year changed. The day passed by and as the afternoon drew to its end, Eide found her in front of the fire, holding the sword upon her lap, lost in quiet thought.

Eide's thought formed in her mind. "Your heart has found peace, little sister."

Yurah smiled into the faint blue eyes.

"I am glad," the thought continued. "and I know the silence of winter will keep the secret of spring."

Yurah glanced to the withering light outside the long windows. "A secret I do not yet understand."

"The time needed will be given," Eide assured her silently. Yurah looked toward the door and noticed that two traveling packs lay next to it. She knew the answer before the question rose in her mind.

"You are leaving for the Mountains with Driin."

Eide nodded before speaking aloud. *"Yes. We will be traveling together. There is a subtle quiet which dwells in the Cold Mountains. It is what gives his folk their graciousness. Someday I hope you may meet his kin. They are fair folk and have many wonderful things to share with those who are willing to know them."*

"I would like that, Eide. But for now another road lies before me."

"The moment is not yet upon you. Prepare for what lies ahead, husband your strength and practice your swordplay. We will return before the year's end."

Her voice passed through Yurah's heart like the fluttering of wings. Its echoes moved through the walls and onward into the forest and for an instant Yurah wondered if the sound reached on forever. Driin was waiting at the threshold. His thought ran clear in her mind.

"Farewell seventh daughter. My blessings go with you in all that you do. And someday, if fortune may have its way, we shall sing together upon the Cold Mountain and our voices will carry forward upon the path of stars." Then he bowed low before her.

"I wish for such a day." she answered, bowing in her turn politely.

"Until the turn of the year Yurah." Eide bent to kiss her forehead as they set out on their way   Yurah stood in the cold and watched until they were out of sight.

"Do not be troubled." Iao voice stirred behind her.   "Change is a part of all that is."

"I am not sad father, though I shall miss her gentle company and the quiet ways of Driin. It is more the bond that exists between the two of them that leaves me to wonder. It is a thing I have yet to know."

"Such grace is the hope of the every heart. But that sweet thing may wear many guises and can oft be found in the most unexpected of places."

"Have you known that grace, father?"

"Yes, I have known it as I have walked the never-ending paths of Raldabon. I have tasted it in the air and felt it in the earth. I have beheld it in the eyes of my daughters and ever so sweetly I have known it with Sro. But such a thing can be known in every place, and in every time, for it is always there."

"Will I find it along my way?"

"In time all will find it."

"If it is in all places and at all times, why do I not know it now?'

"It is not always an obvious thing."

"Then is it a secret? And if it is, how shall I come to know it?"

"Is it a secret? Perhaps. Will you come to know it? To me it seems you already begin."

"But Father, I do not understand."

"It is not the sort of thing that lends itself to many words. Trust yourself and you shall know."

The twilight deepened. Fragile shades of indigo spread its shadowy fingers and the stars peeped through the curtain of heaven. Yurah looked after the path they had walked turning round in her mind what sort of secret could hide in all places and in all times. She wondered if Eide understood the answer to Iao's riddle. Watching the fire burn, she ran her finger along the runes of the whispering scabbard.

"May the wanderer remember" . . . the scabbard murmured and she allowed her mind to roam the darkening night. Silent she held her thoughts and listened. First to the sound of the gentle fire and then to the voices as they drifted down the hall; further on, a door opened and then clasped closed. She bent her mind upon it and the sound of the night wind moving papery leaves that brushed by her waiting mind. The cry of a night bird moved in the trees, pulling her ever outward, she passed along the path Eide and Driin had taken. The swirls of snow hissed, their icy breath moved over the bridge, and under it, the waters thrashed toward the sea. She perceived the pair as they walked among the trees. The sound of their voices singing to the rising night was music sweet. Its warmth spread through her and she opened her eyes.

Iao was bent down tending the hearth. "You see Yurah, you already begin. You find it simple to travel upon the threads that bind all. Trust yourself, child. Trust yourself and you will know. Come and eat if you wish. The board is laid once more. We shall sup at our leisure this night."

'I will be along soon, father. The fire is warm and I have thinking to do."

"As you wish, child." he answered. "Call if you have need."

"Yes father, I will."

"Good night then, Yurah."

"Good night, father." Iao smiled and walked down the windowed hall.

She sat by the fire until the night grew old. One by one she heard as all took to their beds. The flames kept her company and she did not grow sleepy. She drew herself into the Riverman thoughts.

"He is never weary," she realized, watching the water thunder under the cold sky. At length she returned to her body and went to her bed, lying under the thick coverlet she rested until the morning came.

And so the days rose and fell with the sun. She slept little and spoke rarely, noticing when her thoughts ebbed to silence was the time she could truly listen. Sothis faithfully kept Yurah intent to her lessons and Raeyn kept to the task of training her to the sword. The weeks passed swiftly as the nights grew ever longer and they practiced for hour upon hour. Never did they hurt, nor bruise, nor did they draw blood as they moved swift and sure with the sharp blades. But ever as they parried, Yurah discovered there was still one who did dominate and one who did submit under the Dance of Blades. Yurah learned the lessons well and the days passed quickly as the turn of the year pressed upon them.

The Cold Moon waxed full as she sat before the hearth, softly playing upon the silver flute. Sweetly the notes swelled before they faded into the room. Yurah laid down the reed and looked out the window upon a new carpet of fresh fallen snow. At the edge of the lawn a group of deer had gathered. Two of them drew away from the herd to walk slowly toward the door. As they came close, their shapes changed and Yurah saw that it was Anath and Garan who stood in the snow. Garan was tall, with a broad back and short cropped hair; Anath only just reached his shoulders. He held her hands in his own as they spoke for a moment more. He raised them to his lips kissing them gently before stepping away. In an instant he was once more the stag; turning swiftly, snow spraying behind him, racing to join the others. Anath opened the door.

"Anath!" Yurah cried, throwing her arms around shoulders.

"Greetings Yurah!" she replied rubbing her frosty hands. "Aye it is warm here, I had all but forgotten the feel. How lovely to be indoors."

"Indeed!" Yurah laughed.

"Where is everyone?"

"Oh, they are near!" Yurah exclaimed taking her hand. "Come we will find them." They passed by the hearth and through the dim alcove to hurry down the hall. They found Sothis in her study bent over a parchment with a writing pen in her hand.

"So you have returned and before the new year!" Sothis laughed rising from her desk. "Hathor has done well in his predictions."

"Hathor! Has he been much trouble?" answered Anath as they embraced.

"No more than usual. Tyla has caught the most of it."

"Then I shall hear of it in great detail."

'Yes, in terrible detail I am sure. Come on, they are clearing the dinner dishes."

They went to kitchen and when Anath's plate had been filled, all retired to the great room to sit before the fire. Iao wanted news of the forest.

"Though the cold is bitter, the wood fares well. Heavy snows have kept roots warm and beasts dry. All that slumbers, slumbers deeply. Though our work has been steady, we have had much time to at gaze the heavens.

"And what do the heavens tell you, Anath."

"The stars murmur of many things, father." she answered softly. "Strange stories stir in the far deep and there is news of the Little Kingdom."

"What have you seen?" asked Lyli.

"Have you news of our mother?" cried Tyla.

"It has always been that star-gazing delights the mind of an Amadryade" she said, ignoring the twins and setting her eye upon Yurah as sadness filled her face. "We have lain beneath the clear cold nights and blended our minds into one, listening to the images the light brings us. By this we have been able to reach further and further into the deeps hoping to hear her voice."

"Anath?" pressed Lyli.

"Please!" continued Tyla.

Anath looked to her sisters and despair trembled in the room. "It was just two nights ago that this tale truly begins. We lay under the night stars and pain-filled sound reached us. It was dreadful. The cries were deafening. It was difficult to not become confused. But we gazed on, gathering strength from one another, hoping to understand and at length we located the center of the uproar. The cry came from within the Little Kingdom of Erda."

The images of the scrying glass pressed vividly into Yurah's picturing mind. She wanted to run to her chamber and hide away under her blankets and hear no more of what Anath had to say.

"I am not surprised." Iao's clear voice broke her frantic thought. "The Little Kingdom has suffered before."

"And it seems it suffers still. It was the summoning cry of the Malkians that spilled across the stars." she shuddered as a breath of cold passed through the room. "The sound of a door clasping shut echoed from down the hall .

"Eide has returned!" exclaimed Lyli.

"And Driin is with her." chimed Tyla, rising to her feet. The gentle pair entered the candlelit hall and Yurah ran to meet them.

"Greetings, little sister. The longest night draws to an end" trembled Eide's words of silent welcome. Driin bowed courteously; his eyes as bright as a lamp.

"I am glad we are all together." said Iao, kissing Eide upon the cheek. "Anath has news we have long awaited to hear."

So they shed their damp cloaks and Anath began once more.

"Images of smoke filled our minds. Beneath the sullen sky we saw a barren land, parched with lifeless clay, spreading in all directions. Along its edge a red horizon burned. It was from here the desolate cries drifted. We gathered our courage to press onward. When we found them, the Malkians were paralyzed but fully aware.

Their garments lay in tatters along the dead ground. We grieved for there was nothing we could do to change their fate. The lovely winged ones had fallen and only the hands of a Greater Weaver could put them right again, so we warmed them as best we were able, wrapping their garments about them and holding them gently until they fell into sleep. The dead land ceased its clamor. No speck of life, nor wind of hope, stirred in its stifling air. Silently we began to summon the bones of the land, coxing them to unveil the story it held within and at length the Little Kingdom stirred. Though as frail as paper, familiar and sweet was its sound. The warmth of her breath had made answer to us and we knew that Sro was kept within the core of that battlefield."

Yurah's mind rushed with nightmare images of broken seraphs and fire stained skies.

"Finally, we know for certain." Iao whispered rising from his seat to stand before the warmth of the firelight. "What came next daughter?" he said as the firelight danced over his face. What else have you seen?"

"Such strange things father, strange things indeed." Anath explained with a shudder. "We joined our minds to her. To help her, to draw her to us but instead a great quaking began to shake the ground and the sound of a thousand, thousand warriors droned. Heavy footsteps were drawing swiftly nearer. Men, both living and dead were coming for us. They wielded lightless swords and began to spew evil verses. Their hideous strength severed our bond and we were hurled from that world. All that remained of our connection there was a name."

"What was name?" asked Sothis.

"Ildabyth. Ildabyth is the daemon's name."

"Ildabyth." said Iao, grimly. "The greatest of deceivers."

"But father, how can this be possible!" Yurah cried out, unable to contain herself any longer. "How can any daemon hold her against her will? How can such a thing happen to one so true and wise under such ordered stars?"

"Ildabyth is also part of the ordering stars." Iao whispered to the fire. "In the first moments of all forming things, Ildabyth was there, watching alongside the Annyd." answered her father, gently. Then he rose from his chair and began to pace before the dark glass. "but Ildabyth has ever been the brooding sort. Always preferring to amuse himself in darker thoughts, and he often used gifts of persuasion to bend others to his will. Sro has known him since Time first entered the Everlasting Dark. I do not believe that she was deceived. I believe she traveled to the Little Kingdom by her own free choice." then Iao stopped his pace and spoke to the moons. "Though why she would chose such a path I have yet to understand."

"Soon that will change father for now we understand far more than we once did. Finally we know that Sro lives and that precious knowledge had once been a wistful dream. In time's order we shall have answer to all our questions. I know it to be so." answered Sothis.

"The fates have opened the way for us." replied Anath solemnly, looking into the cold sky. "And as I breathe the sweet airs of Raldabon, she will not long be without aid."

"The longest night is passing." said Tyla

"And the frozen ground dreams deep." continued Lyli,

"By the morrow the Sun shall be reborn" said Tyla

"And that graceful light will bear upon the sleeping seed once more." replied Lyli

Eide drew close to Yurah's side to whisper in her inner ear. *"The song of home within ever lingers in the heart. Listen and it shall guide you."*

"You are Sro's heir, little daughter." said Iao, "You bear the Sword that was once her own." then he placed his hand upon her shoulders. "Upon the morrow, as the new year returns, you shall begin your journey upon the Endless Sea. Remember Yurah, the dance is the battle and the battle is the dance." he touched his forefinger to her lips and ancient call of the Riverman murmured under the dark. "He shall be waiting when the morning comes,"

"And I will heed the call of the Riverman." she said softly. "But father, I shall not accept this heirloom as my own. Instead, I will follow Sro's path to Little Kingdom of Erda and I will return to her the ancient Sword of the Annyd."

"So be it, Seventh Daughter of a Seventh Son." said Iao, his eyes reflecting the firelight. "Your destiny rises with the new dawn." And the father bowed low before his youngest child.

CHAPTER V
THE WANDERER

The sound of water crept into her dream. She waited upon a spiraling stair, its steep treads winding through the center of a tall rocky pit. Above, a faded light gleamed through the murky air but the beam from above brought no comfort. A freezing wind blew through her thin garment as her path spiraled downward into an infinite blackness. From above, the comfortless light showed the great lengths she had to climb and into the below the darkness beckoned. Endless hours passed and always upward she toiled; the sound of water was ever present, the shrill wind was unrelenting, and the light above drawing never nearer. Still the bleak glow was better than none at all so she quickened her pace. As she hurried she sensed that she was no longer alone. Something was creeping from the bottomless black. A stab of fear raced through her and she began to leap up the stairwell. But the unseen thing matched her every step. Its foul breath was close behind her and from faraway the cries of birds echoed down the well. She wanted to be with them and she raced up the narrow treads. Then, from the depths beneath her, another sound cried out. Someone was calling her name. She froze upon the stair with the beast just behind. She knew the voice. She drew her sword and turned to face her pursuer. Its back was gruesomely twisted. Its arms were uneven. Its leathery skin was pulled taunt over thick bone. The beast stank of burned flesh. It bent forward, revealing rows of teeth that swelled outward from the wide mouth. She could smell its sour gut as it mocked her. A clawed hand lashed forward but the sword stood ready. She leapt toward the creature, never giving the strike a chance to meet its mark. With one fatal cut the blackened breast was cleaved apart. The ugly head rolled backward and pulled the body with it. The creature dropped into the endless dark. She never looked back to the wan light that hung over the well but raced instead into the shadows, following the voice that had beckoned from the dark.

When she opened her eyes she was gasping for breath. Traces of a queer melody lingered in the air. She cast the coverlets aside and dressed hastily. Golden firelight spilled over the gifts that rested upon the hearth. She fastened the sword and scabbard about her waist. The box of stone, she placed over her heart; the crystal flagon, with its spark of sun, she carried across her chest. Anath's scrying glass was wrapped thrice and tucked safely into her inner pocket and next to it, rested the Book of Secrets Sothis had given her. The silver flute she settled against her back as she looked around the room, wondering what she could have forgotten. Her father's gift sat upon her window sill and quickly she placed Wind of Raldabon over her shoulder.

"It is time." she whispered to the lightening sky. "I must reach the Riverman before sunrise." She hurried down the back stairs, to fill a satchel with traveling food, and was just finishing when she heard someone stir behind her.

"All is well, child." said Iao, "It is only I."

"Father!" she cried, throwing her arms around him. "I have seen. No. . no, I mean instead, I have heard . . in a dream, . . ."

"I know your vision, child." he said taking her hand. "The call sounded in my mind as well."

"She called me, father. She called out my birthing name." she shuddered then, letting her shoulders drop. "And I touched the burden she carries inside her heart. It is the lament of the Little Kingdom of Erda which draws me to her." she trembled.

"And the choice to go remains your own."

"I do not understand it father." she answered softly. "Only the pull of the Riverman is clear, nothing more."

"Then the next step is before you, to heed it or no, is the choice."

Yurah shook her head. "You say this burden bears choosing father, but I say it does not. I either I choose to follow the call or I choose to wait. But to what ends would waiting lead. I would only be choosing to wait until an unknown time, an hour, a season, an eternity perhaps; and I again I would be confronted with the same choice to reject or accept anew."

He smiled, "Then your clarity is not diminished by your lack of confidence."

"No, I fear it is not." she answered, smiling back at him. "Then I suppose that makes me as ready as I shall ever be."

"Not quite Yurah, there is yet another token meant for you to carry along your way." and it was then that she noticed the deep blue cape he had draped over his arm. He held it out to her. "The way before you will have many turns and twists, this will help with your comfort and remind you of those who hold you so dear. It was a gift to Sro from Derdekea the day you came to us. Long ago she said to your mother how it would suit you both well." Carefully he placed the blue cape over her shoulders and clasped the silver pin fashioned as a silver flame at her neck."

"It is beautiful." she said, touching the delicate flame. "Thank you father."

"The Riverman is preparing the way my daughter."

"The orbs of light he carries will take me to the road I shall follow" she said softly, worry knitting over her brow. "I must not arrive too late, father or all will be lost. I must reach him before the sun touches the southern slopes. "

"You will not arrive too late." Iao answered calmly. "Come."

Yurah slung the traveling sack over her back following him down the hall to front door. A tall man waited upon the other side.

"Hail Master Garan." said Iao.

"Greetings." he answered in a curious accent. "Is all prepared?"

"Yes, it is ready." spoke Yurah, checking her few belongings. "I have yet to say farewell to my sisters, and time is short."

"They are full aware of the moment. They have been up all night Yurah, preparing for the dawn." said Iao, taking her arm to lead her down the stairs onto the lawn. "Look upward." The gables of the upper garret faced to each of the four directions. A peculiar light poured from the narrow windows and a strange melody was upon the air. "The six are there, building the bridge that will not be broken and weaving the threads that will connect us as you wander the stars. Soon I shall join them to hold the seventh note. Remember Yurah, we are with you through each step along your way" then he paused and shook his head. "The Endless Sea ebbs and flows with force of many lives. It can be a perplexing place and there is no time left to explain further. You must be on your way."

Yurah turned to speak to Garan but he had changed. A silvery horse stood upon the lawn. The Amadryade bent his neck into a graceful arch and turning his head slightly he beckoned for her to come. Iao lifted her upon his tall back. "Remember," he said stepping back, "Remember we are with you, ever listening to the spiraling stars." With those final words, Garan reeled about. In an instant the lawn flashed behind her. The forest passed like a graying blur. The long hill that reached under the waterfall was but a brief fleeting glance as the Riverman's valley fast came into view. Deep snow was thick amongst the trees and clear ice clung to the steep path. The way was treacherous but Garan's feet did not falter. He came to a graceful halt at the edge of the riverbed. Yurah leaped from the horse. She turned to thank him and he changed before her.

"May I be of further service?" he asked with a low bow.

'No Master Garan. I know what I must do."

"She is just beyond the ridge," he said casting his eye toward the sky.

The forest frost paled from gray to shades of rose and thundering water filled the valley. The Riverman knew she stood upon his shore.

"Thank you Master Garan." she cried looking toward the mountains. I could never have arrived in time."

"It is my pleasure, Lady. But you must make haste." he said as a ray of sun glimmered his black eyes.

"Farewell Garan. Please tell them they are ever in my heart." she called, sliding down to the frosty stones.

He raised a solemn hand in farewell and in an instant he was out of sight.

The light of Taygeth burned just beyond the new horizon as she made her way over the slippery stones. The minute globes were all around her. The cold water reached to grasp the hem of her cloak. The echoes of his bewildering freedom soared around her. Moving further into the churning froth she peered into their translucent light. Their reflections held within the Riverman's globes consumed her. She found herself pulled within the fragile lights. Suddenly she understood the attention of the probing root as it pressed ever-outward, chewing the solid stone. From within those fracturing bones there settled the writhing worm, the bite of frost creeping down to still its pulsing vein and the sleeping seed burrowed inside the rot, only to rise once again with shafts of sun.

The thought was broken as another globe passed her by and it pulled her to it; the dark was everywhere and sound was all things, moving through the thin skin spread the sticky, sweet taste. Others, close and safe, huddling in the night; claw and tooth. A flock scattered into the dark; fluttering wings against the waning moon.

She drew her gaze away from the globes and focused upon the Riverman. The crystal white cold caught the rays of the new morning. He seemed content, knowing he had her attention.

"I have heard your call Riverman!" she cried across the torrent. "What do you want?" Her call was abruptly answered by a thundering wave. The Riverman was not gentle, and though his riposte seemed courteous, it hinted of danger. Beneath her a face appeared in the spume. His bright eyes held her in his sharp gaze. The Riverman's beard was flowing around the rock upon were she stood. His words rippled through the unsettled currents.

"Hail, Iao's daughter, Seventh Song of the Seventh Sign,
My path ever flows by your father's door.
I am the humble servant of the Greater Master.
I am the one who never sleeps.
I am the journey ever outward,
I am the way of return.
It is I who serves your need, little one.
You are the pilgrim.
I am the means."

His directness surprised her and he was amused by her uncertainty. The sound of his laughter churned in the water. The lights were spilling from the north. Each one born of snow and stream and dripping frost and the globes were everywhere. A glint of gold caught her eye. She peered inside to see a bear struggling in a raging river. She was seized with the impulse to reach for the globe. Putting out her hand, she reached into the light and suddenly found herself within the run, the creature thrashing wildly next to her.

Choking beside him, she gasped for breath until they rounded a bend and the swift current eased. She reached her hand out to the struggling beast, finding she could swim easily through the shifting water. Brown pools now lay along the sides of the riverbed and soon they were able to scrabble out upon the rocky shore. Resting along the rough beach, Yurah surveyed the strange world around her. They lie under the blinding glare of three white suns. Low shrubs and prickling bush speckled the parched terrain. Broken canyons fractured the land and across the river stretched a bleak expanse of desiccated wasteland. Parched clay, sallow and lifeless, spread in all directions under the relentless glare. The long view ahead was blocked by a winding barrier cliff. Layered sediments striped the ruddy cliffs. Behind her, desolate mountains rose above the plains, their sheer clefts and broken ridges soared high above thin clouds. Worn by wind the barren earth crumbled over the cracked edges, and at their feet was the snaking path of the river run. Gnarled trees dotted the dry ground offering patches of shade from the beating suns and beyond the bleak desert, a city of sorts rose from the flat earth.

The beast was at her side, studying the harsh surroundings in its own way. His gray eyes were alert and she pressed her mind into the creature to sense him better. A sharp jolt of heat shot through her skull. The ground met her knees. The animal's breath was close against her check, a low snarl rattled in her ear.

"I meant no offense." she cried soundlessly.

The pitch of the snarl deepened. Her apology was not well taken. The bite of a sharp claw pressed against her skin. She lie still, careful not think another word. Her heart pounded wildly. Dust crawled into her mouth. The bright day began to fade into blackness as the silent moments passed.

When she opened her eyes, grainy bits of sand had burrowed deep into her face. She brushed the grit away. The bear was watching her from the edge of the water.

"Who are you?" she asked, gripping the hilt of her sword. She would not be taken unawares a second time.

The eyes flickered but he did not answer. A bright current was breathing over the dry land and strange voices began to move upon the air. A great thirst suddenly overtook them and, in that instant, their quarrel forgotten. Yurah washed her face as the bear had waded out into the shallows. The center sun was almost straight above them and the odd pair began to walk toward the city.

They tread in silence. The bear kept his head close to the ground, his golden lashes nearly closed as he went. Yurah pulled her hood over her forehead, to shield herself from the pounding glare. Several times they rested under the sparse shade of the gnarled trees. Sword-like leaves grew in clusters from the twisted trunks. Huddled in the center, yellow fruits drooped from woody stems. As the day worn on she began to wonder if the fruit was good to eat. She reached up and touched the fruit and as her fingers brushed it a dryad appeared.

"It is meant for taking." her voice croaked. "You will need it if you are to reach the city."

"Thank you, mother." Yurah answered, plucking the withered fruit. The stem broke easily under her hand. The sallow peel was thick. She bit into it and her faced soured.

"Not so quick, child. Peel away the skin first." spoke the tree spirit gently.

Yurah took a short knife from her pack. The golden flesh underneath ran messily down her chin. The old dryad stood next to the bear, absent mindedly stroking the space between his ears. The beast seemed to take no notice. Yurah pealed another fruit carefully and laid it upon a flat rock. He lapped it up with his pink tongue, the heavy juice oozed from the black jaws.

After they had eaten, the brilliant light did not burn their eyes and they relaxed under the cool shade.

"What place is this, mother?" Yurah asked the dryad.

"You walk in Rempha's Land." answered the dryad gesturing toward to the west. "I have fed many travelers as they make their way towards him. Some come to seek guidance. While others come to rest from the toil of many lives, then there are those who have lost their way. The travelers come to him by many roads," she said stiffly gesturing to the hills. "The cold north mountains, the broken ground of the southern plains, the arid eastern waste; or as you did, from the river that separates one realm from another. But none of these things really matter child. All roads in Rempha's Land lead to the center place. His city goes by many names. To say them all we would stand until every sun rose and fell once more. Today, its name shall be Mundi." Then the dryad shook her thorny head. "It is a meeting ground of odd companions, if you will."

Yurah looked over the grainy soil and in the distance she could see a bright city, gleaming in the hot air. "How far do we have to go, mother?'

"Distances deceive as you travel upon the flats. But you need not fear any harm as you walk though the desert. All things here are held in good order." she smiled, casting a green eye toward the bear. "In Rempha's lands no wanderer will lose their way and should you choose, make your camp with any sister along the way." she continued with a wry smile as her image faded into the heated air.

"Well, I would prefer to reach the gates before nightfall." Yurah said, slinging her pack over her shoulder. "I hope that suits you."

The bear licked his stained jaws and shook the dust from his thick hide. They struck a path toward the city until their pointed shadows stretched long behind them. As the first sun dipped behind the horizon the air became easier to breathe. The new coolness lay soft upon her skin. The city was close now and she stopped under a stand of trees, plucking a yellow fruit and eating it slowly. The bear lay down near her, panting gently. Yurah peeled him a fruit and handed it to him. He ate it as she stood looked out toward Mundi. The city spiraled gracefully and every set of concentric rings were marked by pairs of low towers. The bleached mortar walls were crestless. The doors of the arched gate stood open.

'We must hurry if we are to make the gate by nightfall." said Yurah. "I fear the desert will be a cold place to sleep."

The bear gave her an unconcerned glance and taking a deep breath he left the shelter of the low trees. They walked in the pale dust until second sun fell from the sky. The air was much cooler and Yurah had to quicken her pace to keep up with bear. He plodded on under the indigo sky, turning his head often to check her progress. As the last light faded behind the northern ranges Yurah could see her breath as she walked. Torches were being set along the edges of the watchtowers and as the night swallowed them the distant city glimmered under a field of stars. Yurah stopped to get her bearings under the canopy of dark. Loneliness passed through her like a freezing wind. Standing under the unknown sky cold crept under her cloak. She felt a warm muzzle push against her. The clear sound of a tolling bell broke across the airs.

"We are too late to enter this evening." his thought said, "But do not worry about the cold, I can provide warmth enough for the both of us."

His unspoken words startled her but more than this, his apparent concern astonished her still more. The bear tossed his head toward a grove of huddled trees.

"There is nothing to fear in this place. Though the land is harsh, Rempha watches over all. No harm shall come to any who walk under his sky."

"You have been here before?" she asked him but he turned his head away. "No matter." she replied acknowledging his mood. "Your past is not my concern, but I would like to know your name."

Again the bear seemed to struggle with an inner dilemma and after a moment Yurah knew she would get no answer to that question either.

"So you have secrets, traveler. That is well enough, your business is your own."

"All will be known when we reach the city," he answered indifferently. "until then there is little to say."

A thin moon crept over the grove as Yurah settled herself under a tree pulling her cloak around her. Opening her traveling pack she found the bread was ruined but the fruit and cheese was fair enough to eat. She offered a portion to the bear. He smelled it and refused.

"I do not hunger." he answered, "It is thirst that burdens me more."

Yurah took a fruit from a cluster of sharp leaves. She peeled it and set it on the ground.

"You have been kind." he said quietly, "My earlier actions I regret. I was startled. Your thoughts surprised me."

"Speak not of it. I took liberties unawares. This journey has not been at all what I had expected it to be," she smiled and then glanced up at the stars. "To tell you the truth, I am a bit lost."

The bear took a seat close beside her, his warm flank pressing against side. "I know the names of the some of the lights." he said looking toward the western sky.

"Do you know of Raldabon?"

"You see that one." he replied, ignoring her question. "The blue star there. It rises just over the horizon. Do you not know him?"

Yurah looked to the blue star. "Yes, I recognize it now. The star is of the Hunter. And there resting on his shoulder, lies the greatest of the red suns. And underneath, are the three that make up his girdle. Indeed, I know them all by name. But it is a far different sky than the one I see from home. The nights of Raldabon overflow with stars and beyond its twin, Taygeth there lays a greater cluster still. The dome is sparse here by comparison."

"And yet it is still the same endless dark we all bide. Look along that horizon. See there, it is the River Eridanus."

"And that is Achernar?"

"And above it is the Phoenix and Ankaa. And see," he said as he turned his snout further south, "within the winding river is Beid and Zaurak."

"Beyond is the Hunter burns the brilliant Mirfak. Raldabon lies near those crossing roads."

"Yes, so it does." he answered softly.

Yurah wondered at the beast beside her. He seemed almost content looking upon the evening sky, naming the stars. She looked out over the night and she laid her hand upon her sword remembering the last words Iao spoke. The soreness of the long days walk had taken its toll but the bear was warm beside her. Oddly at ease upon the barren sand, she wrapped her cloak around her and, keeping her eyes set to the west, she fell asleep.

CHAPTER VI
THE LIGHT OF TAYGETH

The globe filled with mist under Doxomedon's searching gaze. He held his hands to either side, taking care not to upset the fragile radiance that hovered within the crystal. Derdekea was at his shoulder. The form he wore could not conceal him. She would know her son through any veil. Staring into the glass she watched as Kiel walked in the barren waste with Iao's daughter at his side.

"They travel together to Mundi. But what from there, Doxomedon?" she said turning from the crystal. "What advice will the Old One give?" then she hesitated, speaking her thoughts aloud. "and will those words be heeded?"

"The Seventh Daughter now carries the talisman of the Annyd at her side. She is bound by fate to lend her force to Erda." answered Doxomedon broodingly. "But Kiel? How is he connected to this forgotten world? And what strange path could have led him back through the Bear? Alas Derdekea, it has been far too long. I do not know my son all."

"Maybe it has been the realm of Erda where he has hidden himself all these years."

The light within the globe began to pulse and Doxomedon steadied it with his long finger "There is someone who may hold answers to these questions."

Derdekea knit her brow, "Rempha?"

"Rempha's concerns are not the same as our own." he said shaking his head. "But there is another that may understand this puzzle. His name is Mqttro. Since the Annyd first intervened in the destiny of that land, he and his legions have watched over her. If Kiel has walked in that troubled realm, the Malkians would have been aware of him. Take heart, my dear. Finally we may learn something of his dilemma."

The glass trembled as the wizard released the secret sound.

The chamber quivered and a white flame blazed within the scrying glass. The tireless Fates within the inner core of Taygeth gazed back at the old mage. One sister was at the wheel, twisting the cord, weaving and ever weaving the threads of fortune. The illusive substance flowed under their hand. An icy wind chilled the flame of life she held in their hands. Suddenly the door between them flew apart. The Malkian's radiance filled the room.

"Welcome Mqttro." said Doxomedon, rising to meet him.

Mqtrro's brilliant wings murmured like a blending of sweet

voices. Clasping a closed hand over his heart he spoke and his voice was like the tolling of bells. "I am honored, Doxomedon. Taygeth is a flawless star. How can I be of service?"

"We seek news of the Little Kingdom. Her cries have touched our dreams. We have bent our minds toward the suffering sound to find a devastated land."

"The centuries have been bloody." the Malkian replied. "Since Ildabyth has returned to Erda, ruin has followed every turn of her yellow star."

"The weight of a war is again upon your shoulders Mqttro." answered Doxomedon gravely.

"It is not your affair Doxomedon. Erda's fate must lie in her hands."

"So it was once said. But relationships renew as time passes." Doxomedon replied. "We are not called to meddle, my friend, but again our eyes have been drawn to your little world. We believe one, long lost to us, is bound within the inner core of Erda."

The tips of his wings pulsed with flame. "The core of Erda has become Ildabyth's stronghold. He keeps his most prized captives there. And I must tell you Doxomedon, it is a fortunate one who sees the shackles he lays upon them. Most of his hostages are but slaves. They are twisted by his will as they blindly perceive themselves as free." Mqttro's eyes flickered in the crystal light and his heat began to fill the room. "Ildabyth's nature pervades every bit and part of the land. His voice has destroyed both human and Malki alike. He moves through Erda without remorse."

"Has taken to himself a form?"

"He uses the mortal forms to do his biddings. He teases the ignorant with riches and entices the educated with twisted bits of the higher laws. Ildabyth tells them secrets that are not meant to be shared. Not so long ago he succeeded in driving the Children of the Yellow Sun from their sacred city. The Basilian stronghold is now held in his hands."

"And so the visions are genuine." said Derdekea.

"Erda's fate is ever wrought with despair." confirmed the Malkian, gravely. " and yet hope remains with us. Just as all things ebb and flow with the turning of the stars we shall stand with her to bear her burden." and as he lowered his brow the heat within the room began to fade. His clear voice soothed the scrying chamber. "You have spoken of another my old friend and, in that, I believe I may be of help. Many years ago, a wanderer was brought to us. She had been gravely wounded and we cared for her in the Gardens of Urdar. After many months she was restored but even as her health returned the star-wanderer did not remember her origins. Since we did not know her name we called the traveler, Lethe, after the River of Oblivion. Her strength grew and we realized the Lady had great powers over water and fire. We left her often to guard the Great Tree that nourishes the forms of Erda and this is where the trouble brewed. Ildabyth has ever desired the secrets of that ancient one, keeping his priests busy in efforts to attain them and one dark night they almost had their way. In a twinkling it seems, a great storm brewed black over the waters and suddenly battles erupted from every direction. We were pressed to leave our island to fight and the Lady Lethe stayed behind to guard the Tree. In hindsight I see that that was the true nature of Ildabyth's plot. He wished to find her there alone for he sent Valentinus and one hundred of his deadliest warriors to assail her as she stood alone.

When we heard their cries and raced back to the Urdar. His army fled when they saw us taking the Lady Lethe prisoner as they went. In the aftermath we found naught but a single strand of her hair. We pondered upon the shred and saw the nature of battle she had fought alone. Many wounds were laid upon her and in the midst of that fighting heat the memory of her origins had been restored. The recollection of all past things returned and she knew her true name as Sro. She had left the whisper of that name within the lock; and whom we called Lethe was in truth the Lady Sro, consort of Iao and sister soul of the Pleiades."

"Yes, Mqttro. The Lady Sro is the soul we seek." answered Doxomedon, softly. "Tell us what you can. What has become of my sister?"

"Time's wheel is a most peculiar thing." smiled the Malki. "though but a day may pass in these finer spheres, centuries will come and go in the Little Kingdom. Since Sro's imprisonment, Ildabyth has relentlessly sought her secrets. Deep within the Crystal Towers, his Dowerymen mutilate the cause of life within the form. Now they have become able to make life from shadows. Ildabyth steals her strength by perverting the core of Erda."

Derdekea was silent. Sro's plight burrowed like a bitter thorn in her mind and an unsettling question rose within her. "How did Sro come to your gardens?" she asked quietly.

"She was borne to us upon the shoulders of the traveler Kiel." replied Mqttro as Derdekea's face grew pale.

"You speak of him as if you have met before." spoke Doxomedon.

"I have known Kiel for centuries." answered the Malki, keeping his eye set upon Derdekea. "Long ago Kiel lived in our gardens upon Urdar."

"Then tell me what you know of him Mqttro, for Kiel is our son and we have not seen him since for many years." she said.

Mqttro bowed his head and he spoke to her in a low voice. "Long ago Kiel walked freely upon the Islands. He is a fair lad, blessed with both with voice and melody. Grace lay within his every movement and when he spoke the beauty of his voice spread over the room like a new day's sun. What I recall most is the stories would he weave. Sadness and joy, dread or bliss, all things tragic and fair could he stir in a heart. Kiel was welcome in every hall but after a time we would see him rarely. Sometimes years would come and go between his visits. It was during one of these long absences disturbing rumors began to reach us. Ildabyth's armies were growing ever larger and our ambassadors would hear Kiel's name spoken in inner circles. It was then we realized he lingered often at Ildabyth's side. But Kiel was a restless child and often the boy would wander. It was more that once that I found him brooding alone in the outer dark of Erda. Each time we would meet I sensed him as increasingly sullen and finally I began to understand his dilemma. I believe Kiel had remained within the shadows too long, listening to the enticements of Ildabyth. The sorcerer's voice had stirred within the boy the heat of pride. Kiel was fed with lies and it was through these wants that he was deceived. "

"Deceived?"

'Ildabyth is the Greatest of Deceivers. Both Human and Malkian alike have fallen into the webs he lays." Mqttro replied, his fiery wings hissing strangely.

The orb upon the table began to glow. The road to Mundi was slipping into darkness and as the last sun set over Rempha's land, the travelers lay themselves down upon the desert to sleep. After a long time, Doxomedon spoke, "I must know Mqttro, did ill come of Kiel's errors?"

"During these years Kiel came and went as he pleased. He used his talents and many were lost to the power of his magical voice. Kiel was torn between the two worlds. It was during these years I often I found him prostrating himself in the outer dark."

"Was his service to Ildabyth?' asked Derdekea.

"I do not believe Kiel knows a true master. Through his frailty he served Ildabyth but I shall not forget that it was Kiel who brought to us the Wanderer Lethe and to that we are ever grateful."

"But how Mqttro?" said Doxomedon shaking his head. "It is only the force brought by a cosmic river and the heart of a living sun that such vast spaces may be mended. By which road did they come to you?"

'That I can not answer. Lethe did not recall her past and Kiel kept his hid. But the story of the Lady Sro and the wanderer, Kiel did not begin nor end within our gardens. As Lethe recalled her true name as Sro, she saw the boy as he is, her deliverer and her betrayer."

"Her betrayer?" cried Derdekea.

"All things have not been said nor done, sister." assured the seraph gently. "Kiel knew Sro's origins, though she did not. Perhaps it was curiosity. Perhaps it was jealousies. Or perhaps it was her great power that intrigued him. I do not know what mind-state served to betray her hiding place to Ildabyth's forces. But even this may serve the Fates of our Yellow Sun, for as Sro was betrayed she was also given back her memory. And the memory of a flawless heart is a most powerful thing. Since that moment, her sacrifice has been our strength. Her grace our beacon."

Doxomedon looked as ancient as his years as he bent to brood over the globe. "I recall what happened in the beginning," he sighed. "When the satellites of the Yellow Sun were whole, and Erda and Urdar were as one world. The perfect design was torn apart. How well I remember well the day we left those planets to heal. But alas, old friend, some did heal and some did not. We misunderstood his cruelty."

"Aye, Doxomedon, the germ slept until it found a new place to take hold. Deceit is its strength and ignorance its blanket. We too misjudged his powers."

"And where are we left, Mqttro? What has happened since? What twist of fate has returned Kiel to Rempha's Land? No one may come to Mundi by chance."

"I can tell you these things Doxomedon, but they may be difficult to hear."

"If healing is to come, I have no choice but to hear them."

"Then you will hear a bitter tale for I have seen much from the upper airs." said the Malkian as the light of the globe flickered, "I watched as Ildabyth imprisoned her, torturing her in his attempts to break her mind. Kiel was ever at his side witnessing the wicked things he did. The Lady knew no relief and it left his heart to burn in remorse. He began to seek refuge in the dark places between the worlds but even here he found not peace. It is the gracious Lady herself who granted him mercy."

"Yes, it would be like her." answered Doxomedon remembering her gentle face.

"She saw how he suffered, hiding himself along the dark edges of the world. When Ildabyth would leave her to herself, tortured and undone, Sro would call to him. At length the boy heeded the voice and emerged from the shadow lands. He came to her willingly, having lost all things. When all was said between them, they devised a plan. Kiel lent to her his perfect voice and she lent to him the powers of the water.

It was enough to reach through Ildabyth's prison." Then a shadow passed over the Malkian's fiery countenance. "It was not a "safe" thing to do. Ildabyth knew the instant that call was sent went forth. He turned his face from his outer business and the earth belched poison fume. Sro saved the boy but at great cost to herself. It is because of her selflessness Kiel escaped his death."

"Did she give him the shape he wears?"

"No, Sro did not wrap him in the skin of the Bear. She had sacrificed all to hold Time's Gate so he could slip though the prison door. The Malki are not the only force that stands against Ildabyth and his armies. There are other guardians. Powerful races, born from the beginning of days, that still bide in the dust of Erda. The Vanyr are the most like we are, living lights born from the ethers of the cold dark. They are eldest in the line of stewards. They are children of the perfect satellites and they are able to serve as seers of the realm. The Alfyr were forged in the core of the Yellow Sun and they are the born warriors of the Little Kingdom. They are fierce and inquiring. But the Drui are the cousins of both, and that leaves them to be the most diverse of all. They are shape-shifters of Erda, understanding the nature of both men and beasts. Each of these lines are all close kin of the first stewards and they heard their cry as it was sent forth from the Ildabyth's prison cells. It was the Drui who had the power to wrap him in his animal skin and send him outward through the Time's Gate. Without them, Kiel would have never made his way to Rempha's Land."

"So this was how Kiel found his way to Mundi." mused Doxomedon, glancing to the globe in the center of the room. "And now he waits outside Rempha's gate with Iao's daughter at his side."

"I saw her face as the suns rose over Mundi. Her name is Yurah. She is the youngest of the Pleiades."

"Aye Mqttro, you have seen true. Yurah carries the sword of her mother, the blade which stayed Ildabyth's hand at last gathering of the Annyd."

"Sro's talisman is a precious thing Doxomedon." replied Mqttro, "But the hour is late in coming and the seventh daughter is still a child. What odds are against her as the greatest of all deceivers takes his place in the fight? Ildabyth is as ancient as the universe. He has succeeded in deluding many of the Elder Race. "

"I will not deny it Mqttro but the child bears the sweetest gifts of her six sisters. She is pure and she is willing. There are many who hold her dear from across the dark sea of stars."

"Then perhaps his shadow shall not be able to still her inner voice." answered the Malkian gravely. "But she travels now with Kiel and he is a fickle companion."

"It is said that the sweetest all things are born in mercy."

"Aye, and the wise do live by it. But even so the Law remains firm. Sro has suffered by his hand and now she suffers still more." he said sadly, "there is little left to do but regroup to fight again."

"The Islands of Urdar shall not stand alone Mqttro." said Doxomedon. "The Little Kingdom will have the aid it requires. Promises once made are not forgotten. The Law can offer no more and hope will not allow for less. Hear the vows renewed, Keeper of the Yellow Sun. May it come to pass that Time's Gate render the key of Victory and may your lands at last know the peaceful fostering for which they were intended.

"May Time's Gate hold the door ajar
As little lives beyond do tremble
Under the threads that bind each star
A shadow cast is light rekindled.
In memory, it is readied.
In moments, it is done.
In motion, it is set
Under star and under sun."

The wizard bowed his head and waited for Mqttro to answer.

The Malki drew his sword. He touched the blade to Doxomedon's forehead.

"As one life, as one mind, as one heart, it is done.
Finis Ahren
Finis Lumin
Finis Aina"

And leaving his farewell unspoken, Mqttro sheathed his bright sword and faded into the airs.

"So another age begins." Derdekea said softly to the old wizard.

"Yes my love and hope remains."

Derdekea did not answer. There was no need; the brilliant glare of clarity was before her. "He is lovely." she thought gazing upon her lost son.

And as she loved him from afar a gentle rustling began to fill the chamber of vision. Along the walls the Muses gathered to hear the news of the boy. Their love of Kiel had never failed. His suffering had but served to strengthen their resolve.

"We will not falter in our vigilance for we love him beyond all things. We do not forget what was given freely. He is our own." rang the voice of Tersicyre and the others murmured in agreement, "Our blessing is untouched by time, unsoiled by tainted circumstance. We reaffirm our vows to the eternal Wanderers, though they may know it not. May we bring the hope that shall never fade."

Doxomedon raised his hands to bless them, "And as beauty and strength remains alive in the Little Kingdom of Erda. May those who wander take comfort in its giving."

"Your gifts shall not fail those who walk within the shadow realms." echoed the firm voice of Derdekea. "She is not forgotten."

And through the dark glass Derdekea gazed toward Rempha's land, wondering what tomorrow would bring.

CHAPTER VII
THE GATES OF MUNDI

A fierce sun burst over the horizon and Yurah set her eye toward Mundi. The bear stirred behind her. Throughout the night he had shielded her from the cold desert air with the warmth of his body. He opened his eyes.

"Did your night pass well?" she smiled recalling she did not yet know his name.

"Fine enough." came the soundless reply. "And your own?"

"To have no proper bed, surprisingly well." she answered as the tower bells began to chime.

"We should reach the gate in a few hours." he said looking toward the sky. "And if we hurry we can outrun her."

"We will get to it soon enough," she answered gently, opening her satchel. "I have food to share. Surely you have need."

"It is thirst that presses me more." was the staid message sent from mind to mind. "There is a spring just beyond the next grove. We can break our fast there. And you can fill your bottle if you wish."

"A spring you say. Indeed a wash would serve quite well before we reach the city." she answered brushing the dust off the cloak. "In fact I believe that a wash might serve better than a meal."

He cocked an eye and began to lumber from the grove. They walked until they came to the next stand of trees. In its shady center a rocky hollow had been carved into the land. Small yellow flowers crowned the rude stair. A spring gushed from the ledge forming a pool at the bottom of the ravine. They climbed down and she sat alongside the water. The bear stood as her side and drank as she washed. When they had finished, Yurah opened her food satchel and laid out some morsels. Again he smelled the fare and again he refused it.

"Take no offense. It would be best if I refrained from foods of other worlds until I pass through the Gates of Mundi." was his wordless reply. Yurah did not press him further, but as she stayed near, hoping to understand him better. With each thought that had passed between them he had told a little of himself. The form he wore did not suit him and brief glimpses of a human shape began to appear in her mind.

"A boy, or possibly a young man," she mused, careful not to allow her thoughts to touch upon him. Patiently he watched as she finished her shallow bath, dunking his head in the cool water and shaking his wide black jaws. Then he lay down along the stones to wipe the dust away from his face with his great paws.

"It is only a few hours to gates you say?"

"No more than that and maybe less."

"This is a certainly a strange place." she said adjusting her satchel.

"Far stranger than you might imagine Lady." murmured his whispering mind as they climbed the stair.

They walked the pathless way toward the gleaming city. The first sun glittered behind them as their shadows reached far ahead. Images of home filled Yurah's mind. The face of the Riverman forming among the stones came and went as she set one foot before the other. The bear kept his head down. His golden lashes were nearly shut to keep the bits of dust from his eyes. After several hours they drew near to the western gate. Other travelers were gathered there and a guard waited at the open door. His tunic was a dull white and emblazed across its front was a circle enwreathed in flames, divided evenly by two intersecting lines. His breeches were the color of the pale desert clay and his black hair hung straight to his waist. He had a silver chain draped loosely about his shoulders. One end was gathered at the collarbone, and upon the loose end hung an oddly shaped cross that rested against his chest. In his right hand he carried a staff. The rod was fashioned of a pale, bleached bone and bound at its top was a faceted white stone.

The guard was speaking to group of men in a language she did not know. They were dressed in bright robes bound with wide golden belts and carried their curved swords unsheathed. Standing along side were several stout dwarves. Their business was brief and soon the guard stepped aside allowing them to pass. A pair of children came next. They were frail. Marks of old wounds marred their milk colored skin. The guard knelt down addressing them in a strange songlike voice. Whatever words he said the children seemed much comforted for their worn expressions had faded into relief as they passed under the arched way.

A clatter of voices then rose as the small group of short, hooded wanderers began to argue. They spoke brusquely and their manners were rude. But the Guard remained courteous and after a time it seemed their dispute had been settled. The tall warden stepped aside and the troupe passed through the Gate to the streets of Mundi.

"Hail Gate-Keeper!" said Yurah, bowing politely when he turned to face them. "I am Yurah, Seventh daughter of Iao and Sro's youngest child. By your leave we seek entrance to Rempha's city."

"Hail Yurah, youngest of the seven maids! To both of you I bear a message" he answered glancing to the bear, "You are expected in the Master's hall this very evening and at his humble table you will be provided with the council you seek." The stone upon the staff glowed

61

as he stepped aside to grant them entrance. "You are free to pass the First Gate."

"My thanks." Yurah answered courteously. She stepped up upon the low stair and peered to winding paths of the bright city, "But sir, I do not know the way." she said. "How will I know when I reach Rempha's Halls?"

"Rempha dwells in the upper house." the guard answered gesturing to toward the climbing alley. "All roads lead to it. In Mundi none can lose their way."

Yurah gazed along the ascending paths. Faint melodies lingered within the mortared walls. The shade of a full green tree danced over the finely cobbled stones leading to the first tier.

"The day is young." continued the Guard. "May I suggest you follow the road that leads to the first circle. A meal is soon to be laid out for all that seek their way."

"Again I thank you sir." she answered.

The Guard nodded a polite farewell as another group gathered at his gate. They left him to his work and walked under the shade of the green tree. Lilac scented the air. Its leaves rustled above them, and as they looked closer they saw that minute birds hovered within the flowers. Fleeting and fragile like a new beating heart Yurah reached her mind to the one nearest her. Shades of violet sweetened with cool winds filled her thoughts. The exquisite creature understood the voice of the sun that danced with the glowing leaves but then a sudden gleam caught her eye. The bear was leaving her behind. She hurried to follow him upon the first alley road.

All along the streets of Mundi were clear fountains and shady places to rest. The warmth of Mundi's second sun had begun to fall about her shoulders and she realized that this light was inherently different from the one before it. The first sphere brought the release of darkness but with this second sun was a healing light. She walked wordlessly, following the bear as he led her between garden rows and long faced dwellings.

After a time they reached what seemed to be a common garden. Lines of trees in even rows ran along its edge and a well worn path twisted its way through their shadows. The thick gray bark and the hand shaped leaves reminded Yurah of the great oaks that surrounded her father's house. The white stone she carried near her heart hummed softly as they walked under the canopy of green, the tall trees rustled above her in response. Colored pavilions were set and cooking smells drifted upon the breeze.

"The midday meal will be soon be ready." the bear informed her silently. "It is the custom of Rempha's folk to provide for those who pass through his Gates. Here we will refresh ourselves before the next step comes." and he walked on, knowing more but not telling it.

Music played in the grove ahead. Harp and lute; voice and drum blended in unfamiliar rhythms as they drew closer to the crowd. Half-grown children, dressed in pale yellow breeches were beginning to carry platters to the waiting travelers. The young servants were just as the Gate-Keeper, uncanny in their ability to speak with each visitor in their own language. Light of foot, they kept the flow of food and drink steady. It was not long before one of them approached Yurah offering a cool pitcher with cups and bowls.

"It is a lovely place." said Yurah studying the others travelers that were settling around her. She hesitated a moment and then lowered her tone so those near did not hear. "It is odd to me that I did not notice it yesterday but the light around us most strange. What I mean is it seems to change as voices pass through it. I can see it, moving from yellows to blues and now to green."

"Such is the nature of the Rempha's land." the bear answered, lifting his head from the bowl "The third has not yet risen. She is the nearest of the three and will blend the light of the first and second. It is the balance held between the three lights which allows Rempha to open and close the gates of Time. The center realm holds threads to every star. It may be used to travel to any place and to any time."

"So from here I shall be able to reach her." she thought, looking to the place where the third sun would rise.

"You speak of Lady Sro."

"Yes," she answered. "How did you know?"

"I have known her for many years," the frail message drifted, "Sro knows no fear but it seems her choice of friends brings her nothing but grief."

Yurah opened her mouth to speak but a serving child stood at her elbow. The plate he carried was laid with warm bread, a bowl of butter and a small wheel of cheese, then he opened a bulging satchel that was stuffed with red pears. She took enough for both of them and thanked the boy.

"Will you be requiring anything else?'

"No, we are well set." she answered, noticing the small silver ring set in his dark brows.

"There is other fare that may be more to your liking set up under the tents." he said motioning toward the pavilions. "And the music will begin soon. You will like it."

"Thank you. We will come to hear it."

The boy bowed low and he took his leave. Yurah had wanted to ask the bear more questions but he had pulled his mind far away from her. She broke apart the loaves and laid the fruit and bread upon the plate between them. She ate slowly, deciding it was best to leave her questions until later. She was intrigued by all the strange creatures that rested upon the lawn. A large centaur lay quietly at the tree closest to her. His golden beard curled over his bare chest. The bronzed flanks were thick with muscle. The creature had no interest in the food left by the young serving folk but drank freely the flagons. Leaning against the tree she buttered another slice of bread. In the leaves above something stirred. Balancing carefully along a thin branch was a beast hardly larger than Hathor, her sister's cat. Its scaly skin glittered green and gold. The wings were not feathered but covered with a thin webbing. It lowered its bony head to glide effortlessly to the tree just above the centaur's shaggy head. The muscles rippled as he settled himself along the bough and turned to meet her gaze. She knew in an instant it was an intelligent beast and then she remembered the creature's name. She knew it from the books Sothis kept in her library, though it was far smaller than any picture she had seen. "A dragon," she said, forgetting all regard for his privacy. "What an exquisite and tiny thing."

"In our tongue we are wyvern." answered the creature letting a snort of flame escape. "And in my own realm I am considered quite large! I am Huaynjyn, Master of Deep Mountains, Treasure Seeker and Keeper of Gold. Take care not to compare what you do not understand!"

"Begging your pardon." she replied, scrambling for words. "It is just, well that would be no excuse but! I mean I have never seen a dragon before."

The centaur snorted its disgust. "Huaynjyn! In your realm you are a nuisance! Not a Master, or Seeker, or Keeper of anything of that sort. An overheated lizard is closer the mark."

Huaynjyn sputtered a tremendous heap of black smoke. Turning himself upside down he hung by a single claw and pointed the other at the centaur.

"I demand apology Nessus!" he exclaimed, his yellow eyes bulging with fury. "What resolution to our woes will ever come to pass if a Centaur's arrogance can not be subdued?"

"Such a temper, Huaynjyn," answered the centaur flicking the ground with a smack of his tail. "I was merely making the point that exaggerations will not serve us now. A clear perspective must be kept in these trying times." he replied as his eyes narrowed. "Remember Huaynjyn, though our problems are the same, we share little else."

"Decorum and tact are not the least of which." said the dragon fluttering to the ground to stand nose to nose with the enormous beast.

"Decorum and tact you say! Are those a lizard's words for pomp and flatteries?"

"Flatteries! Flattery is the life blood of a centaur. Oh golden beast, how strong you are! Oh how virile! Oh how you carry your four legs under your bulging chest!" he continued in an acerbic lilt. "It is only the pride of a centaur that knows no bounds, for the dull edge of their intellect is quickly reached."

"Please sirs." said Yurah, taken aback by the exchange, "I did not mean to invite discord."

"The discord between us is not yours to invite Lady." answered the dragon still bristling. "It was the grandfathers of our grandfathers that had the first quarrels and long history is hard to put aside. Circumstance has bound us but that does not make our past any easier to swallow."

"If dragons had let alone the gold of men our lands would be peaceable still. Sneaky stealths, your people are! Tell me Hyaynjyn, how many moonless nights did your folk steal unseen into their villages carrying away their shining things?" said the centaur dryly. "But your people depend over much upon cleverness for you are too weak to defend what you have taken and when the men came to find you, you found you needed us. It was only then that you did not resent our presence in the foothills of the mountains."

"But in the end Nessus," answered the dragon shaking his head, "in the end it did not help us; for men have other possessions that glitter in the eyes of beasts and men! Your folk have slain hundreds only for the joy of doing it. You have stolen their women and are all too fond of their drink." A wisp of dreary smoke curled above his head and the dragon lowered his head and muttered to the ground. "The two-footed ones love your kind as little as they love us."

"They are foul folk with few virtues." stated the centaur proudly. "But the two-footers have grown great in number. It is our land and our homes that they desire now." His voice deepened as his lips curled. "We have paid twice for each one we have taken."

"And of late the two-foots have joined with the evil one," replied the dragon grimly "putting put both metal and ritual at their command. They are spoiling your meadows and pillaging our lairs. This is why we must mend our differences Nessus. If any of our folk will know peace again it will be because we have found a shred of it between ourselves."

The large centaur made Yurah nervous. His calm demeanor could barely hide the well of arrogance that flickered behind his eyes. And though the small dragon seemed intelligent, it was easy to see the creature held few regrets of any past offenses. Thievery was his nature and he did not deny it. Yurah was frightfully aware of his tempers for, during their brief conversation, the wyvern had left many blackened scorch marks upon the grass. The bear paid his own sort of attention. But Yurah felt his mind upon them though they knew it not. He was licking his paws and eating his fruit, seeming oblivious to the quarrel around him. She knew his silent question though the dragon did not know it. The wyvern thought that Yurah had spoken aloud.

"Nessus and I are the emissaries appointed by our people to seek the wisdom of the Center Land." he answered. "It is our hope to carry back solutions so we may survive and prosper as the days pass under the sun."

Yurah posed his next question for him. "And what is it you expect of Rempha? He does not give favors." she asked, finding herself uncomfortable with the bear's words but the dragon did not seem to notice.

"All roads meet in the realms of Mundi. Time does not carry in this land so we will be patient and wait for his wisdom to be bestowed to us. Though Rempha is a grim master he will offer wise words." he sighed, with a dreamy look in his eye. "And I for one am anxious to hear them." he said cutting his eye about to stare the Centaur just as the sound of drums pounded the airs.

"The pageant begins." the bear told her silently and the dragon mistook the unsaid thought for Yurah's words.

"You know much of this realm, Lady. It is fortunate we have made your acquaintance. Shall we go see what the festivities hold?" he said smoothing his wings. "Your companion seems much like my own, burly yet dim." The Centaur's stare ran over her skin like oily water. She took her hand and laid it upon the bear's shoulder. "My companion is not what he appears."

"They never are. Beasts must be watched with great care. Their lower natures hold sway over every deed." said the dragon half-closing his eyes. "I may be able to shed light upon your problems. I am very learned in these matters and you are young and inexperienced."

Yurah imagined she heard something resembling a chuckle in the mind of the bear as the dragon rambled on. But the mind of the Centaur was an entirely different thing. A cold notion, like a grinding wheel grated in her thoughts. She held her thoughts close as the four began to walk toward the bright tents. The three suns had fully risen. The greens and blues; yellows and shades of red blended in ways she had never imaged possible. The group of men and dwarves they had seen earlier lunched together. Large platters of meats and flagons of ale were spread around them. They were smoking pipes and jesting amiably with one another as they passed by. Just beyond a group of tree-spirits and fire sylphs were walking together. Their fair voices rose and fell in diplomatic discussion. Rich aroma's swirled in the airs and everywhere around them thronged with life. Her companion seemed unconcerned and Yurah wondered how many times he had walked the spiraling streets of Mundi.

"Rempha's city is wealthy." the wyvern mused with a gleam in his eye, "It is said that the northern mountains hold riches beyond all the imaginings. What lies there has ever been a source on ongoing debate amongst my people. I would like to put the matter to rest and have a look at them before I return home. Of course it would be a purely intellectual endeavor. It is likely he would grant me audience if the request was put forward to him." his yellow eyes flickered red as he said it. Suddenly the centaur made a loud smacking sound with his mouth. "Look Hyaynjyn!" he exclaimed pointing to sky. "Look up and see your better!" And they cast their eyes to the treetops to realize an enormous dragon was settling among the multitude. Its ebony body gleamed and, along the tips of its wings, an indigo light glowed. It landed gently amongst the crowd. A great gathering had begun to assemble around the glorious beast but Hyaynjyn showed no interest. Instead he flew to Nessus' broad back, pretending to ignore the giant creature.

"Rempha sets a fine feast for his travelers." he continued looking to the other direction with a wistful sigh, "I must say such abundance reminds me of my father's time. How our halls would gleam! What a table we would set! We were rich beyond all accounts before trouble came. Oh how I long for such days again."

The centaur walked on, acknowledging the unasked for hitchhiker by the smirk on his face.

"It is a wonderful place." agreed Yurah, gazing back at the dragon. "The music here is beautiful. The melodies are so strange. The sound of it reminds me of the sunlight."

"Oh, hmmm, yes of course." remarked the dragon, rudely unmindful of her remark. "But as I was saying, my father's halls were bountiful and as a young sprite I," and just as Hyaynjyn was about to tell her of his childhood the boy who had served them earlier hurried by. He smiled when he saw Yurah and pointed to a small yellow tent.

"There you will find food to your liking. Sweets and breads, cold drinks and healing salves are available for your comfort and beyond is a place to wash. Do not be shy sister. All things are meant for you here. And for you Master Hyaynjyn, the stone building at the edge of the next stair holds elixirs designed for your kind. I am sure you will find them most refreshing. And Master Nessus, look just beyond the fountain there along that wall both greens and meats are offered to please either of your natures. If you need anything just call. I am Leo." He bowed and then hurried to an ailing woman that lay upon a litter.

At the invitation Yurah politely excused herself, saying that a place to wash away the dust would be most welcome. They were most happy to oblige her for the boys offer had intrigued them as well. As the group parted company Yurah and bear walked on to the yellow tent.

"This place is overrun with odd companions." she said.

"Centaurs and dragons are unaccustomed to working together. But here all things are possible. Old hurts can find ways to be mended."

Yurah noted the remark and took care with her response for the bear's mood was as changeable as a summer wind. "Then as evening falls I might come to know your true name?"

"My name and more, Lady. But the story is a unhappy one and only Rempha can tell it well enough. So again I beg your pardon, I do not mean to be trite." and she heard him chuckling as a picture of Hyaynjyn appeared to her mind.

When they reached the yellow tent Yurah went to the baths and when she finally rose from the steamy warmth she found a clean tunic and blouse had been provided for her. The blouse was a snowy shade with a silk ribbon that tied loosely about her throat. The pale tunic was smooth and finely threaded. She ran her finger along the faint blue edges touching the silver cording that bound the silken seams. A fine embroidery curled gracefully around the neck and covered buttons slipped through silver loops. Her cloak had been brushed clean and her boots were neatly shined. The clothing suited her perfectly and, after she had dressed, she spent time brushing out her auburn hair. She gathered her birthday gifts and thought of her home. When all was to her liking she picked up her pack and went to find the bear.

He lay in a bit of sun, his head resting upon his paws. He rose to his feet when he saw her and shook out his golden coat. A spray of water scattered everywhere, leaving him damp and ruffled.

"They provide for all here, even a hairy beast like myself," he answered lightly. "If we are to reach Rempha's halls by the setting of the suns we must begin. He lives upon the uppermost level of the city. So if you are ready Lady."

"Yes Master Bear, I am ready to meet the Lord of this city." And for an instant she could see someone else was standing before her. The bear felt the intrusion and his sullen mood returned. "Come my friend," she said with a quiet smile, "Let us be off!" and leaving the satisfied crowds and fair music behind them, they began their climb.

The homes of the city dwellers were thin buildings nestled between terraces and rooftop gardens. The streets were unnaturally quiet but the silence brimmed with an expectation. They climbed the steep paths and winding alleys turning always upward.

It was bright afternoon when they left behind the dwellings of householders. The next level was more formal with great pillars and wide stairs leading to grand halls. Among the walkways and buildings Yurah now caught glimpses of other folk. They moved swiftly, with the hoods of their sand colored robes pulled over their heads to shield them from the bright sunlight. Most wore no shoes and if it were not for their hurried motions she might not have noticed them at all.

"They are Rempha's pupils." stirred the thoughts the Bear sent her. "It is a final chore they choose to face. Such a thing might take lifetimes to complete by our reckonings. The task of ordering the city is theirs but there is more that happens here as the suns rise and fall."

As he finished speaking a robed figure approached them. Piercing black eyes peered from under the hood to revealing the face of a girl, not as old as herself. She gestured her welcome and indicated that they should follow. The girl moved quickly, leading them through open doors and sunny lawns. Yurah drank in the sights as much as the hurried pace would allow until a shining building caught her eye. The structure was peculiarly symmetrical. Thick crystal walls were clear as a polished diamond. Within the device, gears and chains, whirring motors and turning spheres, churned in constant motion. Shadows danced upon the lawn as the mechanism rotated and spun. Yurah stopped to look into the walls and inside the center of the soaring structure burned a brilliant lamp.

"It is a timekeeper." the familiar voice echoed in her thoughts. "The source of its power is the center sun. His apprentices use it as necessary. But come now Lady, we must go," he motioned with a slight toss of his head. "She is growing impatient."

They caught up to their guide along a tall flight of glistening stairs A broad dais opened out. Tall fluted columns flanked the wide esplanade. They walked between them as last of the suns shown directly above. Yurah kept her head bent leaving her plenty of time to study the walk beneath her feet. The stone was perfectly fitted, holding no crack nor blemish even under the fierce heat of Rempha's Suns. They followed the walk, passing beyond the gracious buildings and sullen statues, until they found a massive ziggurat which waited at the end of the boulevard.

Their shadows were long as they reached the well kept oak grove surrounding the pyramid. The shade was refreshing and Yurah wished she could take off her heavy boots and walk freely under the rustling leaves of the grove but their guide turned sharply as reached the end of the walk. Soon all other buildings were lost from sight and only the oak trees and the shadow of the ziggurat remained. Nestled in the midst of the forest Rempha's house stood alone. It was an austere building. Its base was a perfect cube and its walls a brilliant white. High, steep roofs rose from each equal side and set within the hard angles were narrow sharp-faced windows. They approached from the east and, when they reached the top to the bluff, they could see how far they had truly come. Behind them the northern peaks blazed and, to the west, the City of Mundi glistened under the last settling rays. Perfect walls encircled the city and beyond their glittering stone the desert lie starkly sprinkled with twisted trees and scrubby brush. The stained sky burned with streaks of red and tongues of gold.

As they came closer, the wide doors slowly opened without making a sound. Low couches and lamps were scattered idly about the empty hall. The shining floor captured bits of firelight flickering under a thick stump of wood. Then suddenly the hearth leaped up into a dazzling burn. Yurah blinked in surprise for now, were no one had been before, a young boy tended the fire. He was fair with gleaming blue eyes.

"Greetings guests! I am pleased you have come. I am Rempha! Your humble host for the evening." he smiled, looking almost roguish as he rose from the hearth. "Long has it been since I greeted a child of Raldabon." he paused looking to the bear. "And longer still since we have spoken my friend." Then the boy fell silent, probing the bear's thoughts and after a time the boy spoke to Yurah. "My pardon Lady I do not mean to be rude. This evening is intended to bring calm and clarity to you both. The time has come to set things right with your companion. I beg your leave to restore him. Sudra shall show you to the garden. There are refreshments waiting. We shall not be long in joining you."

They left by the wide hall along the north side of the great square house. Rempha, seemed fragile compared the lumbering flanks of the bear. Yurah watched until they turned the furthest corner and as they were lost from sight she noticed her guide beside her was barely visible.

"I will show you the way." Sudra spoke as her solidity returned. "The night flowers will have opened. It is a lovely time." and she took her hand and led her down the opposite hall.

CHAPTER VIII
THE BINDING FORCE

The white flames formed a perfect circle and Anath peered over its edge to look into the mirror glass. Slowly a mist grew over the dark face. The wandering melodies of her sisters spilled into the circle and, bit by bit, the mist cleared until a barren desert landscape appeared within the pool.

"She has found her way," spoke the green-eyed seer. The others drew near, quietly taking turn to look into the glass.

"Who is with her?" whispered Tyla.

"A beast." said her twin.

"It is no beast." answered Iao. "That is Kiel who walks at her side."

"Yes. It is Kiel." replied Anath, her eyes growing wide. "I can see it now."

"What strange tales might he have to tell?" mused Raeyn watching them walk across the bleak landscape,

"How far are they from the Gates?" asked Anath.

"The Suns are setting. They will not reach them before the bells sound." Sothis replied.

The images before them began to blur. Fleeting glimpses of banners and dragons; suns and mountains, towers and gates, sentinels and dancers, leaf and twisting vine, passed though the scrying glass as bits of the story began to unfold.

'They will enter Mundi on the morrow." said Iao watching the stars form in the night sky. "Then Rempha will send them on their way."

"And what way, father?" asked Lyli.

"To the land of Erda." interupted Tyla, "It must be so."

"It lies centuries from us," worried Raeyn. "there is little we can do to help her."

"Mundi is a meeting ground. There is no place that cannot reach it." Iao explained, "The star is riddled with portals and curves of space. Rempha is its Master and he holds the key to every opening of Time's Door."

"And what of her companion?" asked Lyli.

Iao looked thoughtfully into Anath's mirror, and finally said. "He will walk as she goes"

"He is more a burden more than a boon." said Tyla pointedly.

"I do not trust him. Nothing about this is safe at all." said Lyli.

"A vast battle rages in the land of Erda." answered Anath, her thoughts far away. "It rises and falls. It is a tempest howling in the dark."

"Kiel could prove to be a useful companion. He understands the dual nature of that world. As an infant the land of Erda was fractured by Ildabyth's intent and its stewards were driven from her perfect waters. But you are right daughter, he is not blameless." replied Iao, "And all along the Little Kingdom has ever been a battlefield."

Eide drew near to the mirror to look once more into the glass. Harsh stony peaks appeared in the reflecting pool. Beneath the gray cliffs and glimmering snows, deep green trees covered the desolate rock. Their thick boughs kept hid the earth but her eye was keen and pressed into the protecting shadows. A sweet music filled her mind and long years of suffering entangled her heart. Then a face appeared. The eyes were clear blue and the skin was fair. Dark hair flowed over his shoulders. He put a flute to his lips and its melody poured from his world and into her own.

'They are Driin's folk!" she said softly as her mind soared over the pain-filled world. "Is this real what I see, father?"

"Yes, it is real. The ancient stewards of Little Kingdom are of the line of Oiolosse." he explained. "Long ago the elder race was left to manipulate the strange stuff that formed her bits and parts. In time their lovely creations rippled upon its waters and filled the airs and earth." Then he turned away from the mirror and walked to the window. "Ildabyth watched the work. Intrigued, he concealed himself in the outer shades, as they teased the combining bits. He became enthralled by what could be molded from those few things and he used his will to turn their fragile experiments to his own designs." Iao turned back and looked upon his beautiful daughters. "When they saw their lovely works ruined they fought against it. Their wars lasted for thousands of years and the first race saw many of their people destroyed. Finally the wounded fled the ravaged land and the original lines were fractured. But those that wandered did not forget their struggling kin and sought aid among the powers of Endless Dark. Rempha was among these folk, as was Doxomedon, and Mirfak. And your mother children, she too was one of that number." he told them watching their eyes widen in disbelief.

"Yes daughters," Iao said sadly, "Long ago Sro traveled to Erda and the folk of the Little Kingdom called those warriors from across the milky stars, Annyd. It was the Annyd that summoned the Malkians to be recreate what had been made before and it seemed Ildabyth's hand had been stayed."

"Did you know her then father?" asked Eide.

"It was not until that work was done did Sro come to Raldabon, soon after she bid Oiolosse and his people to come and dwell in the Cold Mountains. All too well Driin's kin understand Erda's unhappy fate for they are ever bound to that far place."

"And what was its fate, father?" asked Raeyn.

"The realm was left with the task of mending the frailties within it." he answered softly. "The Malki stayed to guard the Seed of Life. They stand before the Great Tree feeding it with the sacred waters of the River Urdar." Iao then looked into the mirror glass and seeing, that Yurah stood before Rempha's hearth, hints of what was to come formed in his mind. "The chance to succeed again stands by Time's Gate." he considered, but he kept the thought to himself.

CHAPTER IX
REMPHA'S TABLE

Shadows danced along the empty walls of Rempha's house. The windows bore no curtains and Yurah drank in the sights beyond every open door. The room to her right was all but empty save for a silver harp standing alone upon a pearl colored rug. She wished to pluck its waiting strings but her guide hurried on. A long low table made of a light colored wood was in the next. The wall was covered by shelves filled with tear shaped jars. As they passed Yurah noticed a strange odor wafting through the open doors and when she looked back, the table had been suddenly set with colorless bowls filled with colorless sand.

The next series of chambers were almost alike, each holding only a narrow bed and unadorned trunk. A large window ran from ceiling to floor and in every one of the odd little rooms a thin stair descended from the corner.

Soon they reached a great glass hall. The first stars twinkled above the domed ceiling. Clay pots, bursting with leaf and bloom, sat upon every wall and, upon every ledge, briary vines curled around metal trellises. Invisible hands opened the garden doors and she was called to follow. The terraces of Rempha's garden were layered. Cascading blossoms fell over low walls of climbing vines and night birds sang to the twilight sky. Sudra led her down a long set of stairs until they reached a broad dais that overlooked the city. A gentle stream flowed by the edge of the garden and a group of golden fish were waiting at the edge. They rolled their bulging eyes to stare, expecting something to eat as the girls hurried past. An oddly carved table waited at the center of the dais. The tower bells signaled the closing of the gates and, as the tolling bells rang, bowls and platters began to move through the air. Warm bread and soft butter, roasts and jams, bowls of fruit, platters of corn and wheels of cheese floated by to settle on the table. Sudra smiled as the Rempha's clear voice broke the silence. From the stairs of the terrace beneath the pair came to join them. A tall young man with sullen gray eyes now walked next to the pale Rempha.

"So we have arrived just in time for supper." said the boy happily but Yurah hardly noticed their boyish host for the change that had come upon her companion had left her spellbound. When she looked into his face she knew his name.

"You are Kiel."

"Yes Lady. I am Taygeth's wandering son." he answered with a graceful bow. His voice was rich as if wind and water and heat had combined into a single perfect sound. She remembered the stories her sisters told of the restless boy and she wondered what fortune had befallen him in the years since he had left his father's home. He knew her thought and he answered quickly, "Of late I have wandered in the lower realms of Erda," he answered, avoiding her gaze.

"And there is much to tell." said Rempha motioning gently toward the table, "So please sit my guests and we will talk as we refresh ourselves." He reached for a pitcher and poured a thin golden fluid into their waiting goblets. "To the future." he said nodding toward Sudra. Holding her cup to the skies, the girl's hood fell away to reveal her thick golden hair and she repeated. "To the future." Then she lay her hand over the mouth of the goblet murmuring words they did not hear. Slowly the glasses began to glow. Rempha smiled and drank from his cup, the light setting his face aglow. Yurah and Kiel followed and as they sipped of Rempha's wine they found it difficult to decide if the taste were bitter or sweet.

Rempha raised his hand and in no particular order the platters rose from their places. The lanterns' glow began to reveal wavering images of bright-eyed children carrying the platters. They moved soundlessly about the table, offering food and pouring drink.

"You are becoming accustomed to the upper airs." said Rempha noticing Yurah could see the young servers. "True vision returns as the days of Mundi pass."

Yurah savored the odd taste of the wine, wondering at Rempha's strange words. She felt her companion pressing for her attention.

"She lives." she heard him say, "She lives, though until this night I did not know it.

The sword at Yurah's side pulsed with heat and the scabbard that kept it repeated the odd words.

"*Cuimnech. O traod annrach, Cuimnech. Cuimnech an.*"

"It is a restless flame that will fill the dark spaces" Rempha's thoughts answered the sound. "And it is a wanderer that shall remember what is lost." he said aloud. "Such is the hope of the Little Kingdom."

"Hope? Erda holds little of that precious thing." replied Kiel grimly. "Soon there will be nothing left and he is saving her until last." he said hanging his head.

"There are those who stand against him." Rempha answered gently. "Remnants of the first race still dwell within high mountains and others lie hid upon the desolate shores of her green sea. They are strong but few. Many have been lost in battle and many more have fallen victim to the treacheries of his voice."

"It is all too simple to do." whispered Kiel.

"And you know this better than any my friend. Though much is ruined, new time has been offered for the healing of that world and must I remind you that old allies are again drawing near." Then boy turned to face Yurah knowing she listened intently. "But be aware, Seventh Daughter that the way is not sure. The choice to go on remains your own."

"In dreams I have seen it." she answered softly. "I know my mother waits for me in a darkness I have yet to know. For me choice does not remain, only the call to follow."

'To follow her is more dangerous than any death you may have dared to imagine. She has been taken by something more hideous than anything you have ever dared to dream." answered Kiel darkly.

"I will not leave her to suffer alone."

"If you are to follow Sro's path you must bear the same burden that she took upon herself." he replied with a glow in his eye. "The Higher Laws will not be broken, for good or for ill."

Yurah did not answer. Instead she watched the candlelight dance in his pale blue eyes.

"Many have tried and failed." She heard him saying.

"Then if I too shall fail, I shall fail trying." she answered solemnly, "All doors are closed to me save one and I hear in your voice that you know it too."

Rempha smiled a bit. "Some things I know and some things I do not." he said gently. Then, like a crackling heat, she caught an inner glimpse of the boy. She was left with the impression of fierce expectancy and she wondered what was really hidden by that childlike form.

"Iao raises his daughters well." Rempha replied. "I will tell you what I know of her. Sro understood the costs as the Annyd delved into the substance of that realm and Ildabyth knew these things as well. For long years he lurked about her Yellow Sun. It was his hand that played the greatest role in the fall to lesser things. Since that time the Little Kingdom has remained a fractured place. But I must remind you, Sro's child, there are many lives within Erda which foster good. While there are others," and he paused, looking to Kiel tense face. "there are others who have done great harm."

Though he spoke no word Yurah knew Kiel suffered. Somehow he was aware of every hurt Ildabyth dealt her mother and somehow she knew he too carried the burden of Sro's bondage. Suddenly she felt herself rushing toward the dark. A furious wind rushed through her. Pain rent her like razors and a merciless sound echoed inside her mind. Above her a great light blazed and she felt herself breaking into parts.

She felt a cool hand upon her brow.

"What is the burden, Rempha?" she gasped, returning from the vision.

"It is the past child," he answered solemnly. "But all recollections will fade as you as you walk upon her shores. Upon Erda far-memory is all but forfeit. Even the voice of your undaunted faith will be but a whisper. Just as it was with your mother when she entered the Little Kingdom, so shall you be."

"My memory?" she said. "Why?"

"To say it most simply, it is the substance of that world which forces it to be so. Her dark light hides the finer realms," he answered, looking to stars. "And where the two meet, the memory of the higher airs is obscured. It can be no other way, at least not yet."

"Is this why she left us?" she asked him anxiously. "Is it why she sent no word?"

"In part, but there are other factors at play."

"Pardon me sir, but I do not understand? Again it seems, all that concerns this Little Kingdom must be spoken of in riddles."

"Then let it be enough to say, her memory was wiped clean," he told her sadly. "but such a thing is oft a mercy"

"Sro's plight is my doing." Kiel interrupted starkly. "It was I who lead them to her and she remembered all when she saw me there standing with his army." He pushed his chair aside and stood against the garden wall, looking over the city.

"Do not take all blame Kiel. All evil is not of your making. Good has come of your acts. Look around and see what fortune has once more been bestowed. Again we meet, do we not? And at your hand is a companion truer than you have been to yourself. Be still now. There is a plan and, with resolve, it may yet succeed."

In the distance, music drifted softly upon the caressing wind. Rempha sat quietly, his calm permeating the night. Yurah held her tongue as her heart raced, waiting for him to speak, and after a time Kiel turned around.

'It is a long tale and much of it does not bear repeating." he finally said, turning round to hold her gaze. "I traveled to many realms during these wandering years and what I searched for still I did not know. When I happened upon the Little Kingdom of Erda I met folk that reminded me of my home. They welcomed me making me into their lands, treating me as one of their own and for a while I found happiness among them. But soon old stirrings welled again and I would hear strange voices calling from across the upper airs. So once more I began to wander. Often I would travel to the edges of that world and wait in the cold upper winds. It was in this place where I first met him. Kindly he looked in his robe and beard. I suppose he reminded me of my father. He was clever and willing to chance. He talked of things I had never considered before and when he was near I had sensations I had never known. As time went by I found myself much intrigued by the lower realms where he was called Master and I began to follow him there. This was my first real error though I see now that it was the restlessness of my own thought had led me to it."

"Did you know that your father sought you and your mother grieved?"

"It was always my intention to return to Taygeth."

"My mother beckoned to you, Kiel. She summoned you for years, believing that you lived but knowing not of your plight."

"It tormented me to deny her voice." he answered grimly, "Day by day, my heart grew more burdened and finally I told Ildabyth of her call. We began to talk of Taygeth and of Derdekea and Doxomedon. I told him of Raldabon and of its lovely daughters. Only later did I realize he would often lead the conversation back around to Sro. He had always known who she was. He remembered her from the ancient war and when the Annyd finally succeeded in his exile. I see now why he was so intrigued. He extended to me a false pity and I did not see behind his pious words. I allowed myself to be made blind." he sighed.

It was Ildabyth who led me across the stars. She was calling to me on that morning, surrounded by the Riverman and his lights. He told me to speak to her and I hid myself behind a cloud and called her name. She lay down her sword because I explained that I feared it, and I asked her to do it." then his gray eyes grew dark his voice shuddered. "That was when they appeared. A legion of fell things poured from a sudden rip in the sky. Raw and withered, they were. Their skin hung in tatters and they stank of death. They fell mercilessly upon her and smothered her cries for help. The Riverman fought them. He raised up and called the wind and she came to aid him. Together they reached for her but it was too late. The shades had pulled her from the world. Ildabyth stood at my side, holding my arm, telling me not to follow, saying that I would not be safe. Still I did not see his true intentions and I fell victim to fear.

'When I awoke, I was in his castle. Feigned tears poured from his eyes when he told me of her capture and of the battle that followed. He said that the forces that surrounded him were too strong and he did not have the strength to take her from them. When I heard the bitter tale I was stricken to my core. Finding no courage within me; my mind grew weak. I chose not to seek her but instead to lose myself in the forgetfulness of the lower lands. There I did not have need to recall that Sro was gone and that I was to blame." he said sadly. "And that was yet another fatal mistake."

"Tell her what came after." reminded Rempha. "It is necessary that she know the truth."

"But this too is spoiled," he sighed.

"Do not fear your past." he encouraged him. "Go on with the tale."

"Here at your table Rempha, every regret is all too clear and still this the story has not yet ended."

"Then tell her what happened next, Kiel?"

"Little and much I dare say." he replied drawing a heavy breath. "Ildabyth saw to my comforts. There were maids, and song, and strong drink always close around me. It was simple enough to could go from one day to the next with only a dull ache to remind me of her loss." he said softly, shaking his head. "But time passed as it seems to do and old longings returned. I would leave the city to go to the upper airs and listen. There Sro's memory could return. It blew through me in that cold place and I was racked by its icy hand. The world beneath turned from day to night and night to day. I was alone with my pitiful self and the wind would not stop blowing and I watched as Ildabyth made busy with his wars. He had won many campaigns, and when he took the Ringed City, it seemed he needed me no longer. So I sat for years, looking out to the starry sky, and finally my isolation overwhelmed me, so far from home was I. Desperately I cried to the heavens in hopes another would hear and as I called out a traveler happened by. I recognized him immediately for once I had regarded him as a friend. He was Malkian and dwelled upon the perfect Isles of Urdar. We talked long and he laid out no judgments. He spoke to me fairly, stirring in my heart whispers of things forgotten. I returned to the Ildabyth with a new calm. He gave me clearance to go anyplace with his city I wished. None thought it strange when I began to frequent the highest levels of Basilus. I enjoyed walking within its crystal towers and speaking with the priests and the learned men. It was in those lofty halls where I first heard the whispers of dissent."

"The Dowerymen had been given the highest offices in Basilus. They serve as discoverers, collectors, observers, and inoculators of the natural laws. It was from those men that I learned of a mysterious prisoner concealed beneath their towers. When they spoke of their work and I heard their cold, reasoned words my heart grew troubled. So secretly I viewed their minds and when I saw into their thoughts I knew their prisoner was none other than Sro. I followed them to where they held her waiting in the shadows until I found a moment to slip through their locked doors." he paused then, staring into his cup and remembering, "She had become but a wraith of her former self." he said finally, "They tormented her; stealing bits of skin, straining her bones, piercing her hands with metal rods, bleeding her veins. So intense was the suffering they laid upon her, my heart became filled with blind rage and I seized a rod."

Kiel bowed his head and stared again into the still goblet. After a time he raised his eyes and met her gaze. "I broke their skulls across their filthy altars. Then I gathered Sro in my arms and fled the city. I went to find my friend, the Malkian. I did not tell him what I had done and he asked me not. I left Sro upon the Isles of Urdar to be healed as I sought exile in the cold airs. I watched their battles play out from above and would take neither side."

"Then why do you despair, Kiel? asked Yurah. "You saved her from Ildabyth's prison?"

"Save her? No, I did not save her, at best I only spared her for a time. I still trusted him. I believed him when he told me his men had acted without sanction. I did not know what was in his heart and before all was said and done, it was I who delivered her to him. "

"What?" Yurah whispered in disbelief.

"I left her with the Malkians and over time their powers healed her. But there was one thing that their powers could not do. Sro did not remember herself. She had spent too long trapped within lower lands. I did not have the courage to return to her. I could not tell her of the past and of those who loved her and missed her. So I grieved pitifully in the outer dark. The universe became a wretched place and the years passed by. I spoke little for only a few wanderers would dare pass though that warring realm. It was Ildabyth who finally found me in my hiding place. He spoke to me as a child who had once erred. He told me such things could be mended and reminded me that he too had been deceived by the treachery of his ministers." then Kiel laid his head into his hands and shadows spun round his dark hair. "I cannot understand why his words rang true. I suppose I wanted to go with him. I was weary of my isolation and he offered me those comforts that had once pleased me. So again I returned with him to the lower lands and I was stunned by what I saw. War had taken its toll upon Erda. The people of Basilus suffered dearly. The priests would use their powers to incite them to battle time and time again." Kiel paused and took a long drink from his cup. At his side an urn stood ready and unseen child poured the empty glass full.

"Ildabyth began to tell me stories of a Great Tree that grew upon the Isle of Urdar. I knew that this was so, for I had seen it often when I lived among those folk. It reached from a snowy peak that shadowed the Northern part of that realm. It bent and twisted its mighty limbs far into the heaven. A powerful life flowed through it and it gave the skies of that fair realm is unworldly glow. But Ildabyth knew more of that tree than did I. He told me that the tree held the spiraling secrets of all life and with this he could put all things that were wrong back to right. But the Tree was guarded by the Malki and they had refused to give its secrets to his suffering folk. And as I listened to him it seemed that the Malki erred and their wrongs should be undone. So I ate his food and drank with him as he spoke to me of his plans. They burned into my heart until no other thing seemed reasonable to do and finally I agreed to go with soldiers; to help them take the thing they desired and the thing they believed they deserved."

Kiel sighed. No longer could he hold his eye to hers as the last part of the tale unfolded. "Ildabyth had told me often that I was his favorite and if harm would ever come to me he could not bear it. He laid his hand over my own and said I must remain safe from the Swords of the Malkians but he needed my skills to help his people. He wanted me to ride with his warriors as they fought for the Great Tree. He wished for me to play the battle-drums and inspire his armies forward. So again I listened to his counsel for I had grown to love him too. The day of that Battle soon followed. He sent his men and beasts and flying machines over all parts of the green sea and upward to the coldest mountain. But this was but a ruse to deplete the Malki of their forces. He knew their numbers would be spread too thin to protect the Great Tree as Ildabyth sent the mightiest of his warriors to battlefields of Urdar. I went with that battalion, playing the drum and enraging the men with its murderous rhythms. As we approached I saw that the Tree was guarded by but one soldier. And as we came near it became clear that that this one soul was mighty warrior, perhaps mightier than all of Ildabyth's forces combined. None could draw near, so I played the drum with all my skillfulness and the battle lust poured through Ildabyth's soldiers. But still, his men were driven back and it seemed the single warrior would win against the legion that Ildabyth sent. Then Valentius took me from my place and pulled me to the front of the line. He thrust me before the other warriors, pulling off my helm to reveal my face to the mighty solder that guarded the Great Tree. When I saw her my will shattered for I knew the warrior. Before me stood the Lady Sro, bloodied by their assault and weary from battle. She gasped when saw me there unveiled and revealed. For but an instant her sword wavered but that was all Ildabyth's forces needed. They fell upon her and she was lost from sight. His army swarmed the Tree and Valentius grabbed me as we fled the island."

"Ildabyth was delighted at our return, but not in the ways he had before. He treated me differently, like a used plaything. Openly he distained me for now he had something he desired more. Sro was his new captive and he focused his all attentions upon her. I was confused and my jealousies amused him. He called me a fool. He kept me locked in a tower room, visiting me often, telling me stories of the war and how things were now to his favor since Sro belonged to him and no longer lent her strength to the Malki. He savored in my grief and sometimes led me to watch as he tortured her."

"Ildabyth's destruction was laying the land to waste. In the streets of Basilus the folk celebrated for victory was surely at hand. As the tide turned to his favor, Ildabyth became preoccupied with his brutal games. He was not aware that Sro had called me and we revealed our hearts to one another. He did not know when we became able to draw upon each other's strength. It was through this exchange, she became able to use her powers once more. It was Sro's soundless call that went forth from the deep prison of Erda and now the eye of the Annyd turned back toward the Little Kingdom."

"We heard her!" exclaimed Yurah. "And you were there! You were with her! But how did you come to be here and she did not?"

"It takes great force to use the portals that lie between the realms." he explained. "Through the incessant torture, Sro had lost the use of her body. It was only her mind that remained untouched. What I know next was that I was safe and hid in a golden skin." he said, once more holding her gaze. "I knew help would come but I did not know that it would be you. Sro's heir, I did not expect."

"Who did you expect?"

Kiel rose from his chair and looked down over the soft lights of Mundi. "I do not know. I suppose I have given it little thought. I do not know how to mend these ills. They stretch too deep into the past. The very fabric of Erda seems to be at fault. Errors in that realm are far too easy to make."

"Eons flow in their own fashion, Kiel and Time has been promised," Rempha replied, "but Time alone will not save her. Sro knows these things. She very wise, from a time so long ago even Ildabyth is but a child by her reckonings."

"Then what shall we do, Rempha?" Yurah asked, "How do we begin?"

"To enter the Little Kingdom without Ildabyth's eye upon you will the first challenge." he said. "He has many servants that read the stars as accurately as any of the Elder races of Erda. Travelers from the arm of Mirfak can not be hid from those with eyes to see, no matter which master they may serve."

"I can help her. I understand the customs of Basilus." said Kiel.

"But Kiel, there are things you do not understand. You did not escape his influences," Rempha answered, "Ildabyth's dungeons leave no one unmarked. You have been undone, Kiel. Reformed, so to speak. Such things happen when the body is forced through the lower portals. said Rempha slowly, shaking his head. "It will not be easy. In fact it shall make your task all the more difficult. Your former self has been undone but your acts have not. Again far memory will be forfeit."

Kiel's face grew pale. "Then I shall make the same error, over and over, without end. Every flaw will be revealed. I do not have the strength, Rempha."

"You have more strength than you know. Take comfort in my house. No harm can come to you here. I know you are weary, Taygeth's son but you are much loved. Forget this not."

Then Rempha turned to Yurah, "Alas Seventh Daughter, the burden of the Greater Law is also yours to bear. But you are Sro's child, and a pure heart will find its way through dark places. Remember." he whispered faintly, putting his finger to his lips. "You are not alone."

Then Rempha raised his cup to the night sky, "Tomorrow a noble destiny awaits. When morning comes may your Fates find you willing." he said, drawing a deep breath of the sweet night air and blessed them.

"To the Flame that fills the dark spaces,
May the Heart be ever drawn
To the Sword that leaves the seed unfettered,
May the Living Sun reveal the dawn. "

So they put the cups to their lips and drank of Rempha's wine. A silent peace pervaded his lands and there was not a way to avoid its power. So they finished their meal without fret, and when the last of the brew was poured, Rempha bid them a fond good-night and Sudra showed them to their rooms.

CHAPTER X
THE DOOR OF RETURN

Her dreams were scattered like disorderly stacks of parchments. She opened her eyes and cast aside her coverlets but as her feet touched the floor she realized the room was not as she remembered it. The chamber had become unusually long and a strange light was pouring from the corner. She turned to look behind her but the bed had disappeared into a fog. The curious substance of Rempha's land was losing its defined shape. The light ahead was the only choice so she walked toward it. When she reached the corner she found a long flight of twisting stairs. She touched the smooth walls and she caught a glimpse of a robe. Compelled to follow, she raced after it, but the stairs were deceiving; first leading sharply downward and then twisting suddenly upward. She hurried on, trying to catch another glimpse of whoever moved just ahead. She stepped without faltering, faster and faster she went until the stairs became a blur of gray and the walls long streaks of white. After a time the trek became effortless and the guiding light led her further in. Suddenly a sharp crack echoed through the stone passage and Yurah drew to a quick halt. Minute sparks were passing through her.

"Peculiar." she considered as the sparks flowed into her body. She stood fully dressed in the strange stairwell, her sword at her side and her boots and cape brushed clean. "Very peculiar?" she wondered again, knowing well she had leapt from her bed in only a long nightshirt.

Just around the bend, two voices spoke in soft conversation. One she knew immediately, but the other she did not recognize. She moved slowly, cautiously peering into a simply furnished room. It was much longer than it was wide and along each side were a series of small windows pressed tightly together. They had no blind, nor shutter and outside them blazed an absolute dark. A simple bed stood in the corner. Upon the rumpled coverlet were open books and scattered papers. Much of the stuff had fallen from the bed and was strewn along the floor. A metal lamp burned upon a narrow table which sat askew in the middle of the room. Oddly simple machines were clustered around it, all moving of their own accord. The chamber was cluttered with measuring devices and cutting blocks. The air smelled of spice and, at the far end of the room, a fire glowed. Kiel was sitting upon a low stool, poking at the flames and speaking with an old man.

"Ah, you have arrived!" the old man exclaimed happily. The sharp gleam of his eye caught the firelight. "Are you ready to begin?"

Kiel snickered softly but did not turn from the fire.

"I suppose sir." Yurah answered, wishing Kiel would turn to look at her. "But I am not quite sure where I have arrived."

The old man chuckled. "Come child." he said pointing his staff toward the windows. "I will show you." Kiel stood up grinning and joined them at the windows.

"There! See there!" he cried, shaking the tip of the staff toward the lower edge of the glass. Yurah leaned forward and her eyes widened in disbelief. The chamber was suspended in the empty space and beneath them a giant blue planet turned.

"Where are we? What type of place is this?'

'A provisional lodging my dear. Do not be concerned. It is a working hostel of sorts. We use this place to attend to the affairs of the system."

"What affairs?" she thought pressing her face closer to the glass to watch an enormous cloud swirl over the face of the indigo world.

'That is quite a storm isn't it? It has raged there for centuries." said the old man placing a seeing scope to his eye. "Here child, would you like a better look?" and he handed the scope to her. "Like this." he said, reaching over to show her the adjustment rings. "Move them just a little. Take your time." Yurah took the scope. She moved the rings slightly until the surface to the blue sphere was plain.

"Today the winds are very potent. That is how I knew you would be coming."

'Is her name Erda?" she asked taking the eyescope away and peering into his wrinkled face.

"No, child. But that place is not far. We must take care to stay hid from Ildabyth's gaze and the Blue Lady," he explained tipping his staff toward the stormy planet. "she is always glad to shield us from his eye. Here we may work undisturbed, covered by the airs and moons she holds close to her bosom. She is known to me as Phanuel. She is without flaw and over her he can never have dominion."

"Then this is a traveling ship?" she said looking again over the books, and maps, and urns, and chests.

"Aye, but only small one. It is Rempha's work, or I should say his students. They enjoy structuring the transports. This ship has proven useful by countless standards. The portal is there," he said, pointing. "just behind the crook of the wall. Such a blind is needed for any coming and goings upon Erda. The Little Kingdom is such a dangerous place. But do not worry, all is well in hand. Come child, I will show you something quite interesting." he said running his long finger against the window sill. At his touch the wood seamlessly moved back into the lower sill and a series of copper shaped disks emerged from the lip. He adjusted them, always checking outside the windows as he did. A slight whirr soon became apparent within the room and under the glass a translucent sail mirrored the image of the small craft. The man was muttering under his breath.

"It only takes a bit of sun." Yurah thought she heard him say.

"Master Elus," said Kiel, "What of the upper sail?"

"It is rising now! We have but a moment to be ready." he replied waving his hand toward the other wall. "Go now, Kiel. Do as I tell and be quick."

Kiel took a position upon the opposite wall as similar disks emerged from the window's lip. He touched them gently, waiting for instructions.

"Degrees 45 to the north, Kiel. Eight to the east. Take care now. It is coming!" Elus cried.

The whirring became louder. Kiel finished setting the dials. An odd pressure began to push against their bodies. Yurah leaned against bedstead as something else caught her eye. Thin as the wing of a dragonfly, a sail began to unfold from the flying ship. Then it came. A bright flash caught the vaporous wing and a wind, quick as a beam of light, swallowed them up. The view outside was instantaneous and different. She had felt no jolt but now startlingly near, hung a glistening moon. Great valleys, cracked the pitted land and icy crags rose perilously high. She put the scope to her eye and watched a geyser blast forth from a crack in the lower shell. The Blue Lady had her eye upon the little moon. Holding the contrary sattelite close, she spoke to him as if he were a child and the moon trembled at her touch.

"Phanuel holds the mystery of Triton." Elus said adjusting the copper dials. "If you dare, you may enter the Little Kingdom unseen by his eye. Ildabyth is not aware of the secrets the Lady's satellites hold."

"It is what I have to do." she answered. "Really, I do not see it as a choice at all."

"And I shall help you do it." he said. "But first, please sit at the fire. It is important to understand the nature of the descent into Erda. I am not the only one who has anticipated your arrival. What is good and what is ill awaits you in the lower world and as you walk upon her lands and sail upon her waters is difficult to separate one from the other." The teapot began to whistle and Elus motioned to the fireplace. "Here, the tea is ready, and we must wait a while until she steadies him. Alignments cannot be taken lightly. Errors are too easy to make. Come on, please now. Sit."

Kiel busied himself with cups.

When she had settled her teacup in her lap she asked the old man what was on her mind. "How did we get here? We slept in Mundi and now the Little Kingdom is nigh. What power has brought us here?"

"The Gates of Rempha's lands extend to all places." the old man answered. "Though he appears a child he is the eldest of Time's children. Rempha understands better than any the mysteries of Old Ones realm. Only a portion of this knowledge is known to me. What I do know is that the Vanyr, and their cousins, anticipate your arrival. But you must understand that they too are limited by the nature of Erda. They may not recognize you. You will have to prove yourselves to them."

"Prove ourselves?" said Kiel.

"Rempha told you of the forgetfulness?"

"He did."

"It is the only way error may be undone."

"But any errors are of my own making. Yurah has no part of them. Why will she be burdened?"

"In the dense airs of Erda all far memory turns into dreams. No one is exempt. Yurah will bear the pain of exile with you. There is little that can be done of it. It is the task before you both."

"For myself I am willing." he answered looking into the flames. "And you Lady?"

Yurah set her cup along the mantle and placed her hand upon her mother's sword. Elus understood. He looked back to Kiel who was brooding before the fire.

"Kiel." he said softly. "Are you ready?"

"Yes. Of course I am. Where shall we find ourselves, Elus?" he answered standing slowly.

"The portal is located south of Zelmisso's summit. There you will find refuge of Odyn and the Alfyr. That warrior clan now dwells alongside their ancient kinsmen. Trust to the grace of the Fates and you will find your way though his forest. But after this I do not know how much aid they can offer. All folk of Erda are failing people."

Kiel walked to the glowing portal and thanked the old man.

"Stars whisper." Elus said, answering their unspoken doubts. "The Lady watches; as do I. What is not expected is always there to guide you. No more than this can I say," and the old man stepped aside. "It is time."

The portal ahead was pulsing with warmth. A filmy web of light spilled into the room. Kiel's glowing silhouette was just ahead as the light entered her body.

She hit the ground with a jolt.

"Get up!" said Kiel scrabbling to his feet. "Hurry, there is no time to waste."

They were upon a wide hillock. Just beneath her a narrow gorge dropped steeply into grove of struggling trees. Beyond the rift, snow covered mountains stretched to north and west, their stony peaks guarding the grim face of the summit, Zelmisso. The cold crept under her cloak. She glanced around her, seeking signs of the portal that brought them to the icy world.

"Come Yurah! We cannot stay here." he cried looking around the deserted slopes. "We must find them. Already I can feel it. The airs creep like a disease. Hurry." and he began to climb the tall rocks. A falcon flew overhead. Calling to the strangers beneath her, the bird's voice rang harshly through the fields of stone. They set a hard pace hoping to keep the chill at bay. They scrabbled down the small canyon to where a grove of study evergreen waited. They walked under the sheltering branches until they reached an older wood sprinkled with oaks and maples. The Tree Summoner Yurah carried whispered and the trees rustled in response. The branches moved revealing a faint path among the piles of snow and bracken. The beckoning breeze called her and she made her way to path, Kiel following behind.

Lower they went into the sheltered dell, finding the land strangely riddled with stone walls and hollows. They slowed their pace and walked warily until they came to the spring. Kiel filled his hands with the cold water and then paused to look about the deep wood.

"The trees have eyes." he whispered.

"I see him." she said silently, turning half around but Kiel gave her a curious look. Yurah wondered why he did not seem able to read her thought. "I see him." she repeated, softly mouthing the words. Still as a stone, a half grown child peered from a high branch. They pretended not to notice and continued to drink from the spring. After a time the boy moved from his perch and a moment later he stood solemnly before them. He carried a small bow and quiver of arrows. A short knife hung about his belt and his dark hair was pulled tight from his face.

"Why have you come to my forest?" he asked slowly setting an arrow to his bow.

"We seek the warrior, Odyn." answered Kiel.

"Odyn." he laughed, "That old goat! He is only a legend. Pathetic stories told by old wives to whimpering babes. It is said that Odyn's folk were ruined long ago and they ran from this wicked world." he winked, casting an eye to sky. "What need have you of such cowards?"

"My business is my own." Kiel replied, impatience creeping into his voice.

"You are mistaken traveler. You have no business here. These lands are under siege and none are permitted here, save those who have leave of our Lord" he said sharply, a sardonic smile curling around his lips. "And courtesy permits me to tell you traveler, that such freedom is never rendered without a price. I have followed you since you entered this valley and you thought you saw me by chance. You are very conceited." he scoffed. "And you, Lady? What are your intentions? Veiling yourself with silence, allowing your companion to blunder on like a fool." the boy's twilight eyes blazed. "What device have you under that lovely cloak? It has strange powers and I am interested in it. Show it now or he will pay for your error." and in an instant the arrow's path lay in straight to Kiel's heart.

"Do not show him!" cried Kiel, "He does not know who he insults."

"I understand his concerns." she said quietly. "We mean you no harm, boy. Please put down your weapon."

The boy relaxed the string ever so slightly. "Then show me what you carry, Lady. I am waiting."

"I will. When you lower your weapon."

He thought for moment and then lowered the arrow's tip, "As you wish." he replied with a gleam in his eye. Yurah cast the folds of the robe aside, revealing the hilt of her sword as she reached into the inner pocket of her vest. The tip of his arrow steadied again upon Kiel.

"I mean you no harm boy." she repeated, removing the stone-case from her shirt. "and neither does my companion."

"Open it." he said. Yurah did as she was asked feeling Kiel's silent fury as she undid the catch. The golden light poured from the stone. The trees drew nearer and the wind began to sing. A smile spread slowly over the boy's face.

"A Summoner." he whispered. "I had thought them to be only legend. What a treasure Lady. How did you come by such a wonderful thing."

"It was a gift." she answered.

"And the Sword? Was this too a gift?"

Yurah touched the hilt and the scabbard murmured. Like an breeze it swept around her. "The sword is from my mother," she said as if she understood a thing for the first time. "It is my heirloom."

"You are a peculiar one, Lady. But I believe you mean no harm." he said lowering the bow. "And you Kiel, if that be your true name?" Kiel flashed him a dark glance and the boy grinned widely. "Since you keep the company of this fine Lady, I will not kill you today. I will take you to my father. He will be most interested in the White Stone and you will be interested in his council. So put aside your doubt and follow me," he said with a wink. "But hurry travelers for I am light of foot. You will have trouble keeping up. Come now, Kiel. Be quick." and the boy sprang from the glade disappearing into the thick wood.

"He knows something and is hiding it." said Kiel, "He is over there, I see him." The boy moved quickly, just in and out of sight, teasing them from behind rocks or jumping out from the undergrowth always staying just ahead.

"These games infuriate me."

"He is just a boy."

"He is a rascal and needs to be taught a lesson."

Yurah caught a glimpse just ahead, "There." she pointed. When they caught up to him, they were panting and hot from their race.

"Tired?" said the boy, eyeing Kiel. "The airs of my mountains are a bit thin. But fear not stranger, soon you shall have a chance to rest. My folk are near. So mind your manners and make no sudden moves. Remember you must show them what you have shown me." Then without a sound they found themselves surrounded. A host of tall men and women were aiming their crossbows at their hearts.

"What have you brought us, Urion?" a gray eyed woman said suspiciously.

"A courteous Lady who bears at her breast the stuff of legends," grinned the boy cutting his glance around to meet Kiel's. "and a lout in need of a lesson."

"I am Yurah." she said stepping ahead of her companion and bowing to the tall warrior. "and this is Kiel. We have come to seek the counsels of Odyn."

"Odyn. What would you know of such man?" replied the lady, looking intently into their faces.

"I know he leads a wise people, well learned in the ancient mysteries and battlelore. And what I know best is that those folk resist Ildabyth and his tyrannies."

A subtle restlessness stirred the group.

"Quiet." commanded the woman gravely. "And so, Yurah. Who told you of this place?"

"The trees know her, Lorya." spoke the boy out of turn. "She carries a Summoner,s Stone. It was the trees that drew her deeper and deeper into our wood. I watched them move. I heard them call. "

A new light came into the questioner's eye. "A Summoners Stone? Have you seen this thing Uri?"

"Aye, I have seen it. And I know . ."

"When to speak and when to hold your tongue." she interrupted gently lowering her bow. "I would like to see this stone, Lady."

"Of course." Yurah replied taking the white stone from pocket.

"Open it." Lorya asked, a note of wonder in her voice. "Please."

As the golden light poured into the deep forest the trees answered the note. The boughs moved gently. They spoke softly among themselves using a pleasant tongue she could not understand. Kiel was quiet, covering his inner discomforts, and after a time of long conversation Lorya spoke to them once more.

"This is not the place where all things may be said. You may walk with us, if you choose, and join us this evening in our retreat." then the tall lady bowed to them and said finally. "I will give you a moment to consider."

"It seems the irksome child has led us right into a trap." said Kiel looking after the lady warrior. "They hear our thoughts. At least that is so with the boy."

"He did as he said he would. I think they are the folk Elus spoke of. The trees do not fear him."

"I was expecting something a little less rustic." he answered heatedly. "These folk seem little more than wandering hunters. What power could they possibly wield against the likes of Ildabyth and his armies. If they are the allies we seek we have little hope of fulfilling our purposes. Ildabyth commands legions of fell things. They will squash these pitiful hunters like insects. If the Malki could not save Sro then what can these wood folk do?"

"If the Malki could not save Sro then what do you think that we can do?" she replied softly.

He turned his eyes away. "I suppose I had hope this contest before us would be more just." he said faintly. "But even if these folk have an army hid in these mountains, hope is small indeed."

Yurah looked through the trees at the group that waited for them.

"I am not yet sure what to think. It is a strange place we find ourselves in Kiel. The question of the moment remains to go with them or not? "

"I do not believe they will be much help. Nonetheless, we have been politely asked and they may provide an adequate dinner." he said, "So I will follow as a willing lout. If you think this way may prove best." and he smiled at her.

"I think they offer more than you believe."

"What I believe is best kept unsaid."

She pondered the remark watching Lorya leave the group to walk toward them.

"We will join you in your retreat." Kiel replied stepping up to the tall warrior. Thank you for your offer."

"Then follow with care strangers, the way is steep."

The silent band wound their way along the gorge. Uri was no longer in the mood to taunt and he spent his time listening to the rustling breeze. His feet were noiseless and often he would turn to smile at Yurah.

After a time they came to a steep cliff and the company formed a half-circle around the face. Lorya stepped to the center and opened her palms toward the sky. The language she spoke was a living thing and her vibrant chant was soon joined by the voices of the others. Sparks began to fill the glade, clustering along the gray stone. The song began to draw to itself other lights, pulling the sparks from the highest parts of the green canopy and, a moment later, an opening appeared in the center of the wall.

"Walk close." Lorya said as they passed through the new formed arch. A soaring ceiling curved above and long spires descended in tapering threads. Uri handed Yurah a torch and lit it easily with a flint piece he carried in his pocket. The woman faced the forest, shaping a symbol with her torch and the wall of stone joined seamlessly behind them. Uri ran ahead but the rest of the band moved unhurriedly, speaking politely with Kiel and Yurah, explaining to them the nature of the caverns. After a time, the stone corridor narrowed and they had to walk in a single file. The path was polished smooth and along its side queer paintings were stained into the walls. She did not have time to look at them for Kiel pressed closely behind her. Soon the tunnel opened out. The settling light of the evening sun spread over a broad ledge. Beneath them now thundered a rushing falls, crashing along the tiered steppes as it quarreled to a valley below. A chill drizzle scattered through the trees. Lorya was at her shoulder.

"You look upon the Vale of Odyn. Long has it been since this fair place has welcomed travelers. Uri has gone ahead of us and by now may have already reached have the retreats."

"The boy told us of his father. He said he would be interested in the Stone."

"Urion is a not a child of Odyn. His parents no longer bide upon the lands of Erda but keep watch upon him from afar." she said with a strange tone in her voice. "In fact there are few children here, so each must be raised by all that abide in the Vale. Uri has many fathers, and many mothers, as you would think of it. All here serve as the Stewards of Erda. We will meet in council before the old sun has set. There what "interests" us about the Summoner's Stone will be made known you," she paused to look to Kiel but she did not allow him time to reply and pointed to stone path. "The way is slippery. Move with care, travelers."

Fine steps were cut into the ravine but soon more well-wore paths could be seen. Water flowed from the cliffs, pouring into pools she had seen from above. Now it was clear the lakes had been contrived, their weirs built by skillful hands and upon the still basins floated lovely gardens. Low boats glided among the flats shifting them from shade to sun. Yurah looked on with interest as they passed. The fair folk watched them with bright, clear eyes touching her thoughts as she walked on, stirring within her a memory she could not find a name for.

Lorya led them up a shadowy lane to a small cottage. Its door was open and an empty stool was sitting against its sill.

"They are the ones! They are the ones!" shouted a familiar voice. "Atyn! Atyn! They are here. Come and see them. These are the folk that have fallen from the skies." He cried as he ran down the path and grasped her hand. "Come Lady and meet my kin. You will like him. He is my closest friend."

Atyn stood in threshold of the door. He was tall, with silvering hair and deep gray eyes. A large dog heeled at his side the intelligent face waiting for his master's command.

"Greetings wanderers." he hailed. "Come and refresh yourselves. Urion has already told me much of you and I dare say that most of it may need to be told more perfectly." and he smiled warmly, standing aside allowing them to enter.

The house was a long single room with resting lofts tucked under the low gable ends. A kitchen board was cluttered with plates and cups. The small fireplace burned low. A kettle spit a thin stream of stream into the homely space. A quiet corner held a writing table, pens and unrolled parchments lie waiting under an expectant candle. Atyn offered them chairs and Uri sat down the cups and loaves upon a clean round table.

"I will return shortly. You are in gracious hands. And Uri," Lorya said from the door. "Do not weary them with questions. The airs of Erda are difficult to those new to it, so listen instead and help your brother as he asks."

"No bothersome questions shall pass my lips." said the boy happily. "Do not worry Lorya. I will help."

"See that you do." she replied before slipping under the shadows.

"I am Atyn. And you are Kiel and Yurah." said the tall man, "Uri tells me you entered by Elus' portal along the southern mounts. He was not to be that far from home and finds trouble for himself in not heeding his own rules. So he will be waiting upon us and please, do not be shy in asking for anything we may have to offer. I enjoy watching Uri fetch. He needs much practice at it. And seeing that he is forbidden to ask questions we shall have time for quiet talk. I shall do my best to answer your questions though somethings may be better explained in council."

"We are obliged." said Yurah courteously, "This valley is a beautiful place. I have seen growing things the like of which I have never seen before. But how do your gardens survive, sir? The sun is so cold and the land so rugged. I would like to understand that, if there be time."

"What do you wish to know?"

"I saw gardens floating upon the lakes. Your folk were tending them from their boats. What type of plots are these? " said Yurah taking the cup of tea that Uri offered."

"The flats are built upon a lathe of light wood. We wind them tight with an oily vine and when they have cured and dried, we heap it with lichens and soil. Our folk tend them by boat, pulling the beds through out the day, keeping the growing things under the sun as it moves over the skies. But you are right lady, there are other arrangements that must be made if we are to grow the things we are accustomed too.

"Arrangements? Accustomed too?"

"This rugged land, as you say, is not the land of our birth. We are immigrants here, driven from our green and graceful shores as bloody years have passed by. During these times of struggle we have retreated into these wood. My kinsmen, Odyn, maintains this refuge. It is necessary to retain the quiet we need for our efforts."

Yurah was about to ask another question but Urion was standing at her elbow.

"More honey?" he said innocently.

"No, it is lovely. Thank you, Uri."

"And you Kiel? More honey?"

"Yes, just a drop." and he held his cup over to him. Uri carefully spooned a golden heap into his cup. "Shall that be enough to sweeten you properly?" he asked with a wry smile.

Kiel stirred the cup ignoring the younger boy. "What labor drives you from your homeland, sir." he said to Atyn instead.

"Likely that work is the same as your own." he answered, buttering a loaf. Then, with a gleam in his eye, he said to his brother. "Uri, bring me some of that honey, please. For you shall need none of it, such a sweet-tongued darling you have become," Uri eyes widened knowing a sting was sure to follow. Atyn's face brightened. "Hmmm, it seems to me that you grow a bit pale. Having walked too many miles in the wilderness must not have agreed with you. A cup of dandelion should curb both these ailments for no amount of sweetness can stay the bite of that bitter root. It will give you the strength to complete the list of your ever-increasing chores"

Uri opened his mouth to complain but Atyn's face had changed abruptly. Grimly he looked around the room.

"I have changed my mind, Urion. Leave the jar upon the table." he said distantly, "The hearth fire is faltering. Bring in the night wood instead. It will be late when we return home."

94

Concerned flashed across the boy's face. "What is it, Atyn?"

"Do as I ask Uri. I wish to speak with our guests in private for a moment."

Uri frowned but did as he was told.

"I am glad you have come" Atyn said as the door closed behind him. "It is good to know the stars still listen to our little world. We called for aid through we knew not what form it would take.' he said setting his plate upon the table and his hands trembled. "Though they are our greatest hope it wise not to share all that we know with the children. Much of our strength has been spent in fruitless struggle. The battle goes poorly, travelers. The council hurries to table and yet another blow is dealt us." he clinched his fist tightly and blood seeped from between his fingers.

"What is this turn upon you?" Yurah said, taking the bleeding hand in her own. The scabbard at her side began to whisper as the sight came upon her.

The harsh voices were reaching into her mind. Endless chanting of countless names formed the image of a dull red pentangle along a flat gray surface. Through the dismal mist, shapes appeared. A ring of grim men, robed in gloom, formed a circle around an alter of pitchwood. Shadows poured from their long fingers to dance about the alter flame. Their rasping voices called out to the sullen light and the wraiths bent downward to meet them. Their long teeth gleamed in the eerie light as the spirits bit into the bones of the conveners. They burrowed downward into their ruined minds and the chants grew quicker.

"Pawns of a greater hand." her mind explained as she watched them collapse. The energized wraiths began to pour from the alter room. In an instant she knew what they had done and she knew what to do stop it.

"Cover him, Kiel!" she cried out. "Cover him quickly with light! With candle flame! With firelight! With the beams of sun if we can find them! The dark has been summoned to take him."

Quickly Kiel laid Atyn's arm around his shoulder. Together they helped him to his feet. Atyn's face was gray as he stumbled with them. He was speaking in a tongue she did not understand.

"What is wrong with my brother!" Uri cried as the firewood crashed to the floor.

"We must get him into the light." said Kiel.

"Lorya knows. She has helped him before. Take him to the water! Hurry!" he cried as he raced away.

They lead him down the darkening path. Blood ran from his nose and his feet faltered. Kiel pulled him closer and Yurah shored him along the other side. When she placed her arm across his belly as a sticky redness stained her arm.

'We must be swift!" she whispered, watching the creeping flow spread across his gray tunic and they ran to the end of the woody lane. A beam of fading sun rested along the shore where the floating gardens were moored. His folk drew near and gently they placed him upon the garden bed as low boats with many lights began to float toward them. Lorya had come and the others moved aside to let her pass.

Standing over him Lorya held her torch over him and gathering of folk begin to sing a slow chant. Atyn's hands and feet were marked with oozing stains. They watched as the living garden was pulled into the center of the lake and if the moment had not been so bleak, the sight would have been wondrous. Thundering clouds barred the beams of settling light. But at their call a bright shaft gleamed from behind the dark shoulders and rested perfectly upon Atyn's face. A thousand lights burned within the shadows of the wood, golden flames reflecting upon the violet waters. The tall warrior raised her arms and began to speak in a gentle rhythm. He stirred as she spoke. She called his name and he opened his eyes.

"It is over. They are gone." he said softly

She knelt at his side and took his hand. "What did they what?" she asked without sound.

"They are searching for something."

"I wonder what?" said Lorya glancing toward the shore. "But there is time for that later. We must get you home." And she signaled for the raft to turn around.

"Galen, fetch a litter and take him to the cottage. Be sure the fire burns high all the night. Take seven others and post watches in the wood."

"Uri, do not leave him for a moment. Make sure he drinks before he sleeps."

"I will, Lorya." answered the boy.

"Travelers, you must come with me. Time is shorter than I had thought."

And as they made ready to follow her, Uri came and touched Kiel upon the arm. "I am sorry sir. I meant no harm by my careless words but harm I have done. Accept my apologies if you be so inclined." and the boy bowed low.

"It is forgotten, Urion." said Kiel "Someday we will understand each other better."

"Thank you for helping my brother." he whispered then he returned to Atyn's side and they disappeared under the shadowy trees.

CHAPTER XI
ODYN'S HALL

Twilight had given way to night. A young girl greeted them at the doors of Odyn's Hall. Smiling shyly, she took their cloaks and hung them upon pegs beside the kitchen. A robed man watched the fire blazing in the corner of the room.

"How is Atyn?" he asked without turning around.

"The morning will see him on his feet again." answered Lorya.

"I owe you a great debt, travelers." he said laying back his hood. His face was long and his gray hair in the flickering light. His left eye caught the flame and reflected it oddly back into the room. "Atyn's fate may have been far worse without your quick work. I am ever grateful." He said looking at them with his other eye. "Welcome Kiel. Welcome Yurah. I am Odyn. It is an honor to have you in these humble halls but the night has brought us extra duties. Make yourselves comfortable and the others will join us soon."

The girl who had met them laid a flagon and cups upon the table. "Thank you Circe," Odyn said handing each one a full cup. "The wait shall give us time to speak uninterrupted."

They stirred uncomfortably. Not because they feared to answer his questions but because the shadowy presence of hate-filled malice still lingered in their thoughts. Kiel shook off his doubts and answered all that he knew. "I recall there was a man, sir. And he seemed a man much like yourself. He was the one who sent us here."

"Much like myself so you say. Do you recall his name?"

"It hangs like a prickling thorn but I do not remember."

"Then allow me to ask you a question Kiel. Is Elus the name you struggle to recall?"

"Yes. His name was Elus." said Kiel, unsteadily. "And just hours ago I knew it."

Odyn nodded thoughtfully, "The airs here are heavy. It is burden we all bear but there are ways to counter that force. Elus is my Elder, if you will, but we share not the same fate. Long ago Elus chose to be the explorer of the endless vault and only seldom will he descend low enough to touch this ravaged land. We had received a sending from him. We knew you were coming."

"Elus said there were star readers in the lower world."

"Aye and that there are, but as ever, it is the Oracle that must decipher what is given and that is difficult thing for all eyes do not see alike. But tonight we are the fortunate ones. The full moon is upon us and we shall join her as it rises over the birch grove."

Odyn's eye then to turned to Yurah, "Lorya tells me you bear a talisman. The Summoning Stone is but a myth too many of my folk." and the strange eye flickered. "But I am more ancient than myth and I recall when it was sent forth from the battlefield. So, if you please Lady Yurah, show me this thing you carry."

Yurah opened the stone casing and laid it upon the table. It quivered then began to glow. Odyn smiled as the stone swelled with light and the forest outside trembled in joy.

"Aye traveler, it is real." and the hum of the stone grew louder as he spoke. "Surely you are my kinswoman, if such an amulet you bear at your breast. How did you come by this gift?"

Yurah tried to explain but found her thoughts difficult to connect.

"Worry not, child." said Odyn reaching out and closing the box. "I can aid in your remembering." and Odyn called for the serving girl.

"Circe, bring me Memhir's wine." and child rushed to do his bidding and when she returned, she was carrying a clear vase and a clear glass. Odyn poured the glass half full.

"Drink this. It has the power to uplift that that is drawn downward."

Yurah drank until the glass was empty. Its water spread through her like a fire. Raeyn's face appeared inside her mind. "It was a birthday gift from my sister." she gasped , "She told me the stone was formed in the heart of eldest tree of my father's land. She said it held the power to summon its descendants in times of need."

"And where is the realm that holds this ancient seed?"

"Raldabon. My father is the steward of that sun and I am his Seventh Daughter."

"Iao." The old man answered wonderingly. "Indeed you have traveled far child. That land lies past the Hunter and even beyond the great star, Mirfak. Not since the exile of Ildabyth have any born of that realm traveled to this land?"

Yurah gazed at the Summoner's Stone in a new light. "I have come seeking my mother's fate. Her heirloom has been bequeathed to me. I have come to Erda to find her, for I know in my heart it is not meant to stay in my keeping. I come to return it to her." Yurah replied unsheathing the blade. The sword caught the light and burned like a torch.

"The Sword of the Annyd." Odyn whispered, "So much has changed since I last laid my eyes upon it. Ahh child it was long, long, ago when this world was young and I was not so old."

"Then you must know my mother."

"I can tell you little of your mother child, but I do know the blade. This Sword is also the stuff of legends. It bears the mark of the

Ancients who came to aid this realm as Ildabyth spoiled the first work. It was their efforts which abled all to begin once more." Odyn then turned his gaze to Kiel. "But little word has come of them since. It would be heartening to believe the Annyd have turned their eye to us once more. Times have been difficult for the Clans and the Malkians alike. War is hard. It is a Fates blessing that you have come. Perhaps we might still be able to the stem the tide after all." He said staring into the fire. The shadows of light danced over his face and, after a moment, he spoke again. "And you Kiel, you seem much more familiar to me. Have you walked in the airs of Erda before, or are you a child of the far stars as well?"

Kiel gazed at the old man. "I have walked in this land before" he said haltingly. "But I am born of the star Taygeth, though that place has become but an empty word to me. Now I am but an vagabond, having no real home within any land."

"Taygeth is Doxomedon's realm."

"Doxomedon is my father and the Lady Derdekea, my mother."

"Then you are a high born son, Master Kiel no matter what past you carry. It is truly said that what has come before spirals faithfully in history's telling. Did you know that Doxomedon was among that great gathering at the turn of the Age?"

Kiel could not answer and stared into the glass.

"What has drawn you back to this forgotten world?" Odyn replied softly,

"I have come with Yurah, to help her seek her mothers fate." he replied firmly, "And may it suffice is to say I have an obligation to clear."

Odyn nodded, a knowing look in his eye, "You are a guest in my hall, Kiel. You are welcome here no matter what burdens you bring to my door. Lorya has said that,"

But Odyn was interrupted. The door opened and the chill air poured in. Several folk were hanging their cloaks upon pegs by the door. The serving girl put her head around the corner and counted them quickly.

"Hail Odyn." they said, bowing courteously.

"Welcome friends. The board will soon be laid and our refreshment we will take together. But first allow me to make much needed introductions." and he looked down at his guests. "Before us it the Lady Yurah, Seventh Daughter of the light of Raldabon and her companion, Master Kiel of the Star Taygeth. These are the travelers we have been expecting." Kiel and Yurah stood.

The group began to murmur between them but in a moment the tallest of the men spoke up. "I am Theo. Counselor of the Drui, at your service." and he bowed low before taking a seat next to Lorya.

"I am Dorig. Holder of the Cross. The honor is mine." said the soldier at his side.

"I am Istah. Keeper of the Trinity." spoke a fair faced lady, holding Kiel's gaze in her bright eyes.

"I am Varda, of the Water." a pale nymph said, lowering her brow.

"I am Inrih, Archer of Delphi." said a dark-eyed man with a solemn jaw.

And the door of the hall opened again and more folk entered and each spoke their name and title aloud until every chair was filled and each glass was poured. Then a hush fell in the room as Odyn took his place at the head of the board. The candlelight burned quietly and all became still. Finally the old man spoke.

"Hail Kinfolk. This is an evening long awaited and it is shared with company long sought." and he raised his cup to his lips and took a long sip and the others drank with him. "The bitter stage has been set sooner than we supposed. But take heart, my children. Atyn rests with his brothers and should be about his duties by the morrow." and at those words murmurs of relief passed through the hall. Odyn raised his hand and quieted them. "The Shadows took us unawares. But by good fortune and quick work, we were saved from greater harm." and again the table whispered and every bright eye looked to Yurah and Kiel. Odyn waited until the whispers passed. "The dark work has been undone but our vigilance must be doubled and our resolve must never fail us. Tonight the seer shall speak to the white light of the moon. So I call upon you to set aside a troubled mind and may her words bring us the far memory and greater wisdom."

Then Odyn raised his hand as a half a dozen children entered the hall carrying platters of bread and cheese, meat and fruit. And when the plates were filled and glasses were poured, a harper put his fingers to the strings and began to sing.

"Is the fare to your liking Kiel?" asked Lorya, offering again the plate of bread.

"Yes Lady," he answered, taking another piece. "I find it to be much more than "adequate". But just as fine as the fare of your table, is the music of your harper. Truly Lady, this is what sets my mind at ease."

"It is said among our people that when the Harper plays the Malki look upon us and smile."

"The Malki?"

"Aye, you know of them?"

"It seems I do but only from a distant dream."

"And that would be a fair dream indeed. Odyn holds that they still dwell upon the Isles of Urdar."

"And from this place they smile?'

"The Malki are not as we are." she replied warmly. "They dwell in a finer substance, seeing what we may only hear. They are the shape-builders and, too this end, they guard the Great Tree that makes all forms. I imagine them to be a perfect folk but I have never been so fortunate as to encounter one. It is only a True-born Seer that are able to do such things."

"Odyn made mention of the Seer" he said looking around the crowded room.

"Odyn was speaking of the Oracle of the Valkyries. She is Alfyr, just as he, and tonight she will not sup. She remains within the sanctuary, tended by her ladies. But soon now, as the night grows older she will come forth to listen to the Full of the Moon. We will stand together and hear the words she brings down from the skies."

"Does the Seer guide your people?"

"Guide? No, we have our own ways. I am Drui. We are distant cousins to the Alfyr. In the beginning all the Clans were once one people, but time has changed us. You can see it best here," she smiled pulling back her hair. Her ears were graceful and long. "We must each make our own choice when we listen to the words of the Odyn's Oracle. The White Lady understands many things. Some of her visions clear as a cold winter morning but other images she brings are more difficult. These will be the things most important to ponder. Often I have deemed that every seer is ever bound to speak in riddles for lives are filled with both choice and fate." then Lorya looked over his shoulder to Yurah who was sitting quietly, sipping a steaming cup, and listening as the harper's song filled the room. "As with your companion there, upon one hand she was born to bear the weight she carries but upon the other it is naught but her own free choice that holds her to that path."

Kiel was about to answer but Odyn rose from his chair and held his cup high above the table and declared. "Hail Kinsfolk! The Moon draws nigh. So let us make peace with ourselves and stand ready under the endless sky."

The children came as the plates were pushed aside and the cups were emptied bringing each one a fat stump of candle wax set in a silver bowl. The tables were cleared as cloaks and hoods were donned. Yurah touched Kiel upon the sleeve and he took her hand. The moon was rising as they went. Its full face was shining brightly through the tall spires and between the flimsy clouds. They walked long under the night. Their candles flickering like fireflies through the forest shadows. They walked until they reached an open glade surrounded by birch wood. In the center of the circle a great mound was laid high with dry limbs. The Moon peered over the cathedral of trees and under the light there stood a women garbed in white. Her silver hair was unbound and at her side, her attendants waited. The maids were six in number; standing three along each side, elbow to elbow and one step behind the other. They were dressed in the same pure cloth and each carried a token in their hands. The first to her right held a silver bowl and the first to her left a silver flagon. The second to her right carried a linden wreath and the second to her left a scepter and the last set of attendants were candle bearers. As the light of the rising moon filled the circle, the silver bowl was placed upon the earth and filled with the pure water of silver flagon. The linden wreath crowned the Seer's brow and the White Lady took the scepter in her hand. She stood before dark waters and as the moonlight touched the watery mirror, she began to speak.

"Night breaks and the light that was is revealed
Holding the future yet unset
And what lie incessant and ever tumbling moves into the moment
Drawn to the ceaseless yearnings beckoning through the dark
It is a Sword that shall cleave the shades in parts
Rending shadows in its sound
It is a Word that shall pierce the moment
To leave its stains upon the ground."

A cloud moved over the face of the moon and its light was lost from view. The seer placed her hands along either side of the mirror and she breathed upon the water. The ripples spread over the mirror's face and the gloom faded from the sky. The Seer spoke once more.

"In fierce countenance comes the weathering storm,
Through fire born of sky,
And to the breast of she who waits,
The weary lay their burden down to die.
And what is between the land and sea is swallowed by the womb.
In Zu, in Mithra, in Ganymede,
Lingers the binding tomb,
But higher than this, a Queen of Stars, her blind will to preside.
The scales held by that subtle hand
The lower doth despise."

"It is the dance, oh Wanderer, of that that is undone.
The song is raised and the milk is poured by the lighting of the Suns,
The Gates that lie between the Groves, open shall remain,
It is the Hand that is ever masked the Uroborus does unchain.
It is the Eye that is the Storm.
It is the Sound that cleaves to heal.

The Sword of Sorrows now reborn
In the Renting of the Years. "

The ribbon of light that had filled the mirror faded. The candle bearers came forward and between them walked a child. A silver circlet banded her fair brow and her golden hair brushed the ground. She stood before the gathering and, alone and unaided, by any instrument save her own sweet voice, the child began to sing. The song spilled into the night and the words like spidery threads spun themselves under the light of the moon. Yurah listened, realizing she knew the verse before the child sang, for the words of her song were the same words the Seer had spoken. When the song was finished the Candle Bearers came forward and lit the bonfire. Yurah stood with Kiel, glad of the warmth and the company, as the song repeated in her mind. She did not notice when Odyn came to stand near them.'

"The Oracle holds a message for each one." spoke the old sage.

"It is so, Odyn." answered Kiel, "Every portent will first stir the memories of one's own road." answered Kiel. "And what is heard is ever different for every heart."

"And what did the augury say to your heart, Kiel?"

"To my heart Lord," he said looking deep into the flame, "my heart is reminded that a tempest awaits and the outcome is not yet sure."

"And is that all your heart told to you?" he pressed.

"No Lord, it is only the surface." his reply becoming a whisper, "The Seer's words hold an ocean of suffering, and a night that swallowed all hope. I heard the lament of Erda calling to the stars."

"And did answer come?"

Kiel looked upward to the bright round moon. "Answer came Odyn, but not without a price." and he hung his head for the cries of the dying rang in his thoughts.

"This storm has brewed for centuries" said Odyn, laying his hand upon his shoulder. "Look upward, my young friend. Look upward to remember. Remember the sprinkling stars serve to remind us that what is unseen also holds oceans of life. Though we stand upon this little world, and we hold but a little time in our possession, all is possible under these skies."

And for a long time they were quiet, remembering the Seer's Song. The fire was blazing high when Odyn finally looked to Yurah.

"What stirrings did the song bring to your heart, Yurah?

The voice of the man carried an ancient beauty and when she opened her mouth to speak it seemed there was nothing she could tell him that he did not already know.

"There is little that I understand well, Lord." she said meekly turning her eyes into the fire. "the song was haunting but its words brought little comfort. The vision came to me as an endless rippling tide, deep waters ebbing and flowing, with all that is good and all that is evil blending into each other. Such a thing seems too large to fight. And still fight we must and we must do it because the chance of victory remains," and looked into his face and her voice diminished into a whisper. "but then, what would victory mean? Could it be no more that the rhythms of the greater stars? It is naught but the light that creates the dark. Alas Odyn, what the Seer's Song revealed to my heart was that is made here is only made to be undone."

The old man smiled tenderly, "Circe's Waters have left you uncomfortably clear-headed child. Indeed we live in a world of two Parts, both absolute and both contrary. We walk on a thread between the two and where it leads; in that each one must decide alone."

"Such is my dilemma?" she said softly, her eyes alight. "I carry a Sword upon my girdle and it bears a name that breaks my heart to remember. I do not believe I hold within myself enough strength to bear it, and even if I did; how would I understand its true nature. To me it seems to carry the best and the worst of all things. How can I know if the power of the blade is meant for the healing of this world or if its strength lies instead in the ability to break it apart?

The night was silent. Even the fire ceased its crackle. Every eye had turned to Odyn, waiting for his sign. The old man breathed deep the night air.

"Such knowings do not lie in the past or future set." he said quietly, in her ear. "It is only the moment that extends to us a chance of understanding what might, or might not, be real."

Yurah looked into his face. His left eye was strangely clear and she realized then that it did not see. Odyn felt her know it.

"It is so child. My left eye is sightless. But that is another story, better left until another time. For now I will say you that it happened long ago, when Ildabyth came near to undo the work of our hands, I was a young boy when made a bargain with the Lady of the Grove" and then he smiled. "Her name was Menhir and when she spoke of hidden things, the blind eye would fill, like a glass. But the Lady is no longer of this world, making her gift all more precious to me." A tear then welled in the blind eye. It caught a glint of firelight before falling upon the ground. The sound was sad and soft. Yurah looked into the old face and the other eye stabbed sharp into her own. "But now I can help you with your choice. The gift of Menhir gives me sight in all directions of time." and the old man stood before the assembly and in a great voice, Odyn declared.

"Look upward Stewards of Erda! Look upward and call to the hearts of Stars." And at his command a cold wind swirled into the glade. Odyn raised his arms and the voice blew through him.

"The Sword of Sorrows has returned to Erda. Again the shades will tremble under the power of heaven's dark. Its sound will rend the coming storm. Draw your blade now, Seventh Daughter of a Seventh Son."

And so it was that Sro's heir drew the Sword under the full of the moon and, as it gleamed in the light, the Eyes of the Stars and the Stewards of Erda set upon it the best of all they had to offer.

CHAPTER XII
THE QUEEN OF STARS

The sun teased the shifting leaves. Uri was sleeping curled in a chair. The cottage door was open, letting in the chilly morning air. Galen stood at threshold looking down the lane. He gestured for Kiel to join him upon the stoop.

"Good morning Kiel." he grinned, his curly hair straggling into gray eyes. "Do you sleep enough? You returned quite late."

"Quite enough. I appreciate the bed." he answered, looking back over his shoulder. "How is Atyn?"

"Uri fretted over him all night." he replied uneasily. "And he will be up soon, acting as if these bouts mean nothing. But I know these battles take their toll. Atyn is always the first to meet the shadows."

Kiel shook his head and frowned. "But I could see no shadow Galen. In fact I could see nothing at all and yet I knew he was dying."

"Atyn is the eldest of our line. I believe it is the only reason he can survive these assaults."

"Your line?"

"We are Vanyr. Most of our clan perished in the first of Ildabyth's wars, and those that did not, were gravely hurt and the Annyd led them to other realms. Atyn is the eldest son that still walks the land of Erda. He is closest to our father. This gives him the ability to be in several places at the same time. He is at ease in the cold upper airs and one of the few that speaks to the Malki. He keeps watch over Odyn's hold so we may know when the Ildabyth's Priest start their work." Galen picked up a stone and threw it into the wood. In the distance the sound of its strike was muffled by the leaves. He looked after the noise. "To lose him would prove disastrous. It is my duty to protect his body while he heals from those hurts. But it was different this time. The shadows were searching for something. I could feel it."

Kiel's mind crawled with discomfort. Shame suffocated him, but he kept the sensation to himself and replied. "I will help you if I can Galen. What would you have me do?"

"You are a considerate one, traveler." Galen smiled. "And perhaps there is something that you may do. The guards are still in the wood. They will not leave their posts until Lorya bids them to do it. But they have had no bread this day and I would like to bring them their morning fare. They should not be far." and he whistled into the wood a soft bird call. Its sound was quickly answered. "That is Taryn. So, if you please Master Kiel, stay near to Atyn and Uri while I gather some apples and loaves and see to their need."

"That is easy Galen. Have no worry."

"Thank you." he answered stepping softly into the dim lit room. Quietly he gathered loaves and fruit. "Take care, my friend. I will return in shortly." and without another sound he slipped into the wood.

The quiet of the new day and the soft breathing of the sleepers left Kiel alone with restless thoughts. A loathing had settled with him. He wrestled with his fear and doubt and could find no peace. Uri groaned. Kiel rose from his chair, wondering if it was his own discomforts that troubled the boy's sleep. He went to the cupboard, hoping perhaps that busy hands might drive away the restive waves. It was well stored with bacon and onions, and the fire was perfect for cooking. He took out the slab and began to slice strips along a marred cutting block and he looked up to see Uri at his elbow.

"So you know a little about cooking, eh?" he quipped.

"A little." replied Kiel, "Why?"

"Well, might those strips be on the thin side?"

"I do not think so, that is if you like your bacon crispy."

"Oh, do I." he said smiling widely. "Crispy is my favorite. I know quite a lot about cooking. Atyn lets me do it all the time. Here let me slice the onions." and the boy grabbed a knife and began to peel away the papery red skin.

"Urion, will you not give him any peace."

Kiel turned around to see Atyn sitting up with his feet on the floor.

"He has not gotten himself into trouble, yet." Kiel said with a wink. "I might even teach him a thing or two about making breakfast. He can not know it all just yet."

"No, not everything. Not just yet. But to hear him tell it is quite another story."

"You wait, Atyn. You will see. It will be delicious." he replied, setting aside his knife. "But these onions must wait. You must have some water Atyn. Lorya's orders, so keep yourself still another moment and I will fetch it."

Atyn laughed. "I am quite able to see to my duties this morning."

"I am sure you are brother. Here drink this now." he said, handing him a cup. "Are you warm enough? The morning is cool, I shall build up the fire."

"I am warm and the fire is right for cooking." he said, draining the cup. "Help me to clear this bedding so our cook may reach the fire."

Uri happily obliged, folding blankets and putting the pillows back into the lofts. While the cottage filled with the scent of frying bacon and onions, Atyn sat at the table making light conversation and looking out toward the path. When they sat down to the meal Atyn wanted news from the night before. Kiel repeated the words of the Seer and he was attentive to every detail. He was especially interested in the nature of the skies and he pondered every word. Finally he wondered if Odyn had made further mention of the Queen of Stars.

"No, he did not speak the name again." Kiel answered, being sure to recall each of the old mage's words. "Only the Seers' song spoke that name. Who is she Atyn, the Queen of Stars?"

"In the skies of Erda she lies just past the constellation of Erigone. She is of little notice and one must look to find her there. Perhaps you know her by another name Kiel, more often she is referred too as Astraea."

"Astraea." he repeated the word trying to remember.

"She has many titles. The Malki speak of her as Libera, the Guardian of the Seventh Hall, the Starry one and last night this Lady was in my dreams. I sat with her before her homefire and she spoke to me of many things" then he paused and his gray eyes grew troubled. "but I did not understand the most of what she said and I fear that do not understand any of it better in the light of day."

"Can you recall any of the dream Atyn?" asked Uri.

"It is difficult to put her words into our own. The best I may tell is that the Lady held an image before me." he answered grimly looking again to the path outside the door. "Ildabyth searches for something familiar and he is confident that he shall have it."

The words tore into Kiel's gut like a blade. It left him hollow and Uri stared into the hole.

"All of this you have heard before." intruded the boy into his unspoken thoughts, "You know Ildabyth. I can feel it inside you."

The boy's directness was startling. Loneliness consumed him. Suddenly his mind was filled with fire. His body was gone and he splintered apart. Again he was alone struggling in that dark. "I am but a wanderer in this land." he heard himself say.

"But you know him." the boy continued.

Atyn laid his hand upon the Urion's shoulder. "You see much little brother, but you do not see all. Do not judge what none of us have yet to understand."

"I will not pry," Urion replied with a curious look. "Through there is more to you than you have told."

Kiel was trying to think of a reply when Galen opened the door. Atyn went to greet him.

"I have seen Lorya." He told them, "The Council met throughout the night. It seems, at least for the moment, the danger has passed. She has dismissed the guard and is sending folk to fetch you. Odyn wishes to speak with you, and the traveler."

"And your companion waits in the Odyn's Hall." he said to the Kiel. "So make ready. The horses will be here soon."

Uri was suddenly at Kiel's elbow, his eyes dancing with mischief. "Well it seems you have business in the Hall, Master Kiel so do not concern yourself with the ordinary work of cleaning up your messes. I shall see too it. I am childish," he smirked, cutting his eye round to Galen. "or so I am often told by those more steadfast. It seems there is much to learn in the doing of mundane tasks and I can not wait to know this thing for myself."

"Well now you have heard it." laughed Atyn. "You have been graciously released from service that was never yours to have. Take advantage of his goodly nature, Kiel for no one may say how long it might last."

Uri laid a cloth neatly over his arm. "Master Galen, there is bacon and there is toast. And I believe the coffee pot to still have a cup or two left in it. And worry not about the bother, another plate, another cup, another knife, are all such small things. In truth these small burdens shall increase my value in the eyes of others."

"Well Uri, while I am honored to increase your value, a full plate and cup I would appreciate more."

"Then you will have it. And please understand I have ignored your lack of manners." He said genteelly before he turned away and returned to hearth to fix Galen a plate.

"I have not heard the end of that." said Galen making himself comfortable at the table. "It is good to see his humor back. Last evening he was as pale as you were. He never left your side. He is coming into his own. It will not be long now."

"No, it will not be long at all." Atyn answered, watching the boy whistle over the washing pot. "His powers are growing each day."

Uri looked up. "The horses are coming." he cried, tossing down his cloth "Galen can help me finish after I have seen you to your mounts." and in an instant he standing on the stoop watching as the riders turn the bend.

Kiel recognized one from the night before. Her name as Istah and she rode with a younger girl.

"Hail Kiel. Hail Galen." The gray-eyed lady called, springing lightly from the pony. "Are you well enough to ride?" she asked taking Atyn by the hand.

"I am quite well enough, Istah." he answered gently and then he nodded to the younger girl. "Good morning, Rhea. You are on stable duties today?"

"That I am. Leading the horses to your door is only one of my many errands. My other chores await in the higher hills. I am on my way to fetch the nannies and the kids. I was wondering if Uri might like to join me there."

Uri's face brightened at the invitation but he shook his head no. "I would like it Rhea, more than anything I would, but I can not today. I have to help Galen clean the dishes and when Atyn returns he may need. . . I mean it may be that we have to and because, well perhaps, Odyn may . . ."

"You mean you what to stay with your brother today?"

"Yes, that is what I mean. I would like to stay near home today, until I am sure."

"You may be sure, Urion." answered Atyn but the boy shrugged, ignoring him and grinned widely at Rhea.

"I would do the same." she replied. "I will be going again next week maybe you will join me then."

"Yes, I will join you then, Rhea."

Atyn mounted the pony easily but Kiel struggled. The horses wore no saddles and only a soft rope was bound lightly around their muzzles.

"Are you alright there, Kiel? Shall I fetch you a stool?"

"I need no stool!" he said, swinging himself up and turning the pony round to face him. "I am quite able to manage!"

"Well take care then. That one is known to scrape her riders along the trees, if she thinks she might lose them that way."

"And why not tell him how you know this Uri?" replied Galen chuckling as the others readied themselves to leave.

"Farewell Rhea." he waved, ignoring Galen's remark. "Come back as soon as you may! Take care of Master Kiel!"

"I will Uri." she said, winking politely at Kiel "I will." and she was still smiling as the cottage faded into the trees.

The blue morning held only the barest wisps of cloud in the soft clear sky. Birds called from the upper lofts and through the hollows, dark eyed creatures peered from their burrows. By the time they left the shady trees, the sun was dazzling. The gardeners, with their crafty boats, were out on the lake, moving between one floating bed to the next, tending the growing things. All the folk of Odyn's Hold were solemn and polite but quite different in build and bearing. Some were tall and gray-eyed just as Atyn and Galen but many more wore skin of pale gold with eyes blacker than the night. Still there were others with skin tinted softly as milk, watching with eyes so blue they pierced the inner workings of the heart. Many who reminded Kiel of the solemn Inrih, Archer of Delphi for they carried themselves so regally and their sun-baked skin glowed with vigor. All greeted them kindly and were many well meant words were said to Atyn as they passed.

Finally they turned to the west finding themselves once more under the shadow of trees and it was not long before they reached Odyn's Hall. The dwelling was wrapped in neatly cut shingles of shaggy bark. The eaves hung low over the sturdy walls and high above them, thin streams of smoke curled from cobbled chimneys. The hall was filled with folk waiting for them to arrive.

Odyn grabbed Atyn around the shoulders. "The time was barely enough." He said studying his face.

"But once more it was enough." Atyn replied, "I remain in your service Odyn."

"Aye, and I am glad of it, Atyn. You are the oldest of our mother's line. A grave hurt would have been dealt us to lose another so dear. How the shadows of Ildabyth have breached our most secret places, I do not yet understand but what I do understand is we must act. The battle will not wait."

The Council murmured knowing the old wizard would offer no promises of a false peace.

"Astraea came to me during the long of the night." he said, the unseeing eye catching the firelight, "And it is true that Ildabyth is growing increasingly powerful as the Great Wheel turns. We must act now and seek out his new found strength. Our plans must be laid quickly if hope is to remain."

"Ildabyth is searching for something." Atyn replied. "Something that is familiar to him. Something he must not have. You are my brothers and sisters, my cousins and my kin, and I say to you, a crossroads is before us. No longer can we allow him to linger in Basilus, making his mischief and creating his beasts. The moment has come to make answer to the Fates. We can wait no longer. Time's Gate will not allow this chance again."

Odyn placed his hand upon Atyn's shoulder. "The signs are everywhere. We must seek what little hope remains within the lowlands of Erda. Long ago our families were besieged by his monstrous wraiths, our cousins slowly put to brutal deaths, and our mother saved all she could. You must return to the city of your birth for resolution lies within of the Rings of Basilus. It is the time. Time to finally and for all, penetrate his refuge. We are left with no other choice and we will not despair, Atyn Stormbringer. You carry the power of Minerva's Clan. Her tempest shall clear your way and the flawless light of her flawless star will shine unfettered once again."

Atyn did not smile. Odyn stepped up beside him, knowing well his difficult task and said to the others. "While each of us is willing to make this journey, there are those among us destined to do it. They must speak first for only they know why they would chose such a fortune.

Inrih, the Archer, rose immediately. 'I am one destined for this fate Odyn. I am the only son of Sata and of Delphyne. To this errand I am born. I beg your leave to stand beside Atyn as he wields the storm. I am ready and I will make answer to my Fate.

"So it shall be, Child of the Black Sun. You shall serve as his Deliverer. May the voice of Delphyne be strong in your heart and may the will of Sata be made pure by your hand."

Inrih took his place at the front of the hall. He stood a head taller than the old man and was twice his girth. His ebony bow was slung across his broad back and in his quiver, the silver tips of his arrows were marked by a crimson stain. He stood with his arms folded behind his back, his smooth golden skin gleaming under the lantern light.

Istah spoke next in turn. "I will ride with him, Odyn. Atyn and I can not be separated by death nor chance. We are one and so we shall remain until the end of days.

"The Fates have made it so, Istah. Together you shall enter the Valley of Woe for together you are stronger than you are apart."

She touched her heart with her open palm and she took her place beside the others.

Theo and Lorya then rose together. "We are the First Guard and Counselor of the Drui." said Theo to the group, "Many of our Clan have been lost to Ildabyth's sorcerers. Those who hold the balance outside the walls of Basilus will have need of our strengths as well as our staffs. We wish our leave to travel with Atyn and to aid our comrades in their secret work.

"You will go as part of the company, Theo and Lorya. The Druii hold the balance in the wilderness outside the Ringed City. They will need you as the moment draws to a close."

Yurah then stepped forward. "I too am destined for this path sir." Her clear voice carried through the room. "I bear the Sword the Oracle foretold. And whether it be my good fortune or my bitter fate to join your folk; my lot can not be denied."

"Truth is never to be denied, Seventh Daughter of a Seventh Son. It is written in the spiraling stars that you shall hold the balance of the chord. But there is one who has not yet spoken. One who is destined to carry the burden of the Sixth Cross." he said looking out over the room.

"It is I, Odyn." answered Kiel rising from his bench. "I shall stand as the seventh member of the company. If you see fit to accept my service?"

"The fateful number has been filled, Master Kiel." he said gently and then he pressed his hands against the table he declared, "The

Storm will soon pass through the Gates of Basilus. You who stand before this Council have chosen your way and whether your origins be of Zu, or Mithra, or of Ganymede, it is you and you alone who makes your answer to your Fate." and he paused and looked over the group. "Do not hold back what is in your hearts. There is much to be said. Speak now of your concerns for every moment is precious."

A slender man stood. He wore a plain cape draped loosely over his bare chest. His dark hair hung in a long braid down his back. Painted symbols ran along the side of his face and neck covering his shoulder. He held a twisting staff of rowan wood.

"My concerns lie with my kinfolk who dwell outside Basilus," he said. "My household has sent word that no winged messengers came during the night and none have arrived this morning. My folk are always expected to send a messenger during the full of the moon to hear the words of Odyn's seer. I fear they may have fallen victim to the same evil that touched us last evening. I ask for your leave to take on the raven shape and travel ahead to their hiding places. I will bring word back to the Council and share that news with the travelers as they make their way the sea."

The Drui must always take great care when they travel. Perhaps it was too dangerous to fly under the light of moon." replied Theo gravely, "We will hope that it is caution and not peril that keeps their messenger from our door."

"Indeed." spoke Odyn, "Such is the nature of the world in these troubled days. Go and prepare yourself, Rudra. I will be glad of the news upon your return. The others will set out as soon as they are able."

Rudra pulled the gray hood over his painted face. Theo met him at the door. He took a token from his vest and placed in his hand. Rudra carefully tucked into his cloak and went to his errand.

Varda rose to speak. Her watery voice rippled through the room. "I am troubled Odyn. The Valkyries must keep the armies close to the summit, Zelmisso. It is the task of your Clan to guard the Upper Gate at the top of the mountain. My heart holds a question I have not heard measured by the Council." and her clear eyes focused upon the Atyn at the head of the long table. "Who shall keep watch over the Upper Airs as Atyn travels? Who shall know if the Malkian's call and who shall know if Ildabyth's shades draw near? He is unique among us as he may dwell in the two realms at once. Who besides, the Son of Jupiter is capable of such a task? And if there is none who can do it, how do we handle the dilemma as the Upper Airs are left unattended?"

"There is one among us able to do the work," answered Odyn his bright eye gleaming, "for that labor is fated to the child, Urion."

"Urion." Varda whispered. "but he is still so young. Such a burden could crush him."

"And he is a boy child at that. Mastery will not come easy for him and we have not the advantage of time nor training." croaked the ancient crone huddled near the fire. "What does he understand of the powers of dark sorcerers? What protection has he against their fierce assaults? The priests of Basilus have no respect for that which brings life. What can a child know of hearts so bereft of light?"

"I will not deny it." Odyn answered nodding to the crone. "The boy will have much to conquer. But remember Macha, Urion is Atyn's pure brother and it is by virtue of this birthright that he wields the power to watch in his brother's stead."

"There is much danger in this, Odyn." said Lorya, "Uri is a yet a boy, filled with roguish ways. I must insist upon rethinking. His reason must be safeguarded. The danger points are three in number, first his body, then his mind, and lastly his spirit and each is more difficult to master than the one before it. Though his body is strong and his spirit endowed to him by Jupiter and Minerva, it is his mind that may not be ready. It is crucial that his thoughts remain under steadfast control. The power that comes with the combining of the Three is more perilous to the Magician than Ildabyth and a wheatfield of his wicked sorcerers. I do not wish to see him left maimed. Uri is precious to us all.

"Even now Urion intuits both the living worlds and though he may not be able to clearly separate one realm from the other." said Atyn. "Such confusion is to be expected and it can be overcome with perseverance.

"Is he able to maintain himself at the two places at once? Can he be the point and the wave? " Lorya asked, understanding all to well the subtle magical work.

"I have taken him to the Eye of the Storm and he did not quail. He was in no danger of drowning. The tempest did not fragment his mind and the fire did not sear him. I believe he can do it. I believe Urion has the strength to stand alone."

"A full day has not passed since I watched you fade from this world" said Lorya gravely. "And with all the strength that is endowed to me, I could not hold you from them. You were dying, Atyn and it was not I that saved you. It was the power of Astrea that kept you from that final moment."

He answered by taking her hand, "It is to die and to be born anew which binds us to our Fate. To dare to know it, and to dare to will it; that is all that any of us can hope to do. And through Urion is still a child he will settle for no less than this."

114

"But it is far greater a test to watch those you love suffer than to suffer oneself." Lorya answered. "If Urion be willing I will stand by the decision of the council."

Istah took her turn to speak. "Uri need not shoulder this burden without aid. There is much we could do to help him succeed."

"Urion will not bear the weight of this station alone Istah." said Odyn looking over his folk, "We have many gifts we may lend to the boy"

"I can aid the child," said Dorig without reserve. "I understand the crossing roads of time, I fear that Uri will find those endless hours unsettling as he learns to bear the splitting of realties."

"There is much Urion must learn to bear. He must know the power of listening before the power of Voice may be safely wielded." croaked Macha, tapping her cane impatiently upon the floor. "We will see how quick he is to learn the deeps of silence, for only then may he trusted with the powers of cadence and rhyme."

"I may aid the boy in this." replied Thrae rising from his seat, "The magic of silence and sound are most evident in song. Such knowledge will offer him safety in times of sudden need."

"Uri does not know what it means to be vigilant in every moment of the day and night." continued Theo. He will become weary. It cannot be avoided, and when he does he must be shielded. His Shadows will be quick to perceive any wrinkle that might stir the upper airs."

"He is vulnerable. Any failing, will alert them to him" replied Lorya.

"Then we must see that he does not fail." Odyn answered, "Aside from Atyn, it is Galen who knows him best. In his brother's stead I deem it wise for him to dwell in their cottage. With the aid of Dorig, Macha, and Thrae, Urion will learn the point of balance. This will give him every chance to understand the blending power of the Three."

"The power of the Three." said Lorya, a shiver sounding through her voice. "Though we may be able to bar Ildabyth's hand there is none of us who can shield him from that which is neither Good nor Evil. It is an indifferent strength. How can a child understand its nature."

"Urion was born to the task. He understands it better than he understands himself." Atyn answered. "He has been just waiting for the moment to know it."

Odyn laid his hand upon his shoulder, "Do not fear for him as you return to the Sacred City of your folk. Take back from Ildabyth what was once your own. Our spheres of protection will be steady around him. Now it is your duty to undo Ildabyth's mishandling of Erda's affairs. You are the Stormbringer. You hold the power born from the Upper Airs. You hold the hope of this realm as the steady eye within tempest."

"I will not fear for him, my oldest friend, for I know he is in the best of care." Atyn answered gravely.

Odyn smiled grimly and his blind eye gleamed as he looked again to the council, "The road is long and many dangers will await as they descend to the sea. They will need horses and provisions. The company must shed their woodland cloaks and clothe themselves in the manner fitting of the Basilians. Now is the time to bring our minds together. A carefully laid plan is what we need most." Odyn signaled to the child that waited by the door, "In an hour we shall recount and settle on our parts." and he left to them work and followed the child down the hall.

The Council spoke quietly among themselves. Kiel and Yurah listened with interest as they coordinated the duties of the various Clans. Atyn did not involve himself. He and Macha talked before the fire."

"Though it is much effort, it might be the wisest choice for the Drui to alter their shapes. Those pointing ears are all too easy to spot. Maybe traveling as hunting dogs or beasts of burden would be best." she said squinting her wrinkled eyes, "All roads to Basilus are watched and the Drui have a high bounty upon them. They will be slain on sight. Ears, head and all will be taken to the Priests as badges of honor." she scowled into the fire. "And Inrih! He is a giant of man. He will not be able to slip through any gate without notice." she grunted softly, "He will go as himself, a warrior guard. Maybe then he shall not be pressed to lay aside his precious bow and long arrows. Such a thing would cause him great angst," she cackled, imagining the hulking man mourning for his weapons.

Then her black eyes grew thoughtful as she considered the others. "It will be clear to any with an eyeball and brain that Kiel and Yurah are not of this world. They have airs about them will raise many suspicions. Great care need be taken in their concealment," she murmured, rubbing her thin hands together, and leaning closer toward the flame, "but if they travel with emissaries, maybe, just maybe then, they could pass without notice, possibly a liegeman of the north or perhaps as western merchant, in this their unnatural strangeness might go unnoticed," she stared into the warm light, still as a stone considering the ruse. "and even used to benefit. If it is done well you may find yourselves keeping company with those Dowerymen." then she rose straight in her chair, her thoughts clear and her mind firmly made, "and you, Atyn" she said, "if you could manage to lower your scorching eyes and bow your proud neck then perhaps both you, and the Lady Istah, may not be taken directly to his dungeons for impudence."

'I have no issue with any of this, Macha." he smiled, "I will walk in whatever guise suits best."

"Agreeable boy," she muttered, tapping her cane against the stone of the hearth "for soon you will find yourself in places that even the Malkians fear to go. You must understand, it is not assured we will defeat him."

"I carry no false hope, mother." he answered, grimly. "The chance of defeat but serves to deepen my resolve. My fate is set."

"Fate, you say. What is that? The wind that drives us forth, helpless as leaves? Know what calls you, Atyn Stormbringer. Know this and you will not falter in your resolve. Know this and the form will not serve to deceive." and the old one leaned toward him placing her hand upon the midpoint of his brow. "Know you are blessed Minerva's Son. May your starless night serve to reveal it." And with those words, his mind was filled with fire.

The full of the hour had not yet passed when Odyn reentered the busy hall. Galen and Urion walked at his side, "Hail brother," the boy grinned. "My ears were burning so hot I had thought the Drui were cast a shifting spell upon me so I hurried to the hall, hoping no one would mistake me for something I am not."

"Urion, why do say such things? The Drui are busy folk and only use their powers as it serves a need." replied Galen lightly vexed. "And they certainly have no need of your toilsome mischief."

"Do not deny you were glad to follow me Galen. You were just as curious as I was this morning," he said looking back at his friend. "and just as surprised when we found that Odyn waited for us on the road."

The Wizard laughed, "I knew you might follow the sound of your name. Much has been said and all of it concerns you both most deeply"

"We have much to put in order before it is time," then he hesitated looking at his younger brother.

Urion shrugged, "The trees know as change comes. They speak to each other across the whole of the world. They told me of your journey." he replied, his eyes kindled with light, "and they told me of its reason."

"And did the trees tell you of your reasons, Urion?" asked Odyn, placing his hand upon the boy's shoulder.

"No Odyn, they did not." his smile fading. "I leave that for you and my brother to suggest."

"Are you frightened, Uri? Frightened of the things we might

suggest."

"Yes. I am frightened Odyn. Frightened I may not be up to the task," he answered genuinely and then the boy set his jar firmly, "but I shall not allow such worries to hinder me. I am ready. I am waiting."

"Waiting? What do you mean?"

"I am waiting for you to tell me what to do."

Odyn raised a bushy eyebrow, "Well, I am not the one to do that, my son." he replied glancing to the crone in front of the fire, "But be assured I shall remain near to sustain you through these trials." and from the hearth, Uri could hear the tapping of Macha's walking stick.

CHAPTER XIII
ZELMISSO'S PEAK

The cold crawled under her skin. Her sword was heavy and Kiel was near but had nothing to say. The familiar cloud was cast over his thoughts once more. The Drui came and went, understanding one another without speaking. The harper sat near the fire. His golden hair was pulled away from his gentle face and the shapely ear caught her eye. Thrae's harp stirred a wandering melody through the hall and the voice of her own flute breathed from under her cloak. She touched the case and a gentle song came from someplace far away.

"What music do you hold traveler?" a voice said, "I heard it whisper? Tell me Lady, from where did it come?"

Yurah took the flute from its case and gave it to the harper. He held it in his hand as one might hold a new and fragile life. "How do you come by these precious things, traveler? This reed was wrought by metal sweeter than any silver or gold I have yet to savor. I dare not put it too my lips." he said placing it back in her hands.

"It is a gift from my father's house, wrought by hands much like your own," she said softly as a fragile vision of snow and song filled her. "There are those who dwell in that land that could certainly be your kin."

"There is much about the both of you that reminds us of ourselves." he answered glancing to Kiel, alone and lost in his musings. "As duty unfolds maybe we shall know the secret that hides us from one another."

"Maybe we shall Thrae." she said, placing the flute back in its casing. "And if you should change your mind about playing, you only need ask." she told him as all grew still. Odyn had taken his place at the front of the Hall.

"Your work has been quick." Odyn said gravely, "The traveling plans are made and provisions are gathered. The travelers will ride by moonlight. The ponies are being readied now."

"There are still things left to say before the evening comes and all that is said Uri must stay to hear." Atyn replied, "Istah is readying the ponies now and Galen will show the guards to their posts around our cottage." and then Atyn caught Kiel's eye. "You are free to go with him, traveler. There is a horse waiting."

Kiel bowed. "I would be glad of the work. Is there anything you would like me to fetch from your cottage?"

"Well now that it is mentioned, Master Kiel," interrupted Uri, "there are a few things left undone about the kitchen. I did not have time to quite finish before I found myself here and."

"Urion, you waste your breath. The work is for you to do and no hand will touch it but your own. See to that Galen." said Macha briskly, "Urion shall be quick to learn what it is to be his own master."

"We will not lift a finger to cheat him of his duties, Macha." laughed Galen, "I shall be grateful of the company, Kiel. Let me gather a bit of dinner for my men. I will be back in moment."

"I will be waiting." Kiel answered.

Pulling his chair close, Kiel touched the hem of Yurah's sleeve. "It has been long day and it seems an even longer night is upon us. What have you been doing?"

"I spent the evening in the halls of the Drui. They are lovely folk. Something about them serves to stir memories of our far-away home."

"Home." he answered sadly, "For me all memory of home is but a faded dream. You are able to hold to something to you that I cannot. Will you tell me a little of home my friend?"

"My memories of home are only the faintest of whispers but I will share them with you as we go. Maybe they will bring you some bit of comfort"

Kiel lowered his gaze, "Comfort? I have no hopes of that. There is a battle I fight inside my thoughts. It is a dilemma that I must endure alone."

"But you are not alone Kiel. We made our way across the heavens to find ourselves in this little world. Soon we will go to Basilus and we will find her and when we do we will bring her home."

"Home, Yurah? Again you say it, and again I do not understand." and she touched his hand and he smiled.

"Good day, Yurah. Good day, Kiel." said a firm voice. A young woman, with raven hair stood at the head of the table. Painted designs covered the side of her face. "I am Artemi, Rudra's sister. I have come for Yurah. We must select clothes to fit and instruct her in the bearing of her guise."

"It is nice to meet you, Artemi." Kiel said, rising from his chair. "It heartens me to see my companion in such good hands. And do not worry about my mood Yurah. I will not be left alone to sulk, Galen will soon be along to fetch me. We will return to this hall before the evening meal."

The sky was a gray wash in the setting sun. Sitting upon restless ponies they spoke their strained farewells. Artemi would lead them to the first pass but from there she would be obliged to return to Odyn's Hold. She had taken Loyra's mantle upon her and stood now as the

First Guard. Atyn said his last hurried words with Urion while Odyn stood between Kiel and Yurah, holding her pony's head and stroking the soft muzzle.

"You should be near to the city by the new moon. Listen to airs on the night as she fades to black. The Drui will help you all they can. Silence and stealth are their tools. They know all the whispering rivalries between the Priest of the Towers. They take shapes to keep watch upon the Basilus but it is dangerous work." he said as a shadow passed over his face, "You should have news from Rudra shortly. This will help you in your planning. Our goals are the same, travelers. Find what you seek and set it free; and if this should weaken him, we might regain some of our lost strength and not fail in our stewardship of Erda. A storm is coming; Seventh Daughter." he said watching Urion embrace his brother, "Stand ready; Wandering Son. Our destinies are one."

Lorya gave the signal to follow. Along the shadowed path single candle flames burned and as the shades of night gathered, a lonely song began to fill the dark. Kiel rode at her side guarding his thoughts and Yurah wondered if she would see the fair place again. Through the miles, the melody drifted upon the night breeze as the song of Drui finally faded under the light of the rising moon.

Atyn and Istah rode just behind them, Yurah listened in wonder to the rise and fall of the their voices. The speech was mystifying; not at all like the melodic tongue of the Drui. But even as she did not understand the words she knew Atyn was troubled.

"It is a strange tongue they share," she said to Kiel as the magnetic exchange flowed by her, "Dreadful as it is lovely."

"He speaks the language of the Malki" said Kiel indifferently, "Atyn is telling her of the airs above. He is telling her the shadows seek a prize."

"What do they look for?"

Kiel fell silent. The voices behind them moved in rhythmic speech. "Do you not feel it, Yurah." he whispered finally, "The road ahead is treacherous. Within the towers of the silver city; beneath the gates that lead to her core, Ildabyth holds the keys to the doom of Erda. Unspeakable power is held there, the horror is immeasurable, the pain is." and then he paused, his hands trembling upon the ropes, "And that presence is all around us, Yurah. It hovers in the air, smelling the land we walk upon. Ildabyth's shadows seek what is theirs," and he hesitated, "but as yet, they do not know my name."

The Scabbard whispered and for instant she glimpsed the frailty he bore. "Do not fear." she said, the clarity of the Sensar running through her. "Do not fear what burden lies within you. Though you bear his scar, hope is not left behind. It is the shadow's lies that make it seem so for justice is never divorced from mercy."

"How do you see what I cannot?"

"The gifts I bring from my homeland clear my mind." she told him softly, touching the hilt of the Sword.

"Then you carry with you the sweetest of all things." he sighed, looking upward to see the moon climbing over the mountain.

They had reached the first summit. A chain of grim mountains loomed ahead. Their rough shoulders gleamed under the cold lunar light and the forbidding miles stretched long before them. Artemi lead them south and they held tight to their ponies. In a single file they walked slowly along walls of steep rock. She began to grow weary of the steady trudge of her pony's feet. The group was silent. The airs grew colder still and as the darkness reached its fullest. The icy night had bore deep into their bones when riders ceased their plodding and rested for a while. Yurah touched the welcoming ground finding her legs had grown to numb to hold her.

Artemi was as her side. "Drink this. It will take away the cold." she said, offering her a flask. The taste was sharp but its warmth spread quickly through her quickly.

"Thank you," she said handing back the flagon. "I am better for it, Artemi."

"Rudra made it. Be it roots and bark, bud or seed; he knows them all by name and virtue. He has concocted many elixirs. It is what he does when there is time. Here just another sip, there are still some hours before the sun will return."

She took another mouthful and Artemi then offered the drink to Kiel. He downed a long sip and then looked up to the sky. "How much longer until we pass the peaks?" he asked.

"By morning we will reach the first pass. The dell cuts sharply south through the mountains. It will provide you with the cover of trees. You will rest there throughout the day. Travel is not safe. The Basilians send their carrion birds to watch the mountain trails but those beasts cannot see by night and few other creatures will consent to their bidding. It will take three full nights to reach its end, and after this there is yet another pass you will cross. Snow will mark the way and your going will be slow. You will travel easterly until the summit, Zelmisso. Lorya knows the road. She will lead you to a cavern, hid from the eyes of Ildabyth's spies. Here you will be sheltered but you will walk without the sun. It is only after you have passed through the hidden way will the mountains soften. It is along this road, for good or ill, you might chance to meet others as you go." and she paused looking up into the night as if waiting for an answer. "I hope my brother will find you along the western side of the range. When you reach it, you will not turn your ponies toward Basilus, you will make your way to the retreat of the Drui. You must enter the city by way of the Wildermoors. My clan knows the paths that are hidden from his probing eyes. And remember, those who enter Basilus are not free to come and go as they please. Take care to remain true to your new identities and not stray from them. Treachery lies in every shadow. This is the only thing that you may trust." and she paused, lifting her face to stare into the moonlight. "My brother flies upon a chilly wind." She said, smelling the clear air. "We must be on our way."

They rested no more and the long miles passed slowly. The colorless views of steep cliffs and black ravines rose ominously above their heads. Yurah thoughts dwelt upon the Sword and, as her restive questions formed, the whispering runes of the Scabbard responded.

"It is the Two Fold Fear that wants of union,
As the field of Struggle draweth nigh.
Just and Merciful, stands the Woman who mourns the Sage
His Earthly Dust sown with the blood of innocents.
Her Life Waters to surround them
Her Balance meant to sustain".

And the words went on, evenly spaced and without flaw, as the ponies made their way faithfully forward until the night faded into dawn. Far behind them lie the quiet of Odyn's Hold and still farther ahead lie their noisy fate. They drew their ponies together and Artemi held back her grief at their parting.

"Through every step and every danger, I will be there." she said raising her arms to greet the new morning and spoke to the frigid airs,

"May your earthy hands be graced by the Mother of All
May your brave hearts be blessed by the Yellow Sun.
And may the wings of Etana guide you to your destiny,
Oh precious ones,
We surround."

And she turned her pony toward home.

Sheltering was easy in the evergreen forest. They lay down their blankets upon their fragrant needles and rested through out the day. The afternoon had begun to fade when Yurah opened her eyes. Kiel lie still beside her so she rose quietly and went to find the others. Istah was at the spring making a cooking fire. Lorya had been hunting and had brought down four fat rabbits. They made quick work of the messy chores and soon the smell of stew filled the air. They ate their meal in the settling night and soon after began their journey in the dark. Along the dale they saw no sign of the Basilian scouts. Inrih brought up the rear, speaking to no one as they passed through the fractured gorge. His watchful presence was assuring and the night passed without incident.

They set their camp in a sheltered hollow just before the dawn. A light frost had settled and Inrih walked about the site, uneasy and silent. After a time he spoke quietly to Lorya and she walked with him to the edge of the crest.

"I fear you may be correct, Inrih." Yurah heard her say as she walked toward them.

"I will take the first watch," Inrih answered.

"Do not take on more than your share."

"Do not worry for me, Lorya. I must understand what my ears told me."

"And what do you think your ears have said, Inrih?" asked Atyn.

"It was most like a shudder, born deep into the bones of earth. The sound trembled in my skull."

"What does it mean, sir?" asked Yurah.

"I am not sure, but Ildabyth's mischief must be close to it."

"We can not allow ourselves to be caught by surprise," replied Lorya, "We will have no fire today and we must take our turn at watching. If his spies be about we must know it."

One by one they took their place along the crest of the ravine. Yurah had the last watch. The day was fading when Kiel handed her a flask he had under his cloak.

"Artemi gave it to me." he grinned, "She was concerned we are not accustomed to these highlands. She said this brew will help us to remain clear-headed."

"It also keeps one warm." answered Yurah rubbing her hands together.

He smiled. "We shall travel hard tonight. So drink Yurah, it will keep the cold from the within."

As before the brew did its work and they were refreshed when the first twinkling light appeared in the velvet sky.

Atyn brought them their ponies. "Are you ready for another ride?"

"The night does not worry me. The stars are my companions." replied Kiel

"Then wrap your cloak well around you. It is time to go."

Under the moonlight they made good speed and as the day approached Lorya called them together.

"We shall not reach Zelmisso's peak before day breaks again. The pass is a dangerous place and the nights are frigid. I think day travel shall serve us better. There has been no sign of trouble. Perhaps

Ildabyth is busy with his mischief elsewhere."

Atyn nodded, "There are troubled thoughts drifting from the Windermoors. I agree Lorya, haste will better serve us now." and a swirl of icy wind swept through the leaves.

So it was, they chose not to sleep and they continued on through the day. They walked under the deep shadows of tall cedars. Tuffs of thick moss grew along the shady gorge. Every few hours they would stretch their limbs and eat. The traveling food was hearty; nuts and fruits, dried salted meats and thin cakes, wrapped in a papery cloth.

The sun had just begun to set when they came to a sharp bend. A long low cliff spread before them, running steady toward the north. The barren rock held no cover of trees and great head of the brooding mountain loomed over them. Lorya jumped off her pony and studied the sky. It was clear and pale; showing no hint of cloud, or worse.

"There it is. The Pass of Serico." she said gesturing toward the summit that spread its deep shadow over the gorge. "We have done well. We will rest for now and wait for the moon."

Inrih leapt off his horse with a grunt. "I am glad of it," he said rubbing his pony's sturdy flank. "Though my feet do not begrudge you, my four legged friend, the rest of me is happy to walk for myself a while."

"Well I am glad you feel that way, Inrih." answered Lorya chuckling, "Your pony will not carry you over the pass. You will have to lead him. That road is difficult one." she said, looking around at the high forest floor. "But the day has been fair. The journey is not as harsh as it might have proven."

While they halted, Kiel and Yurah saw to the ponies. They took off their packs and lead them to the edge of the forest where they could graze.

"Atyn has not spoken all day," said Kiel.

Yurah laughed, "How often have I seen you do the same?"

"Yes, but such a mood is different in him." he answered clumsily, "I brood upon my own dilemmas and he, well he is well able to think beyond his own small problems. Indeed Yurah, we are far from alike. Though his body is with us; he is not. His bearing is both, detached and discerning. I wonder what it is that he sees."

"They say he is able to be in two worlds at once." Yurah replied. "But which of these realms is more real, I would not dare to decide."

"They are both real." said Kiel grimly.

She watched the ponies chew considering Atyn's dilemmas and it was not long before Istah came to find them.

"There is food waiting. Do not worry about the ponies. I will watch them."

"Will you not join us Lady?" asked Kiel.

"I helped in the cooking, and had my fill." she smiled. "Lorya consented to a fire, so supper is better than you might have expected."

"I will be glad of a warm meal." and he bowed politely, "We will be back soon to relieve you."

"There will be no need of it. I have the first watch. Theo will come for me when it is up. It will be a long night, rest as you have the chance."

The dark came all too quickly and Atyn was next to her gently shaking her awake.

"It is time, Lady Yurah. The sun has sunk behind the hills." and he handed her the small flask. "Here. It will help put you on your feet."

The drink was surprisingly warm to her throat, "This is not the same as the other." she said, sputtering at the change.

Atyn grinned, "Rudra has many recipes. This one will help you forget your need for sleep and warmth. It will be a cold walk tonight but near its top there is a grotto our folk keep stocked. Inside we will have a warm fire and shelter from the wind. Here take another draft."

And so she did and the second did not bite as bad as the first. Soon they were again in their lines with Lorya in the lead. The broken path led steeply up among the pale, colorless stone. The hours passed by slowly as they walked alone with private thoughts.

Atyn's attentions rested upon the moonbeams as they as they lingered along the crevices of the dark ice. He was listening to the chill winds but what they said to him, he was keeping to himself. Inrih walked behind them. Touching stones as they passed and paying careful heed as to the mood of the earth. He understood what lie hidden underneath the rocky crust and bent his attention vigilantly toward her. Yurah rubbed her pony's stubbly chin, glad of his warm grassy breath on her hands. The weight of the sword never ceased to burden her but the whispering voice of the magical scabbard lead her again into its waking dreams and tonight its vision was sweet. The comforting arms of rattling trees drew near her, and in the distance, she could hear water calling. Kiel kept his eyes straight forward. His mind was far from the monotony of the climb and sometimes, as they walked, he softly hummed a bit of song. His voice was lovely.

The night grew frigid and to linger was dangerous. Finally the pale mountains began to appear around them. Wrinkled ridges stretched for miles, forming rifts and fractures upon a barren sea of stone. Forbidding peaks, fierce with ice caught the first beams of the rising sun. A desolate land was spread under the winter sky. Lorya signaled them to hurry. To one side of the narrow pass lay a sheer drop and to the other a bleak wall of freezing stone. When the sun told them it was half-way to noon, they reached the hidden camp. Lorya spoke the mystic words and a door appeared. The cavern was spacious with smaller coves clustered around a larger room. They led in their ponies and Lorya sealed the stone behind them.

Soon a cheery fire blazed in the back of the grotto. They sat around it, warming their hands and watching the pot heat. After they had eaten Lorya wrapped herself in her blanket and slept in a dim corner as the rest of the company lingered around the fire. Atyn's cheerful nature had returned. He and Inrih told stories of the forest surrounding Odyn's Hold. Atyn described the strange ways the trees and Inrih spoke of the rocks, always calling them the bones of that land, explaining in detail how propagated in the harboring mountains and told of their many virtues in healing. Istah sat wrapped in a blanket and hummed a soft song into the flames. They passed around the flask once more before they took to their beds. As it went round the group Kiel noticed that Theo was no longer among them. He found him sitting in the soft light, fumbling in his pack, his mind upon other things. Kiel took the bottle and carried it to him.

"What is it like? The place where your folk hide from the world. Is it at all like these high woods?"

"The Wildermoors. No Kiel, there is little similarity between the two." he answered in his low, resonant voice. "The wildermoors are a desolate place, lying close to the feet of the mountains and just behind the brackish fens. Years have past since those hills were laid to waste by the first wars and since that time they have overgrown with heaths and wildberry. Our folk have concealed themselves in this rugged place. Though it is impossible to find them you may be assured their eyes are everywhere. They are shapeshifters, as we all are, but they use their gifts to venture within the walls of Basilus, seeing what they can and sending word as they are able. But this is not all that they do in this place. The Drui have other purposes in the Wildermoors." and he furrowed his brow and stared at the mountain. "They keep guard in those foothills, for within them is hidden a precious secret."

"What do you mean Theo?" he replied as troubled thoughts cluttered his mind.

Theo bent near to whisper, "Can you not recall it, Kiel? This is not the first time we have met. This is not the first time you have met my people."

He found himself gasping for breath, a bright searing through his chest. Theo reached out his hand and held tight his shoulder. "You do remember, then?" he said in a low tone. "Do not fear it! I have known for sometime. We are here to help you."

"Help me? Help me how?"

"As we have before," he answered softly, "It was the Drui who rescued you from beneath the Tower of the Basilians. You were barely alive, in fact I do not how you survived at all" then he paused and stared him, "but that was long ago and much has happened since."

"The Drui." Kiel muttered, the pain within him sharpening. "I do feel it. Deep, deep under my bones I do." and the burn of chest grew stronger as he struggled to speak, "I have known the underbelly of the Basilian empire. I have known it both as an enemy and as a friend."

"If you had ever been a friend to Ildabyth's priests, you did certainly fall far from their favor," he answered, sadness filling his gray eyes, "You were barely recognizable when we found you."

Kiel was unable to answer, struggling wildly with his thoughts as Theo continued.

"You were burned. Beyond recognition, burned beyond hope," and he looked deeply into his face. "but I am sure now. I am sure that it was you."

Then all memory returned. A foul reek surrounded him and his lips were bleeding. His skin split with every slight movement and the pain continued on and on, outlasting every sense. He was suffering alone as eternity passed until a calm voice spoke. The voice told him not to fear. It told him to be still and that it would guide him through the pain. And there would be times he would listen and times he would falter from it, but the voice would still be there, reminding once more. Until one day that he heard clearly. He was not afraid and could remain very still, and he did not falter. Then it was that the voice told him her name. She told him of her home, and of her children. And she filled his mind with visions of fair and simple things and he found himself stronger after he had heard it. His strength grew as the time passed by until the day she spoke of the Malki and something new was rekindled. He learned to hold steady through the suffering and strength grew.

Finally the voice told him of Ildabyth and Kiel remembered his captor and his pain overcame him once more. But the voice continued, encouraging him to be still and to listen. She spoke of the plans Ildabyth made for the world above. A world where nothing good, nor free, nor without stain, was offered. Greed and arrogance, lust and sloth, envy and avarice, and violent rage were the fruits of his twisted intent. And when Kiel glimpsed the hideous force all hope died and her voice faded into silence. Utterly alone in the shadowy dark, evil curses began to surround him and after a time a dull light began to spread over the colorless walls. Skinless forms, nothing more than withered meat hanging from twisted bones flew down upon him. They carried curved blades of black fire, edged by a blood red light. They flayed his skin until his own muscles hung tattered and as his bones were splintered under the fierce heat.

Darkness claimed him. The fiery roar consumed his senses. A heated wind was all that remained and Kiel supposed that this was dying. As pain began to fade he heard a small voice whisper. He recognized his name and he knew he had left Sro behind in the dark. Pain and memories flooded back. He was choking upon his own self-loathing as Theo called him into the moment.

"So you have seen the inner core." the gentle voice said. "That place is the very heart of Erda."

"He keeps her bound her there." Kiel said faintly, remembering the bitter battle she had fought alone. "He uses her to bend the earthy fires to his will."

"Uses who?" asked Theo, drawing close so he could hear his whispers.

"Sro." he replied grimly,   "He uses the powers of Sro to dominate the burning will of her centering place."

Theo laid his hand upon his shoulder, trying to ease him. "There is no need for further talk, my friend. We will think of something."

Kiel slept through the afternoon and when he woke the others were ready and packed. Atyn came to speak with him, "We will set out as soon as you are able."

"I am able." he answered, rising to his feet. "My strains are not of the body."

"You are with friends Master Kiel. We will do what we can to ease your burdens." Atyn smiled. "The summit is but a few hours away. We shall travel through the bones of earth under the protection of Zelmisso. When we venture out again under the open sky, we will be near to our destination. Take comfort, Kiel. We will reach her soon."

After a hasty meal they left the warm cave to walk again between the cold stone and the abyss. During the night, as gray clouds obscured the fading moon as the wind cried. They toiled upward steadily until they reached, the Pass of Serica. Looking over the endless ranges, the ice and rock, they saw the un-giving stone stretching from every direction. Under the fading light of the moon, one of the pikes stood out beyond all the others. Far in the distance it loomed touching the sky with its perfect point.

"Odyn's folk oft refer to the summit as Zelmisso." explained Atyn, "and the Basilians call the mountain, Meru, but in the language of my people, the Vanyr, Golgatha is its name. It is the Pillar that holds the havens above us."

"Zelmisso." she repeated, "Somewhere that name lingers in my mind." and she touched the hilt of the Sword.

"Zelmisso is the centering point of Erda." Theo answered and as he spoke a black cloud passed over the waning moon. Rasping sounds began to creak and soon great currents began push up from the crack beneath them. Moaning voices echoed through the abyss. The company grew silent and Atyn stepped right to the edge of the precipice breathing in the churning winds. Then he turned back to face them and put his hand upon Kiel's shoulder, "We must go." he said gravely, "and we must hurry." and they fled the Pass of Serica and followed him to the caves that lead under the mountain.

CHAPTER XIV
THE ANCIENT ROAD

The cold fog was lifting from the gorge below. Its damp fingers feeling their way through the heavy air, pressing the chill deeper under their cloaks as Lorya commanded the stone to move. The shafts of dim light filtered into the vast cavern. Inrih took several stout twisted roots from his pack. Around the top of each he had bound a single clear crystal. One by one, Inrih placed his hands around them and, with a light touch, the stones lit. Kiel breathed a sigh of relief as the sound of the bitter wind faded behind the wall.

"We should rest a bit before moving on," said Theo sending a concerned thought to Lorya.

"Yes, it would be a good time to fix something to eat." she acknowledged, watching Kiel lean against his horse.

"Indeed it would. Walking in the cold is hungry work. I'll do the cooking this time. I have been practicing you know," Inrih grinned. "and I have a secret in my pack."

"We do not allow you to cook, Inrih. It is far from your greatest skill." Istah replied, raising her eyebrow, "But tell us, what is your surprise?"

Inrih began to rummage in the bottom of pack. His black eyes grew bright as he found what he searched for. "Potatoes!" he exclaimed and one by one, he pulled out about a dozen.

"Potatoes!" Istah laughed. "Only you would have thought to stuff those alongside with your cloaks and britches."

"It takes more than cloaks and britches to travel well." he retorted, continuing to root through his bags, "Ahh, the carrots!" holding up a big bunch by their withered tops.

"Well Inrih, they are indeed a lovely sight. But I beg you, let me help to mind the pot. Then perhaps these precious roots may not suffer to burn and we will all be more satisfied with your well laid plans."

"If you must." he replied, winking at Yurah, "but as I said I have been practicing this art and I do not think you will be disappointed."

Istah shook her head and chuckled softly as she went to set the fire.

Theo and Atyn tended the ponies, pulling off their packs and brushing down their rough coats while Kiel arranged the traveling bags against the wall. First the smell of fire came and then the scent of the stew.

"Smells all right." said Atyn.

"Umm, I suppose it could be fit to eat." answered Theo.

"Well, I could eat about anything at this point." said Kiel, looking somewhat recovered.

"When Inrih cooks, "about anything" is most often what you will get." replied Theo.

"We will know soon, Istah is coming to fetch us."

When they sat to supper they were pleased to find the stew quite fit, in fact surprisingly tasty.

"I only had to rescue the pot twice." Istah told them. "Once from salt and once from scorching."

"The pot needed no rescuing at all, but if it makes you feel better to think it, go on and do it." he smirked. "The stew speaks fine for itself."

"That it does, Inrih and I would like to know if you have any other treats hidden away."

The big man laughed, "I might have a thing or two tucked here and there, Master Atyn, but you must wait and see."

"Then keep your surprises to yourself, sir." he said as he rose. "and I will wonder about them as we go."

Within the hour they started up once more. The halls of the cavern were wide and the cold no longer plagued them. The click of their pony's hooves carried eerily along the long hollow corridors and they were careful to speak in whispers.

"Who made this place?" whispered Yurah, "I have never known a cavern to be like this."

Theo held his stave higher allowing the light to play upon the dark polished walls, "Some of these passageways were shaped by the natural rising of the mountains, but most was built by the first race that lived upon the world. Odyn is old enough to have seen that time." Then he nodded to his left. "Look over there." he said as the spreading light revealed a wide arching passage. "And there," he said holding the light to the right and to the other side where there lie an identical archway. "All throughout these mountain chains hidden routes have been hollowed out. But over the centuries many of the corridors have become blocked and other places have become home to strange creatures. We must be watchful as we go. There may be things here we do not want to meet unawares." and he glanced behind him listening to the long hall.

They continued for several hours. Yurah was weary when Lorya finally signaled a stop. Kiel swayed when he touched the ground. He muttered something and began to fumble with his pony's straps. Even Atyn looked pale and Theo did not speak.

"Though haste is necessary; still we must rest." Lorya told herself broodingly but to the others she replied. "We will sleep for a while. We will be safe here. And yet," she paused looking around the dark corridor. "I would feel easier if we set a guard."

"I will take the first watch, Lorya." replied Inrih. "I am not weary. The stone around us is ancient" he said, placing his open palm against the wall "resolute, if you will. It lends its strength to me, if you can understand such a thing."

"I can understand when you say it, Inrih." she answered affectionately. "You may take the first watch but even you must sleep. We will take our turns."

After the order of the watches had been set the effort of cooking seemed too great so they shared a light meal from the traveling fare in their bags. But soon, and to their pleasant surprise, a bright fire sprang into life from a near hollow. Inrig was leaning over it feeding the flames bits of fuel. When they came nearer they saw that one of his traveling sacks was stuffed with short, sturdy bits of wood. Istah was warming her hands asking him why he chose to keep wood and potatoes in his luggage instead of clean clothes. Inrih assured her that his priorities well in order. Yurah smiled at their banter but soon weariness overcame her and she lay her blanket down upon the stone.

"Not quite a feather bed." said Kiel still looking peculiarly pale.

"And I had considered a few piney needles uncomfortable."

"Well I shall sleep no matter how hard this floor might be. Inrih may gain his strength from these stone walls but this sunless trek has tired me to my core."

She agreed sleepily, and using a smaller pack as a pillow, she lay down upon the hard bed and slept soundly until Atyn woke her to watch.

Inrih's fire had faded away, leaving only the most determined embers to smolder under their thin blanket of ash. Atyn had left her one of the crystal walking staffs so she rose silently and carefully began to study the cavern walls. Long fingers of marbled white, laced with fine threads of gold ran through the polished stone. She walked slowly and it was not long before she noticed that fixed upon the halls were a series of raised symbols. The script was formed of simple lines or basic curves and most of the segments ending with a small circles at their tips.

She continued to explore the dark hall, leaving the sound of her companion's soft breathing behind her. Facing the blackness, Yurah realized that other sounds were stirring from the dark corridor. At first it seemed a fluttering noise echoing through the gloom. The back of her neck tingled and a rustling sound like leaves in a hard wind came nearer. She held her staff higher, trying to see in the gloom but the long hall was black as pitch. Then suddenly, a rush of wings was upon her. She fell to her knees covering her face. A sickly sweet aroma filled her mouth and the wind rushed by in a unbroken flood. For endless moments a beating rush of bodies screeched past her until finally another voice that rose above the wall of sound. She was able to lift her head. Inrih was there, helping her to her feet.

"It is the Nykertis. They will not hurt you. They are the eyes of the mountains."

"I do not like it, Inrih!" Theo said uneasily. "What could have disturbed them from the rest."

"I do not know Theo." he answered with a concerned frown, then he turned back to Yurah, "Are you all right, Lady?"

"Fine. I am fine. But do not think you are going without me. It is my watch and I want to see what lies down this hall."

"It is the way to water." said Atyn standing at the opening studying the glyphs that marked the edge of the arch.

"Water." Theo agreed looking at the raised letters, "It has been a long time since I have read the Malkian Script." he said as the others were on their way to meet them.

"What were those beasts?" exclaimed Kiel, "They terrified the horses."

"They are the Nykertis, Kiel but they do not mean us any harm. They serve as guardians to these secret paths. The darkness does not concern them because they sense all things with sound." explained Theo. "The Nykertis are perfect companions to these caverns for they are ever vigilant, even in sleep."

"But they were so frenzied." replied Kiel

"I do not know why," he said looking down the hall. "but I will soon."

"You are going that way?" said Kiel following his glance.

"Yes, we must see for ourselves what disturbed them."

"I would like to go with you."

"If you are up to it, Master Kiel?" replied Theo warily.

"I will be all right. I would like to go with you. Truly Theo, do not concern yourself too much over me. I need to see this for myself."

Theo studied his face. "Then do what you must, Kiel." he answered, "We will leave in a moment." and he went to meet Lorya in the hall.

"They came upon us so quickly." Yurah told him, watching Theo walk away, "I could hear them coming, and then the beat of their wings was all around me."

"The Nykertis dwell under Zelmisso in great numbers." Atyn replied adjusting the water skins along his shoulders. "The common folk of Erda think of them as emissaries to the souls of the dead. Odyn's Valkyries keep their ears tuned to their movements so they will know if the Upper Gate between the earth and air has been opened." and as the sounds of soft footsteps echoed through the stony hall, they could hear Lorya and Theo murmuring in low voices. Atyn lifted staff. "Come now. Light your staves. They are coming."

They shared few words as they moved slowly down the polished hall. This new passageway was quite narrow and Atyn was wary of any lettering that marked the side as he guided them through the sloping hall. The walk seemed endless until the corridor finally opened into a vast cavern. A black lake spread out before them. They held their staffs high to find the shallow edges of a colorless sea.

"This must be the place." said Inrih touching the walls with his open palms. A low rumble quivered from deep within the root of the mountain. Yurah felt Kiel stumble at her side. The groaning swelled and a peculiar fog belched from the waters. The underground sea began to wave under the dismal mist. Inrih strained his eyes to see, bewildered by the wailing sounds. Kiel leaned against the wall, his hands as cold as ice and his eyes stared blankly into nothing.

"What is this devilry?" muttered Theo.

Yurah kneeled at Kiel's side trying to warm him. Rasping voices crowded into her thoughts.

"It is rising from the water," said Atyn watching the waves.

"It is not the dark." cried Theo his voice filling with dismay. "Those are Ildabyth's shades. They have breeched the water! They have found a way into our realm!"

The light of their staffs began to flicker and spit and the air around them grew thin. Darkness swallowed the fading lights. Yurah could smell the shadows as they slowly gathered around them. Soon it was Theo who struggled for breath and even Inrih's senses were filled with the smell of burning stone,

"They are coming Atyn." he cried. "Ildabyth! He knows where we are!"

But Atyn could not answer. He was struggling to his edge of the lake. He crawled on his hands and knees through the smothering dark until he leaned over the churning waters. Through the gloom Yurah could hear him murmuring to the mear. The softly spoken words like a breath of fresh wind through the lifeless air.

"*Lumin hyphaem, Lumin ecgon dio,*" he began to chant softly, "*Lumin aphthit, Lumin clasi eis erebus. Lumin hyphaem, Lumin ecgon dio, Lumin aphthit, Lumin clasi eis erebus.*"

Again and again he repeated the words and the chant reached over the swelling waters. "*Lumin hyphaem, Lumin ecgon dio, Lumin*

*aphthit, Lumin clasi eis erebus. Lumin hyphaem, Lumin ecgon dio,
Lumin aphthit, Lumin clasi eis erebus."*

His call spread over the uneasy waters and it seemed for a moment
that the darkness had begun to give way. Faintly she could see him
standing at the edge of the water but as she rose from Kiel's side the
ground beneath them suddenly began to shift. The cavern groaned as
an acrid smoke gurgled from underneath the churning waters. Atyn
shrunk to his knees and the water began to wave over his hands. He
shaking and his voice began to falter. The shadows were rising from
the deeps. Dark and malformed, the hideous shades covered him. The
gnash of their yellowed teeth echoed through hall. Yurah struggled
over the slippery stone to reach him but darkness knew she was there
and, in an instant, she too was shrouded by the black phantoms. She
could not breathe. Their vile belch had taken away the air. She could
not see for her eyes were seared by bitter fume. She struggled against
the dark and the dark closed in upon her more tightly, choking her from
the within and the without. Her thoughts began to muddy, her breath
would not come and her strength became a distant memory. Her
struggling ceased and a gentle calm passed through her heart. The
scabbard at her side began to whisper and then a deep memory stirred.
A flickering fire, merry laughter filled with warmth, a strand of music,
a gentle face of a gray-eyed man and finally the parting gift of her twin
sisters burned like a fire in her mind's eye. Amidst the choking stench,
the crystal glass began to glow from beneath her cloak. The shadows
hesitated, confounded by the light. A new warmth flowed through her.
Her will returned and Yurah pulled herself to her feet, drawing forth the
brilliant flask that rested against her chest. She held the crystal out
before her and its brilliance poured into the dark abyss.

Suddenly a vast ocean appeared before them, its fitful waves
stretching further than the eye could see and in an instant the glowing
light had done its work. Soon the troubled waters began to settle and as
all grew still, the groaning of the shadows faded away and the dreadful
shaking ceased. Kiel opened his eyes. He put his head on his knees
and breathed deeply.

"It is over." he told her as she knelt beside him.

"At least for the moment. I did not expect aid to be so close at
hand." Atyn replied studying the glass she held and she knew that
Atyn had read into her thought. "I believe I know this light you carry.
It is the fire who leads Pleiads through the night sky." then he smiled.
"but I suppose that would be fitting."

It seemed to Yurah that he too could see Lyli and Tyla, sparkling
in the fiery light of Raldabon, so faraway. She placed the vessel along
the wall, allowing its light to continue to stream into the room.

"What is this new misery, Atyn?" said Theo, washing his raw hands in the cold lake,

"It is Ildabyth. It could be no other."

Kiel rose slowly and stood near the edge of the pool and looked into the water. "Long ago, Ildabyth built his dungeons in the deeps of Erda and he quickened them by the inner heat of her form. It is here he breeds his wicked things." Kiel drew a pained breath, an unnamed dread burrowed deeply into his mind and every beat of his heart was filled with desperation. But he did not want her to know it. He did not want her to see the shame that lived within him. He forced himself to continue, "When I saw her last she was bound in this horrible place. She is surrounded by gates of pain and he holds them shut with hideous sounds. It was Sro's power that cast me from this evil place but the price she paid was high. He is moving her ever deeper into the centering point. Ildabyth is gathering all his forces. He has taken her deeper into the core. I fear we will come too late."

Inrih had been listening as he watched the waters. Suddenly his eyes widened and he pointed into the clear lake. "Atyn, can you see this?"

Atyn looked through the layers.

Upon first glance the pool mirrored a ravaged field, charred with the sickly remains of buildings and woodland. The barren clay was strewn the bodies of hewn men. The grisly battlefield stretched as far as their eyes could see. Inrih touched Yurah's sleeve. "Look on now child. Look through the land."

The soil began to peel away, revealing an underlayment of packed stone, one atop the other, different in both color and direction. Their struggle vibrated the land as the layers lifted themselves upward, to feel the air and see the sun. Strange elementals hummed under the thin crust as the blood of the battlefield seeped under the bitter soil.

"Who are they?" she whispered to Inrih.

"They are the first born of Erda." he answered. "Look now. They pierce the crust to the below."

A great cleavage then appeared before her eyes and, between the tons of stone and grit, an unworldly sound flew forth. The voice was lovely and, like a song long forgotten, its message filled her mind.

"Years I have I waited for you little daughter. Knowing well the day would come when you too would breathe the airs of this Little Kingdom; The time of battle draws nigh. Forget not your true purpose and see not the form. Seek instead the center point. The Power of the Sword will reveal the hidden way, Seventh Child of the Seventh Son."

"It is she." said Kiel softly. "It is the voice of Sro that calls to you. But alas Yurah, the path before you is fraught with peril."

"I am ready for what lies ahead. And there are friends here to help us."

"But Yurah, look around you." he said softer still. "Your friends, they did not hear her voice. They did not know she called. They cannot, for who she is, is not yet a knowable part of them."

Yurah wrinkled her brow, glancing to Inrih who was kneeling by the pool, and realized in her heart what he said to her was true.

"The balance has been restored." the giant man was saying to Atyn. "If we empty this cavern of his poison stench, the Nyketis will be able to return to their homes."

'Then we shall finish this together." replied Atyn.

The two used their gifts to call to the mountain and the rock answered their summons. And when the breach was mended, the sound of beating wings began to clamor down the hall. They cast themselves down upon the stone and waited until the Nykertis passed overhead. Kiel took her hand while they settled into crannies and together they followed the others through the winding corridor.

Istah and Lorya met them at the main hall. The ponies were packed and ready. Yurah's calm had returned and she dreamed of a blue sky and a clean wind as they made fast time to the end of the ancient road.

CHAPTER XV
THE DRUI

Lorya sealed the stone mountain shut behind them. They walked warily, welcoming the sun and listening to every sound. The afternoon had grown old by the time they reached the river. It was a fast run and they went along its edge until they reached a flat place where their ponies could cross.

"The river runs hard today." said Atyn to the swirls of foam.

"And the hour grows late." Theo replied, "It might be best to cross the ford after we have rested."

"If we choose to wait we shall not reach the wildermoors until late tomorrow," said Lorya surveying the shady forest.

"I go or stay by your word, Lorya." he answered

She sighed. "The ponies are weary and it is safer along this eastern side. We will make camp here, and take our turns at watch."

So they set a fire and settled down to rest. When they had eaten they looked over the water to the twinkling sky.

"I shall take the first watch." said Istah prodding the fire with a long stick. "It smells good here. I could stay awake all night if need be."

Lorya wrapped her cloak over her feet. "The walk tomorrow will be a long one. We must take care and avoid the main trails. The hidden paths of the foothills are rugged. It will be a difficult day." she paused then and felt the unsettled air.

Theo placed another log upon the campfire, the struggling flames shadowed his brow, "I am anxious about this plan, Atyn. To enter the Ringed City without an army of thousands is a treacherous thing. Are you ready for this my friend?"

Atyn leaned against a sapling. "I know what I must face. I have known it since Ildabyth drove us from our city so many years ago."

"Let me remind you Theo, Atyn will not be alone. My sword and my heart will stand between him and every spell the Basilian priests may utter." said Inrih, rising up to his full height. "And remember, it is not Atyn who faces the greatest danger. Urion is only a boy, not accustom to standing between upper airs and lower lands. And he is not the only one at risk. Great danger awaits you as well, child." he said as his black eyes turned to face Yurah. "You are the blood and bone of a being not born of this realm and the heirloom you bear is older than all the specks of time this world has ever known."

Yurah felt every eye upon her then. The scabbard at her side murmured and the heavy Sword seemed filled with heat. She also knew that Kiel was pressing his intent inside of her mind, for he understood the ways of Erda in fashion she could not yet fathom.

"I will keep to the path that has been laid before me." she answered quietly, looking to the faces glowing in the firelight, "There is far more to this little world than I had dared imagine."

"That is true Yurah. This little world is not at all as it seems," replied Kiel, "and Sro is able to understand this better than any. It is why Ildabyth needs her. It is why he seeks to control her. Your mother is high born, her essence is not bred of this lesser place."

"But realize Kiel, just as Sro, Ildabyth too, was not born of Erda." replied Atyn, "He too comes from a realm beyond the aeons. Like her, he is older than any form ever made upon this world." Atyn continued staring into the fire, "He is well aware of Rempha's cycles. Soon all will go one way or another. Ildabyth is growing impatient. He is wanting. His mind is creeping over the roots of earth. He is craving a thing he does not have." then his voice fell into the whisper, "And whatever it is he seeks, he knows that it is near."

Silence then fell upon them. Images of Ildabyth, searching and dangerous, pulled them inward to entertain their private concerns. The wind perceived their cares and neither hope nor comfort did its chill voice bring. They drew nearer to the fire to share the last of Rudra's drink and when heady potion had done its work they took their blankets to drift into sleep.

Yurah lingered at the point just beyond wakefulness and the sound of the river filled her mind. Her body began to tingle and, suddenly, she found herself suspended above a green forest. The trees below her were flowing backwards at a great speed as she realized she was flying upon a cold wind. Its bright chill seeped into her bones. The blue cloak writhed in the ever increasing winds and beneath her the forest grew small. It was then that she realized someone had spoken her name.

"*Greetings Seventh Daughter.*" proclaimed the vibrant voice, "*I am Mqttro of the Islands of Urdar. I have been expecting you.*" And a tall being, formed more of bits of sun than skin and bone, appeared before her. She blinked, trying desperately to adjust to the shifting light.

"*Come!*" the voice spoke again and she noticed her feet had no need to touch the ground. In an instant they stood upon the edge of a high precipice.

"*Behold the lands of Erda.*" he proclaimed with a wide sweep of his hand.

She looked down into the lower lands and far below she could see her body lying upon the ground, wrapped in her blanket in the dark glade just near the rushing waters. Her companions were sleeping peacefully, all but Istah who sat at the water's edge watching the moon. Beyond the river a narrow road came clear into her mind.

"The path you travel leads into great peril." she heard him tell her, *"and much that is lovely will soon be lost."* His eyes flamed with a white heat. A vast silence was spreading between them. The cold air grew thin and her fragile thread of consciousness began to fade. Then she felt a familiar touch upon her sleeve and Atyn's bright face appeared.

"So you find your way to the upper realms, Yurah." he said without speaking. *"Do not fear it and do not force the moment. The airs of the above are too thin for concentration of that sort. Spread away from any sense of isolation. I will guide you."*

And she found herself able to do it for Atyn's mind was steady and she was able to follow.

"Greetings Mqttro." said Atyn to the Malkian, *"What is the will of those who guard the Great Tree?"*

"As it has ever been." exchanged the being serenely, *"for the Malki serve only the One who waits behind the Silent Fire."* then he turned his eye again to the lands beneath them and a sea of blackness now belched forth from between the trees. *"The crux point draws nigh. Are you prepared for its coming, Son of Jupiter?"*

"I am ready." Atyn replied watching the darkness grow.

"As are we," answered the Malki. *"Though we can only proceed as the laws demand."*

Yurah felt the heat of his fiery wings upon her face. *"Sro has spoken to you, has she not little sister?"* Mqttro said. Ice and snow began to hiss about her feet running in rivulets over the edge of the chasm. *"Are you willing to answer a Warrior's demands?"*

His intensity shook her calm and she struggled to maintain her attention. Atyn was steady at her side. *"You alone choose your path."* was the thought in her mind.

"I shall answer. I can do no less than this. It is the only means that her freedom may be won."

"But Freedom may not come, child. There is no thing in the lower world that is fixed."

"Still I am willing." she said, her voice crackling in the cold. "I am Sro's heir. The Sword that she once carried now hangs at my side."

"I know what it is you carry." and the Malki grew greater in height, flaming like an inferno upon the edge of the airy world. *"It was with the greatest of hope I perceived it moving within the dark wood of Odyn's Hold.. The Sword of Sro has traveled far, passing through Aeon's Realm, to once more touch this Little Kingdom. But its nature*

is not of the lower world. It is not of this world at all. Do you understand this Seventh Daughter?"

She stood before the flaming being, knowing she could hide nothing from him and she answered. *"Not so long ago, I was only a child until the moment I remembered her forgotten voice. Since that time, I have left my home, choosing to answer the call. Now her burden is mine to bear. More than this I do not know."* and she looked downward as the green forest was smothered by the black fume. *"More than this I do not seem able to know."*

"Then I shall explain some of its mystery to you." He answered *"The Sword you wield is not of this world. Long ago, when the Annyd first came to this realm, Sro was among that number. Your mother carried the talisman into Erda. It was this Blade which undid Ildabyth's twisted designs but as this work was done, its true nature remains cryptic. Its clear purpose is mercifully hidden by the shadows and fogs of Erda. Only in the ever changing moment will you understand its real intent. The Real can be known no other way. The point between time and form is where true victory is wrought. Draw your blade now Seventh Daughter and hold it under light."*

The Sword flashed, sending its prismatic lights forward to dazzle the airs. But below their feet a mournful earth began to groan and a desolate wailing rattled the airs. The blade became heavy. Her hands trembled under the weight. She gathered her strength and held the point steady. Mqttro watched intently as she mastered the moment and, when she had done it, his voice shook the upper airs.

"I shall ask you once more, Seventh Daughter of a Seventh Son. Are you willing to answer to a Warriors demands?"

"I am willing Mqttro." she answered.

The winds began to speak, intently they told their tale and Mqttro listened. After a moment he replied. *"So shall it be, Sro's child. Your fate is set in the spiraling stars. May your willing heart guide your willing hands."*

Yurah felt his heat upon her face and the Blade was suddenly filled with a myriad of images; Gray stones, soiled with blood, cried under an ashen sky. Burning grasses spilled smoke into the acrid clouds; a treacherous sea of churning dark waters mingled into a swirling mist. The Malkian watched as the girl slowly sheathed the blade.

"Be it in the light of day or in the deep of night." Mqttro implied with a gentle touch of his mind. *"I will know when you call."* and the fiery being faded. Kiel was shaking her awake,

"Yurah, what grace has touched you?" he said leaning over her, his voice was filled with awe.

Atyn knelt down and answered for her.

"It is the Upper Airs you perceive." he began to explain, shimmering in the same unearthly glow.

"I know the one who called to you. I have longed to walk in that place once more. It is like water to a dying man. The fairness of the Malkian Isles lingers all around you. " Kiel said reaching out and touching a lock of her hair. "His name was Mqttro, was it not?" but he did not wait for her reply, he shook his head knowingly, "It was Mqttro that called." he continued. "Long ago we could have been considered friends. Then came the troubled days and our conversations changed. As did I, Yurah. As did I." and he let the strand fall away. Then he took his bow from his shoulder and set the string. "It is my turn to watch. The dawn will soon be here." and he left them and went to sit alone beside the water.

"He understands what is coming." replied Atyn looking after the silhouette moving quietly through the trees.

"He may understand it." she answered, casting off her blanket. "But he need not be alone."

"No, he need not." Atyn smiled. "Goodnight Yurah." and he went to his rest near the others.

So they took the last watch together, sharing few words but looking often to their home shimmering in the twinkling stars above until the gray dawn stole the dark from the rolling hillside.

They were on their way before the sun crept over the edge of the hills. The waters of the ford had come to the ponies' shoulders and its chill lingered long after Lorya led them into the wilderness. The morning had grown late when they stopped to rest for a time, sharing food and giving their ponies sips from their water-skins.

"The wildermoors lie just over that far ridge." said Inrih looking over the bleak landscape. "It was not that long ago these hills were filled with growing things. The battle for this land was a bitter one. Neither side was able to see the good in the other. They destroyed everything, even themselves."

"What do you mean Inrih? Who razed these lands?" asked Kiel, kneeling to touch the rocky ground.

"Work such as this is best done by men," Inrih said, shaking his head, "but in this case it was not just men but beasts and dragons as well. Once these hills were rich and living was a simple thing. The Asvins made their homes upon these grass highlands. The Asvin's were in truth, wizards who had shaped themselves as both horse and man. They hated the clan who lived in the lower vales. Those folks called themselves the Lapiths. They were ignorant people and the Asvins thought themselves the better of the two. The Asvins taunted and mistreated them. The Lapiths became vengeful, spending the better part of their time poisoning these mountains and its waters until no food could grow. They fought until they lost everything, each blaming the other for what was amiss. The dragons lived in these mountains and they witnessed every battle between the Asvins and the Lapiths. But alas, dragons are greedy creatures. They believed they could find advantage over the warring clans below, so under the cover of night they scorched the dying earth, believing it would drive both the Lapiths and the Asvins from the land. In the end, the Asvins proved to be the strongest of the three. They used their elemental magic to raise a poison mire from the marshes. They felt if the lands were not theirs, the land would belong to no one. Here in the uplands, all that remains is the faithful stone. Hate and violence still hold tightly to this place. Their war created a tainted barrier that none may travel along the seashore. Though it is a wretched place, it is this very dyke of rot that helps keep the Drui safe in their wilderness."

"Are there none left in these mountains?" asked Yurah. "None that sought a better way?"

"Legend holds that there were a few who tried to mend differences. But the hate between all sides ran deep and when one faction would move in good faith, another would take advantage and start the violence again. If any survived I do not know of it."

Just as he finished the tale, a raven's cry pierced the air and a great bird landed at their feet and in the next instant Rudra was standing before them in the noonday sun.

"Rudra! It is so good to see you!" Theo cried, pulling him close in a fierce embrace.

"So good you are here, finally with us again. How fare our people?" said Lorya as she stood upon her toes to kiss his cheek. Her eyes widened when she saw the dark bruise that stained his face. "What has happened to you, brother?"

"It is a just a little bruise. It is nothing, really. It happened two nights passed." he answered.

"Two nights passed." said Atyn, remembering the frightened Nykertis.

"Yes. A horde of Umbra came upon us unawares."

"And then what happened." Lorya said suspiciously, stepping back to get a better look at him. Rudra swayed as she let him go. Inrih caught him by the shoulders.

"What is the matter with you Rudra? Where are you hurt?"

"There has not been a moments rest for any of us lately. I suppose I need a nap."

"A nap?" Inrih grunted, "Humph. You have never been a good

liar, Rudra, so why don't you tell us a little more about this fight."

"I was getting to it, Inrih. I was getting to it. Let me see, we were sorely outnumbered and all was sure to go badly." he continued agreeably.

"Please Rudra. Sit down before you go on." said Lorya, "Shifting is dizzying work. Drink this."

He took the flask and smelled it, "As you wish Lorya," he grinned and after taking a long swig he continued. "Like I said, we were outnumbered and all was going badly. The Umbra fell upon us unexpectedly as we were returning to the caves and they were carrying weapons we had never encountered before. As the shadows fought us, the strikes of their swords created a wall of deafening sound. The hideous roar stayed our best offences and with alarming ease they had soon pushed us to the edge of the cliffs. It seemed that their grating blows had the power to call to the winds and soon a storm began to blow up from the sea. Really Inrih, I thought our end come but then something quite strange happened. Suddenly a peculiar light was among us. It was as if the world had split into a million dazzling parts. The brightness spread through the squall like a wind carries away the blinding fog. The shadows could not stand under it that brilliance and, in wink, the dark was released into the light. But just as quickly, the light too was gone and the ordinary day was all around us. We rejoiced in the gift the fates had given and rejoiced still more when we realized that none of our kin had perished." then he shuddered and pulled his cloak closer around him. "But the time of joy was short lived for, as we turned toward home, we found that even the smallest notch from those wretched blades bought with it great pain. Our hopes drained as brothers and sisters collapsed. The Umbra's blade had brought with it mortal wounds by the force of those hideous sounds. We became disorientated, feeling as though an iron hammer had broken apart our very souls; so we stumbled in agony, not knowing which way we traveled. I recall seeing Tristan fall, and as I tried to reach him, just as suddenly as before, the brilliant light was once more upon us. I found myself walking away from the others for the light was calling me into a sheltered cove. The brilliant glare soon forced me down upon my hands and knees and I was made to crawl over the dusty earth until I reached an outgrowth of rock. It was there I found an herb I had never seen before. Its odor was pungent and as I knelt to it the plant spoke to me. The leaf guided me through its preparations. Since that night I have spent most of my time amongst the injured." then Rudra's face grew pale.

Lorya knit her brow as she watched the color leave his face. "What are you leaving out, little brother?" she pressed.

Rudra sighed, and glanced to Atyn, "It was the same evening the shadows came for you Atyn. That night the Drui were also assailed and Alberich was lost to the fight."

Lorya shuddered at the news and Inrih's dark eyes grew blacker. Rudra took her hand and continued the tale. "It was that same night that Alberich was hidden within Basilus. He sat near the upper towers, transformed as a nighthawk, listening as the chanters did their work. The Umbra found him there and stripped him of his guise. The Priests used their chants to work those below into a frenzy and then they left his fate to the people. The mob tore him apart, limb by limb and bit by bit with their bare hands. And after this they carried his pieces through the streets cheering their gruesome prize." and he hung his head and spoke softly . "Clare saw the all of it and barely escaped with her life."

"Where is she now?" whispered Istah

"She is keeping her eye upon the Pool of Reflections for he whispers from the other side."

"He was the First Guard of our Order." Lorya said, solemnly.

"The Umbra have grown more daring. They are able to do what once they could not. We must find out what has changed if we are to stand any chance at all.

"Then the rest of the tale must wait." said Inrih, gravely, "We can not stay here. We are not safe."

Atyn laid his hand upon his shoulder, "And we will find out, my friend. Besides, you look terrible."

"Do not worry over me, Atyn."

"I will worry or not, as I choose." he answered taking a small vial from his vest. "Here, just a few drops, under the tongue. You will recognize it."

Rudra waved it under his nose. "Hmmm, I do recognize that." he sputtered as the tincture went down.

When they started out again, Atyn insisted that Rudra ride his own pony and Rudra, again, did as he was told. Kiel rode at his side.

"The Drui are fine musicians," he said lightly, "do all of your folk play?"

"Most. It is a thing we learn when we are quite young and then we pass the gift on to the children."

"Children? Where do they bide? I saw only a handful in Odyn's Hall."

"And there are a handful more, here and about. Far to few too replenish the numbers we have lost; but far too many to watch suffer as darkness covers these lands." he answered sadly. "To call children to us is not a thing we take lightly, even under the best of circumstance. Our lives are long. We breathe for thousands of years by the reckonings of men. It was when Odyn was young, many left this realm to find other places to live their lives. Those of us who came after are well aware of our plight and the ordeal of Erda."

"Then you are a valiant people," Kiel answered earnestly, "still choosing to continue under such hardship."

"It is a lovely place. So much could be made perfect here." he answered, smiling easily. "And I am not willing to give up that vision so easily. She is far too fair for that." and his bright eyes drank in the sight of a young forest clinging to the austere hills."

Birds were circling the crumbling cliffs and not to far ahead, a thin waterfall splashed down the stones, forming a clear pool at the base.

"We can rest there and let the horses drink." said Lorya pointing the water.

"We must not tarry." Inrih said restively, "Even in the light of day."

"We will not be long," she assured him, "We shall reach the heaths within the hour." but even as she spoke the sun was veiled by cloud.

Inrih washed the dust from his hands. Rudra spoke softly with Atyn as they watched the ponies drink. Kiel climbed up the flowing fall to fill his water skin. The land sloped backward into a narrow gullet. Barely hidden by a stand of brush, Kiel saw shadows stirring under the thorny briars. He waved his arms and called out. Instantly, Istah's crossbow was upon her shoulder. Theo drew his blade and Yurah stood at his side. It was then they realized, it was not the Umbra of Ildabyth but ordinary men that hid themselves in the shadows. They cried out as they rushed from the bushes. Their faces were covered by dark hoods pulled tight around their heads and necks. Some were brutishly tall and wielded their swords with a deadly strength but others were much slighter folk, clumsy and uncertain of their blades.

Kiel put an arrow to the bow as Rudra stumbled backward over a stone. A hooded brute lifted his sword arm to deal the death strike but Kiel's arrow stuck him through his thick neck. Choking upon a spume of bloody vomit, he drew his last breath and the giant collapsed over Rudra's still body. An arrow flew past Kiel's shoulder, snagging his clock as he set another to his string. He let the shaft fly and another man fell to the ground. Kiel looked over the fight and realized Atyn was surrounded in a circle of sharp blades. They sneered as they held him trapped and they began to lash at his legs, shouting out in their harsh language. Kiel put another arrow to the string and struck the largest brute in his sword hand. The blade clattered on the stones as Atyn dropped to the ground. He drew his long knife as the swords cracked over his head. Rolling low, Atyn struck the bandit closest to him, slashing the connecting cords behind the knees and then heaving the man over his back. A curse hissed behind him as the wind of another blade brushed by his face. Atyn turned on his back and his long knife struck bone. The man fell, breaking his arm under his own sword. Two others fell at Atyn's feet and, while Istah was setting yet another arrow to the bow, others turned to run.

Theo's blade was smeared as he helped Atyn from the dirt. Istah held her bow steady looking grimly after the thieves that crashed gracelessly through the brambles. Yurah stood with the tip of her sword pressing into the back of a prostrate form. Lorya leaned over the prisoner asking him questions.

Kiel cascaded down the rocky slide. He raced to where Rudra had fallen and he pulled the dead man away.

"Does he breathe?" Theo cried running up beside him.

Kiel gently put his hand under his face. His fingers were sticky as he felt the warm breath upon his hand. "He lives Theo. Maybe his head hit a stone."

Gently they ran their hands along his back and neck until finding the skin split open upon the skull just above the temple bone.

"The cut is not deep." said Kiel.

"If I know him as well as I do think, he has kept hid another injury from us." Theo said pushing aside Rudra's cloak and under it they could see his light blouse was wet with blood. "What have you done to yourself, little brother?" he gasped.

Carefully they began to tear away the ruined shirt and found his side was wrapped with binding. Kiel gently cut the away bandages and revealed a deep gash.

Theo pressed the clean edge of his cloak gently against it, "This wound is not fresh and these ribs are broken. I do not see how he could walk, nor ride."

Inrih handed Kiel a clean damp cloth. He wiped the blood from his face and slowly Rudra opened his eyes.

"You have always given advice better than you have taken, Rudra." said Inrih. "When did you receive these injuries?"

"A scratch and a bruise hardly compares," he complained trying to rise from the ground. "I was one of the few able to walk at all."

"I will decide what compares." said Theo, his hand gentle against his shoulder. "Bring a blanket Inrih. He is growing chilled."

"So this is what happened two nights passed?" said Atyn.

"Then, yes but I bound the bones and stanched the wound. I have more of the herb here in my vest." Rudra replied patting his inner pocket. "It is right here. Use it as you like."

Theo grunted and began to cut away the rest of his clothing.

"That is an ugly gash, Rudra." Inrih snorted, covering his legs with the blanket. "and is filled with dirt. It will hurt when we clean it."

"I have something for pain." he said reaching for his vest.

"I am sure you do." he grunted, "Now lie still. The stitching is torn."

Rudra did not argue. He drank his elixir and stared at the sky as Atyn cleaned the wound. Theo had just finished closing the hole when Rudra closed his eyes to sleep.

"It would be best not to move him. I fear the bones of his head may be cracked."

"To stay is more dangerous," answered Inrih looking around at the dead that littered the stony lot, "those bandits are sure to be back to claim their own."

"Have we a prisoner?" asked Kiel, watching Lorya hold her sword to the captives back.

"That remains to be decided." said Istah gazing upon Rudra as he lay still and wrapped in his blankets. "How is he?"

"He will live but he is not fit to travel."

"He was not fit to travel when he met us."

Theo agreed but did not answer.

"Would you like to meet our charge?" Istah asked them then.

"I would like that very much." answered Inrih rising to his feet.

Kiel looked at Yurah leaning over the prisoner. "I will come too."

As they drew close enough they were surprised to hear the strained voice of a child answering their questions. "I shall have my revenge upon you infidels!" they heard the voice say as he struggled under his bonds.

"The clash is over now." Yurah answered gently. "It is not our intention to hurt those who mean no harm."

The boy spat at her. "I curse you! And I curse your children. May Ahriman strike you down. May he send you to his Rivers of Fire and may you burn forever. May he crush your bones while you still live. May you die in agony until he reforms you so He may have the pleasure of watching you suffer again," and then boy's tears fell freely as he struggled with his bonds, cursing in his harsh native tongue. Lorya sighed.

"He is distraught but if I loose the ropes I fear we will have to kill him." whispered Lorya as Kiel came near. "They are mountain bandits. The boy was raised to this life and sees no harm in it. We cannot murder a child in cold blood no matter how ignorant he may be."

"Nor how ignorant he may remain." answered Inrih, looking sadly at the boy.

"There is another pass through that ridge of mountains. I believe his folk may dwell in the caves to the north. I think it is best if we leave him. His kin is sure to return for him."

"Yes, they will come back for him." said Inrih looking down the rough path. "And it may not be long. Go now to and speak Rudra. I will watch boy." and he settled himself against a slim sapling, waiting for the boy to tire of his rant.

"I will take him with me upon my horse, at least this way I will be able bear part of his pain." Atyn told her, reaching for the bottle that sat upon the ground. "There is a little left." he said shaking the flask. "It will have to keep him until we arrive."

So they finished watering their horses and laid the dead out in respectful repose. They checked the boy's bonds, making sure they were not too tight and offered him a drink but he spat it in their faces.

"It is the best we may do for you." said Yurah, placing a loaf of bread upon his lap. "Your kin will be here soon." she continued but that began another rant of cursing and spitting so she left him in peace.

To her surprise she found Rudra once more on his feet. Theo had bound a clean bandage around his bruised forehead and was in process of wrapping his ribs with long bands of soft cloth.

"Just another minute." said Kiel holding his shoulders as Theo neatly folded the last of the wrap, "Finished now, Inrih will help you up."

"You are quite the mess!" said Inrih gently easing him upon the pony. "Can you do this?'

Rudra weakly raised an eyebrow, "Do you mean can I flop about like a broken toy upon Atyn's pony until we reach the Wildermoors? It is not a problem, Inrih. I will do quite fine at it."

"Give him the last of the brew, Atyn. Maybe it will put him back to sleep. Then he can not weary my ears his mulishness."

Rudra almost chuckled but stopped himself and put his hand around his side. "I think I will wait a day or two before wearying you more than this, Inrih."

"Aye, that you might have to do." he grinned, climbing upon his horse, "Call if you have need."

So in a single file they left the stony hollow, listening to the fading curses of the young bandit as the foothills closed in around them. The sapling forest shaded their way while sun set in the western sky. They went slowly as the shadows grew and soon the smell of the sea began to ride upon the wind.

CHAPTER XVI
OIOLOSSE'S MOUNTAIN

Driin lingered under the night sky, his thought resting far past the bright Mirfak in a beleaguered realm where his distant kin struggled. The wide doors of his father's hall stood open. Strains of flute and subtle drum drifted through the papery leaves of the aspen grove. The crisp smell of winter filled his senses. A fresh fall of snow lay about his feet. With each spinning breath the cold breeze whirled the icy crystals in tiny cyclones of white. He looked through the frozen world to see Eide walking slowly through the sparkling night.

"The coldest night is upon us. Does her bitter wind sting not the Vanyr?" her eyes smiled.

"No more than it must sting a daughter of Iao." he answered *"Your robes are marked with frost."*

"Her chill brings clarity."

"Aye, and her clarity clears the airs." he responded gazing upon the multitude of lights spreading over the trees.

"Can you feel them there," she asked looking toward the above.

He nodded, keeping his eyes fixed to the skies, *"Yes, their whispers carry. It is a their faint song drifting that haunts my heart."*

Eide listened through the winter cold, reaching to the stars until the hints of a strange melody began to form in her mind. In delicate bits of song, the tragic and lovely tale of Erda spilled into the black havens. They waited until the gray clouds came again to cover the stars and the snow began to fall thick around them. The whispering melody faded as the threads of song were obscured by the fog. They joined hands and returned to the warmth of Oiolosse's Hall. His wide hearth burned brightly and many of his folk were gathered round. Oiolosse sat close to the fire and at his side was a gentle woman playing sweetly upon a harp of clear ash. He acknowledged his eldest son with the bright glow in his clear gray eyes. He welcomed Eide taking her hands in his own.

"I was hoping to see you this evening, my dear." he said pressing her fingers to his lips. *"Your hands are dreadfully chilled,"* he acknowledged, keenly glancing to Driin. *"and though a winter night is matchless for star watching, you must take care. But worry not, I know just the thing to comfort you."* and he reached to a low table and poured from the tall pitcher that waited there. Eide sipped the cup.

"As always your wine is exceptional, Oioloose."

He smiled widely, *"It is a art I much enjoy."* pouring Driin's goblet full. *"and may I fill your cup once more, Niobe."* he said to the harp player and she laid the instrument aside accepting the newly filled glass.

"Your mother has been waiting since nightfall in hopes that you might share a song with our people on this Festival night."

"Certainly I will do it, though it would give me greater pleasure if you would join me, mother." he answered bowing low.

"Imbolg's feast is a fine one for both food and song." she smiled at her clear-eyed son, *"Such a night is intended for closeness. A time to renew the ties that bind."*

"It is such night mother, Driin answered reaching down to softly pluck the strings of the harp. *"The stars softest whispers tremble under her dome."*

"It is our kin of Erda you hear singing. The saddest of all melodies rise from that little world." she answered gently, "Then she looked into the flames and sighed, *"I was but a babe when we left them to struggle. Promises were made and sacrifices given. Those first blessed with her stewardship could not leave her to his torment and those born under the Warrior mark deemed it worthy to try the experiment again."* Niobe's voice trailed off into a whisper and she walked to the window watching the thick flakes cover the slender trees. *"The time of tears is upon us once again. Change is coming and nothing will hinder that work. Our kin will not put duty aside for suffering or for pleasure. The snow ever reminds me of that grief.'* and for a long moment she stood with her hand upon the dark glass and when she finally turned to face them her eyes were shining with tears, *"But within these troubled thoughts a song waits. We shall play it together my son and may it send a thread of hope to those who need it most."*

And as Niobe took to her harp, Driin placed the flute to his lip. The melody moved into the room, touching the sparks of candlelight, caressing the bright flames of the bold fire, thrilling the hearts of all who listened. The quiet night hummed in union and after a time others picked up their instruments changing the song into something new. The airs became liquid and a misty form appeared before Oiolosse's fire. Driin put down his flute.

A tall woman shimmered before them. Her face was marked by twining symbols and her burning eyes were as black as coals. She carried a staff set with a crystal stone, while upon her shoulder hung a bow and quiver. She looked over the hall until her dark eyes rested upon Driin. She bowed her head and placed her closed hand over her heart. Then raising her noble head her eyes met his. Images poured into Driin's mind; faces, familiar yet unknown. The sounds of harsh chanting and the clash of swords came next until the scene grew red and he caught a fleeting glimpse of Yurah turning to look behind her, her face filled with despair.

"Hail Cousin. Clear your heart and sharpen your mind," the *black eyes flashed pushing the telepathy deeper into the center of his thoughts. "Look keen upon the Head of the Dragon as it moves to the yoke of the world. Then you shall hear us call."*

He did not reply. Within the chill night an answering note filled the sparse wood, blending with the music of Oiolosse's Hall.

"The time draws near," the sending spoke aloud and the room trembled pulling the night closer together, *"Please remember our people. Please. Remember me."* it whispered and the image faded but the light that had brought to them remained.

"Who was she?" whispered Driin to his mother, but Niobe did not answer for she could do naught but weep.

CHAPTER XVII
THE WILDERMOORS

They climbed to the top of the ridge as the sun faded beneath the horizon. Brooding clouds had spread across the choppy sea. Layered beneath their tired feet, the long miles gradually ebbed into a grainy beach. Lorya picked her way though the pathless moor with Rudra slumped and still on Atyn's pony. She pulled to stop, uncertain of which way to go. A flutter of black suddenly rose from the spiky heathers. The birds raucous cries blended with the sounds of the surf. Rudra straightened himself in the saddle and surveyed the dim countryside. After a moment he pointed to a knoll jutting from the northern slope.

"They know we are near." Theo whispered to Kiel. "Be aware. Soon they will give their signal." and as soon as he had spoken the rustling leaves stirred.

"Aeoli!" said the wind.

"Be swift." said Theo, turning his pony toward the sound. A faint path appeared between the sheltering shrubs. Again and again the windy voice encouraged to follow until finally leading them to an opening within the hillside. There were folk waiting to greet them. A grim man took their horses while the others helped Rudra to the ground. A tall warrior spun a pattern of symbols in the airs and the mountain closed soundlessly behind them. They were led along winding stairs into a spacious hall. Its floor was laid in blocks of ebony and its smooth ceiling arced gracefully above their heads. Against the polished walls, broad columns carved with the images of fire sylphs and air naiads, reached up to touch the ceiling with outstretched arms. Along the side of the chamber a fire burned in an ebony hearth. An inky black mirror lay under the flames but it held no reflection of the firelight above.

"It is a scrying pool." Theo whispered as they passed by and Yurah felt a waft of fresh cool air brush by her face. Their guides turned sharply north and soon they came upon a smaller chamber. A woman, enough like Lorya to be her twin, rushed to meet them.

"Lorya! How I have missed you." she cried as they embraced. "Since Rudra returned, I have thought of little else!" but when she turned to greet him her smile faded away. "What has happened?" she said pushing back the hood of his cape to look behind his ears. "These bruises say it all. Marial, fix another bed. It seems that Rudra will be staying with us for a while whether he means to or not." and as she steadied his elbow she saw the bandages under his cloak. "What else have we here?"

"A sword wound, Yanhe at least two days old." answered Lorya, "and with it, go several broken ribs." she nodded, her face smugly set.

"I did not know it! There were so many to tend," she sighed. "You should not have hidden such a wound. Take a bed Rudra. You will not heal yourself alone. You know better than any the strange nature of these hurts."

He almost looked ashamed as he sat upon the bed and Marial began to strip his soiled bindings. "The stitches are torn," she frowned, "and it leaks steadily."

"Have you had supper?" Yanhe asked them as she dabbed a bitter smelling fluid over the cut.

"Not a bite," winced Rudra ignoring Marial's stare. "We were wondering when you might ask?"

"Then is fortunate that you have not arrived to late for it." she said, not taking her eye from the wound, "you shall take your meal in here, Rudra. The others are fit and they have been summoned to sup with Tristan. Believe me little brother, I am grateful I have no more than one new charge to lie in my infirmary."

"Well I am pleased you are with us, Rudra." said the man lying in the next bed, his head wrapped with bandages. "I have had no news for days. With you ordered to bed as well, I can be caught up in the happenings of the world."

"So once again you notice that days do pass, Adon. When last I looked in upon you, you could not recall your name." Rudra smiled, glancing down at the ooze that still leaked from the wounds upon his chest to grin up at Yanhe. "And it looks as if we might have plenty of time to talk."

"Indeed." she answered, catching the stream that ran from the gash with the soft cloth, "But even still Adon, you might have to wait for his tales until tomorrow." and she pulled back his dark hair knitting her brow, "Marial, bring the scissors. I fear Rudra must lose these dark curls if we are to care for his brains properly."

'The scissors! Really, I am quite myself Yanhe, and I see no need for brains. No, that is not what I meant. I meant, well what I mean is, I see no need for scissors!"

"Hummph, you are quite yourself!" she said, taking the scissors from Marial and quickly Rudra's bloodied locks began to fall upon the floor. "Worry not, Theo." feeling his eyes upon the back of her neck, " I will take good care of him. Marial will show you to Tristan's chambers. There is much to tell. I will meet you later in the upper hall."

"Then soon." said Lorya, bending to kiss her brother. "We will look in on you before we sleep Rudra. Be at peace, and do as she bids.

"And do not be troubled about losing that lovely head of hair." smirked Inrih, rubbing his hand over his smooth scalp. "You will like it in the end."

"Oh Inrih. You have misunderstood me." Rudra answered cocking an eye, "It is not that I am troubled! It just I do not see how anyone shall be able to tell us apart?"

Rudra looked small in the clean white bed with great Inrih towering over him and Yanhe rolled her eyes,

"You forget Rudra. Your ears will give you away in a moment." and she picked up the bottle of disinfectant she dabbed a bit over the cuts along his scalp.

"Ouch!" he complained. "I shall not know any peace, Lorya."

"I think you are in good hands, Rudra." she grinned, "We will return as soon as we are able."

Inrih made sure Rudra caught his doleful glance to the newly shorn curls lying upon the floor before following her down the hall.

In the dim light of the amber globes Yurah looked through every opening they passed. The walls were smooth and perfect, with no seam nor catch. Strange glyphs marked each hall and she became sure the refuge was made by the same hands that had fashioned the passage through the mountain range. Soon they began to descend another long flight and when the stairwell ended the sound of falling water echoed in the smooth stone halls.

"It is not far now." said Marial as the hall opened into a wide chamber. A fountain splashed from the smooth stone high above them, filling a broad basin at their feet. Along the side of the pool were walkways, edged by low stone railings, and every few feet the rails gave way to sets of easy stairs. The apartments were positioned, one above the other, overlooking the water. Yurah noticed Marial was leading them up yet another stair and she hurried to keep up with the others. They did not stop until they reached the highest level, finding themselves eye to eye with the spring at the top of the waterfall. Tristan was waiting upon the balcony. He was much like the other Drui, tall with a smooth fair face, but his eyes were neither black nor gray, instead they were clear as a crystal glass capturing the bits of candlelight that flickered along the rails. He wore an ivory cape and under it flashed warrior's mail. She had the sense she had met him before and that left her unsettled.

"Once again it has been too long my brothers and sisters. There is food set upon the board." he said graciously, extending his arm to the brightly lit room behind him, "Please join me."

The table was set with fish and fresh yellow loaves, bowls of a tart red sauce, leafy greens, and saucers of butter. Tristan poured a clear wine into each glass before taking his place at the head of the table. He put the glass to his lips and the others drank with him.

"You are Kiel and the Lady Yurah. Rudra has spoken well of you. Travelers as he put it; though that leaves far too much unsaid. It is a rare thing to have crossed the dark current of the heavens." and then he paused to again pour his glass half full before addressing Kiel decidedly, "And many years since you last walked in the streets of Basilus Master Kiel." said Tristan and Kiel's face grew grave. "Time is indeed a different thing in the outer realms and much has changed." he continued before Kiel could answer, "You were all but dead when Theo and Kirkos laid your scorched body at our feet. Do you recall that it was Alberich who restored you?" he pressed him, "and it was I stood at his side to aid him in the shape he spun. Those threads of life were given to you by the Greater Bear. It was that essence which sent you forth upon the spiraling dance. Even then, we knew but a little of your purposes in our realm," and his voice faded as he paused to finish his wine, "and days now prove even more difficult and still your fate remains concealed. But we are without the pleasure of many words. Your fortune, or your doom, awaits the turn of your hand." he said grimly as he bent his gaze upon Yurah. "And you child, it is known to me that you carry an ancient sword. The amulet you carry is archaic and though you may not know it, it too has been seen before in our little world. This heirloom you bear, do you know its origins?" he asked sharply.

"The sword was once my mothers and for now it is in my keeping. I hope to return it to its proper owner. But how she came by the blade; these are things I do not know."

"There is much about it we do not know." he answered casting his translucent gaze to candle, "The blade came to us when some of the Elder Folk made the decision to continue the work of Erda. To those who elected to remain, a promise was given to us by the starry Annyd. And that promise I believed was long forgotten," and his eyes grew more colorless still as he repeated a bit of an ancient prophecy, *'Its voice is a tinkling bell as the feet pass lightly o'er the radiant path between our world and hers.'* So it said but again the same war is upon us and too long have the Ancient's had kept their attentions turned to other games. Truly child, I had thought every oath abandoned. I had come to accept that this Little Realm would always be alone." and again he appeared like a warrior lost in an unsettled memory. His tone was gray and his mood was dark as he sipped his wine and allowed his food to grow cold.

"Forgive me, my guests," he said after many moments of heavy silence. "There is much that weighs heavy upon my mind. The Priests of the Ringed City are more dangerous than ever. Ildabyth is unraveling the deepest of secrets. This was the work that Alberich witnessed, losing his own life in that undertaking" then he sighed and Yurah could see a thin mist had formed about him, his vital life was hovering about his form. "and I believe that it is this new work that leaves so many of our folk maimed In my mind I hear Him taunting. And searching. Searching for something, something to make them stronger still."

"Our plans are to leave for the Basilus at once." said Atyn firmly, "The sorcerers of Ildabyth can be destroyed. We have that power at our command."

"I know well the powers you wield, Atyn Stormbringer and such power unleashed will reap many consequences, much of which will be unlooked for. Who will hold that balance, my friend, when all is turned upside down."

"Odyn shall be able." Atyn replied, " and all the folk of the Upper Hold. The Malki shall stand with us as they have always done. And your people Tristan, between us all we will hold the force in check."

"I do not think you understand, cousin. We are vulnerable, now more than ever before. And what, in truth of Odyn's Hold. Urion is but a boy attempting what is meant for a seasoned Elder. I have of late watched the visions play within the Reflecting Pool and I have seen the Malki. They too have known the potency of Ildabyth's new strength. They have suffered grievous losses upon their Islands."

Kiel shuddered. The memory of Mqttro, standing with his legions, knowing he was the one who had betrayed him flooded his thoughts.

Yurah knew his mind and set loose a gentle thought toward him, Tristan turned to face her, perceiving what she had done to comfort him.

"Then it may be that chance lies with you, Daughter of the Pleiades. It is written in our sacred scripts that the Sword you carry was forged from the First Word of Aeon and was reborn of the Mother of the Sun. Perhaps in this some faint hope might yet remain," The shimmering glow was about him once more and this time, Yurah saw the bitter wound that wept beneath his breastplate. Gently she touched Istah's sleeve.

"Or it may be that no hope is left at all." Tristan was saying. "Long have we fought this battle and many we have loved have been lost. We are in truth a failing line. Do you not see it, my brothers. My sisters?"

"I see the point between the light and the dark. The place we must stand upon the gathering fields. More than this I can not know

Tristan." Atyn answered solemnly.

"And more than this we are not permitted to know." he said drawing a painful breath, "I apologize for my mood Atyn. I will dwell upon these things no longer. Tonight we shall do our best to put aside our troubled thoughts. Soon we shall hear music such as has not been played in long and careworn days," and again his pale eyes burned into Yurah's open mind, "We shall join our people under the tabernaculum and weave our voices into the winter sky."

Theo was wondering grimly of the change that had come upon Tristan. His thought wandered back to Rudra and the strange wound that had pierced his side. How oddly the skin had frayed under the touch of his hand. Never, in all his healing days, had he seen such a thing. It was Istah's voice that interrupted his troubled reflections.

"Truly Tristan, your likeness to young Rudra is unequaled. Why do you hide your hurts from us? What good does it do to bleed alone when there are those among us who may help."

Marial's face fell. Pushing her chair away she hurried to his side. "It is the nature of the wounds. They are not like any we have dealt with before." Taking him gently by the arm she said, "Come, I must have a look at it once more."

Reluctantly Tristan rose from his seat, "Again I beg your pardon. I have spent much precious time in being tended when there are more pressing things at hand. Please finish your meal. I will be back shortly."

"I would like a look at the injury."

"It matters not to me, Atyn." Tristan said, "Many a healing hand has laid me bare in these past days. Another prod and poke shall make no difference to these sore bones."

"I would be glad of it." Marial answered him, "We tend the wounds only to find our work undone. Progress is slow." then a grim anxiety clouded her gray eyes. "and for some we have not been able to stem the festering at all."

The scabbard stirred at Yurah's side and she found herself rising from her chair. "I may be able to help." she said softly. Tristan's clear eyes widened, "I would be obliged." He answered following Marial to his chamber.

Carefully Marial slipped the silver breastplate over his shoulders, revealing the growing red stain upon his bandages. She cut away the wraps and the deep slice across his breast gaped wide apart.

"It has deepened Tristan," she whispered low, looking into the gash.

Atyn bent over her shoulder and gently touched the skin. Angry red stripes spread from the hold and Marial shook her head with

159

concern, "I fear my skills in this are not enough, Rudra was faring better with his concoctions." she said sighing with frustration, "Maybe he has spoken of them to Yanhe."

Atyn stared into the festering wound, "Rudra's plants are potent but these hurts were not made in this world." he whispered laying his palm over the gash. "Such things must be dealt with in other ways." And Atyn rested his hands just above the wound. In a moment the misty force that wavered along Tristan's torn chest, flowed into a concentrated stream. Atyn breathed evenly holding himself in the two places at once. He was in the lower world, guiding the healing currents into Tristan's body while he watched from the mountain top of the upper airs. The scabbard at Yurah's side began to whisper. The misty energies began to run in shimmering threads along the length of Tristan's body. The gash grew darker as Atyn worked until finally a thick shadow quavered upon the open edge of the flayed skin. A strange hum began to disturb the healing flow. Yurah set her hand upon the hilt of the blade and a stream of words came from it. The silvery threads of the scabbard flowed in restless chant. She drew the sword and held it in the candlelight. In its reflection she saw herself upon the cliffs, standing with the Malkian. Atyn was at her side and above her head the sword was raised up in a wild torrent of wind. A white sun pierced the shimmering metal and a perfect sound poured through her; coming from the above into the room where Tristan lie bleeding. For an instant the room was lost in its glow. When sight returned Tristan was sitting up upon his bed, the wound neatly sealed with only a pale red line to show where it had been. He held her gaze and silently returned to her words she had known before.

"It is a Sword that shall cleave the shades in parts,
Rending shadows in its sound.
It is a Word to pierce the moment,
Leaving stains upon the ground."

He allowed the perception to linger before he pressed her again. "The rhymes of the Augerian are known to you, are they not, Pleiad?" he said without speaking.

Yurah kept his gaze steady, "They are."

"Then the Eye of the Storm is truly upon us." he said rubbing his hand across his smooth chest. "and now I am ready. We shall raise the song to cross the havens. My deepest thanks, daughter of Raldabon and son of Minerva. By your grace I am whole again."

Marial leaned down to study the pale mark, her thoughts quickly running to the others that lie suffering in their beds.

"We will come, Marial," said Atyn knowing her mind. "and we will not wait."

"The Druii gather in the Upper Hall." replied Tristan lacing up a clean shirt and stretching his stiff arms. "Truly now we have reason to sing. We will wait for you there. Come as you are able."

And so they left the meal half-eaten to follow Marial back to the infirmary. Yurah worked by Atyn's side and, one by one, they sealed shut the wounds caused by the Umbra's Black Swords, leaving each of the wounded in a better spirit and many well enough to rise from their beds. Finally they came to Rudra. He was gray and motionless under the white sheets.

"The cut has re-opened and I have not been able to stem the bleeding." said Yahnee, adjusting the poultice upon his head. "His sense comes and goes. When last he woke he did not seem to know me."

"We will seal the hole made by the black magicians. This should make your other work easier."

She nodded, gently pulling away the sheets to remove the pressuring wraps. Rudra's bright blood pulsed from the disintegrating skin. Steadily Yurah held the sword over his chest and Atyn placed his hands in the air just over the wound. Together they worked and again the healing flash filled the chamber and when Atyn moved his hands away, only a pale scratch remained. Rudra stirred uneasily.

"I have been traveling, Atyn." he whispered, struggling to return to his body. "Artemi and Urion are calling to us from the Hold. We must answer." he said swinging his legs over the edge of the mattress.

"You will answer to me. Rudra. Now stay still."

"The gash is healed." he said softly feeling the knitted skin, "and the pain, it is not so bright."

"I will explain all to you but first you must lay quiet."

"It was not a dream, Atyn. They were there." he pressed again, "They are calling and we must answer."

"And we will answer. Loose your cares Rudra. Tristan is healed and together we shall all see to it."

"Tristan," he answered his eyes beginning to gleam. "but he was the deepest cut of all. How is it that he is well again?"

"For now you must take my word. He is waiting for us in the Gathering Hall."

"Then you must go to him. A moment approaches. I have seen it. Hurry on, I will cause no one trouble."

"And that would be a relief to us all." replied Theo leaning over his bed. "but be assured little brother, I will come back as soon as we are finished and tomorrow, if you are well enough, I will tell the tale as many times as you wish to hear it."

"And I will hold you to it Theo, but go now. He is waiting."

Again it was Marial that lead them and when they reached the upper hall they found a host of Drui had already gathered there. Harp and string, reed and drum were sweetly tangled in melody and rhythm. Vibrant voices wove their mystic chants into the airs. One by one the Drui greeted them and through warm thoughts and gentle words they made their way to the center of the large chamber. The high stone ceiling had been pulled apart and now lay open to the outer world. The night stars and the thin moon shown above them. Beyond the pool Tristan waited upon a tall chair and, sitting at his side, were two others. Lorya whispered into Yurah's ear that the two were Clare and Kirkos, just returned from Basilus. They took their places close by as the music swelled into the night. Yurah looked into the reflecting pool to see that no sliver of moon shone within it. To her surprise it was the music of the Drui that was taking shape in the black water. Shimmering sounds of color flickered in perfect rhythm across the dark face.

Yurah took her flute from its casing and joined in with the rising song. Voices layered in clear counterpoints grew in number and sweet harmonies layered into the work. Next to her she heard Kiel begin to sing. His voice was radiant. Fading notes, merged effortlessly into many rhythms. The hours passed and a deep peace settled among them.

Time was held rapt in the melody and in the reflecting waters, images began to drift in the skies above. Shadowed in gray fair faces came and went in the mirroring glass. She looked to Kiel and read the vision of her mind in his own. Image after image stirred in the pool and gradually the song became more sorrowing. A stark image of Zelmisso appeared into the still water, Urion stood upon the peak and behind him a shimmering image of the fiery Malkian, standing before his legions. A brilliant sun dazzled the valley beneath but the forest churned in dark fume. A band of Artemi's warriors were battling an army of bleak shadows. The ground trembled and Yurah's tone faltered. Kiel took her hand, whispering in her ear the soothing harmony that was his gift to give. Lovely as the music that surrounding them and as perfect as the numbers that form the spheres, its sound flowed over into the dark waters. Steam poured through the rising mist and far away in a distant sky, a new sun burst forth in the haze of milky stars. She looked round the cavernous hall to find that every eye was drawn upward to the havens.

The night was old when the music ended. Tristan had left the hall promising to meet them at the morning breakfast and that time came quickly. They dressed hurriedly and went to speak a brief farewell to

Rudra before travelling on to Basilus. They found him, still confined to bed but sitting straight upon his cushions.

"Greetings my friends." he smiled, "Marial said you would be leaving early."

"You look better." said Atyn, pleased with the new strength in his voice.

"I am." he answered rubbing his bandaged side. "It is a sweet relief to breath without pain. Thank you all. Last night I was not clear-headed enough to say it nearly well enough."

"And how is your head, Rudra?" asked Inrih.

"Sore." he grinned. "Sore and shorn. But as I have pondered the situation, I believe that matching heads might not be as difficult as you believe. I will look forward to your return for when these bandages are lost we can then compare our heads properly. "

Inrih laughed loudly, "But Rudra, the two can never be compared. Remember, my bruised friend, I do not grow ears aptly as you."

"Ah, but they could be arranged. Do not forget how skillful we are with shapes."

"My ears are fine as they sit," he replied, knitting his brow.

"I will think upon it while you are away. Adon shall assist me. He is a master of detail."

"Worry not, Inrih," said Adon, chuckling in the next bed. "you will be consulted before the final designs are in place."

"Again you leave me without words, Rudra."

"Do not worry your pretty head about it Inrih." Rudra winked, "Trust me. You will like it."

"Hummph. When I return, and your bandages be lost, I will put an end to this absurdity."

Rudra settled back upon his pillows, "I will think of it every day until we meet again." and then he grew serious and without his smile his injuries were obvious, "I am more than willing to help you in this task but that is not my lot. As soon as I am on my feet again I must return to Odyn's Hold. Last night I wandered in my bloody dreams and Artemi spoke to me. I will go when I am able."

"A day will come when we shall be one people once more." replied Atyn.

"I hope it will be short in its coming," said Theo, "but I must remind you now that Tristan awaits. We will stay here for a bit and help the others see to the breakfasting of this hall. We will meet within the hour to say our final goodbyes."

So one by one they said their farewells and left the healing hall to find Tristan's chamber. They shared a fair meal under the candlelight of his dining table. Clare and Kirkos gave Aytn a map.

"Ildabyth has rebuilt much of Basilus since your people were driven away, Atyn. The three towers have been reconfigured according to his design and now a new force pulses from the core of Erda. He has dug deep into the inner fires." Kirkos told them sternly. "From these depths the Priests of the Towers pull the Umbra into life. It is a horrific sight to behold. The shadows are perilous. They are undead and without mind."

"To misjudge Ildabyth's shades will be your final error." replied Theo as Clare touched his shoulder.

"Let us not forget there is another that waits within the center." she reminded him softly. "Deep within the core there breathes a pure life. Bound and caged, she dares to stand within the pressures of this vault. It is because of this he has not been able to take all."

Yurah stirred restlessly in her chair. The scabbard murmured and out of the corner of her eye, she saw the grim Drui, who had taken their ponies the long night before, waited outside Tristan's chambers.

"The time draws near my friends." said Tristan rising from his chair. "Come. I will show you what path you shall take."

And so they walked together, following along the grottoes and precipices, until they reached a wide space of rock where their ponies waited for them. With a word and symbol Lorya opened the wall and the morning sun poured over their faces. The vast knoll beyond seemed to spring straight up from the sea. Its straight cliffs towered above the shoreline to crawl along the treacherous beach. Along the tor, stands of lush trees gripped the narrow ledges. The eroded stone stood like ancient sentinels against the long backbone of the snow covered mountains. All around them the birch leaves rustled and below their feet the tides echoed. They lead their ponies out upon the rough ledge to see that just below them, clinging to hill stood a vast building. Once tall and well-made, hints of decay now lingered about its roofs and windows. Long arms of cobbled stone stretching as gray wings, clung to the desolate cliffs.

"It is the ancient Hall of Healers." explained Theo, "Many of the younger Drui were raised within those walls, and will tell you that both Rudra and Artemi know those countless chambers well. By the reckoning of ordinary men centuries have past since any of our folk have lived there. It is little used now, kept up by a few crones of the wild forestlands. It is a sad thing that the Priests of Basilus have ruined this too. Hurry past it and do not linger. It is not as it seems." he said kindly, embracing them each in turn, "Farewell my friends. May the heart of the Yellow Sun ever burn within you."

Tristan waited quietly as their goodbyes were exchanged, turning his face unto the light. He listened to the voice of the sea and said. "Upon the gathering fields of battle we shall meet anew. The Drui will be among you, through you may see them not." and without a sound the mountain closed around them .

And so they left the refuge of the Drui, to descend the narrow steeps. The grim shadow of the Healing House loomed above. Its narrow empty windows pressed down upon them like hollow eyes. Hurriedly they walked along the twisting road, always striking the path that led them closest to gray ocean. Fitfully the waters churned as their destination drew nearer with every steady step.

CHAPTER XVIII
THE RINGED CITY

Inrih cast a stern gaze over any they chanced to pass along the coarse highway. Istah rode with her bow and quiver hung loosely upon her shoulder. Atyn was lost in thought, keeping pace just behind her. Kiel and Yurah were draped in yellow robes and guided the pack ponies. Grime filled the heavy afternoon air. The sun was low on the water when the ringed tiers of Basilus finally loomed in the distance.

Winding their way along the base of the mountains, the travelers entered a sprawling encampment. Stained tents stank as fish and rotting shells mingled with reek of body sweat. The people kept their distance, watching through narrowed eyes while they picked their way through the putrid litter. Yurah wondered why so many lived in such squalor but she kept her dismay to herself and rode dutifully behind.

At length they came to a long bridge and far beyond, piers harbored sailing vessels of every size and shape. Banners of far-off lands waved in the evening wind as their ships tossed upon the restless waves. The shining walls of Basilus lay beyond the boats. A series of arcing roofs lined the spiraling roads and beyond the silver domes, soared three translucent towers. As they drew close to the gatehouse they could see a bridge ward waited outside the door. He stepped forward with a young guard to either side.

"The levy for passage is twenty pistolets for the women and forty for the men. Pay it now or you are welcome to return to Penury's Village." he shouted as the guards put arrow to the string.

Inrih removed a bag of coins from his cloak and handed to the tollsman. "Count it and be brief. My Master has pressing business. And it best not be you who makes us late," he answered showing his teeth in a terse smile, "or you will be the one to pay."

The man bristled but even so he counted the coins speedily and in a moment the guards stepped aside. They climbed the ramp, with the sharp eyes of watchmen staring them from their high bridgetowers. The bridge was laid with thick green stones, and over it all graceful metallic ropes reached from parapet to parapet. The damp spray of the sea climbed into the fine weave of Yurah's cloak and she pulled it in close around her. The evening stars had begun to sparkle and lights from the city flickered from beyond the wall. At the end of the bridge they were met by a flight of wide marble stairs and an alabaster colonnade spread its graceful wings over the waters. Statues of imposing, robed women looked down upon the unsettled sea. The massive walls of Basilus lie beyond the broad portico and upon those causeways waited a legion of soldiers but Yurah was taking no heed of the guards, wondering instead at the marvelous carvings that held the grand arcade above them.

"They are the Caryatides; the Women of the Menhir." Kiel whispered as she gazed at the huge stone figures. "Long ago starry eyed artisans filled the streets of Basilus, by their grace the Caryatides still remind us of what has now faded into myth." then his voice sank to a whisper and he cast down his eyes, for a emissary approached, flanked by men at arms and their pages.

"Hail Lord. Hail Lady." The Captain said, looking skeptically upon the group. "What business brings you to Basilus?"

Atyn slipped lightly from his pony and bowed low to the wary man. "I am Atyn Ceranus, a practitioner of the healing arts and this is my collaborator, Istah Deii. We have journeyed from the Greenlands to speak with your Dowerymen. We come to Basilus seeking advice."

"These are difficult times. To enter here is a privilege only given to those laudable means. What do you offer in return?" the emissary replied sharply, eyeing his finely made robes, "Surely you are not loutish enough to believe our skills are given to any who might happenchance to our gates. We have our own problems. We do not concern ourselves with charity."

"Then we are folk of like heart sir." said Atyn coolly, "for generosity leaves the giver bereft of his assets. We have many in our service to mine the riches of the deep mountains. We understand your dilemmas. You may rest assured that your Dowerymen will be well paid for their hospitality."

A dull gleam spread through the eye of the herald and he gestured to the pages.

"I will show you to the Strangers House. My attendants will take your beasts to the liveries. Your animals are not permitted in our streets. They will return your luggage when that errand is done ."

"Then allow my bond-servant go with your men. Though I am sure your facilities will prove adequate." replied Atyn dryly, "He is familiar with the habits of our beasts and will assist their stabling."

The Captain nodded and Kiel, playing the part of an obedient serf, took his place with the horses to follow the men to the stables. The guide lead the others up the stairs to the open portico. Kiel turned his head to watch them go but the soldier spoke to him sharply, "A slave's eyes are not made to wander." and he leaned close, his sore breath filling his face. "Or they shall be plunked from his head like a plum."

167

Kiel cast his eyes downward and the guard scoffed. "See to it that none of you forget your place!" he shouted to the others, "Now come quickly!" They followed him to the lowest level of the bastion walls. A sealed entrance waited. He barked out a password and a metal door slid apart, revealing a wide hall. Pale lamps glowed from the copper-like walls as they walked through the chattel passage. Kiel noted the corridor held an uncanny resemblance to the interior mountain tunnels of Drui. After a short time the tunnel ended and they entered a small paddock, barred with metal gates. The brutish guard unlocked the bolt and they followed him toward the soft lantern light shining through the doors of the livery.

Yurah stepped softly, stealing glances as she could of the broad veranda. The last rays of the evening sun clung to the horizon. The subtle rays of light played upon the delicate features of the Caryatides as they cast their gaze over the troubled tides. Beyond the gallery, broad marbled steps loomed and, just as the westerning sun lost into the night, they entered the gates of Basilus.

Their envoy led them through the brick lain streets to a spacious house with handsome windows. Its wide porch was set with oversized chairs and its rail was covered in a sweet smelling vine. The guard opened the door without knocking and they found themselves in a fine parlor. The emissary rang a small bell and immediately they were greeted by a robed man. He was not tall, though he was quite broad, and he wore a long chamois of deep blue. Along the hem of the wide sleeves, fine silver threads curled about above the elbow. His eyes were black as bits of coal and upon his head he wore flat cap which, by more than just chance, perfectly matched the embroidered brogues upon his feet.

"Oh my! Oh my! Dare not say it aloud, Gorgun. What a dear friend you are. Could it be you have brought into my most excellent inn these regal patrons." he cried, throwing up his hands in feigned delight, "Greetings fair folk!" he smiled, lightly grasping Istah's fingers, "and who have we here. Ahh such a sweet lady!" but as he spoke to her hand his eyes strayed to Atyn. "What a lovely thing to turn my hard heart."

"Control yourself, Argut." replied the emissary icily. "These folk require accommodations. I have no time to waste in folly."

"Folly! Love is nary considered folly." sniped Argut grinning brazenly at Inrih, "I think you overlook your sweetest desires Gorgun. Such tension will make you rude. Come by my kitchens later, I will have something special ready for you."

"I will be back, but only to be sure that your work is well done. My sentry will remain through out the night."

"As you wish, good sir. But now it is you who delays me. Run along so I can show my guests to their chambers." he tittered, shooing him out the door, "Remember, I will wait up!" he cooed, leaning after him. Then he latched the catch behind him and smiled at his guests, "But alas, my heart tells me that Gorgon is right. You must have the chance to freshen yourselves before another moment passes. Come now. I will show you to your rooms."

Their feet made no sound upon the thick carpet as the fat man presented their chambers. Atyn's was a large handsome room with a tall posted bedstead thick with coverlets. Along the eastern wall a long windowseat overlooked a cheerfully lit cloister. After pointing out the closet and wardrobe, the waterworkings and the lamps, Argut opened a curtained door to reveal Istah's adjoining chamber and when he was finished explaining the history of the tasteful decorum, he curtly directed Yurah to a small cell conveniently connecting the spacious apartments. Then he led on, insisting they follow him to Inrih's chamber. It was oddly shaped room, with angled ceilings and randomly set columns. The chamber was sparsely furnished, excepting a sizeable bed and ornate dressing table and at one far end a series of long thin windows looked over the kitchen gardens. Upon its largest wall a dark mirror glass reached from ceiling to floor and along the other side of the wall was a series of strangely set doors. With a heavy set of keys, Argut unlocked three of the passage entries, showing how each could provide a hidden access to the connecting rooms.

"Fear not for your safety my gracious guests. I am always certain that my Guardsman are well equipped." said Argut standing close enough to him to press lightly against Inrih's shoulder. "So if there is reason for concern, he can check upon you without disturbing their slumber."

From an expressionless face Inrih affirmed the remark with a slight nod of his head.

"There is another in our party, sir." interrupted Atyn as Argut started an account of the Inn's history and the tragic, yet fortunate, circumstances surrounding his family's inheritance the building and grounds. "He is a younger man. He has gone to the stables to tend our beasts. Have you another bed available, one close enough that I might keep my eye upon him?"

"Keep your eye on him, hummm, a young man; well that is easily enough arranged." said Argut with a new spark in his eye. "But I must ask, is the lad some type of rascal?"

"No indeed." replied Atyn, "But he is unfamiliar with the ways of large cities and I worry that he may be easily taken in. I do not want him finding himself among rouges; or worse."

"Oh I understand. Indeed I do. The lad can stay here," he said unlocking another of the chambers doors. "It is rather small but that window; you see there at the back, holds a fine view of the upper towers and the bed is good. That stair leads down to the kitchen," he said, bouncing playfully upon the mattress, just as distant bell-cote chimed. Argut leapt up and motioned impatiently with his fingertips. "But I have rambled far too long. You must excuse me. I will send him up when he comes. If you need anything, just call out." and he bowed, allowing his belly to flow over his belt, before scurrying down the servant stairs.

'This is shifty place and he is most peculiar man," replied Inrih pensively, "I will be more at ease when Kiel returns."

"Yes, so shall I." Atyn answered softly and then he lowered his voice further, "I would not be surprised if these walls have not only eyes but ears as well. We must go quietly about our affairs and hope he returns before trouble finds him."

So they returned to their chambers to wash away the stains of travel. Golden spouts spilled clear water into deep basins that emptied through golden drains. Thick towels waited along side lubricant oils and downy robes. While they had freshened themselves, they could hear Argut's shrill voice crooning commands from up the back stairwell until, suddenly, a great clatter interrupted him.

"Woe to my mother's dish." the fat man bellowed. "Woe to my merry dinner! And woe to the ignorant dog who will pay dearly for every shard and crumb! They are ruined!" he screamed. "Ruined!" and his wails became confused with loud crashes.

Atyn leaped to his feet finding himself the first to arrive at the bottom of the stairs

"Satis! Satis!" he thundered. "Leave the child alone Argut."

Argut looked up, the beating stick over his head, bloodied and ready for another strike. The child cowered, too fearful to look up at his rescuer. The fat man wiped a string of drool from off his folded chins,

"You catch me by surprise traveler," he hissed. "How does the fairer tongue fly so impeccably from your lips? The Hibernicis are not known for their letters" and his eyes narrowed to squint, "nor for uncommon judiciousness. I am surprised to hear you carp over the treatment of a dredge. But if it bothers you," he said, turning his bilious belly to face them. "I shall take it up with the little wretch's master instead. Not only has he ruined my dinner he has served to make me late." and he spit at the boy that lay at his feet. "My apologies for any inconvenience but appears you will wait a bit longer for your supper." and with a contrived bow he left them standing upon the stair.

Yurah knelt at the boy's side, "Do you have pain?"

The boy did not answer and clamored to his feet."

"Wait a moment." said Atyn sternly, seeing that his arm hung useless at his side.

'I meant no harm sir." he choked, wiping the blood from his teeth. "But the plates were hot from the oven. I could not hold them."

"Plates do not concern me, lad." he said looking carefully over the boy, "but your shoulder. It must have a least a little pain?" placing his hand over the unnatural bulge.

"Aye Lord, more than a little in fact."

"And it will take "more than a little" to repair it." he replied gently as he positioned himself. "Are you ready?"

The boy raised his slight chin and nodded.

"Inrih, help me hold him."

And with a sharp gasp the shoulder was reset. Atyn looked over his wounds. "You are quite bruised. You will be sore for many days. Come upstairs and we will soak them and then you may be on your way."

"On my way," the boy shuddered inadvertently, "Argut is a kind man compared to my master."

"What is it that you fear boy?"

"The whip sir, by the time morning comes I will not walk again for a week."

"There are ways I may help you." said Atyn.

"Not unless you choose the same fate. Compassion is weakness here. You can be assured, even as we whisper in this empty hall, that knowledge of your flaws are being made known."

"Well then, I will concern myself with that presently but for now you must come with me."

After they had wrapped his wounds Inrih saw the boy through the main door paying no heed to the guard who watched before the fire.

"Farewell, young sir." he said placing his hand upon the boys shoulder. "And remember lad; no man is bound to the words of any master, a man is bound only to the words of his own heart."

The boy paused to look into the grim, noble face and then he turned away to fade into the shadows.

Kiel followed the young attendants through the stable gate. Some of the horses stomped as they passed by, a few tossed their heads, but most simply turned back their ears and set their attentions back to their mangers. He led his pony to hitching post and removed the bulk from his sweaty back.

The tallest lad brought him a currying comb, handing it to him with bland indifference before slipping away down the long corridor. Kiel murmured into the beast's ear as he cleaned the dust from his coarse coat and two other lads tossed the bundles upon a cart.

"You take it, Nestor. I have carried your share of work all day!" said a frail pallid youth. "It is time I have my just rewards!" and he leaned back upon a stack of straw closing his eyes.

"You best rise up, Pytios. The guards are heading this way," he whispered, "and you! You had best cease that racket if you do not want a taste of the leather strap across your mouth.

Pytios leapt to his feet and began to fill the watering buckets just as two soldiers turned the aisle spitting into the pile of straw as they looked upon them.

"What have we here?" said the tallest, his dreadful leer spreading like an oily stain over a badly set chin.

"Gorgon's littlest soldiers and they look rather hungry this evening." spoke the other.

Nestor's voice was tense. "We are to bring this luggage back to Argut's Inn"

"Hmm, no time for refreshment. That is a shame. I suppose there is never any rest for wicked lads."

"Gorgun would not like us to tarry."

"Ahh, but it would be a cruel thing to have our goodies spoil, wouldn't you now lad?" replied the first, grabbing his collar and drawing the boy close under his chin, "or worse yet, wait until next time."

Nestor grew pale. Kiel put down the brush and walked to the guard. "My master travels in good faith to your city and does expect us back at the inn promptly." he replied allowing the hilt of his sword to peek from under his yellow robe.

"What type of master allows his servant to carry a weapon?" said the guard sharply.

"I am sworn to his service by life or by death. It is love of duty which binds the sword to my side." setting his feet wider apart as he studied the man.

"Strange affections you highlanders hold." the man sneered. "No slave loves his duties or his master! Such notions will be your downfall. In our city it is said, 'Let them hate as long as they fear!'" and he pulled a dagger from his belt running a slow finger across its edge.

"Stand down good soldier and allow the boy to finish his labor." Kiel answered civilly. "Timeliness is surely a virtue in your land as well and as I said, we are expected back shortly."

The guards hesitated, looking upon at the fine weave of his robe and the bright sword that hung at his side, "Let it not be said that the Guard of Ildabyth, is unkind to strangers." the tallest soldier spoke finally, "Go about business but leave all things as you found them. Volos!" he shouted into the barn, "You have guests in your stables."

"And all I hear is your babbling." came the reply. "Pack away your misguided attentions and return to your duties. Here! Here, young sirs! Bring the beasts to me." the strong voice commanded as a man, with a broken gait, hobbled from the far corner of the stalls. "I apologize for their cheek." he said to Kiel, "They fill themselves up on drink when they think no one watches." then he hissed at the sentries, "Go now, or I shall inform your Captain of your gaffe." and the soldiers laughed and mocked him as returned to the yard.

"As they said, I am Volos, keeper of the liveries," he said rubbing the smooth flank of Inrih's pony. "I must warn you stranger, though there are bolder men in this city than these worthless brutes, take care what you say, for even the sneaking dastard may prove deadly."

"I did not wish to offend." replied Kiel. "but it is not my habit to stand indifferent."

"And I thank you, sir for I have met that guard before" Nestor said with a tremble. "and though Gorgun is not a civil man. He does not mistreat us without cause. We are lucky in that regard."

"Lucky! How can you say it! His treatment of us, lucky! We are no better than beasts. In fact beasts are treated better than are we, at least they are in your stable, Volos." said Pyrios ardently, "Only the few have luck inside these city walls, and they are the cruelest folk of all."

"Quiet! Someone could hear you." whispered Nestor anxiously.

"You must heed his advice, Pyrios and learn to be silent when you should. Now see to your work. And you traveler, to stand indifferent to the sufferings of others is a trait you must soon acquire if you are to survive long in Basilus."

"I am sure your advice is well meant, sir and I will do my best to keep alive within these hard walls."

"That is good to hear." the old man replied with a grin, "Now let us tend to these tired beasts. The dark is upon us now and the streets the most dangerous when covered by shadows."

"The Umbra," muttered Pyrios looking about uneasily. "Those creatures are worse than any loathsome man can be."

"Only fools name their doom." growled Volos, "Do not utter that word here!" and Pyrios cowered, covering his ears as if he had been stung by a switch.

"Too much has been said here tonight." Volos hissed and without another sound between them the work was finished in silence.

The band walked in quiet. Street lamps burned from ornate posts giving them some comfort from the dark as the boys showed him the way back to the Inn. Kiel kept a sharp ear tuned to the night for in the distance an unsettled music was playing. Its steady drums pulsed with a fervent chant. The odd melody carried an alarming fascination.

"Where does that song come from?" he asked Pyrios.

"It is the House of Feasts you hear. The music has only just begun. Do not go near that place. Strange habits are made in those walls. It is not safe." then his voice fell to lowest of whispers, "The foolish are calling to the shades. They are seeking favors from the Umbra."

"Do you learn nothing from Volos?" muttered Nestor as he began to run from the sound. "Hurry viator. Do not be that fool!" he cried, and together they ran to keep up.

CHAPTER XIX
THE ACADEMIES OF BASILUS

Disturbed conversation came from the kitchen downstairs. Kiel rose from his bed, feeling as if someone had been watching him sleep.

"Master Kiel! Hurry up now. We will be leaving shortly." said Inrih poking his head around the corner.

Kiel pulled on his breeches and went to meet him.

"Are you feeling better this morning?" asked Inrih when he saw him at the door, "You did not seem yourself last night."

"I had a run-in at the livery."

"The same happened here," Inrih replied, "I fear we draw more attention to ourselves than we had intended. It appears young are treated poorly in this land."

"It is a cruel place," Kiel answered trying to clear his muddled thoughts. "And in the night, even stranger things wait."

"Hullo! Hullo! Good morning sleepyhead!" Argut's trebly voice shouted. "Ho there! Young man-servant; go to your masters and tell them to hurry to the garden. Breakfast is waiting!"

"Breakfast is waiting young man-servant." said Inrih raising his brows.

Kiel looked at him, a bit confused, "I found him on the stairs last night, watching as you slept. It took but a glance to send him scurrying along his way." Inrih confided.

"Thank you Inrih." replied Kiel worriedly and he went to tell the others about breakfast.

The meal was good, eggs and muffins with jam. Argut hovered about them, pouring tea and chattering incessantly, giving no indication that anything out of the ordinary had occurred the evening before. Kiel stood at Atyn's side, playing his part well even when Argut would pinch him and ask him to fetch something from the kitchen. Inrih gave no sign that he noticed Kiel's dilemma and Yurah hid her dismay by keeping her eyes fixed upon her plate. In the corner, Gorgon's sentry waited for them finish. Kiel was relieved when they finally followed him through the gate and on to where a open coach waited.

"Orders are that you will be taken to the Academies. This is where the Dowerymen teach their students the virtues of the body. They are located to the top of the second tier. An envoy will be waiting to meet you."

"We are grateful for your courtesies." answered Atyn.

"I was also to remind you that these considerations do not come cheaply. Compensations will be sought promptly."

"I need not be reminded of my commitments. The Dowerymen will be amply rewarded."

The driver made no reply and set the horses to a steady pace. Graceful halls and shady parks, waited beyond every turn and often the sheltered lanes would join in a clustering of shops and eateries. It was early yet; the sky was the palest of blues and the smell of the sea was light upon the air. Only a few patrons busied themselves along the polished stone streets. Yurah watched discreetly, perceiving the ways of the folk that worked and shopped in each of the unique districts. But as she watched the flawless shops and perfect walkways flow by she caught brief glimpses between the narrow brick alleys at what festered behind the bright storefronts. These were dreary depots piled with refuse and weary vagrants toiled, their betters tossing them scraps for their morning labors. The sullen coachman appeared to see none of it, keeping his eyes to the highway which had begun to lead sharply upward.

When they reached the second tier of the city, the fantastic grandeur of its wealth gleamed from every polished corner. Robed men and women walked under the covered passages followed closely by bound servants. The carriage stopped at a broad gate and keeper came to meet him. The driver exchanged few words with the man and the gate opened, allowing them to pass. Students walked upon the grassy lawns between the imposing buildings. Tall oaks and cypress gave shade to bright gardens and trimmed walks. They rode on until they reached a columned hall and above its wide doors the words *Philosophia Naturalis Librarius* were set in stone. The coach pulled to a stop.

"Your guide will be waiting inside." he said glancing back at them impatiently. "I will return at sunset to carry you back to the Inn."

"Thank you. We will meet you here as the evening sun sets." replied Atyn helping the others from the carriage. The guard bowed his head slightly and set the horses to a fast trot.

At the entrance of the massive building, statues of great men were carved into the supporting pillars of the main arch. Above were elaborate garrets, resting one atop the other over the main cornices. Kiel gently touched her arm and Yurah realized the others had walked ahead and were waiting for her at the top of the stair.

An elderly man stood with them. His red mantle was draped about his shoulders and a great mane of finely combed white hair fell loosely about his shoulders.

"I am Baebys, Keeper of the Books." he said haughtily, "I am told

176

that you are a healer from the north and desire access to our libraries. I am here to help direct in your search. What is your title sir?"

'I am Atyn Cernunas. I am a healer to my people. Our lands have been stricken by a strange disease. Ultimately sir, I seek a remedy to our troubles. I have come to your fair city to study the texts kept in your learning halls."

"All diagnostic works are located upon the upper floors." he said abruptly and set off at a great pace down the wide hall. He led them through dim corridors and stone stairwells until they reached a long room filled with leather-bound books. Baebys pointed out a large cabinet set with dozens of small drawers.

"Information is indexed in these catalogs. Seek your text by symptom or by disorder. Either way will lead you to the proper shelves. If you need further assistance I will be in my offices. I am a busy man but willing to serve if you find it convenient to disturb me.

"We appreciate that sir." answered Atyn, noting his sullen tone.

"I will send an assistant if one comes available. The physicians often have their apprentices in my halls. Perhaps, I may find one able to help you in your searches."

"If it is convenient." Atyn replied back with measured courtesy.

"Good day then." the man acknowledged tersely before closing the door.

"Quite the raconteur," said Inrih dryly.

"All the better for us and if fortune holds we will have no assistant come to our aid." said Atyn going to the door and casting a concerned look down the empty hall. "Now the most difficult part begins. The higher tiers of Basilus will not be easily accessible. Come with me Inrih." he said motioning to table hid from sight of the door. "We must take a hard look at Kirkos' maps."

"I will stay here. The Basilians are a greatly learned people, and these records should not prove middling." replied Istah taking out parchment and pens from her satchel, "and if one does come to watch us, we must make this ruse believable."

"Keep an eye by the door Kiel." whispered Atyn, "None must know of these maps we keep."

But Yurah did not hear their words, for she was walking among the tall shelves, breathing in the aroma of old pages and polishing oils. Bronzed letters were inlaid at the edge of every case to better guide the seeker through the endless reams of information. Volumes, great and small, were snuggly set from floor to ceiling. Pulling a text from an upper shelf she gently opened its pages. A detailed rendering of a skull was laid out before her and for the first time she looked upon the furrows and channels that marked the internal surface of the bones within the head. The finely etched protrusions were labeled and explained at length. The meticulous observations continued until the whole of the human interior, and exterior, had been precisely detailed within its yellowing pages. Carefully tucking the text back in its place, Yurah went on to explore the cases. Amongst the anatomy and histology, she found a book entirely dedicated to the nature and health of the blood.

" 'The Circulating Fluids' how interesting." she mused as she opened the first section.

"The nutritive fluids which subserve the nutrition of the body are the blood, the lymph, and the chyle. The blood is an opaque, viscid fluid of a scarlet color. It is salt to the taste and has a peculiar faint odor. Dark red when flowing from the arteries and a purple color when it flows from the veins the general composition of blood consists mainly of plasma and its red color is due to the minute corpuscles that float suspended within this faintly yellow fluid."

"Such lifetimes of work; one after the other, shelf upon shelf," she thought looking down the long row and placing the book back in its place. Along the corridor of texts and ladders she slowly ran her finger against their bindings reading the titles as she went, "Histology of the Skin and its Appendages", "Nervous Tissue," "The Articulations of Human Form", "Surgical Anatomy", "Chronological Tables of the Development of the Fetus." and for an instant her hand paused there, almost pulling it from the case but then she hesitated and continued down the row.

When she turned the corner she saw Atyn and Inrih sitting at a long table. Sun streamed through the paned window and leaving only dark silhouettes against the bright day. She went to Inrih's side and glanced through the tall casement. The library window faced north. Stately trees and trimmed shrubbery marked the paved walks and covered arbors. Beyond the buildings, a speck of horizon glittered along the flat sea. Against that broad sky the three towers of the highest ring cast their shadows to the ground. Fixed in the center of the tallest turrent was a crystalline spire. From the maps she knew that between the towers were maze like by design. A legion of men and gated entrances kept all common folk from moving freely within their grounds.

"There!" said Atyn, pointing to a row of structures near to the wall. "That is the place we must make for first. Long ago those buildings served as casting houses for the metal smiths. There are old tunnels still within their basements that the ore was brought from the inner mines. We could breach the barrier from underneath we would be able to slip past any upper guards unawares."

"What role do those buildings serve now?"

"According to these notes," Atyn answered running his finger along the edge of the map, "ore is still worked within these walls. Look here Inrih! The symbols for Mercury and Sulfur, indeed the Alchemists must labor there."

Yurah was listening to their talk as she looked to the towers that sat atop of the grand city and she wondered what fate would hold when she would finally walk within those dark halls. Glancing back to the Academy lawns she saw a young woman, her arms heavy with books, hurrying to the Library stairs. The head-scarf slipped and fell upon the ground and Yurah caught a fleeting impression of her weary face. She bent to retrieve the hood and the books spilled upon the walk. Gathering them quickly, she rushed on as if a demon was at her heels.

"Perhaps we might have them design a remedy for us?" Atyn was saying.

"I suppose that could work, if we do not run short of gold. I do not think the Dowerymen put much faith in charity."

'That they do not." he agreed with a grim smile, "They prefer to keep their faith in their wallets. Do we have any more information about the tunnels, Inrih?"

"Aye, right here is something," he answered shuffling the papers upon the table, "Here it is! Look now at this, I believe that we might,"

"Someone is coming!" Kiel was standing at the end of row of books. "Hurry. Put the maps away."

"Find a way to look busy" said Atyn placing the maps in his satchel. "Straight away!"

Yurah hurried away down the row and grabbing several of the books she had just seen she rushed back to set them at the table. The Articulations of Human Form, Surgical Anatomy, and The Spinal Column and its Membranes were among the selections offered. Inrih picked up the nearest sat in front of the window to read. Atyn took the others and went back to where Istah worked.

"Here take this parchment and make some notations." suggested Inrih pushing the sheet over to her. Yurah opened the book of anatomy she began to diagram and label the structures.

"What should I do?" whispered Kiel.

"Pretend to look for something." said Inrih impatiently, "But do it near enough so you may hear what is said. Then come back and tell us! Hurry now."

Kiel took a long way through the shelves of books until settling himself just out of sight. He was well within earshot of their conversation.

"What symptoms are manifest?" he heard a soft, voice ask.

"A gradual crippling," Istah was saying, "striking mainly the children. Many of them die and the few that live are horribly maimed."

'I have heard mention of such a thing before. From the southern lands of Kham there have been scarce reports of writhing of the limbs and, as you say, it is primarily the children that fall victim to it."

"Have you referred to catalogs?"

"We have made some try at it. We have spent most of our time making ourselves familiar with what is here," replied Atyn, "there is so much here to search."

"Well in this I might be able to assist." she replied with a slight smile, "I have often rooted my way through these libraries to find all sorts of things I was not looking for. What books do you have?" she asked looking to the small stack he carried.

"Hmmm, The Spinal Column and its Membranes, yes this one may help you." she said musing as she turned the thin pages, " If I am remembering correctly the disturbance is thought to begin in the fibers within the central canal. When the inflammation begins spread it starts often with the lower limbs. But neither lung nor heart are exempt from its creep and when it stills those muscles, the victim will die. Is this what you observe?"

"It would fit with what we have seen." he quickly followed, playing his role deftly but something else had his attention. There was something quite unusual about the girl. He opened his inner vision to see her hands glowed with a strange light. "The Healer's Mark" he noted silently and he knew she was not bred from Basilian mores.

"It you do not mind my curiosity Lady, what is your background?" he asked politely.

"As yet I am student of these halls sir," she answered with a soft sigh, "I have learned much in my years here but my benefactor keeps me to a hard pace. It seems today he owes the Librarian a favor and I was summoned to assist you."

"Indeed you seem well informed. And now as I understand your duty, may you also grace me with your name."

"My pardon sir, of course you might have my name. I am Tamil of Karuna. It is a warm and gracious land not too far to the south of us." she began to explain.

Kiel dared a better look from around the corner of his hiding place. The woman was slight of stature and dressed in pale layered robes. Her black hair was tied loosely back from her face and her wide eyes were a deep shade of sparkling green. But then he startled as a large hand softly touched his shoulder and he realized that Inrih was at his side.

"I could not wait." Inrih whispered with a finger against his lips.

"If I may make a suggestion," said Tamil, "the texts that might better serve will be located along these rows," and they realized she was pointing toward their direction. Looking frantically to the shelves above they began to read the titles nearest and without thought Inrih plucked a volume from its place and opened the cover just as they turned the corner.

"Ahh, Kiel. And Inrih! So there you are?" Atyn said, a hint of surprise on his face, "Have you found something for us?"

"I can not be sure, Master Atyn," Kiel answered quickly, "Some of these titles I do not understand."

"It is of no matter, Kiel. We have other help now. This is Tamil. She is here to help us in our search. Lady Tamil, this is Kiel Kadmon, my trusted servant. And this is Inrih Bharata, our guard."

"Most honored," she answered, but instead of dropping her gaze she stared directly into Kiel's face. "My apologies sir, I did not mean to stare you, but you seemed quite familiar. Please forgive me. It seems I have quite forgotten all civility this morning."

"No offence is taken, Lady." he said.

"I believe the book is along this aisle," she answered but as she passed by him and he could feel her attention set upon him. "It should be right near here," she said, touching the bindings with a gentle care, "No. It was not this far." and she turned to see the book Inrih held in his hands. "What book do you carry sir?" she asked politely.

"On Airs, Waters, and Places," he answered, reading the cover.

Again Tamil looked surprised and shook her head slightly, "Though you may not know our libraries it appears your intuition serves well. That is the title I am seeking. Come and I shall show you what little I know of the ailment." and they followed her back to the table where Istah worked. Tamil sat down and begin to turn the pages, "It is not by chance I choose these texts. In my homeland there was a string of summers when our folk would fall to the strange malady. It would begin with a high fever and an unbearable aching and shortly after would come the heaves and flooding. I thought often, the source must enter through the mouth to settle in the gut and then move to the limbs. It was after these sufferings the paralysis would begin. Many died from the disease. This particular book I found most interesting. The healer proposes the origin of the plague would reach us though the river in the growing heat of the summer." and she began to read.

 ' "Whoever wishes to investigate medicine
properly, should proceed thus: the first place to
consider the seasons of the year, and what
effects each of them produces, for they are not
at all alike, but differ much from themselves in

regard to their changes. We must also consider
the qualities of the waters, for as they differ
from one another in taste and weight, so also
do they differ much in their qualities. These
things one ought to consider most attentively,
and concerning the waters which the
inhabitants use, whether they be marshy and
soft, or hard, and running from elevated and
rocky situations, and then if saltish and unfit
for cooking.'"

Atyn watching the light in her green eyes grow and wishing (for
other reasons) to hear her thoughts spoken aloud, "So he believed
source of the blight was your riverbeds."

"It could have been," she answered cautiously, "or may be it was
not. We were never sure. More certainly we knew as one began to
suffer, others close to them would fall ill within that same moon. Then
almost as strangely as a change in the weather, the blight would leave
our lands."

"Did you find ways to help them?"

"There was little we could do but relieve their pain and attempt to
exercise the frozen limbs. Still it was more personal to me yet. My
younger brother was one of the stricken. We laid him upon his funeral
pyre before he had seen his ninth winter. It was then I knew I would
become a healer and do whatever I was able to prevent such
sufferings."

"Then our meeting is truly fortunate." answered Istah, perceiving
the sincerity of the girl, "Did your folk figure ways of dealing with it?"

"I kept a journal of my brother illness, keeping good account of
the times and places of the other outbreaks. Still it is very interesting to
me. Sometimes, as my benefactor feels charitable, I am allowed up to
the Alchemy rooms." then she stopped herself and looked nervously
toward the door, "But I have talked to much. Come, I will show you
the places were you might study and cross-reference. It is not wise to
jump hastily to conclusions until more is certain." and she looked back
to Kiel, a concern knit to her brow.

Kiel felt her glance and he excused himself and returned to the
window to sit with Yurah. They worked together quietly until Atyn
and Inrih returned to say that they were again alone in the hall.

"She is an interesting girl." said Atyn.

"She is not Basalian by birth. Her appearance leads me to think
she bides from near the realm of Kurukshetra." replied Inrih, "They are
a wise people, not at all like the servants of Ildabyth. This girl is
different, Atyn. Her desires are pure."

"Then perhaps there is more help in this forbidden place than we had figured upon." said Atyn and Yurah could sense Kiel next to her, desperation fluttering in his uncertain heart.

CHAPTER XX
A WAY THROUGH THE DARK

It was cold when they returned to Inn and Argut was waiting at the door.

"Ohe!" he called out in the sweet acidic voice. "Ohe! I have waited all day to tell you. Hurry inside. Dinner is prepared. I have a surprise for you all."

Kiel jumped out as the horses came to a halt.

Inrih whispered to him, "You may sit next to me, Kiel. I do not believe he likes my look at all. In fact I think I frighten him a little."

"Then I can only hope that you frighten him enough." Kiel murmured, looking back at Argut's silhouette barring the light of the door. "My arms are blue from his breakfast pinches. It might be best if I find a way to excuse myself from dinner all together."

"Hmm, it might indeed. Wait here." and Inrih opened door to the carriage and sharing brief words with the others he returned quickly.

"Atyn will send you on to check on our horses. That should be enough to keep you from his clutches. Do you recall the way to the stables?"

"Oh, I can find my way. I will leave as soon as you settle to dinner."

They could hear the rustle of the kitchen servants just beyond the atrium door. A harper sat before the fire. At her side a young man held a lute and between them was a girl child, neatly dressed, was ready with a flute.

"Tonight we shall have music!" Argut cried waving his arms and almost striking the flute from the child's small hand, "It is by the grace of my good friends, who owe me much I will say candidly that I have arranged this entertainment for you all." and his face swelled as he smiled at Kiel.

"How kind of you Argut." replied Atyn. "It has been too long since we have enjoyed such comforts."

"There are many things to enjoy in my hall." he answered pertly, his ruddy forehead glistening with perspiration.

"The servants will bring in the platters while you wash. But make haste. I am ready to begin!"

"Then if you might be so kind Argut to prepare my man, Kiel, a satchel of dinner. He is obliged to return to the stables this evening and see to our beasts."

"Master Kiel shall not be dining with us tonight!" he replied with dismay.

"I fear not. The health of our beasts is central to us. It is necessary to see to their comforts often." Atyn replied gesturing for Kiel to be on his way. Kiel traded his light cape for a warmer robe and collected his dinner satchel from a young cook. Argut was waiting in the kitchen giving orders to the small staff.

"I will save you desert, Master Kiel. I have planned a creamy scone, sweet and sticky with honey and covered in fruit. I can be sure that it will be hot when you arrive, so do not keep me waiting too long." he shouted as Kiel disappeared into the shadows of the patio.

Grateful to be alone under the chill evening sky, Kiel made his way along the well kept streets of the upper gentry. Through the windows he could see many meals being catered to finicky diners. Looking in his satchel he found a warm roll and he ate as he walked. At the end of the street, he had a long view over the streets of Basilius. The city was designed as a spiraling ziggurat. The upper levels were beautiful and well kept but the lower levels seemed dirty and dismal. In a moment he had found the familiar landmarks from the evening before. Turning south he headed toward the stable yard several tiers beneath him. Soon he found himself among a lighted street of shops and grocers. The owners were putting out the last of their customers and leaving the shops tightly locked they made their way along the cobbled walkways. Further down, in the lowest levels of the ringed city the sound of raucous laughter and threads of fractured song filtered into the night airs. Smiling women looked down from the windows above the main hall waving to him as he passed. A group of men waited outside the door, smoking long pipes and sharing a bottle between them. Kiel hastened by, keeping his eyes to the path beneath him.

The gates of the stables were locked when he arrived. He rang the bell upon the post and watched through the cracks. The lantern bobbed its way through the paddock and Kiel recognized the hobbled gate of elderly livery man.

Volos greeted him warmly. "So you survived your first night among us, eh young sir." he grinned "Are your virtues still intact?"

"I suppose they are as intact as they ever were." he answered lightly, "However, I did find it necessary to escape the company of our host. He seems a most peculiar man, with most peculiar habits"

"Many of Basilus choose peculiar habits." Volos replied, looking over the settling night, "And you must trust me when I say that stranger things roam our streets than the pathetic Argut. So I advise you to take care, young Kiel. I have seen what they like and they are clever. So clever you might not be aware when they set their eye on you."

"What is it you know that I do not Volos?"

"I know no secrets lad. I am only man but a man who watches much and speaks little during unsettled times. And times are the most unsettled in Basilus after the sun sets." he answered looking up toward the three towers that stood high above the city. "Late, into the night, strange lights will pour from that peak." he said pointing to the center structure. "And strange sounds come as well. The horses hear them and it seems I can hear as they do. I suppose you might even call it a gift. But let us get to business now and see to your ponies. That is why you are here? Right Master Kiel?"

"Yes sir. I am here to see to our ponies." he replied wondering what Volos had on his mind as he followed him into the stable.

As he had expected the horses were well cared for and after he had checked their feed and looked to the care their feet he returned to Volos. He found the crippled caretaker comfortable in backmost part of the stable. He was sitting in an ancient rocking chair with his feet near the fire, sipping a mug.

"Would you like a taste of this?" he asked his guest graciously, "Over the years I learned quite a lot about the nature of grains. I make a good brew, you can be assured."

Kiel agreed that likely he did and sat down upon a stool next to him with the chilled cup in his hand.

"Go on now. Try it!" encouraged Volos, "Tell me what you think."

Kiel tasted the draft. The beer was smooth and its color almost black. "It is good Volos, some of the best I have ever had." he replied taking another deep drink. "Maybe you could share your recipe with me sometime."

"So you are looking to apprentice? Then surely you must realize the knowledge of a perfect brew can not passed on hastily."

Kiel laughed, "It would be an honor, but I fear I am not the man to do it. I hope we will not linger too long in Basilus. We made much progress today."

Volos turned to face him and Kiel noticed once more the strange look in his face. "Progress, so you say. Long to wait. Hmmm, what is your errand here Master Kiel?"

"I have said too much," he thought allowing no expression to stir upon his face, "I have come with my Master to seek medical advice. Some of our clan has stricken with a strange disease. I expect we will return to our lands as quickly as we are able." he replied taking another sip from his mug.

"Oh." he answered staring into the flames, "Our Dowerymen do

186

not concern themselves with the people of the lower tiers. The folk here wait weeks, and sometimes months, for their aid. I am surprised they are helpful to you at all."

"As yet they have not been, though today we worked with the help of one of their students. She showed us how to find what we need in the Libraries."

"Then you are lucky indeed. You have an air about you, Master Kiel, something familiar. Have you ever visited Basilus before?" he asked.

"No. No I have not." he answered, feeling the old man probe his thoughts.

Volos studied his face for a moment, "Where is your home Kiel?"

Kiel felt himself shudder as he told the lie that must be told, "The greenlands to the north, Volos. Our country is lush in the summer and quite cold in winter."

"My mother's folk are from the north. Maybe this is what I see about you." then he smiled, "and I also see that your mug is almost dry. Let me fill it." and he poured until the froth spilled just slightly over the top.

For hours they drank Volos' brew and talked. The night had grown old when they made their final rounds about the barn. The air was sharp when the old man took him to a smaller stable set off from the main barn. He made a soft whistle as they drew near and his sound was met immediately by a low whinny.

"This is Valraven. Come closer. He will not hurt you." instructed Volos as the great black horse pressed his wide chest against the rails. "He is the pride of my house" he continued, "and he has fathered some of the finest steeds of Basilus.

Kiel stroked the soft muzzle. The horse widened his nostrils and his warm breathe smelled sweet with grain. "What a beautiful creature, Volos. So he is yours and not just one of the keep. Where did you get him?"

"He was a wedding gift from my wife's folk. A noble dowry indeed. In her land, horses are thought to carry the souls of those recently dead. They are sacred creatures, believed to be the bearers of both sorrow and hope."

"I did not know you have a wife, Volos."

"I have no wife. She left this world, along with my infant daughter, twenty years back. Her name was Lona. It was she who taught me how to understand these beasts. Still as I work among them, I can hear her voice."

The horse shook his head smartly and pawed the ground.

"Steady lad," he said stroking the glossy flank and then he

hesitated, listening to the quiet. "Come Kiel. The hour is later than I thought. We must return to the fireside." but before they turned to leave Volos broke the crust of ice from Valraven's watering trough. "There old friend. Have your drink. I will be back before the sun." and he gave the horse a final pat.

The freezing dirt crunched beneath their boots. Kiel shivered without meaning to do it and Volos' sharp eyes caught his eye.

"So you hear it as well." he said, "I thought that you might be able."

Kiel questioned the man and Volos continued, "Some things I am able to see. They are calling, calling to what they want, Master Kiel. Now is the time when they take what it is that they desire. Look up there. The sound comes from the middle shrine."

Kiel felt the pressure in his head rise uncomfortably as he looked toward the upper ring of the city. A long faceted crystal pulsed with a cold violet light under the night sky. The airs were disturbed and they vibrated with a hum so deep the ears could not truly hear it. It was the body which resonated with the pulse without knowing why.

"What is that sound Volos?"

"The priests are calling the dark spirits to the towers. Come on now. Let us be swift to the stable. We will not be harried there."

Volos pulled the doors shut behind them and they returned to his fire. Volos brought out a small loaf of bread and a bit of cheese. "It would be best not to venture into the streets so late, my friend. There is room in these quarters for several others. Often the younger lads come here to help me in my work. They welcome the time away from their masters." he grinned.

"I am expected back." he replied courteously, "I have dallied too long. I do fear my companions will worry over me."

"That you have lad. This city is a treacherous place when the Umbra pass from the towers."

"They will send someone for me if I do not return shortly. I have enjoyed your hospitality but it is time I find my way back to Argut's Inn. " he answered, "Do not worry, Volos. I can keep out of trouble's sight."

"As I said before, I know what they like. If you have not already noticed there are few lads of your age in these streets. Believe me, they will have an eye out for you."

"I will be fine." Kiel replied, rising from his chair and brushing the crumbs from his lap. "I will come back tomorrow. To check on the ponies, of course."

"Do you have your sword?"

"I have it." he answered pushing back his cloak and revealing the blade.

"Then keep it out of sight, my young friend," he affirmed, "and stay to the quiet streets. Venture not into the places where the chants are raised. I hope you understand me."

"I think I do." he answered, wondering once more at his over-concern. "Thank you for the brew, I will let my companions know what they have missed."

"And they will be sorry for it" he grinned. "I shall expect you again tomorrow, Master Kiel."

"Aye Volos, tomorrow." and he bowed courteously and left the man sitting in front of his fire.

The crystal spire glowed above. Kiel set a quick pace though the uncomfortable dark as he considered Volos words of warning. He followed the better lit lanes and quickly found himself where the houses stood close together, separated by small, well kept gardens. But soon the streets were changed and every home was shut tight, their shutters pulled closed and the gates of the grassy patches sealed with heavy locks. Checking his sword he pulled his cape tightly around him. The road had turned sharply upward. He could hear other voices now calling along the icy breezes. A long row of sleeping shops lay upon the other side of a narrow alley. He slowed down to peer into the shadowy lane recognizing some of the stores from his walk earlier. He thought of the others, looking from the windows and worrying over his whereabouts. The wind howled and its freezing fingers pulled his hood from his head. The hour was late and his ears burned as Kiel decided to take the shorter way, through the dark.

CHAPTER XXI
THE SHADOWS OF BASILUS

Inrih crept down the back stairwell. The fat man was sitting in a chair beside the kitchen door. His swollen chins were spread flat against his chest.

"So I am not the only one who waits up in the night." he thought with some hint of despair. "I should not have allowed him to go alone." he mused looking though the parlor windows to the street beyond, "What is this mischief that spreads through the dark? What is this evil creep that crawls?" he asked the cold window panes as a new unease began to settle upon him and his face grew grim. "No need to answer for this night holds no mercy and I fear I have met this gloomy shade before. Soon the earth-bound dead will not be still in their wormy vaults." he whispered touching the dark cold glass with his fingertips, "they are out there." and Inrih returned to the bed chambers to wake Atyn.

"I did not think we would use Kirkos' maps for these reasons." he mumbled adjusting the map under a dim lantern.

"Kiel has known the interworkings of Basilus." replied Atyn softly, "I am not surprised that would be the one first to perceive Ildabyth's work. It will take every skill we have to find him."

"My sense tells me it was Kiel who was noticed, my friend. I sense he was the one who was sought out and he answered the summons though whether it was by will or by fate, I can not say."

"Fate or choice, either road leaves him in grave danger. Do you know where we are, Inrih?"

"I know where we stand. Now we must find out where he is." and they looked down the broad sloping hill to study the intertwining streets below. They spread their attentions over the sleeping city waiting to perceive the spidery web of intent. Then silent and almost unseen they hurried through the perilous streets of Basilus and they did no slow their pace until they entered the lane of shops.

"He did not return by this way." said Inrih hesitating in front of a dress-makers window.

"And yet he is near" Atyn replied. The ground under their feet trembled and, in the alley just beyond, a living shade passed into the shadow. "There Inrih." he pointed, "What do you see?"

"What do I smell is the better question." he shuddered, and they hurried past the shops to enter the deep gloom of the alley.

"It is colder here." said Atyn, looking up at the sides of the building.

"Go with care. Something watches."

Stepping carefully through the dark they ran their hands along the grainy surface of the bricks and studying the walls for openings.

"No windows nor doors, where then do they hide?"

"In this black hole, I dare not say." answered Inrih softly, "Look here. There is another lane."

"And I did not think this hole could get any blacker. Dare we light a flame?"

But before Inrih could answer a low groan came from down the lightless path.

"What do you think that was?" he asked drawing the small crystal lamp from the folds of his cape and with a sharp snap of the sparking stone a flame burst into life.

"Light our way, little fellow." Inrih whispered to the glow and they made their way toward the sound. The alley was narrow and all along its sides were piled with refuse. The muffled cry grew near and Atyn was the first to see the crumpled figure lying face down among the waste.

"It is a boy." he said kneeling to the ground.

"How badly is he hurt?"

"He is very cold and I think his leg his broken.

Inrih frowned at the twisted shin and covered him with his cloak.

"Put the light up here Inrih. I need to see his face." Atyn asked as he gently pulled back the sticky matted hair. "His head is injured and his nose bleeds."

"I know this lad, Atyn. It is one of the Gorgon's young unfortunates from last evening. He went with Kiel to take the horses to the livery."

"He is in poor shape. Do you happen to have a flask?"

"Of course I have a flask." he said, pulling it from his belt pouch. "But it is strong stuff."

"Then it will be the perfect thing to clean this nasty cut." he said, pouring a draught upon the edge of his coat and gently wiping the gash along his brow. The boy stirred at the sting.

"Lie still."

Thin streams of blood ran through his broken mouth. Atyn put the flask to his lips allowing the smallest sip to pass. "We will bring water as we can." he said softly, "How did you come to this end boy?"

"They are not finished." the boy choked, "The light has not come. We must hurry. Soon it will be too late."

"Too late? What do you fear child?"

"The Umbra. They move in and out of who they will." he cried.

"Calm down boy. Can you tell me where they are?"

"They are all round us." he gasped, "Do you not hear them sing?"

"He is right, Atyn." said Inrih listening to the cold wind blow between the closely set buildings. "I do hear it." and Atyn turned his ear to listen.

"It comes from beneath us." he whispered. "They are drawn to the calling."

"Who boy? Who are they calling?"

"The others. Those with no hope left. I followed my sister here seeking refuge from my master's whip. She was my only living kin but she does not know me anymore. She has become as they are."

"We have got to get him out of here, Atyn."

"Yes but still we must find Kiel. There are still hours of dark left ahead."

"Kiel." the boy groaned, "Kiel is in there. I tried to tell him but he could not hear it. They were all around, stealing his breath and singing his name. I saw as he faded."

'Where did they go child? We need to find him."

"At the end of the way. The opening is there. They dragged him through it. They uttered a chant to breech the wall." and the boy coughed and choked a bloody mouthful. Atyn put another sip to his mouth. "The words are old. I knew then once, at least a part of it. She spoke it aloud. The phrase has not always been evil."

"She? he asked.

"My sister. She is one of them now." and the boy began to shiver.

"What did she say? Can you recall the words?"

"Aye, I can remember it." he answered, struggling to compose himself, "'Manus o terra', was the phase she spoke. Yes I believe that to be right. 'Manus o terra'."

"Hand of Erda." repeated Inrih in the common tongue. "Is that all she said, lad?"

"No, it was but the first part. Then she moved her arms up and she touched the keystone of the hidden arch and said, 'mors janua vitae'."

"Death is the gate of Life." nodded Atyn, "You are right lad, not always has it been an evil phase. But as ever all things hold the intent of the utterer."

"And the Umbra's words hold only death."

"Not if we can hold it back, lad. The door is at the rear of this alleyway you say."

"It is, and so are they. Do you not fear them? If you do not, you are either a god or a fool."

"I am neither boy." answered Atyn, "Stay with him Inrih. I will go for Kiel."

"I believe the boy truly understands the nature of these shades Atyn. Can you do this without me?"

"This is only the first of many trials." he sighed, "The boy can not be left alone. We must choose the least of each evil. I can see to Kiel."

"Take the lamp, sir." said the boy. "It is your only hope."

Atyn took the flame, "I will be back." he said as he turned to go.

He found the dim arch in the end of the alleyway. Speaking the words of the boy had told him he touched the central stone and the solid wall faded into gloom. The unsettling hum echoed through the stony corridor. Strange chants crept from around unseen corners. He kept his pace, waiting for some inward sign to tell him that his companion was near. Uneven stairs bent around damp walls; slanting ceilings and barricaded doors created a tangled maze under the city streets. Still he listened. Through the groans and hums of the shadowy warren he recognized the sound of labored breathing. Atyn pulled his blade from his sheath. Water leaked along cracks giving the underground a smothering air. He ran his fingers along damp wall until he found the keystone buried into the rock. Stepping back, he spoke the words boy had told him and the wall separated slowly. Oily fumes spilled along the floor. Hissing like serpents the mist grew until shadowy ghouls began to pour from the hole. But the flame and the bright gleam of sword of Atyn's sword would not let them pass and the whimpering dark bled back into the cracks between the clammy stone

Kiel was sitting slumped in small chair. His eyes were fixed and a crust of blood was caked along his mouth.

"Fear no more, my friend. I am here." he said placing his cape over bare shoulders. "What have they done to you." he whispered noticing the tight cord binding his waist. In the instant his sharp blade had severed the knot. Atyn caught him as he slipped to the floor. Kiel's warm blood seeped through his fingers,

"Kiel. Do you hear me?" he called, trying to warm his freezing skin, and after a long moment Kiel drew a ragged breath.

"How did you find me? I do not even know where I am."

"I had some help. Shh now. I must see how deep these cuts run."

"It is awful to take a breath."

"Your ribs are broken. Can you rise, if I helped you?"

"I will. I do not wish to linger here."

"Then take a drink of this. It will help you stand."

"Rudra's?" Kiel asked recognizing the flask.

"And Inrih's," Atyn replied, "They are in cahoots."

"How do they come by these awful concoctions?" he sputtered as the fluid seared his throat.

Atyn smiled, glad to see him complaining. "They try and fail, then try again."

'I wonder what Inrih thought of it."

"He was not complaining."

"Not complaining, indeed." he grimaced.

Atyn helped to his feet. "Are you all right?"

"Yes I think so, at least I will be as soon as this room stops moving." he answered as the floor trembled eerily under their feet.

"Take the last of this." Atyn said watching the floor shake. "We need to be out of here." and they left the prison hole to make their way back to the streets of Basilus.

Kiel muttered nonsense as they walked through the dark places. Finally the last gate was opened and the starry night appeared over the alleyway but Atyn kept hid his small relief as Kiel stumbled into the night air.

"It is not that much further to light, Kiel. Steady. Lean on me." he encouraged as the chill wind wailed and the sound of beating hooves filled the night.

"Ohe! Viator!" a voice boomed over the freezing drafts. "Ohe Kiel! Is that you boy?" and a wagon pulled to a stop in the middle of the lane.

"Volos?" Kiel answered, softly raising up his head.

"You know this man?" questioned Atyn looking to the rider.

"He is the stable master." Kiel replied, "He will do us no harm."

Inrih jumped from the wagon's seat and went to help them.

"Your friend does not seem to have fared any better, Nestor." said the older man, as they lifted him gently upon the hay.

"Still we are lucky, Volos. Our fate would have been awful, had fortune not turned her eye to us." said the boy. "Thank you. Your timing is impeccable."

"I should have never let him leave the barns. The night is a dangerous time, particularly when the Priests of Ildabyth are at work. This city has become a strange place."

"Indeed it has." replied Atyn. "And to think it was once so lovely."

The stable master gave him a strange look. "That was long, long ago sir. Even before my father's time. It is funny you should know of it. My name is Volos. I have met your charge, Kiel and your guard, Inrih. Fine men both, I can tell it. You must be Atyn."

"I am." he said with a slight bow, "and I am grateful to find a friend here, Volos. It is a long walk to our lodging. Our wounded would not make it without your help."

"I will take it slowly but their sakes but we must save every moment we can. The dark is still on us."

CHAPTER XXII
TAMIL

Kiel tried to turn over in his bed.

"You are in pain?" said a voice he could not quite place.

"It is hard to breathe." he answered opening his eyes.

"Your ribs are broken. Here now, drink this tea." and a young woman put a cup to his mouth. "It is knit-bone."

"I know you?"

"Yes, just yesterday in the Libraries. I am Tamil."

"What are you doing here?"

"I brought some comforts for you and the little boy."

"Nestor?"

"On the couch by the window. He is sleeping."

"And the others?"

"I am with you Kiel," and Yurah's face appeared next to Tamil. "Atyn and Istah will returned as night falls."

'Try not to stir much," said Tamil.

"How long have I laid here?"

"It is two hours past noon" said Yurah. "You arrived back quite late."

Kiel's face grew distressed, "but I can not stay and be idle. There is much at stake."

Tamil laughed, "And there is little you can do about it."

"I am afraid she is right. You have nothing to do but heal."

"You can rise tomorrow for a bit, if you are up to it. We must wait and see how fast you mend."

A soft knock told her Inrih was at the door.

"Where is Argut?" she asked looking around the big man's shoulders.

"I have sent him to fetch some fresh fruits. He should not be back for some time."

"Does he suspect that Nestor is with us?"

"So far our secret is safe. The boy's life would be forfeit if Gorgun found him among us." Then the great man smiled, "but after I told Argut how catching Kiel's ailment might likely be, he was not in the mood to disturb our privacy. How is he?"

"I am awake Inrih. And please tell me now, besides these broken bones, what other ailments do I bear?"

"Enough to keep the noisy Argut from prying?" he smiled graciously, "It is good to see you awake. How do you feel?"

"I have been better," he answered.

"And you could have been much worse. Those foul creatures

intended you no kindness. If it had not have been for Nestor we might not have found you in time. Do you remember anything?"

"I remember nothing before Atyn." he sighed.

"You are talking too much Kiel. You must rest." interrupted Tamil pouring a small amount of powder into a scrap of parchment. "Place it under your tongue and hold it for a moment. It will take away your pain." she instructed, folding the paper in half. Kiel made a face as she poured it in his mouth. "I know it is bitter. Hold it there just a moment. All right. Do not choke on it. Here, have another sip of tea. It will not take long."

"Remedies are hard." Kiel sputtered as the bitter dust spread through his mouth, "but at least it does not burn." he complained, looking at Inrih and taking another sip of his tea.

"You could come to appreciate that burn, Kiel. You can even grow to like them, over time." said Inrih.

"Too much sampling of your own recipes have left your senses altered. Tastes can become scorched from too much use, Inrih?"

The big man did not answer but chuckled to himself as he watched for Argut's return.

Tamil pulled back his sheets and began to inspect the bindings around his sides. "Shhh now. Lie still." she told him sternly. He was miserable the entire while as she checked the wraps and felt under his arms for swelling but as she was finishing Kiel realized the ceiling above his bed had begun to wave, "The powder; I think it is working." Was the last thing he heard.

Yurah watched his steady breathing and though he seemed at peace she perceived a frailty clinging to his skin. She reached out and touched the hand that lay outside the blanket.

"It is not the cracked bones that concern me most. He has been with the Ildabyth's ghosts and they do not ruin with ordinary weapons. It was their sound that broke him." Tamil said softly, pressing into her worries. "He is too weak to remember it but they were trying to make him as they are."

"The Umbra did this?" she replied, remembering the morbid hurts of Tristan's folk.

"Yes, they were intending take him and use him, like they do the others."

"And Nestor?"

"Nestor is not yet of age for their fight. They had left him to die. The Umbra take mostly young men and only the soundest of the women. The shades never take the old and never take the children."

"Why? What do they want with them?"

"Alas I fear I know too well the purpose of the nightly raids. Ildabyth's priests are building an army. They use their spells to create the Umbra. They shape the creatures from the elder youth of Basilus. Just as they are entering their physical peaks, they find it easiest to bind them to the shadows. And of late these unfortunate souls have been armed with strange new weapons. Kiel is the type they seek. He was drawn to them, like a moth is drawn to a flame." she said glancing to Inrih, "And now they have been inside of him, and he inside of them."

"How did you learn these things, Tamil?" asked Yurah.

"My benefactor is a blind man. He teaches me and in return I serve as his eyes and hands. I am in held in their confidence, of sorts; though they pay little heed to me. But all too often now I have heard the excited whispers of the Priests of Ildabyth." she explained grimly,

"Over the years my benefactor has grown quite bitter from his loss and as those days have passed, his activities have caused me more and more concern. The Priests and the Dowerymen trifle with the most sacred of things. Last night I knew they would work their spells once more. I can not sleep when they set to it. I know there is little time left to act. What is valued in my homeland is quite different than what is valued in Basilus. My people do not seek to prevail over another's free spirit. I am free-born daughter of wise women. I was still a child when I was taught the natural powers contained within the hand and eye. Though our conversations were brief yesterday, I sensed that your company might grasp some of these more noble truths." and then she looked deep into Yurah's face, "But hope in Basilus is in short supply and as the troubled night held no rest for me, I found myself wandering in the dark. The Fates must have guided me for I happened upon your companions returning from their errand." and she adjusted the coverlet over Kiel's bruised shoulders.

"You must understand. It is treason to meddle in their designs. The people of Basilus have long lived in fear and there is little that can be done about it. When I witnessed this quiet rescue a cloud was lifted from my heart. I can put my greater duty aside no longer. I shall help all I can. The works of the Towers must cease. All who linger within them have become the darkest of conjurers, draining the world of her goodness to suit themselves. They will destroy everything that has ever been fair and lovely to look upon. By all the powers of Vac, the mother spirit of my homeland, these hands are yours to wield." and she held out her upturned palms and a light glowed from them.

"But you put your life in danger by helping us." spoke Inrih, gazing at the radiance that gathered about her hands.

"There are greater dangers than the death of a body. I am sure you understand this, Inrih. Likely you understand it better than do I."

"I would hesitate to put my understandings before your own, Lady Tamil. Your essence shines from within you." he replied.

"As does your own, Inrih." she answered kindly. Nestor stirred on his couch and the big man kneeled next to his bed.

"How is your head, boy?"

"Not so bad." he replied, trying to moisten his bruised mouth with a dry tongue.

Yurah filled a glass. "It is only water." she assured as she put it in his hands. "Are you hungry?"

"Not enough to eat."

"Then I will make you a broth, boy." replied Inrih glancing to the street. "If another will watch the window?"

"I will do it." answered Yurah, positioning a chair to hold long view of the road, "We can talk while we wait."

"Kiel will not wake for sometime yet," said Tamil "And Argut likely has a goodly supply of kitchen herbs. I know some blends that should ease them further."

Inrih smiled, "I will be glad of the company, Lady." and quietly they left down the back stairs.

Yurah took the empty glass from the boy's hand and helped him to adjust his broken leg amongst the pillows. "Is that all right?"

"Fine. I am fine." he said shyly. Yurah smiled at his awkwardness.

"It is safe. No one will hurt you here."

"Yes ma'am," he answered casting his eye away from her gentle face, "but that is not a situation I am accustom too."

Yurah did not reply. She reached up and pulled the curtain back, allowing a ray of light to fall across his bed and she felt the boy wince.

"Does the light bother you, Nestor?" she asked.

"It seems to burn." he answered wearily. She leaned over to close the drape but he put up his hand to stop her, "No Lady. Leave it. I will not fear the sun." he answered just as peculiar whisper rushed through the room.

"Did you hear that sound, Lady?" Nestor asked, wide-eyed.

Yurah put her hand to the hilt of her blade not sure how to reply. Nestor did not seem to notice. "Strange my dreams have been. It was likely just the wind" he said to the window, "Will Kiel be all right? I thought for certain he was done."

"No lad, he is not done. He is resting." she assured him handing him the glass, "He will be able to speak with you when he wakes."

"I owe him much. He stood up for me before the guardsmen." he said looking admiringly over to where he lay. "I warned him what end his rashness might bring, but he did not listen."

"And it seems you follow his steps. Venturing into the dark without aid, it appears to me that you hold much in common with him."

Nestor's brows perked up, "I was only doing what was necessary, Lady. Courage is not a thing I have ever known."

"Courage is more the doing of what is necessary than it is anything else. Likely you understand it better than you realize." she smiled and sniffed the air. "It seems they are cooking something downstairs."

"Something quite nice by the smell of it. I might be hungry after all."

It was not long before Tamil and Inrih brought up a large platter of toast and warm broth. Nestor ate his share slowly and when he had finished he was filled with questions.

"When do you think Kiel will be up?"

"Kiel should mend quickly, once he sets his mind to healing. He is of a different fiber than most?" answered Inrih.

"I have noticed it. There is something rare in him." Tamil mused looking at him as he slept. "And yet he keeps himself so guarded, somewhere so far away. He is not what he seems." then she laughed, raising her eyebrows astutely, "as none of you are quite what you seem. Someday you might tell me the whole of your stories."

"There will be time for all of it," Inrih answered looking down the street, "We must wait until we are all together."

"Yes, there were two more." said Nestor, "A tall man and his lady. Where are they?"

"They are at the Libraries working on our problem, lad. We have no time to waste and error we can not afford."

"If error you can not afford then how do you plan to keep me hid here? I know Argut. He is a gossiping man and he will tell any tale for a price."

"Volos will come as the twilight falls. You will accompany me to my quarters. The others of my block know I am partial to the street orphans particularly if they are sick or wounded." Tamil explained. "I have taken them in before. They will allow me my 'conceited impulses' as they put it. You will not be bothered there." then she frowned watching Argut plod into the yard with his bag of fruit. "We will find a way to slip past him."

"We must keep our voices down," said Inrig looking over her shoulder, "He enjoys listening through keyholes."

"How much longer before Atyn's return?" replied Yurah,

"Just as the sun is to set." answered Tamil, "I sent them to search a most ancient part of the Libraries. The language spoken in the ceremonies of the Priests is said to be kept there. It is the most ancient of all worldly tongues. Those sounds contain the secret of combining intention with form. It will be important when we are ready to stand against them."

"Stand against them! You cannot mean it! What madness has come upon you?" Nestor interrupted. "Stand against the Priests of Ildabyth? Our only hope is to flee them, not to fight them!"

"There is no hope in flight, lad." said Inrih gently, "A moment of reckoning awaits. We must be ready when it comes and that, my young friend, is the only hope that remains." And from the stairwell beneath the kitchen door slammed shut.

CHAPTER XXIII
THE KINDNESS OF STRANGERS

The evening light was stealing the color from the skies of Basilus as Atyn and Istah made their way back to their companions. Stubborn leaves rustled in a worried dance, bearing the threat of sudden change in their rattling voices. Atyn settled back and looked to the first stars.

"What secrets dare you tell as this dark night falls?" he asked silently, drawing his mind to the place between worlds. In an instant a mountain vista appeared and a song filtered to his waiting ears. He listened for a word of counsel.

"I have been waiting." A voice said and he turned to see the Malkian standing next to him.

"What is it, my friend?"

"There is something you must see." answered Mqttro, gesturing to the layered realities.

Atyn looked down from the middle place to see a shadow of a man walking along the edge of a brackish fen. A broad green-glade was wreathed by fierce mountains shrouded in sparkling snow. A wild river flowed between the rock and meadow. Its frothing head, enraged and elated, following a path to the sea.

"What is this place Mqttro?"

"These are the lands of Iao."

"And who is there; walking in the fenland?"

"It is Kiel."

"But Kiel lies in Basilus, mending from his hurts."

"Yes, his body rests in Basilus but you must understand his plight Atyn. All wounds must mend from the inside to the out. The origins of these injuries began long ago.'

"I know he carries the burden of regret, Mqtrro and I know that memory must grow more acute if he is to recover.

"Indeed, it is so." the Malkian agreed, "Listen now. It has begun."

Atyn turned his ear to the faraway place and a sound, filled with longing, began to move between the land and sea.

"The voice within is his true strength, though he has yet to understand it." said Mqttro softly.

"It is beautiful." Atyn answered, listening as the delicate song rising from the valley.

"He is calling to his past; and to every call will come an answer." and as the Malki spoke, Atyn saw a tall figure coming from the mountains. The man walked more swiftly than the river did run.

"That is Iao who goes to meet him." Mqttro continued to explain. "He knows him well, though ages have past here since the last time they laid eyes upon each other."

The song became more bittersweet as Iao approached the mouth of the river. The sorrowful notes hung in the air like bits of ice and after a long moment another voice joined with him. Lingering at the edge of the riverbed they studied one another, the despairing shadow and the flaming father star and the sounds of the two songs blended in every lovely detail.

"You have returned." was the message sent.

"It is necessity that has drawn me." came the grim reply.

"So it would seem." acknowledged the man, standing now a head and shoulder above the boy, "You are injured."

"Another circumstance of my own making."

"Such things can be mended."

Kiel did not answer and the song faltered.

"I can draw away the shadow that binds you. Such things have no power in my world. Come closer and be whole again."

"But I am no longer of your world, Iao. I left this place long ago and have done nothing but damage since. I am a shade, only a ghost of what I might have been," he said casting down his eyes, "I am not a man."

"You are like a son to me Kiel. Lose your fear and discard your loathing. Come closer and be whole once more." and as Iao's hand gently touched his brow a warmth flowed. The shades of gray that shrouded Kiel's form began to glow. A light filled the marsh and when it had faded, Kiel was gone. The mountains and the sea of Iao's Lands dimmed from sight.

"He has mended him, at least in part. It is a gift to your advantage."

"But will he remember this dream?" wondered Atyn,

"Memory will linger as he returns to his form. Iao has done what he can. It is Kiel who will finally remake himself."

"We will care for him, Mqttro as if he is our own."

"Indeed old friend, Kiel is a part of your world now, ever-entangled in its burdens and its choices. But none of that changes his origins. Kiel was born of Elder Stars just as Yurah and her sisters, the Pleiades. The turning point of this little realm is part of their path. Distant eyes are upon us. Look to Raldaban of the East. He shall lead them true."

"I will remember it, Mqttro." he answered as the Malkian fade from sight.

The carriage turned the corner. The lights of the Inn's long porch were blazing. The fat innkeeper was pacing up and down and when they pulled up to walkway, he ran to meet them.

"Have you found it?" he cried, running to meet them, "Please say you have found the cure I need. My fair house reeks of illness. I am not well! Not well at all!"

"Not well at all?" replied Atyn, "What do you mean?"

"My stomach! My head! That is what I mean!" Argut wailed miserably, "Ever since Master Kiel has become stricken with this disease I can do nothing but fear my own house. I have not be able to find a moment of peace."

"Oh, well then, you should take to your bed early tonight. Undisturbed rest is by far the best remedy I might offer."

"Surely you must have another cure! You are a healer, are you not?" he cried. "A powder, a tincture, anything to help me? This will be very bad for business. Very bad indeed. Word must not get out of a catching ailment."

"Do not worry, Argut. We will find something to ease you and protect your affairs."

"I do expect it, of course. After all I have done in good faith for you, Master Atyn. Turn about is fair play and you know I am a fair man. A very fair man!"

"Yes, certainly I do but being out here in the chill will not help matters. You should get inside Argut and have a cup of warm tea."

"I should go inside. I am catching a chill. Oh my. This is upsetting. Most upsetting!"

"You go in, Argut." said Istah. "I will fetch your tea and I believe I have a powder in my luggage that will help you. I will bring it to your chambers."

"Sweet lady." he said, bending down to kiss her hand lightly. "I will be waiting. It is warm inside and it is so cold out here. So very, very cold." he whined as he hurried through the door, leaving them standing next to the carriage.

"Shall I come back at the same time tomorrow?" the driver questioned.

No sir, leave it to us to reach the libraries." Atyn answered promptly, "I have other errands. We will be on later in the day."

"Very well, then." smiled the man, happy to have his morning free. "I will be waiting at the library stair at dusk."

"So you will see to Argut?" said Atyn watching the cart roll away.

"I have a sleeping powder." answered Istah "That should help with his fretting."

"I wonder what Inrih told him to make him so nervous."

"I would not venture to guess," she smiled. "but it certainly has scared him off from his eavesdropping.

"Come lady, we must go find out." he said taking her arm. "And I am certain that Argut's fire will feel good to us."

Yurah was waiting as they climbed the stairs. She took Istah's satchel and looked inside.

"Those are the texts that Tamil asked us to find. They were not easy to come by. How has it been here?"

"Uneventful. Argut has kept away from these upper floors and Kiel has slept for the most of the day."

"And what of Nestor?"

"He is resting too." Yurah answered opening the chamber door. Tamil eyes widened when she saw the satchel. She took the bag and immediately opened the heaviest book of the lot. Knitting her eyebrows, she sat down on a couch she began to read along with her finger.

Atyn walked to Kiel's side. Gently touching the palm of his hand to mid-brow he murmured a slow rhythm over his head. Inrih pulled the curtains almost closed and kept his eye set to the small crack that looked over the street. Yurah leaned against the threshold and waited.

Istah began to read over Tamil's shoulder. "Oh my, I had already forgotten about Argut. I promised him a cup of tea and a potion. He is expecting me any moment." she exclaimed.

"I can see too it Istah." answered Yurah, glad for something to do. "Tamil will be filled with questions when she pulls her nose from that book. I will make sure Argut stays put downstairs."

"Very well then but bring this with you," Istah said, pulling a vial from the pocket of her luggage. "It will solve at least one of our problems for this evening." Yurah took the bottle from her hand and shook the powdery substance inside. "It has no taste." Istah explained, "Put it all in his tea. He will be sleeping before the hour has turned."

Yurah heard Kiel stir as she passed by his bedstead and an impression of a rushing river poured into her mind. She lingered at the top of the stairs hearing the river's song carry into the room. She could see what Atyn was doing. He was drawing Kiel back to his body and she wondered where he had been.

The potion worked just as Istah said it would. Carefully she took the cup from Argut's chubby hand and left him snoring peacefully. Returning to the kitchen, she poured her own cup and, while it steeped, she wiped down the table board, wondering where Argut's usual servants had been all day. A soft knock came at the door and through the glass she could see a tall man. He was well-built though no longer young.

"It is all right, Yurah. That is Volos. We have been expecting him." said Atyn hurrying down the stairs. She opened the door and the man stepped inside, dragging one leg slightly behind the other. "Good evening." he said bowing graciously, "You must be the Lady Yurah."

"I am sir. And you are Master Volos."

"At your service." he smiled.

"Everything is almost ready." said Atyn, stepping lightly from the hall, "Tamil is helping the boy dress but I need to know if you could carry one more in your carriage this evening?"

"I can certainly. Who else will be coming?"

"Kiel. He is awake and well enough for a short ride. Tamil has offered to tend them both," said Atyn, "I think he will be safer further away he stays from Argut's waggling tongue."

"The innkeeper is a dangerous man and he is no idiot when it comes to keeping his pockets, or his belly full. But hurry up now, I feel a storm brewing from the north. We could see the snow by morning."

A spidery line of frost crept about the edge of the window glass. The moon was fading under a deep gray cloud as Inrih's heavy steps came down the stairs. He was carrying Nestor and Tamil was close behind him. Wrapping the boy in blankets, they settled him in the carriage.

"The ride could be difficult for you, Nestor. I fear your leg will know every bump between here and my apartment." Tamil said fussing over the boy.

"Volos' knows every rut in Basilus, Tamil. I doubt my leg will notice any bump at all."

"Indeed, Volos you are a fine carriage man," she said, smiling at the horseman. "may the journey will be quick, and safe."

"Over the years I have become able to smell trouble. A gift I acquired from the friends, I suppose." Volos grinned warmly and scratching his pale horse behind the ears, "It is most fortunate that the moon hides her face tonight. The Umbra will sleep and the tower will not summoning up more trouble. We should not be bothered and besides, I have known many of these guardsmen since they were just lads. See to your patients without alarm. Strange as it might seem, there are still those in this world that can be trusted."

"Trust is a strange sensation to me." Tamil answered softly as a beam of lantern light spread over the yard, Atyn and Inrih were helping Kiel through the garden walk just as the first flakes of snow drifted silently to the ground.

He was ghostly pale, and Yurah could feel the pain that rushed through him as if it were her own. He did not mention his discomforts but joked with Inrih instead.

"Will you be tucking me in my bed again tonight?"

"All you need do is ask, Master Kiel. I have a pocketful of remedies that could set you back on your feet in no time at all. We might just have to try out a few. You know, just to see which one works best."

"Well now, really." Kiel stuttered. "I can always send word if I am in need."

"Ahh then, you are trying to be rid of me? Not so fast, my hobbled friend, I am going with you tonight and I will make sure that you are both properly settled and tucked before I return."

"Well then I am a lucky man. But could I ask you for just one more favor my generous friend. Would you mind leaving your pocket of remedies home? It would be wrong of me to become a burden."

"A burden! You are light as a feather and sweet as a lamb. I have never considered you a burden, Master Kiel."grinned Inrih. "Actually, I have come to think of you more as an endowment, if you know what I mean."

"An endowment? Humph, well that was certainly nicely said." replied Kiel, "But alas Inrih, I fear you are too sweet-tongued for me to match wits with tonight. I will consider myself as "safely kept" for the time being and I hope someday I may return the kindness."

"You shall be on your feet soon enough." Inrih answered, gently placing his hand on Kiel sore shoulder. "Do not despair."

Kiel smiled up at the big man. "I will be fine." he told him and if it were not for the cold shudder that swept through her heart, Yurah would have believed him.

"I would like to come with you." she heard herself saying aloud. "I can care for them while you are about your daily errands, Tamil. Who can say how long it will be before either can move freely about. You do not need me loitering about in the library halls, pretending to be something I am not. Besides Nestor can barely walk and someone needs to keep an eye upon Kiel."

"Someone does indeed." agreed Inrih, "Indeed you are a lucky man."

"Yes Inrih, I suppose I am." he answered pressing his troubled thoughts of the night's ride into her mind, "It suppose I am."

It took Yurah only a moment to fill a traveling sack and soon they were on their way. As Volos had said, any guardsmen they met nodded an amiable greeting and allowed them to pass unhindered. Tamil's apartment was located upon the second tier and just outside the Academy Walls. The well-kept buildings surrounded a common garden and the fresh snow was beginning to cover the benches and walkways.

"Take the carriage around to the back." gestured Tamil, "There is a patio there and my door is not far from it. We may slip in unnoticed, if our fortune chooses to hold."

Volos followed the signal to the rear of the building. Pulling the horses to a stop, he grabbed up the bags. Inrih already had the coach doors open and quickly the big man gathered Nestor up in his arms and hurried after Tamil. He was back in moment and found Kiel waiting against the side of the carriage.

"All right then, suit yourself." he said cautiously, taking the bags from Volos. "It is the first door down the way."

Kiel slipped his arm over Yurah's shoulder and he leaning lightly against her they followed Inrih through the door. Tamil showed him the small room he and Nestor would share. Nestor was propped upon some pillows and seemed no worse for the ride but when Kiel sank down upon the edge of bed, his hands trembled. He clenched his fists to hide it.

"I will make you something Kiel." Tamil said with some concern. "Be comfortable. I'll be but a minute."

"It is more than just broken sides." Yurah said softly after Tamil had left, "I can feel it. Your pain creeps under my skin."

He looked up at her, troubled by her abilities to read into his nature. "It is not my body that pains me." he answered finally, "This pain hovers here, just a few inches above my chest. Sometimes I can almost touch it. I do not understand what is happening but something I can not see is crushing me."

"I can not understand it now either." she replied, helping him pull off his boots. "Take some rest now. They will not come for you tonight." and all the while she settled him into bed, the scabbard was murmuring a forgotten rhyme, in a forgotten tongue.

Tamil returned with a large tray filled with steaming cups and bowls of herbs. She smiled approvingly when Kiel raised it to his lips and then went to tend to Nestor's bandages.

"Do you ever rest, Tamil? Or do you ever ask for help? There are willing hands here. You do not have to shoulder these chores alone." said Inrih, placing a hand on her shoulder.

"These things are not chores to me." she told him gently.

He did not answer. He understood. And seeing she had all she needed he called to the others. "I think there are few things left in Volos' wagon. I will fetch them and then we must be on your way."

"I will come with you." Yurah answered, "My satchel is there and I would like to say a proper goodbye to the horseman."

"Very well, Lady." he turned then and spoke to Kiel and Nestor,

"Stay to bed and do as she tells you, for it you do not you will answer to me tomorrow."

"We know how to follow orders." said Kiel, "Besides, we have little else to do."

"Nothing but mend." added Tamil. "So drink your cups and say your goodnights. The sun will be up before you know it."

"I will be waiting right here." said Kiel.

"As you should." Inrih said with a bow, "Until tomorrow."

"Save the mess, Tamil." Yurah said, "I will help you clear it when I return."

Tamil smiled and went back to wrapping Nestor's bruised head. The snow was falling heavily. They spoke their brief farewells, promising to each other to be wary and safe. Yurah took her satchel and watched the carriage pull away into the cold night.

"And what pretty thing have we here, trying to catch a death of cold?" said an unfamiliar voice.

She could smell the clean aroma of fresh soap. A tall figure stood just inches behind her. He was wearing a heavy robe and his feet were bare in the chilly hallway. He leaned over and stared at her with his clear blue eyes. Then, placing his hand against the wall, he barred the way to Tamil's door.

"Who do you belong too, Lady?"

"I belong to no one, sir." she replied curtly.

"Is that so? Then where are you from, stranger?"

"It is no business of yours, Dion. She is a guest in my house and I suggest you dig up your manners, if you could only remember the place you have buried them."

"Oh Tamil, you are such a grouse." he grinned slyly, "Must you always see the bad in me. I was only jesting with the little lady, just trying to help a stranger feel at home. And anyway, she told me she belongs to no one. She might like to let go of your apron long enough to come up to my door. There are a few folks over she would enjoy meeting. Come on now, Tamil. Put down your books. Just for tonight. We will go up together."

"You do not listen, Dion."

"Only because you do not tell me what I want to hear. Try changing your tune and you might find I am not as deaf as you think."

"No Dion. Not tonight and not tomorrow."

"Then the day after." he suggested pertly.

"Goodnight Dion." she answered sharply, "Come inside Yurah. Do not let his nonsense trouble you."

"Yurah." he repeated sweetly, stepping close enough as she passed by that his robe brushed against her own. "Goodnight for now,

Yurah. I will see you tomorrow."

"No Dion." Tamil replied.

"Then the day after." he answered with a tidy bow and Tamil closed the door.

CHAPTER XXIV
THE NEEDLE'S EYE

Snow covered the garden outside of Tamil's kitchen window. Yurah put the teapot on to steam. She had found little sleep during the frosty night, spending its long hours huddled on the couch, watching the white flakes fall. It was Kiel that had kept her worries alive. All through the dark he had tossed fitfully, calling out for folk she did not know, and sometimes he would call out her name. She would go to him then and sit next to his bed and hold his hand. She had waited for him to quiet and the images that tormented him would form in her mind.

Acrid smoke drifted through the corridor. The stone floor was slick with oil. Mournful echoes clamored through the walls. He could not tell which direction the sounds came from so he grasped the gritty stone and stumbled on. Too often he would loose his footing, slipping hard to the oily ground and soon blood began to mingle with his body sweat. Sick with fumes, he dragged himself further down the hole. The walls glowed dimly orange and the heat grew more stifling with every inch. Finally, pulling himself around a corner, he came to the edge of deep cleft. A black mist moaned beneath him. Searching for a way to cross he began to crawl along the edge and after a few moments the ground began to tremble. The shaking grew stronger and he pressed himself against the wall. The choking mist belched from the crack. The canyon rumbled uneasily. He felt his way along the jagged rock, his bloody hands leaving a trail along the stone. Rounding another bend, he could make out a thin bridge stretching through the smoke just ahead. The wailing grew louder as he came closer to the bridge. Swelling into a deafening roar the noise battered the inside of his head. Again he crawled through the smothering fog. The canyon's edge grew brighter as flames began to lick along its sides. The bridge lay just beyond the next bend. Choking on the ash he crept to the edge of the crack.
When he reached the hole he saw a robed man waiting at the neck of the bridge. He was sitting with his back to him, looking down at the flames and rocking back and forth on his heels.
"Hello Kiel," came the strangely familiar voice, "It has been far too long." The shadow hissed as the old man turned to face him. The hollow eyes stared from the wrinkled face. A jolt of terror shot through her just as Kiel cried aloud.

She shook him then and offered a sip of water. He murmured something but he never fully woke and Yurah lost all hope for sleep. The empty eyes plagued her. During the black night she sat with the sword in her lap. She ran her finger along the runes of the scabbard but the whispers of the intertwining letters faded into a mist of confusions. She did not understand the isolation that swept her, and as the morning was gathering she went to the kitchen to set the teapot to boil.

"Are you always up before the dawn?" Tamil asked, standing at the door, barefooted and wrapped in a blanket. Her hair was loose from its braid and the dark ringlets hung to her waist.

"I am always glad to see the morning." Yurah smiled, setting another cup upon the table.

"I will make the toast. And," Tamil winked pulling a covered jar from the cupboard. "I have sweets." Yurah looked inside and selected a sticky cake from the pot. Tamil busied herself about the small kitchen while she sipped her tea. Gathering herbs and powders together, she gave Yurah the day's instructions for each of her charges.

"Nestor has trouble getting about but it is Kiel who concerns me more. How did they pass the night?"

"Nestor was quiet but Kiel's dreams were troubled." she answered, the image of the hollowed eyes still lingering in her thoughts. "I have not spoken with either this morning."

"I would like to look in on them."

Yurah wiped the gooey sweet off her hands and followed. To her surprise Kiel was leaning against the wall and looking out of the window. He looked as if he had not slept at all.

"Good morning Kiel." said Tamil looking him up and down. "How was your night?"

"It was fine Lady," he replied politely.

Tamil did not answer and frowned instead.

"Actually I have had better," he admitted turning his gaze to the snowy garden. A bright sunbeam was climbing over the edge of the tall buildings and suddenly the courtyard burst into light. "but maybe the day shall prove different."

"How is your pain?"

"A little sore." he answered, putting his hand gently to his ribs.

Tamil raised a brow.

"Very well then, quite sore."

"At least I have something to help with that. Your injuries are the work of the Umbra and there is little I can to do about it. I will meet your companions in the Libraries today. Maybe they will find the way to make you whole again, Master Kiel."

"Will you be going with her, Yurah?" he said, idly looking over the court.

"No, I will remain here." she answered, surprised he did not seem to remember, "It is a quiet place and good for healing."

"Let us hope it remains so," replied Tamil, "Running into Dion last evening will likely prove to be a nuisance. If I know him at all, he was up all night with his cohorts. It will likely be late in the day before he drags himself from his sheets. He is very dogged when he wants something and I fear he was quite taken by you Yurah. But let me caution you, do not think of him as only a simple rogue. He keeps true to his work in the Healing House. One day he could prove be a most brilliant surgeon but not for now. For now I believe he cares mostly for himself. Take care if you run into him again," she smiled, "and do not be concerned about offending him. I have come to believe that that is quite impossible."

"I do not plan to go out. It is cold out there." she said following Kiel's distant gaze. Then glancing over her shoulder at the Nestor, sleeping soundly in his tangled blankets, she added, "and there is plenty of work here."

The sound of the tea kettle drew Tamil away to the kitchen. Yurah walked to the window and stood next to Kiel wondering if she should say what was on her mind. He was lost in thought, somewhere in that familiar place she could not reach. In the distance a bell was ringing, the people of Basilus were soon to begin their day.

"I have seen inside your dreams Kiel?" she told him as the ringing faded into the morning. Despair washed over his face. "Do not worry. I am not harmed." she reassured him. "But there is something I need to know. I saw the one you met at the bridge. What is his name? Or can you even remember these things?"

"It seems my memories are returning Yurah. And much I would like to forget, I can not. These dreams are living things. I can feel them crawling inside me." he said placing his hand against the window. "And I fear they are becoming more real than the sun that shines outside this glass."

She took his hand, noticing its coldness. "You should get yourself back to bed. You have pushed yourself too far. Come on now. Lean on me. I will bring more covers."

It was a struggle to help him to bed. His thoughts wandered strangely and for a moment she wondered if he even knew she was there.

"I do not forget you." he told her plainly as he lay down upon the bed. "Alas, I can not forget anything." and he tightened his grip upon her hand and turned his face toward the sunny window. The sun was quickly climbing over the buildings and soon the light spread over the floor to touch his bed. It seemed to comfort him and as his breathing grew even, his fingers loosened from her own. He seemed familiar as she watched him sleeping, so familiar and yet so unreachable. Then she heard Nestor stirring behind her.

"Good Morning, Yurah." he said quietly.

"Morning Nestor. Did you sleep well?"

"I did, Lady." he smiled looking out over the sparkling snows, "It is lovely out. Did it snow all night?"

"Yes," she answered, remembering the silent flakes falling through the dark, "It did snow all night."

Tamil came and together they helped him from his bed. They laid him on the couch and set his breakfast before him. He ate everything, including most of the sticky cakes, and when he had finished he stretched his injured leg as far along the couch as it would go.

"It is itching," he grumbled.

Tamil laughed, "It is healing. You are a lucky one, Nestor. You are mending swiftly. I am sure your suffering will be brief."

"Well I will be grateful for that," he answered, twisting around to scratch, "and if I could just reach around this splint, I would be satisfied."

"Take care that you do not pitch yourself over on the floor." Tamil told him, placing her books into her worn satchel. I must be going. I have an errand to run for my benefactor before I can meet the others in the library. Do not be shy about looking for things you need."

Yurah opened the door.

"And remember, do not let anyone in." she whispered before hurrying down the hall.

Yurah spent the morning playing card games with Nestor. He was easy company but as the day wore on he became restless.

"Do you think we could go outside?" he asked, looking out the window.

"Snow and broken bones, Nestor. That is asking for trouble."

"But it is the first snow and it is so lovely. Just a few snowballs, I could sit on the steps and make them. My leg would have nothing to do with it. I promise you, nothing at all."

"It is more than a broken leg, Nestor. Your eyes are bruised black. And your face, it is cut and swollen. You are not fit enough to leave the couch, and we can not chance anyone else having a look at you.

We do not need to draw attention to ourselves."

"But the courtyard has been empty all morning and besides, no one would notice me there, or even if they did they would not care enough to look twice."

"Then you have not seen yourself." came a voice from the corner, "Trust me, Nestor. You look awful."

"Kiel!" he cried happily, "How long have you been there?"

"Long enough to know complaining when I hear it. Resign yourself to it now, you will be going nowhere."

"He seems almost himself." she thought watching him walk alone to the chair. "Could it be those wicked dreams have lost their hold?"

Kiel sat down carefully and picked the cards up from the table.

"What have you been playing?"

"Here, I will show you. Deal out five." smiled Nestor, forgetting about the snowballs. "Are you ready for another game, Yurah?"

"Not now. Play this one without me. Tamil has left your things in the kitchen. It will not take long."

They spent the rest of the day playing cards. Yurah carefully followed Tamil's instructions and both of her charges, seemed in good spirits. The room became pleasantly warm in the light of the afternoon sun and is not until twilight when Yurah got up to tend the fire. For the first time, all that day, they began to hear other folk moving up and down the halls outside. Laughter and light conversations echoed in the corridor. Out in the courtyard, students heavy laden with books, left their footprints in the wet snow. The new fire had cast a subtle glow across their faces when Yurah finally pulled the drapes closed. Kiel rose and went to the window. Pulling back the curtain he watched the last of the sunlight fade. A shuddering ache moved through his chest and he lingered at the glass, waiting for the pain to ebb. In the patch of sky above, a star twinkled through the naked limbs of a rowan tree.

"Good evening, Raldaban." he murmured, letting the curtain fall.

Yurah had seen Nestor to his bed early but Kiel held no wish for sleep and had refused the painkilling herbs. Pulling his chair close to the fire, he stared into the flames and lost himself in thought. The moon was high when Tamil returned. When she turned the latch, a melody drifted down the hall.

"Who is playing, Tamil?" he asked, stirring from his dream.

"It is coming from upstairs. It must be Dion; or one of his companions. It is not unusual to hear them play this time of the evening. Is it disturbing you, Kiel? I will interrupt them if it is."

"No. It does not disturb me, in fact I recognize the piece. It is a tale of the perfect islands that lie in western seas. The goatherds sing it to the stars when their beasts have strayed away."

"It is strange that you know it, Kiel. A common Loremaster might have trouble placing such an obscure tune."

"I know many songs." he said, looking into the fire.

Tamil paused for a moment and then glanced down the corridor. "Few wander the halls this time of night." she said. "It will do no harm to keep the door ajar. Dion always presumes he has an audience, even if any listen or not."

That night seemed endless. Kiel stayed close to the fire, tending it when the flames grew too low and wrapping himself in his blankets when dread overwhelmed him. Yurah was resting on the couch and he did his best not to disturb her with his unease. Images of faraway stars plagued his mind. He could not sort the thoughts fast enough and disconnected notions would tumble through him, leaving him frustrated and answerless. Then the moments of pain would come upon him. Pain like he had never imagined possible to withstand. He had been set ablaze upon a funeral pyre. His skin was peeling away in sheets and his body fluids were moving through him like steam. But death would never come, only loneliness. Isolation spread through him like a disease. He was empty, with no color or sound to comfort him. But the door to the hall, Tamil had kindly left ajar. Through the night soft strains of melody would draw him back from the waking nightmare. Again he would feel the warmth of the fire and the soft sound of Yurah's breathing was steady behind him.

Tamil had told him some of what they had done that day. They had found their maps and ancient books and would be using the night to study and plan. Part of him had found their news hopeful but deeper he understood more than he dared to say. He knew well the impasse before them.

"How comforting it is to be naive." he mused, tossing a bit of wood on the fire. Glancing to the window he wished the sun would come to claim him and then the music drifted through the door once again. Someone was singing. It was a girl. He wondered what she might look like as he closed his eyes and fell into a dream.

The smoke curled over his boots. The dim glow of the furnace glowered from the crack. The thin stone bridge stretched over the hole and he blinked his eyes to adjust to the light. Along the other side, lay his destination. Someone was calling his name, he knew her voice. She was the one who had called him home so long ago. He would find her and he would bring her out of the burning hole. He began to run. Time was short. His feet touched the thread of stone that led the way over the pit then a cold hand grabbed his shoulder and the fire beneath came to meet him.

CHAPTER XXV
THE DAUGHTERS OF IAO

Iao walked along the edge of the salt marsh on his way back to the river. The tide was ebbing, abandoning its lonely grains of sand about his feet. The foam swirled behind him and he hurried on. The Riverman was waiting. He could hear him complaining up ahead. With a few broad strides Iao climbed the ridge that separated the marshes from the mountain gorge, and from the top he had a wide view of the upland valley. The river poured down the canyon spilling its icy waters into the Endless Sea. He rose up from the edge when he saw his Master there. The Riverman was an ancient thing, who knew no purpose but the one for which he was made. Taking whatever form that suited the instant, he was as rash as he was enduring. His voice trembled like a storm.

"They have been stirred, Iao." he called out. "Her song reaches through the starry river. Nothing will rest. A finishing point approaches."

"All was set into motion eons ago." Iao answered, "But you know this as well as I, old friend. What is really on your mind?"

The Riverman shifted in the stream bed, pulling his watery robes more strongly about him. "Long have I lived upon this edge of land bearing witness to the starry seas. I have seen what is coming. I am your eyes, Iao. Do you not shed a tear for the Little Kingdom?"

"I have shed many tears for the forgotten realm."

"It was greater beings than I who chose to leave the orphan to strive alone." he recollected, "A dear price has been paid for that decision."

"It is true enough and little has changed since. Then, as now, the folk of the Little Kingdom have been fooled by their desires. But this is not a new thing. And though they know it not, they too are part of heaven's game."

"Indeed they are." answered the Riverman, eddying restlessly about the stony edge. "The universe is fated to all of its parts. Erda is no different." Then he looked over the reedy place to where the waters fell into the dark airs of the Endless Sea. "And I am not different either, old friend." he continued thoughtfully, "Past these cloudy headlands and under the deep ethers lies the first dwelling place. If you are willing to allow it, I must return there. The time has come for me to speak with my forebears."

"So this is your dilemma, Riverman." Iao answered with a low bow, "Your leave is granted, my most faithful servant. Indeed it is the pull of Rempha's Waters which shall bring us all to the centering point. You may go as you see fit."

"The moment draws near." he answered slowly as the wind began to rumble in the airs behind him, "The Old One's plea has touched what makes me. I will take my leave before this night has chance to fall." and the faint mist began to fall about his broad shoulders as he pulled himself up higher above the stony bed. "My daughters will tend your shores in my stead. Call upon the Naras if you have need. They are always close. They will aid you."

"Have no concerns for me. Always it has been your fate to serve the Starry Queen. Fare thee well, Varda's son."

The Riverman bent gracefully, his reedy hair touching the waters. A breath of fresh wind swept the filmy mists from his shoulders. "I will return Iao. I will return as soon as the work has been finished. Farewell, old friend and know I shall keep an eye turned your way." The sweet wind descended. She pulled him through Pillars that marked the way toward to the Endless Sea. Casting themselves into the havens, they broke into starry bits and joined with Eradinus to move through the stars.

Deep in thought Iao walked toward home and shortly he noticed that the Riverman's daughters were following. The Naras whispered words to comfort his troubled heart. Night was drawing close around him as he crossed over the bridge leading to his door. Anath was waiting the threshold, holding a lamp in her hand.

"Good evening, father. I have kept your supper warming. Has all gone well?"

"Well enough. I have done what I can. The moment rests in his hands."

"And Yurah? What news of our little sister?"

"A shy child she will not long remain." he answered, a hint of sadness in his voice, "She was born to be a warrior and she will hold true to that cause."

"But does she yet understand the cause?"

"Her mother's sword hangs at her side and its scabbard bears the Gift of the Senzar. But alas, far memory is all but a fleeting dream to those of Erda. It is a difficult road to travel." then he paused for a moment and listened to the sounds of the crackling fire before he continued, carefully. "To understand the true cause of her dilemma is to understand much. The Old One's purpose is enduring and so few of Erda's people ever see more than a glimpse."

"But there are those of the Little Kingdom who do see." Anath answered. "I peered within the eye of such a man. Jove, is the name that lingers. Mqttro brought him here. He is aware we exist. He is now aware of our presence here in Raldabon and he seeks aid in his work. Who is this being father?"

"So you have seen Atyn. He is a true-born child of the Annyd." Iao replied, "He is known to me as the Stormbringer. He is the keeper of the Vanyr. In the beginning it was the Vanyr that were given stewardship of the lands of Erda and the airs of Urdar. Even as Ildabyth tampered with their first good works, they have remained a peaceful folk. They have no love for war and are only called to it when the need is great."

"But war is near. I feel it when I think of her." Anath answered grimly. "My every dream is filled with battle. The shadows are moving deeper into the core of the Little Kingdom. Need is everywhere."

"And that need will be answered too." said Iao, "There is another that stands by Atyn's arm and those folk are rightly warrior born. They are the Asyr and they too are sons and daughters of the ancient ones. They are guided by the old mage, Odyn. The Asyr are ever a persevering folk. For centuries they have sought the unseen knowledge and are not opposed to taking it by force. It leaves them able to do what many can not. Odyn and his Valkyries will prepare themselves for this fight as will their elven cousins, the Drui." he explained thoughtfully. "And there is more too it all than this. All of Erda's races, Asyr, Vanyr, and Drui are bound by blood to Oiolosse. This is why the folk of the Cold Mountain are ever looking past Raldaban in hopes of saving the lost children's children of Niobe."

"Father, how have you come to this knowledge? Have you been using your own scrying glass?"

"I leave the scrying to you and your sisters." he laughed, "In recent days, I have spent my time walking with Doxomedon. We have talked long of her history."

"Well father, what I have seen of her history is most cruel. It is not the severity of the elements, nor the balance of nature's spirits that brings trouble to the little realm. It is the power mongering of men and gods. But above all else father, I have seen a lovely garden, filled with the most incredible things."

"It is the Malkians that care for the Tree that creates the forms of Erda but it is the Vanyr who have loved the nature spirits longer than any of their magical cousins. They understand the severity of her nature and rejoice in the balance it brings. Under their guardianship the rain is sweet and life flourished."

"Do all the Vanyr understand the work of the Malkians?"

"So much has changed since that beginning time. Even the Vanyr suffer from the forgetfulness bred by that realm. Now only the eldest child may converse with the seraphs and the Stormbringer is that one. Yurah travels now with him and I find that most promising.

"But what of Kiel, father? My dreams of him are the most disturbed of all. Often I see him wandering and alone in a deepening shadow. A battle swarms all around him."

'The first war came to Erda long before Kiel's birth. Kiel's betrayals are but part of a larger deception. Never has a tearless battle been fought in her realms of opposites and never has that victory been certain."

"But cycles have turned, and change draws near." Anath answered

"All things change daughter, and we must be able to change with them. This morning the Riverman joined with the Four Rivers of Mundi. The Little Kingdom will face their battle soon. We must be waiting ready when we are called upon to act."

"And how shall help her until then?" she was about to ask but the words did not leave her lips for Tyla and Lyli came storming into the room. Hathor raised his head from the couch and looked at them sleepily.

"What have you done with it now?"

'This creature is not a beast at all. He is Boobach! He takes what is not his. And not because he needs it. Not even because he wants it! His desires are far more shameful. He takes it because he enjoys watching another endure his mischief!" exclaimed Lyli.

"What curious things have you taught this creature Anath? Tell us, what is his true form? Whatever it is, he gives his kind a bad name." continued Tyla.

The cat spread his toes and began to lick between them.

"Hathor. What have you done now?" Anath answered, scratching behind his ears. "though I can not believe it is worth all this ruckus."

"He has taken the Firestones again! We have turned everything upside down and they are not to be found anywhere." Lyli said, glaring at the cat. "He knows where they are. That blameless face does not fool me."

"The Firestones you say." mused Anath. "What would you want with those, Hathor?"

The cat looked over his toes.

"Perhaps he is concerned about what his Fate may hold?" chided Tyla. "But he would need no runes to it that for I am about to show him."

"Be still, little daughters." said Iao, a slight smile lighting his face, "Hathor is twice times both your ages. If he has taken your firestones, he has some reason for it."

"Then we can hope it is a good one." answered Lyli.

The cat turned to the twins, and flipped the end of his tail. He jumped lightly to floor, dashing up the stairs, knowing they would follow him. He passed every flight with the twins close behind and when he reached the garret room he pushed the door open with his head. Sothis was waiting for them. Hathor sauntered up to her and rubbed against her legs.

"You are looking for this, I imagine." said Sothis holding up the pouch.

"The firestones!" answered Tyla, taking it and pouring the runes into her hand to count them.

"Why does he bring you his booty?" asked Lyli.

"I am never quite sure what is on his mind. He carried it too my study and when I tried to take it, he ran away and came up here. I believe he wants the stones to be cast."

Hathor wore a peculiar smile upon his reserved cat face and pitched his tail back and forth along the floor.

"I believe you have guessed rightly." replied Anath. "That whipping tail, it is his victory sign."

"Then I believe that victory sign could use a bit of wrenching." suggested Lyli as Tyla swooped down to grab the oversized cat. Hathor rubbed his head against her chin and began to purr.

"Come now. You can not be mad at that." said Anath, scratching behind Hathor's ears.

"I could be indeed and he deserves every ounce of wrath! He is not to take what is not his to give." answered Tyla, scolding the cat, "But maybe Sothis is right. It is long past time to read the runes. We should see for ourselves the possibilities the future holds for the Little Kingdom. So that would mean, at least for the moment Hathor, you have been given the benefit of the doubt."

The cat looked smug and jumped lightly to the floor. Prancing to the edge of the scrying pool he peered over the edge and pricked up his ears.

"The waters are perfect. When I arrived, the pool was inky black, so I lingered and the Abyss appeared in the mirror." said Sothis, "I have been preparing for the rite since. Clearing away the dust and waiting. I thought he might be bringing you up soon."

"And we followed like sheep to a fold."

"It could be to your benefit, Hathor not to be such an arrogant escort next time." suggested Anath and Hathor lashed his tail.

"He has done his work," said Lyli rolling the stones between her fingers. "now let us get to ours."

The firestones were twenty-three in number and each was scored with a twin symbols. The markings cast a flickering light as she breathed upon them. Along one side, burned the arcane letters of seraphs and upon the other, the symbols of alchemy. Faster she rolled the stones until each letter set alive with a flame of its own. Lyli nodded with approval. "They are ready. We can we begin?"

"When the others arrive." replied Anath looking out the upper window. "I can see their lanterns crossing over the bridge now."

"Is Raeyn with them?" asked Sothis looking into the dark lawn.

"No. I came ahead." said Raeyn. She was standing at the door and Iao went to greet her.

"Raeyn, where have you been? You have not been home for days." exclaimed Sothis.

"The trees have much to say this time of year. But had I thought you worried for me, I would have sent a messenger to ease your mind."

"I can not set blame for this uneasiness. I have only wanted us to be together. I am grateful to Hathor for arranging this gathering."

"He has taken quite a lot on himself. But I would like to know how he managed to bring those two back from the Oiolosse's Mountain." answered Tyla, watching them come down the lane. "Anath, this creature of yours becomes more curious with every season. What are you teaching him?"

"I never gave claim to owning him." she told her, "Hathor is his own beast. He has his own purposes and a will I do not bother to control."

"Hiding under that cat skin will only serve you so long, Hathor." teased Lyli, gently placing her foot on the tip of his tail. "We will understand you soon enough." The cat's green eyes flashed and he scampered from the room. They could hear the door opening from below.

"Off to greet your other guests?" Lyli called after him.

"I will light the candles." said Tyla spreading her hand apart. A bit of flame appeared at each fingertip and she guided the each sylph too its place along the recesses of the chamber walls. When every candle was set, the room glowed with their warm light but the pool in the center remained dark and still.

"Which casting should we choose, Lyli?" Tyla asked finishing the work. Lyli pondered the question still rolling the stones in her hand. Eide and Driin silently took a place near the northern window.

"There are eight of us, Tyla." she reflected, "We could cast for the Nine Worlds. One draw for each of us, if Iao will consent to draw both for himself and for Yurah."

Iao nodded his consent and Tyla continued. "I will set the spheres over the water. It will only be a moment more."

They gathered about the pool as Tyla called the Nine realms from the Ethers of Raldabon. White fire flowed from her open hand as the orbs hovered above the dark mirror.

"The Nine Worlds," said Sothis watching the spheres began to spin. "An excellent choice, little sisters."

Lyli placed the runes back in their pouch. "We shall draw in times order." she said holding the pouch out to Iao and he drew forth the first stone. He released it into the air and Tyla called it to the first World of the upper triangle. The fiery symbol blazed within the crystal. The light pulsed over the dark pool and outside the night airs became as still as glass.

"Upon the uppermost point rests Ing, of Erda." Tyla said softly, "It is strong spirit. Love and courage. It is the sign of the homeland. It is realm of the Alfyr that rules the Upper Point." And sensing the meaning of the burning sign, Lyli moved on quickly to offer Sothis her choice. The eldest daughter picked from the bag and opening her hand the rune floated gracefully to the second position.

"The Seraph speaks of sudden change." Tyla continued, the pure light of the runes reflecting gently upon his fair skin. "But as yet, courage and potential are not known. The Watery realm will awaken once more, through the power of strength and the pure hand that shall guide."

Her words faded into silence. Anath trembled as she reached out and drew the next stone. The rune rushed to join the third orb and the first triangle complete.

"The Vital Air joins with the upper world." spoke Tyla, holding the spheres suspended by her outstretched hand. "Transformation and revelation are in motion. The power of the Seraph's sign is harnessed through sacrifice. The Sword is wielded in regeneration." and she knit her brow as the words of the Seraph formed inside her mind. "Justice will stand." she said looking into water below her.

Eide then drew from the pouch and sent her stone gliding to the center of the next sphere. "It is Caph." the seer said, as the symbol took hold within the fourth realm. Hesitating, she allowed its meaning to fill her mind before she spoke aloud. "Breakthrough and change are the message the Seraph brings. It is Time's door turning by cycles great and small. Intuition becomes the primary goal." and Tyla turned her eye and signaled the next draw.

Raeyn' crystal hovered in the air, turning itself, end over end, before being drawn to its place in the Fifth Sphere.

"You have drawn Kenaz through Time's door. Its name is Iod in the upper halls. The fifth Realm holds what is known, but not remembered. It is a dangerous world, even if fortunate enough to bear a Seraph sign. So let not faith be lost, for the heart's beacon inspires the way that is clouded by fog. A torch will enter the shadow realm. It is the place where illusion and nakedness are swaddled by mists." then she paused for the words were difficult to utter aloud. "It is the unceasing labor of the Eater of the Dead to harness that power, creating the place where fear begins."

Lyli held the pouch in her left hand and selected the stone with the right. She set the rune spinning sharply on its way.

"The Wrath of the Mother rests in the realm of men." spoke Tyla watching the light burn. "There the testing will be fierce and only the strongest shall prevail against her storm."

Tyla's vision formed in Raeyn's mind. A tempest pounded a legion of mounted soldiers riding along the edge of a mountain road. The ocean climbed into the arms of the storm, swirling and screaming in frenzied gusts. The waves pounded upon the rocky shores until the raging swells forced their way into the jagged cove, descending upon the soldiers and their horses. When the wave cleared the road was empty and not a cry was heard over the wailing winds. Raeyn shuddered and wondered where any hope might lie.

And without moving her arms Tyla lifted her choice from her sister's hand.

"It is Gimel. A fortunate sign. The Seraph stands in the first sphere of the lower three. The creation, and the destruction, are the sign of hope. Every hope rests in the realm of fire, at the point of eternal creation, in the place of flame and the realms of frost." Drawing a deep breath she rested.

"You will make the next draw, son of Niobe." said Lyli. "Your kin shall ever hold their place in the history of the forgotten realm." Driin looked over the pool and noticed still no reflection was revealed in its smooth surface. He considered the relationships between pulsating globes above the mirror and allowed his mind to feel the intentions of the fiery signs. After a moment, Tyla opened her eyes and he pulled a crystal from the bag. The firestone drifted over the black water taking its position among the others.

"It is the Gifting letter," she said in a steady tone, "but it is at odds from what was once intended. Need speaks. Obligation holds balance. The Gift stands opposed." and the fiery letter flashed with shades of orange and blue.

Iao stepped forward to her warning words, ready to make the last choice. His stone rose slowly and took its position within the Ninth Sphere.

"It too is opposed." Tyla said softly, "Possessions won or earned by such great efforts. There is nothing in the Little Kingdom that is made without tears and toil. Failure waits by the unopened door. But there is still hope, hope in remembering that the lowest point is often the key to the uppermost vision. So it is said." she whispered, cautiously she drawing her hand away from the Nine, allowing the stones to hold them above the pool. "So it shall come to pass." replied the others.

And the pool trembled as the vision appeared.

CHAPTER XXVI
A SHADOW COMES TO CALL

Kiel sat alone in Tamil's kitchen. A candle burned in the center of the small table and the dark night crept along the edge of the window glass. The quiet house breathed gently with sleep's rhythm. The Umbra's wounds would leave him no peace and it was only the daylight that gave brief relief from their merciless summons. He had set the window open a crack. The chill air made it easier to keep awake as most of the dark still lie ahead and the thought of dreaming was terrifying. The repeating nightmare plagued him even with his eyes wide apart. The feel of the icy fingers casting him into the pit and the hideous laughter echoing in his skull was an endless torment. He could feel the skin peeling away from his finger bones and fire searing a path from his throat to his belly. He could not faint. He could only feel an endless pain and the remitting despair of self-loathing and wonder why death did never come.

He considered the pattern made by the tea leaves as they lay in the bottom of his cup but thought better of it. His future was not anything he sought to dwell upon. He went to the window and he listened to the night air. Quietly at first he could hear it, someone was playing strings the on the balcony above. He lingered at the glass and then pulled the window closed. Silently he left the apartment to walk in the cold courtyard. Scant bits of snow still lay along the dry grasses. Wrapping his cloak around him he kept to the walk near the building. He waited under the balcony, leaning against the wall while the sound of the lute poured over him. The song was another he was familiar with. The smooth voice sung of Phre, the son of Phtha and Tiphe. It told how his parents gave Phre the task of creating all of nature by casting seed through the Upper Airs to take hold in the earthy ground. His mother kept watch over him through the starry nights, wisely guiding him through the long slow work. Phre listened well to his mother's song keeping the accounts of their discussions upon pure parchment, written in a script that only the illumined could understand. These were the threads of knowledge that drew Atyn to the libraries of Basilus. Hidden within the Arts, and Sciences, and the Ritual of Ceremony, maybe he could find the way to overcome the Priests of Ildabyth.

"And why do you let such false hopes linger, my son?" the icy sound pierced his thought. Kiel did not answer to the familiar voice. Instead he turned his face upward and whispered to the Tiphe, who rested among the lights of heaven. Staring into the silent night, he traced her garments through the paths of stars and after a moment he realized the music had ceased.

"Ohe viator." A voice whispered from the balcony. "Who walks under the Lady's stars? What business do you have with the night?"

"Perhaps the better question is what business does the night have with me." said Kiel genteelly.

"Well answered." came the soft reply. "But that does stay my curiosity well enough."

"Well sir that is the reason you must accept for I have no better one to give. Sleep is not mine to have this evening so I am left at her mercy." Kiel answered glancing up at the stars.

The player laughed, "That I do understand. I am always at her mercy, stranger. But she is a lovely thing, so I do not mind it. But the night is grows colder as we linger and my fingers are to numb to play anymore. Let me introduce myself. I am Dion. And you stranger, you are one of the folk holed up in Tamil's rooms." Kiel could feel his smile from the balcony. "Tamil thinks she can hide things from me. But I have known her too long and she doesn't seem to appreciate that I sleep by the moment and not by the hour. I see everything that happens here." then he laughed again, "But please do not tell her I said so. It would only serve to provoke her and that, in turn, will leave my already questionable honor in further jeopardy."

"Then trust I will not mention it."

"Trust. You throw the notion about loosely, stranger. Indeed your home must be far from here. There are but a few in all the Ringed City who might understand the meaning of that word." he replied playing a simple line along the strings. "but alas it seems there are many hours before the morning and when this sleeplessness is upon me I know I have all night to listen. Why don't you tell me your story?"

"I fear my story has little in it worth repeating but I will say that once I played the lute, and the pipe, though years have passed since I have tried my hand at them, still I recognize the melodies you play. They are the stuff of legends. Where did you learn them?"

"My, oh my. You are filled with such clever answers, stranger. I suppose your past is likely interesting enough but if you choose to keep it to yourself, I will not press you for it. But let me remind you sir, to ask questions without first giving your name borders upon impudence in Basilus."

"Then I beg your pardon. My name is Kiel and I am traveling with a company from the Greenlands. I have injured myself and, for the moment, I am in Tamil's care ."

"Hmmm, well that is interesting enough alone," answered Dion, rubbing his chin thoughtfully, "and the Lady that is with you. Her name is Yurah, if I am not mistaken. She is one of your band?"

"Yes. Yurah is her name and we are traveling together. She serves us as nurse while Tamil is away at her duties." replied Kiel beginning to feel uneasy at his questioning. Dion noticed.

"Tamil has always liked to take in strays. But enough of that for now. It is impolite of me to let a guest stand in frozen drifts and since I rarely bother with sleep I am known to keep a good fire burning. Come upstairs Kiel, and let us see if you can remember how to tune a lute."

Kiel laughed and the sound of it surprised him. "How long since I have felt cheer?" he wondered to himself as he cocked his brow to answer dryly, "I am sure it will all come back to me."

Dion was waiting in the hall. He was wearing a pair of dark britches with a blanket wrapped around his bare shoulders. He motioned Kiel inside and quietly closed the door behind him. Dion's apartment seemed smaller than Tamil's but when Kiel looked closer he realized it was because so many more were lodged inside it.

Dion whispered loudly in his ear, "Everyone fell asleep and I was left with nothing but the balcony. But I will lay claim to this couch once more." and he roused the girl that rested there. "Go on back to my bed, Minn. I will be in shortly." The girl sat up and pushed her dark hair out of her eyes. She was wearing a long wrinkled blouse that did not look like it belonged to her. "You promise, Dion." she said sleepily.

"I promise." he answered, "Go on now. Here and take the blanket. It is colder there."

"Thank you," she said wrapping it around her, "and remember, you promised."

"I did, and I mean it. I promised."

Kiel stepped lightly over a couple that lie on rug near the hearth and noticed yet another sleeper huddled in the corner.

"I like company." Dion explained innocently, carefully stoking the fire. "I get lonely without folks about. But don't worry much about waking them up. They all have had plenty of wine. They should be able to sleep through anything." he grinned, "Now where did I put that other lute." and he began looking behind the couches and curtains.

Kiel played for long time though his fingers went sore quickly. Dion knew many melodies and he sang them softly, taking some care not to wake his guest with rich voice. Kiel chose not to sing. The music reminded him too much of forgotten things so he focused on his strings and the sound of Dion's clear voice. When the first light began to pale over the Basilus, Dion put down his instrument and sighed. "You are a perfect player, Kiel. I feel as rested as a babe who spent the night in his mother's arms. I had no idea that such musicians were bred in the Northlands."

"I had perfect teachers." he answered, carefully laying down the lute. "But Tamil will be worried. I must be going. Time has slipped away."

"Yes, it has. And I still have a promise to keep." he winked playfully, then his face grew more serious, "And after that I have a day's work ahead. Maybe Tamil could meet me in the," but he hesitated. "No, I will not worry her with it. They keep her busy enough with their errands." and as quickly as it had left, Dion's smile returned, "Come back and visit tonight. Maybe you could meet some of my companions when they are more are a bit more seemly." he said placing a friendly hand on his shoulder as he opened the door.

"Well, I might Dion. But I must hurry on. They will be anxious if I am missing when they awake."

"Just blame it all on me. They will understand."

Kiel laughed at the notion. "I do not think you as my argument will sway their concerns. I have given much reason for worry by not being as mindful as I could have been. Harmful things lurk in the dark of Basilus. Take care of yourself, Dion. This is a dangerous city to be at odds with it."

"But we are all at odds with it." he answered in a distant tone, "I will be home as the sun is setting."

Kiel hurried down the stairs. Silently he slipped inside and hung his cape with the others. Yurah was still sleeping on the couch and Tamil was stirring in her chambers. Quietly he went to his own bed and pulling the curtains back he watched the yellow sun creep over the buildings.

When Yurah went to him she noticed he had pulled the bed to touch against the sunny glass. One of his hands pressed against the window and the light was just beginning to spill over his face.

"He seems peaceful enough," she thought though her nagging doubts still peeved her. "I wonder if he slept at all."

"Good morning, Yurah." Nestor whispered from his bed, "How is Kiel?"

"He is sleeping. Come on, I will help to you breakfast."

"I can do it myself." he answered swinging his leg over the edge of the mattress. "I do not wish to keep Tamil waiting."

"I think it is Tamil's sticky cakes you do not wish to keep waiting."

The boy grinned and picking up his crutch he took himself to the breakfast table. The cakes were set out on a clean white cloth and Nestor's grin grew even wider when he saw them. He sat down and waited politely for Tamil to finish her work.

"Thank you, Tamil." he said when she pulled her chair to the table. "Your breakfasts are so delicious I can hardly wait to wake up."

"It is good to have someone so gracious to break my fast with, Nestor." she smiled, "I noticed you were handling that crutch rather well. How are your legs this morning?"

"They hardly hurt at all. Maybe I could go out for a walk today?"

"It is still icy. You can not risk a fall."

"The courtyard is not too icy. I could stay on the walk and besides, Yurah would be with me. She would see that I did nothing foolish."

"Let me think about it, Nestor. Your face looks better. You might not scare off any that might chance to look at you."

"Oh Tamil, there is not many things in this world that fear me," he answered, sounding a little sad, "except maybe this little sticky cake." and he scooped up another and stuffed it whole in his mouth.

Yurah laughed and handed him a damp cloth, "You have more on your face than in it, Nestor."

"Eat all you will, Nestor. Healing is hungry work. But watch yourself if you do go out." said Tamil rising up from the table and placing her plate in a basin of water, "Stay to the walkways and do not leave the courtyard."

"I will do it, Tamil. I can take care of myself."

"Yes, I know you can, Nestor." she said. "There is plenty of food in the cupboard when Kiel wakes. This habit of sleeping during the day at least will give his body time to mend."

"It is not his body that is worrying me." Yurah answered, looking in her empty teacup.

"It is not what worries me either." she answered, leaving the kitchen to gather her books from her study desk.

Yurah followed after her lowering her voice, so Nestor would not hear. "The light helps him but when it fades he fades with it. He fears to fall asleep."

"He is the most vulnerable then. It is more than a mortal wound he bears. The Umbra did not seek to kill him. They drew themselves into him and broke him apart from the inside. There were trying to make him like they are." answered Tamil, "I have been looking into it as I can. Baebys is such a lazy man and he pays little attention to what goes on in his libraries. But as the Fates would have it, Atyn and Istah have located the maps that show the Ildabyth's labyrinths connecting the lower realms. It appears that certain words must be intoned to open those doors. But here our luck has ended. The secrets of those sounds are well hid. I am beginning to believe that such things were never scribed and maybe the deeper secrets of the lower realms are only be passed directly from one ear to another." she explained pulling the straps of her satchel tightly closed. "but this search, it is not futile. They have found ceremonies for a plethora of things and some few may prove helpful to Kiel. I am concerned when I hear him wandering about like a ghost in the dark."

"He sits in front of the fire most of the night. I hear him whispering to another I can not see," she said, recalling the dream she followed him into.

"Dion is often called upon to handle the injured and the unlucky of the lower rings. The Dowerymen do not serve the common folk. They leave that work to their senior apprentices. I would not be surprised if he has seen the Umbra's handiwork. Dion spends many of his nights in the Healing Houses of the unfortunate ones."

"He is healer then and not a rogue?"

"He is both, and jaded by either standard." she answered pulling on her cloak, "He never had the stomach for the pomp of the Dowerymen but neither has he the wisdom of the sage. When he was younger he would despair at this cruel city and time has changed him. Now he hides in his music, and generous amounts of wine. Oh and let us not forget his women. He is always certain to have several of those about."

"You have known him a long time."

"We were barely grown when we came to the Academies. For years we were close, but things go wrong. Dion is not a cruel man, he just a man that should not be trusted with a heart." she said gently, "He is a skilled surgeon." she told her as she opened the door to leave. "But alas, the Dowery-men of Basilus have become so arrogant they can no longer see when a true healer is sitting among them."

"Maybe you will find what you seek today, Tamil. Do not worry about us. All will be well. The sun is bright outside. Nestor is full, and Kiel sleeps peacefully."

"That we might. The moon has begun to wax again. New beginnings are just ahead." she replied, slinging her satchel over her shoulder. "Good day Yurah, I will be back as quickly as I am able."

Yurah pulled the latch behind her. Nestor was hobbling about in the kitchen, whistling and clearing away the dishes.

"I think he will be fine for a walk today." she thought and she went to check on her other charge.

The sunlight had spread across the room. His blanket, no longer wanted, lay on the floor. She went to pick it up and noticed he was not wearing his sleeping shirt. Laying the coverlet gently over him she realized his boots were still on his feet.

"Walking in the dark?" she asked him silently. He looked almost like himself with the sun warming his face and chest. She undid his laces and gently set the shoes on the floor. "I will ask again later, Kiel." and went to help Nestor with the kitchen.

After the dishes were finished they played cards until Nestor grew restless.

"I would love to go out there, Yurah." he said standing against the window sill. "The sun is bright. And look the birds, they are trying to find something to eat. There are some stale slices in the cupboard. I do not think Tamil would mind if we took them."

"No, I do not think she would." Yurah answered watching the birds peck at the fruitless ground. "We can go for while. Let me make sure Kiel is still sleeping first."

"I will get on my cloak," he answered happily, picking up his crutch.

Yurah stepped to the edge of the chamber door and looked inside. The room was still sunny. A strong beam of light rested across his chest and the blanket was again discarded on the floor. "I will be just outside the window." she told him silently.

It was surprisingly warm when they stepped into the yard. Nestor was having no trouble with his crutch. He followed the birds easily about the lawn, leaving crumbs to tempt them and imitating their songs. She wandered after him, studying the shrubs and seed pods left from the last of the summer blooms. Nestor sat down on a bench and contently began to set snowballs one on top the other. The birds gathered about his feet, hoping for more crumbs. He whistled at them, throwing just enough to keep them near. Yurah walked to the far end of the courtyard. Trailing vines clung to the brick, their pods hanging by a thin black thread. She was wondering what the yard would look like on a warm summer day when a harsh cry broke the silence. A large raven had settled in the upper branches of the ash tree.

"What do you want?" she thought at him but the bird just watched her with his keen black eye. Then she noticed that all had grown dim around her and black clouds were beginning to roll in from the ocean. The bird cried out again.

"It looks like another storm," called Nestor, staring up at the gloom. The sound of thunder rippled through the clouds.

"Say farewell to your snowman, Nestor. He is soon to meet his end." And a cold drop of rain splattered on the sidewalk.

"That outing did not last nearly long enough," he complained, getting back on his legs. "but maybe the rain will be quick."

"Maybe," she said, realizing the apartment had grown quite dark. She hurried to Nestor's side as the rain began to pour

"We should build up the fire, Nestor." she said shaking the mist from her cloak. "The damp will creep into everything."

"I can see to that. Tamil stoked it this morning. It will not take but a minute." he sat down on the hearth and began to poke at the embers. "It is too dark in here. Kiel does not like sleeping without the sun."

But Yurah was already on her way. He lay atop his crumpled sheets, deathly still in the dimming light. A freezing wind drifted by her and her mouth tasted bitter. She glanced about as dread consumed her until, there in the corner she saw it, the shadow hung over his bed. Like a spider preoccupied with its prey, the phantom did not notice her there. A thin arm reached out and pressed its long fingers into Kiel's chest. Yurah drew her blade and caught a beam of light from Nestor's new fire. At the flash, the shadow turned away from its work and in that instant the phantom appeared to be an ancient, withered man. The magical scabbard began to murmur and the ghoulish thing croaked at the noise. Gathering itself into a billowing cloud the spirit began to fill the room. The smell of burning metal was spreading through the air. With a terrible strength, the shadow violently wrenched its hand from Kiel's chest and flung him mercilessly against the glass. His death shudder echoed through the chamber but there was nothing she could do. The shadow barred the way. It hissed as it drew near, changing its shape into open maw, allowing its sour breath to flow over her face. She was ready when the head made its strike and, pulling the sword through the empty air, she cleaved the dark in half. Without hesitation, the shade drew itself together and was formed again. Flinging a whip-like claw, the daemon struck her face. Stumbling, she swung the blade over her head. The creature was split apart once more, but this time the thing groaned loudly.

"I am causing it hurt." she realized, readying herself for another hit. And just as before, the shade swiftly drew itself together. The liquid dark pushed her back, knocking her to her knees. She held the sword upright, allowing the phantom to spill over her. She felt it as it began to pull her breath from her body, and then, with all the strength she had to give, she leaped to her feet and cut through the darkness.

In that instant a dazzling glow filled the room and suddenly the dark was gone. She turned about, finding Nestor standing behind her trying to hold a heavy flask with both his hands.

"Yurah?" he cried struggling to steady the crystal.

"It's all right!" she called out as she ran to Kiel. He was lying

234

against the cracked window. His skin was freezing cold and smoky black wisps moved from between the buttons of his blouse. "Bring the crystal here, Nestor. Hurry, place it over him. A darkness seeps from within."

He was at her side in an second, holding the light over Kiel's chest. She tore the buttons apart and felt him draw a shallow breath when the light touched his skin.

"He is not dead." she whispered in disbelief.

"No he is not." Nestor gasped in wonder, "Again he cheats the Umbra of its prize."

"He is breathing in the light. Please Nestor, give me the crystal." she said taking the clear flask from the boy. She held it close over is chest and his breath began to come more easily.

"You scared it off, Nestor." she said keeping her hand steady.

"Yes, I suppose I did a little. But really it was not my doing. It was the magic glass that did the scaring."

"It is a magic glass, Nestor. How did you know to bring it?"

"It was quite strange Yurah. Really it was. I heard the fight begin and, as I was hurrying to the room I tripped over your case. The crystal rolled out at my feet and it spoke to me. It called me by my name and told me to take it to you. And I did Lady. I had too. I could not refuse it."

"You did what was right." Yurah answered holding the light in both hands. The bright beams fell over Kiel's body and spilled through the cracked glass into the storm that still poured in the courtyard.

"Now that might draw some attention to us, Lady." replied Nestor looking at the multitude of dancing rainbows filling the lawn.

"It might indeed." she answered and Nestor drew the curtains closed.

CHAPTER XXVII
THE SECRET SOUND

Atyn spread the aging parchment along the table and Istah leaned over to hold the corners back. Inrih was at the window watching the gloom roll in from the sea.

"There is storm coming, Atyn. I hear the thunder rolling."

"Thunder?" said Tamil looking up from her book. "That is peculiar for this time of year."

Istah left the scroll to curl and went to watch at the sky. "Look there." she said after a moment pointing to the Tower that stood on the ring above them. A glittering fog flowed like waves from the crystal spire.

"The Priests are working the chants," said Tamil grimly, "It is the first time I have seen it under the light of day. Something strange is afoot."

Istah set her mind upon the menacing waves, intent on feeling the purpose of the work. "They are provoked." she said finally, "Rumors have reached them."

Atyn's face grew grave. "We have lingered here too long." and his concern grew more fixed. "And still I am not certain which way to proceed."

"All this knowledge, the books, the scrolls, the obscured glyphs, they only serve to draw us away from our goal." said Istah returning to the parchment and uncurling it gently. "These riddles deceive. We must find another way to finish what we have begun."

"Yes. These things are leading us astray." replied Atyn. "We have weakened ourselves by standing apart." and at that instant a large clap of thunder shook the window glass.

"What a fool these airs have made of me!" cried Inrih, "They are alone! I have left Yurah and the boy to stand unguarded against the Umbra." and in a single stride he was at the door.

Istah looked again to the peak and a slow terror began to cover her fair face, "The priests have found their prize." she gasped, "and it is Kiel."

"Follow me," said Tamil stuffing her books in her satchel. "I know the shortest way."

She led them through the back stairwells until she reached a narrow metal gate. The rain poured as they fled through gardens. Suddenly Tamil turned aside and pushed open a hidden door. Wasting not a step she led them through the channel until they reached another flight of stairs.

"It is up here." she pointed breathlessly and in another moment they had come up into a small grove of trees.

"That is it!" she cried pointing to her dormitories. Inrih sprang ahead. He was there in an instant, and in another he had broken the door away from its lock. Nestor came hobbling to the bedroom door.

"Inrih!" he exclaimed, "Atyn, Istah. How did you know?"

"Where are they?" exclaimed Inrih.

"In the room." he gestured. "But all is right now. The shadow has passed."

They entered with their weapons drawn. Atyn kneeled down next to the bed.

"What happened here?" he asked her softly.

And when she told him of the smoky mist that had flowed from beneath Kiel's skin his face grew grave.

"How many were there?" questioned Inrih.

"There was but one."

"One?"

"Aye just one, and for a moment I thought it was only an old man." she shuddered, "but I was wrong. All would have been wasted had Nestor not brought the light."

Istah knelt down next and gently touched the vibrant crystal. "This Fire Glass, an ancient Sword, a Summoner's Stone, and a Reed of living silver; such treasures you hold child. Truly it is your innocence Yurah that makes your power so difficult to read. So tell me Lady, are their other gifts you bear from your far-off star?"

"There are two others." she replied, quietly remembering the sound of faraway laughter, "They were gifted to me by the eldest of my sisters."

"Then would you share them with us now, Yurah. We have come to an end and we have not yet found what we came for."

She looked down at the radiance that flowed from the Fire Glass she went to gather the final gifts of her father's house. Feeling through her pack she found them. As Anath's Scrying Mirror and Sothis' Book of Secrets were resting in her hands, the sound of whispering came from far away.

"Cuimnech. O traod annrach," the voices murmured. *"Cuimnech. Cuimnech an."* Her heart trembled at the words. Through the firelight she saw that the fiery sylphs dancing and she realized her sisters were watching her. "May a blessing thrice heard be a blessing kept." She thought she heard them say and pushing back her tears she went to join the others in the chamber.

"It is a scrying glass" she explained, unwrapping the cloth and mirror began to sparkle like the deep night sky. Istah's eyes widened.

"It is a powerful thing, Yurah." the gray-eyed lady said staring into the middle of the silver ring. "But the laws holds true for all who wander under heaven's dome. The wisdom to understand what is seen must be left to the seer."

Istah's truthful words did nothing to ease her uncertainties. She kept her concerns close as she continued to explain, "And this is from my eldest sister." she said touching the plain cover of the little book. She knelt on the floor and looked upon Kiel's pale face. Feeling the deadly light that poured though his body she wished for a cure. She placed Sothis' book across her knees and opened the cover but, when she saw that every page was empty, confusion swept over her. Then softly a message began to form in her mind.

"Hold it close and speak your need." the whisper told her as a blurred image of a cluttered study formed in her thoughts. "From the heart that you will know what is truly real. Do not be afraid, little sister." Yurah closed her eyes and begin to think carefully. She waited for a moment and then looked up at the others.

"Open it." Istah said. Yurah looked down at the simple book and spreading her hands apart, she allowed it to open where it would.

At first the empty leaves held nothing but soon the pages began to stir and slowly the words appeared upon the open page.

'What is dealt from the within may only be healed from the within. The healer shall first determine the correspondences by which the injury was inflicted and then be able to provide the proper environment for the transfer. All work must be done in the presence of the corresponding light. This will provide the healer the ability to witness the disparities within the connecting web which surrounds the form. It is important to note that the body of the injured must not be touched during the transmission. None of his hurt was done by the physical means so all principles of alignment will lie in the finer grades of substance. May the healer also understand that as the balancing force is applied, so will the attracting force be recognized. It is by this act, providing if the patient be willing, and the bestowed force correctly applied, the resulting electric fire shall be made able to consume the dark light.'

She read the words over a second time and by the third time she had begun to understand something of their meaning. She gave the book to Istah.

"The room must be made clean and the airs must be purified." she said decidedly, picking up the crumpled sheets and the scattered clothing.

"Should we try to wake him?" asked Tamil.

"He sleeps without dreams." answered Istah as she held the light over his face. "The shadows can not torment him under the protection of the light."

"Then let him sleep." Tamil replied looking at the dark bruises, "He will ache enough when he revives."

"The physical ache will be the least of his pain." answered Istah grimly.

"What do they want with him? Why Kiel?"

"The old man knew him as he was long ago." Yurah told them, lowering her voice. "I have seen the place where he waits for him. It is always afire."

"The lower realms of Basilus are always afire." said Atyn.

"Well the old beast succeeded in bringing some of it with him. The air reeks. I can taste it. It is like a bitter metal in my mouth." replied Inrih.

"I know how to help with that," answered Atyn. "Tamil, do you have any Olibanum?"

"Only the gum. Is that what you need?"

"Yes." he smiled, "That is the part I need."

"Will you need a censor?"

"Yes, I will need that as well."

"I will be just a moment then." and she went to fetch the herb and the ember plate.

"He looks as if he slept in his clothes." said Inrih after she had left the room.

"Sleeping is something he has done little of lately." said Yurah wiping her hands clean with a soapy cloth. "I found him in his boots this morning."

"Wandering in the dark again? I will hope he did not stumble into too much trouble during the night." replied Inrih as a soft knock caught his ear.

Dion stuck his head through the front door. "What has been going on down here, Tamil? This place is a mess." he said looking at the broken lock.

Tamil could not answer him. She sighed and shook her head.

He chuckled, laying his hand on her shoulder. "Are you worried? Worried what the caretakers might see? Well then put it aside, Tamil. I have been known to have an accident or two occasionally. The damage can be repaired without the steward ever having to know. Trust me."

"Trusting you, Dion, is ever too much to ask."

"So you always say," he quipped, "but I never hold it against you. You are a smart girl. One of these days you will learn better."

"I have errands. What do you want?"

"I have come to see my new friend, Kiel."

"Kiel?"

"Yes Tamil, Kiel." he answered smugly, "Already he is as dear to me as brother could be. He plays the lute like a Malkian and he does not use the night to sleep. We could not help but understand each other."

"Dion I do not have time for this."

"Alright Tamil. Alright." he replied, fiddling thoughtfully with the broken lock. "I did meet him last evening. He was walking the courtyard. We spoke and ended up in front of my fire. But I shall tell you the truth now," and Tamil raised her eyebrows, "Yes I can tell it, if it suits me." he retorted gently, "The truth is last night I noticed how deeply Kiel's injuries went and when the rains set off I started to worry. I thought you had gone off to the Libraries this morning and that there might be a need for my services."

"Well Dion, he is injured," she answered pensively, "and there is a need." and hesitating for only an instant more, she stepped aside to let him pass.

"Thank you, Tamil. I will be good. I promise." he said with a neat bow.

"I can not worry about your goodness today, Dion. I only ask that this secret be kept." she replied, pushing the door shut and frowning at the useless latch. "He is gravely wounded and your services may prove useful. Follow me now. There are others you must meet."

Dion followed her into the bedchamber where they found Atyn waiting at the threshold. Inrih stood at his shoulder, his hand resting on his long knife. Dion paused and waited. Atyn studied his face and when he was satisfied with what he saw, he spoke.

"So you have come to aid us in our work, Dion. Indeed it is by fortune's hand we meet. I am Atyn Ceranus." and he bowed low allowing him to pass.

Dion was shaken. Atyn's solemn grandeur was something he was not accustom too. A blinding light was pouring from the corner of the room and through its radiance he could just see a tall woman standing over a sickbed with a brilliant lamp. But it was Inrih that captured his attention most. The man was massive and his fingers still lay on the hilt of the knife. His black eyes did not turn away. Dion felt himself begin to sweat.

"Trust me, Dion." Tamil grinned, enjoying his discomfort, "Inrih will not slay you, unless you deserve it."

Inrih led him to where Kiel lay senseless. Dion shuddered. All too well he understood that dozens of minute fractures which lie under the dark bruising. Countless hours he had watched the young suffer, leaving him with the bitterest of news to carry to the mothers and the sisters who had waited through the night. Long ago he had noticed that before the wounds appeared there came a sound. Gently he lay his hand over Kiel's chest and the creeping buzz echoed from the within. It was a sound that swallowed hope. Then Dion realized that someone else was at his side but time she wore no long cape and he could see the long sword at her side. Her grim expression matched the dreadful Inrih's.

"These strangers are like no others I have ever met before." he thought silently.

"Everything will be ready soon." Yurah said, looking up at him.

"Ready? What do you plan to do? I have never seen a soul recover after the Umbra have taken hold of the heart."

"They are preparing the room for healing." answered Inrih.

Yurah knelt down beside the bed. "Do not fear." she told him and Kiel opened his eyes. "All is safe now."

A quiet chant filled in the chamber. Atyn gently swung the smoking censor in his hand. The thick odor of the olibanum mingled in the warmth of the light Istah held.

"Lumen soli mutuum das." Kiel whispered in the common tongue, laying his hand over his chest. "Again you have lent your light to the sun, my friend. But do not think you can not stop it. None of you can. He will come for me again." he said as his body began to shiver. "He is calling me back. Calling me down into his dungeons. I will not escape it. I can not escape it."

"The light does not allow the shadow pass. No harm can come. We are going help you." Istah said softly.

"I have seen what they intend, Lady. Do not underestimate them. That would be the most dangerous thing of all."

"Your companions are a match for any them." Dion said earnestly. " 'Do not fear', the Lady told you. Take my advice and listen to her. Resist this despair."

"There is only one thing left before we start." Inrih told him softly. "And that would be you Master Kiel. It seems you went out last evening, and came back to sleep in your clothes. Really, you are quite the mess. So if you are able to stand it, we must clean you up a bit. You can not be the center of all our attentions in such a state."

Dismay poured over Kiel's face

"Do not worry." said Inrih kindly, "We will be gentle."

They left Istah and Inrih to prepare him properly. Yurah settled near the fireplace to reread the instructions once more.

"What does it say?" asked Dion. "Can I read it?"

"So patience is still a virtue you intend to grow later?" Tamil replied.

"Patience has nothing to do with it, Tamil. These wounds have baffled me for too long now. There is something there I must know written there. It is radiating from the page. What is it she holds? I have never seen such a book before."

"It is a gift from her sisters."

"A gift? A gift indeed. Its pages are calling us together like sheep to a fold. What do the words say, Yurah?"

"The words will hold a different meaning for each reader. But each may have way of understanding them could prove helpful." Yurah said, handing him the open book. "What do they tell you, Dion?"

Politely he took it from her hand and, trying not to appear too excited, he read. His eyes lingered on the words "corresponding light," and understanding blazed up like a fire.

"The shadow that smothers life is summoned into the world by the Dowerymen. It is a specific type of force that draws together, like to like. I can not believe I did not see it before?" he exclaimed, standing to pace across the room.   "It is the tones that allow the Shadows to enter the victim and as the dark is placed within fears, loathings, obsessions, jealousies, all set alive. This is what drains the patient. So to heal the patient, Light must be returned to the smothering dark. It must be done in a like way. And more than this it must be done intentionally. Do you see what I mean? That is that kind of transfer the book speaks of. A song, a tone, a word, any of these can be used to pull the illumining force within."

"But how will the light be drawn into the heart, Dion? That is where the shadow lingers." asked Tamil.

"The correspondences by which the injury was inflicted' must be understood. What is the 'Like to Like' that made that pathway possible? We must understand the course the shade followed to the heart?"

"I understand that road." answered Yurah softly.

"Then you understand what it meant by the 'balancing sound'?"

"I know what they touched to reach into him. It is an old conflict. He has carried it for many years."

"So again, we return to the corresponding light." he said, jumping ahead in his thoughts, "And what word shall undo the shadow's work?"

Yurah looked into the letters written on the yellowed page listening to the clear sound ringing in her silent thoughts. Dion leaned over to touch her arm.

"You hear it. I can see you do."

"He is ready." they heard Istah say from the door.

"As are we." answered Yurah, rising from the hearth.

CHAPTER XXVIII
THE NINE GATES

Atyn held the smoldering Olibanum at top of the bedstead. Istah pulled back the heavy curtain and surveyed the courtyard. Yurah called Kiel's name, allowing the sheets of pain that shuddered through his bones to move into her own. Dion knew their suffering all to well. The same leaking darkness had crept under his own skin as he had tended unlucky victims of the Umbra's raids. "But I would favor this death to the alternative." he mused, watching the delirium rise and fall in Kiel's eyes, "The loss of the body is a small thing when weighed against an endless slavery to the Priests of Ildabyth."

Atyn began to speak in steady rhythm. The Malkian chant swelled and the lamp that Istah held began to blush. Yurah leaned over the bed and held the sword over his heart. She did not touch him and no word did she say aloud. From shades of flaming crimson, and then fading back into white, the light pulsed across the blade. Kiel's breathing became steady as the rite continued. Yurah drew closer then, breathing in rhythm with the light carried by the sword. A trembling light formed between them and Yurah sent it forward to touch his living breath. Kiel drew the sound into his heart.

It was then all pain and memory returned. Again he was falling through the smothering hole with the hideous laughter echoing above him. His body was alive with fire. He fell for an endless time and at a point he realized that another voice had joined him. The voice was soothing and as the pain faded he dreamed of Sro. She was bound by a web of black shadowy threads and held deep in the belly of the world. A dark place where sunlight had never known.

"Why did you call me to the Little Kingdom?" she asked from her prison bed.

"I was wrong to do it. I did not understand."

"Well it seems you misunderstand again, Kiel. You did not bring me here. I chose to return. Can you not understand that?"

"Why would you choose such suffering? Why would anyone?"

"The day may come when the same choice shall stand before you Kiel so I will ask my question once more. Why did you call me to the Little Kingdom? How did it serve you?"

Centuries had passed since he considered his motives and he thought about the question for a long time.

"I wished to be his favorite." he told her slowly. "But then I realized that it would never come to be. He loved you best. He was

244

willing to sacrifice everything to have you. All of his trinkets, each of his armies, every resource at his hand, all this he would do, just to keep you near him." Kiel shuddered, remembering every detail of the betrayal. "I was envious Sro. Envious of all your powers. But most of all I was envious of your power over him."

Shame swallowed him and he could say no more. And after a time Sro spoke again.

"There is another question I need answer too, Kiel. If you give me leave to say it."

"I will answer, Lady."

"Why have you returned to the Little Kingdom?"

"I have returned to help you home." he said and at that instant everything turned to fire. All around him voices clamored. People were running in every direction. But he did not run. Someone was carrying him and his skin peeled away from his bones like butter. The reek of burned skin choked him and soon consciousness faded. Then came the sensation of earth and water being wrapped around him. A tender song whispered in the leaves above. He was not dead. He was changed. He was wrapped in a bear skin and drowning in a river. The pain was gone and a bright sun warmed him from above. He opened his eyes and Yurah was there. He reached out and touched her hand.

"Where am I?" he whispered.

"You are back where you belong." she answered.

Istah leaned down. "Fear no more. The storm has passed."

He began to rise up on his elbow.

"You are not to think of it!" Dion exclaimed, hurrying to the bedside. "Oh my, how you misunderstand what has just happened. This work may yet be undone. Do not sit up! Be still, Kiel. Let me take a look at you."

"You will find him intact" said Inrih dryly. "Sore, but solid enough. But suit yourself young master and have your look."

And it was just as Inrih said. Though Kiel was pale and drew his breath lightly, his suffering was unexceptional. The bruising lay deep and, still sore to the touch, but it seemed the bones were sealing even as Dion rested his hands over them.

"What type of folk are you?" he asked when he had finished listening to the beat of his heart. "You are not like I am. This ability to heal is phenomenal, and these treasures you bear." he said glancing down at the sword Yurah carried at her side, "Every Doweryman in Basilus would slay his brother to have them. Where are you really from, viator? And what brings you to this pitiful place?"

"That is a long story, sir." Inrih answered for him. "And Kiel is not the one to share it.   Come with me, Dion. I will tell you all you need to know."

The sun was creeping around the edge of the drape and Istah pulled back the curtain. Anxiety clouded Atyn's face when he looked through the telling crack.

"The Priests become bolder with every spell they cast. And today they are so brash as to steal what they want right under the light of the sun. They are working to gather their forces.   While Sro waits still for liberation his priests seek another prize. I believe the Sorcerers of Ildabyth have set their eye upon the Malkian Isles and neither Odyn's army nor Tristan's elves will hold any hope if the Sacred Isles should fade from the world." he added uneasily.   "And we are no closer to our goal than we have ever been."

"The days spent searching the Libraries have proven of little use. The maps we have found can not help us. Even if we did slip past the guards, the way to source of his powers have been well hid." said Istah gravely. "Only Ildabyth knows where that secret is kept."

"Ildabyth keeps his secrets well."   Kiel said broodingly, staring at the crack, "but Sro understands him. She always has."

"How do you know this Kiel?"

"I know that prison. I know where Ildabyth keeps her bound in his underworld, locked tightly away behind the Nine Gates of Erda.

"Nine gates?"

"Yes. This is the secret you have been trying to unravel."

"How do you know this Kiel?"

"My memories have returned Atyn. I fear I know far more than I wish too. The Nine Gates nourish his desires," replied Kiel ruefully, "He uses that power to delve ever deeper into Erda. They are dear to him and he guards them jealously. But Ildabyth does not let every riddle go unanswered. He has shared the mystery of the Nine Gates with only a few, with those he trusted above all others."

"I have never heard you speak of him with such candor before, Kiel. What has changed?" asked Istah.

"My perspective I suppose." he said shifting uneasily in his bed. "After the Umbra found their way into me so many things had I struggled to forget, I found myself remembering. Ildabyth would come to me, while sleeping and while awake, reminding me of our times together, of my obligations, of my duties." then Kiel hesitated as pain flooded through his chest, "but mostly he spoke of my fate." He turned to the window then and, through the fractured glass, the yellow sun had broken apart into a rainbow. The light danced along the wall. "But the Fates work in strange ways and what was once forgotten is now plain to me." he continued distantly, "Long ago I was the one who Ildabyth trusted above all others. I could come and go anywhere within his Kingdom. I could do whatever I pleased, whenever it suited me. He showed me the pleasures of lower worlds and explained to me many of their secrets. But I did not realize the depth of it until I was saved from his nightmare. Ildabyth intended to bear me home to him. And, indeed, he almost succeeded."

'The realms of Ildabyth are not your home, Kiel. Your home is Taygeth. Your father's star." Yurah reminded him with gentle concern, "Do you not remember this?"

"I wandered from that place long ago. Truly, what type of son am I, Yurah?" he replied with a grimly. "No, no, please. I do not expect another to answer for me. I will tell it. I am a son that is not willing to look into my father's eyes. My greatest hope is to undo some of the harm I have caused before the Fates put me to that test."

'You are harsh on yourself, Kiel." said Atyn.

'Truth is harsh, but very often more practical." he smiled, "And as you have said, Atyn, 'if the Isles of Urdar should fade,' none of your folk nor none of your far kindred will not be able to stand against them. If there is to be a victory in this battle Sro must hold the key to it. This is why tortures her so brutally. For even as he keeps her bound and gagged in her prison room, still she holds the balance of the Little Kingdom within her. "

"Sro sat alongside the Annyd on the first day the new sun shown." Istah replied, recalling the words of her Elders. "The day they spilled their blood into the Little Kingdom."

"And it was envy which spoiled it then. The envy of Ildabyth." said Atyn. "He desired the Little Kingdom for his own. His jealousy distorted the first work, his avarice created the first war, and what has come since is lesser still."

"Aye, envy and hatred. You understand your past well, my friends. Indeed, Erda's history flows like a poisoned river." Kiel answered softly, his eyes clouding with despair, "Her past like an unwanted secret and it is always there, haunting the present."

Istah leaned toward him, reading his worries, "What secrets did your nightmares bring, Kiel?"

His face faded to gray as he explained. "I am left to remember the many times he lead me to her prison bed. He enjoyed an audience when tormented her and I followed behind him like a cur." he told them remorsefully, "Every step of that walk is plain to me now. I can remember it like it was yesterday."

Atyn stood in front of the window and considered the things that had been said. "You are with friends. Cast aside your despair, Kiel.

Tell us what you know."

He sighed and looked out the window. The brown grasses stirred under the sour wind. Above it all, the clouds moved swiftly along their field of blue. Kiel could feel Yurah's hand inside his own and after a long moment he spoke again. "Her prison lies beyond the Ninth Gate. But as the Fates would have it, all hope must be abandoned when you enter that realm. There is no other way it can be. "

We will stand as the Fates see fit." Atyn answered.

"Then your doom is sealed because I understand what you have been looking for. Alas my friend, I am the one who can tell you what you want to know." he told him gravely, looking into Yurah's innocent eyes. "Hmmm, and perhaps you might even venture to assume that my recollection a gift. Oh yes Atyn, indeed I do realize what you must do to reach her for it seems I have remembered every evil word Ildabyth spoke to open those doors."

Then he lay her hand down gently upon the bed, and would not let her help him rise to his feet. He went to the broken window and putting his hand upon the glass he watched the wind blow.

"The Gates are triple by design. And when all points are joined together they form a perfect dominance." Kiel explained. "Though it is the path of descent, its pattern follows the Laws of the higher realms. When the Words are spoken in their proper order the way can be tread swiftly." Then he shuddered. Atyn went to his side but Kiel raised his hand and shook his head.

"There is no help you can offer me Atyn. Just let me finish this. The time has come for you to understand your path." And he turned from him to stare into the troubled sun. "The First Gate is entered through Ignorance. It is a simple thing, one step after the other, an effortless path to doom. Its lot is to see nothing as necessary, exposing itself to a power defined by no rule. It is opened by calling the name, MIYA." and as the sound of the hideous word exploded in his mind. His hands shook. Shame seeped from his gut. He could not hide from himself and there was no empty words of comfort to be said. No thing that could heal him now. His mouth was parched; his bones dry as dust; his intentions withered as the ancient dead. "Really, what could I do for these brave folk?" he considered helplessly and in that instant of remorse he decided. "There is nothing. Nothing at all." and he continued on not waiting for a reply.

"The Second Gate is entered by Neglect." he said "Through idleness and in excess, disease settles and is left undisturbed to its work. It is opened by calling the name, TOAB." and, as he spoke the loathsome word, his mouth tasted of metal. He swallowed hard but the taste lingered. "The Third Gate is opened by the sound, HEVAH." he paused a moment, knowing the sound carried filth. His tongue began to bleed and his heartbeat rushed ahead like herd of wild horse as he wiped a streak of bright blood from his nose. He took a steady breathe, hoping against all hope that the evil sounds he uttered aloud would not be enough to blot out the sun for that gracious light was the only thing that kept him standing. "It is entered in Vanity," he told them softly, "the house where Pride grows into the demon that rages. That is the nature of the first three halls. They complete the first of the triangle. The apex points downward." And from the window he could see a flock ravens gathering upon the rooftops of Basilus as he heard himself say, "The next gate is entered through Envy. It preys upon others by coercion, and by thievery." he explained pushing the sound of the birds away. "It is a straggling passion that does not mind its own affairs. The fourth is opened by calling the name, IANDO." he continued leaning hard against the broken window. "And through this door the fifth gate soon follows. The fifth gate is entered through deceit and in duplicity, keeping itself safe in its narrow room, allowing fickleness to abandon itself to the sweltering heat. Its real name is Betrayal and it is opened by the Word, THA." Something warm ran down his face. Quickly he wiped it away before he turned to face them. "The Sixth Gate is entered in Animosity. Loathing now rests at the feet. Rancor now speaks to the heart and Malice does breed in the mind. It is opened by the Sound, RUBEG."

A cloud began to pass over the sun. His eyes burned, his heart pounded like a drum and as he spoke his voice croaked like the raven.

"The Pressure is terrible at this point. No rest does the orphan know, only longing and yearning. The lost wanderer is solemn and starved and the last of the Halls entices the pitiful creature onward."

His head throbbed and his arms grew numb. He understood the next door far too well. The ravens stirred in the tall, gray tree and several lighted in the courtyard, hopping and clicking they moved in an odd round. Kiel closed his eyes and struggled to keep his wits.

"The Seventh Gate is opened by speaking the name, MIAL." he said to dismal air. "It is entered through Wrong Use of the Law. It is the hand that trifles with what is sacred, leaving behind all greater reason. It is the corrupt seed that mocks its design. And alas, my good companions, it is alarming how quickly the Eight Gate follows. It is a realm entered through Ritual. By good or by ill, the Law is unyielding as its cycles hold all bits of life together. The Eight Gate is opened by the Word, INODI." his voice labored now and something warm leaked down his belly. He pressed against the broken glass and forced himself to continue. "But the Ninth Gate bears no name." he choked. "It is the intent of those who seek to enter which holds the key to that final door. The last realm of Ildabyth can only be opened by forever sealing the Eight Gates behind it."

He thought his chest would burst apart as the cruel images swarmed into his mind. Maiming was ever Ildabyth's preferred practices. "How often had he wished her the release of a sudden death," he wondered through his pain but he knew himself better than this. He knew he was a coward and he turned away from those who had befriended him. He was naked in his shame and closed he eyes and explained to them what he had done.

"I never crossed the gate into the Ninth Hall, though I can not count the times he led me there. I would linger at the threshold and watch his wicked games. Even now he mocks my lack of will." he added wryly, and turned away from the sun. "So my friends, at last now you truly can understand my dilemma. That was how I gained my salvation. I gained my freedom by sanctioning her ruin."

Istah cast down her eyes. Atyn's despair was plain. Reeling with both dread and pity, Yurah looked past him to gaze out the window and she saw his bloody handprint, still warm and moist, remained upon the glass.

CHAPTER XXIX
UNDER THE LIGHT OF THE YELLOW SUN

"Shadows wax strong in the Little Kingdom." Doxomedon murmured staring into the globe. "What new troubles plague your world, Mqttro?"

The tolling of distant bells filled the chamber and the wizard looked up from the orb to find the radiant Malki burning before him.

"The Tree withers in the garden of Urdar." the lovely voice answered. "Ildabyth has taken form within the hollow realms. Now he walks as an old man among the people of the Basilus.

"So I feared, Mqttro. I have seen the light fading as Ildabyth sets his traps. Soon he shall again stake his claim to the realm."

"The Umbra have spread their forces far past the boundaries of Basilus. They lurk the airs over Odyn's Hold waiting for his signal. The Valkeries polish their silver arrows, with only a child to warn them when the strike does come." the Malki said grimly.

"What has been set into motion will not be stopped." answered Doxomedon beckoning for the seraph to peer within the crystal, "but the conjuring of Ildabyth can be amended. Look, an alignment approaches, the moment when the Rivers of Mundi and the Starry Lights collide. It is there Mqttro, where Eradinus is headed by Raldabon and Rempha's Star holds the point at the center of all of it. The Pleiades, the Greater Bear, and Mundi will form the first trine and that strength will touch the planets of the Yellow Sun. The perfect satellites will bring their influence to Erda's children."

The secret burned in Doxomedon's crystal as the old mage explained. "When the lights within the Bear greet Iao's Daughters, Rempha will release the Four Rivers. The magnetic powers of Mundi will pull upon her and her lands will be forever altered. Erda will shudder as her position shifts."

And while he spoke the glimmering lights began to flicker and Mqttro laid his hand upon the crystal to steady it.

"Neptune is the Mystic of the higher Airs and his work has only just begun. He is the petitioner that inspires sacrifice and that work is kept hid by the dark light of the moon." the seraph whispered to mage.

"Ahh, the lovely Moon," Doxomedon mused, "She hangs in the dark sky to remind them of what might have been if the First War had not been made. Such a tragic loss she was. But even in death she is perfect, hiding what is the most pure of all. The moment draws near when Neptune's Secret will be exposed. The Seven Sisters will comfort those who suffer."

The fore-knowing lent to his lovely face an air of grim nobility. Long had the Malkians known the misery of ambush and the horror of the battlefield. "The River Urdar feeds the Tree of Life and when the Four return, it is Urdar who will rejoice. Only then may the tears of Jupiter clear away the taint."

"So finally we can understand it, Mqttro." the old man said, rubbing his long beard. "The Tree will be fed when the Four Rivers meet. There is hope in this. Hope that the life of Erda will not falter and fade."

"Such is the way of things everlasting." he answered as faint bells began to toll.

"May the Four Waters of Life return swiftly to your realm, Mqttro." Doxomedon said with a low bow.

"And may the Hidden Light be remembered by those who wander." the Seraph replied. "Blessed be Light of Taygeth."

"Blessed be, Lord of the Flame."

And in a sudden spark, Mqttro was gone.

CHAPTER XXX
URION

Uri twisted the root in his fingers, peeling back the stringy threads. The old woman watched his hands do their work.

"We can not stay here, Macha. It is not safe. I can feel it. I can hear it."

"But yet you can not see it. The truth remains that you are not yet prepared to see what the future holds. A blind man is no aid to us Urion."

"But shadows can be heard just as they can be seen. Why do you not listen to me? It is real."

"I do listen, child. The work before us all is real and I shall not lessen its difficulties by allowing you to believe you are ready when you are not. Peel the root back and hurry up. The fire is ready."

Uri lifted the pile of threads from his lap. "Isn't this enough?"

Macha looked at the straw and nodded her approval. "It shall suffice. Throw it in."

Uri placed the fibers into the boiling water and immediately the oils were released. Macha stirred the pot gently and the odor filled the small hut.

"The smell is too thick. I can not breathe."

"Shhh Urion. Help me with this. Everything is almost ready."

Uri gave her the rest of the lamps she waited for.

"And the globes. They are over there. You will need the yellow ones."

He hurried to fetch them while Macha lit the lamps. Placing the colored glass over the flame she set the lamps around the edges of the sweat house. The steamy room glowed in the amber light. The old woman searched through the pouches of herbs that hung about her waist and threw a handlful of resin into the cooking fire. The smoke from the pit joined the steam and Uri began to cough.

Macha chuckled, "You will become used to it. Now go over there near the fire. That's a good boy. Lay down on your back. Hurry now. You will be too dizzy to stand in a moment."

Uri was already too dizzy to stand. He sank to his knees and crawled to mat she had laid for him. "What are you doing to me, Macha?"

"Speeding up progress, Urion. It can not be helped. The Fates have left you with responsibilities far beyond your years. There are ways to hasten the process. Do not worry. Try to relax."

He watched as her voice floated by him on the steam. The sound lifted up and flowed through the small hole in the top of hut.

"Good. It's working already." she said cheerfully, her black eyes dancing. "The Malkians 'see' every sound and it is important that you understand how they do it. All words carry intentions. Atyn knows this. It is the natural way of things. But you must listen well or all will be lost in your clamoring thoughts. Be still, Urion. Quiet your mind; but do not sleep. The root will take you to what you need to see."

"What am I supposed to see, Macha?"

"Just follow the rising mists. It is all you can hope to do."

He settled back on the mat and looked upward to the speck of deepening indigo that shimmered above the forest leaves. The dizziness faded as he made himself still. The yellow glow of the room cleared his mind. He focused upon the rising smoke and found he could ride along with it like a wisp of wind. He saw his body below him. The familiar sheath breathed easily. It was not concerned about his return and Urion moved on through the trees. Rising up through the airs he had a grand view of Odyn's Hold. The sun was just lowering its brilliant face under the edge of the mountain. The birds swirled through the green canopies beneath him and the vast mountain chains spread their rocky arms under the sky. Far in the distance he could see the Strait of Sudra and he wondered of his brother's road. Looking down at his hands he realized he could see through himself. The paleness of skin did not hide the bones and blood beneath and with a closer look he realized his body did not hide the turning world below. He was transparent and yet, solid and whole as he had always seemed. The new condition did not concern him. He turned his thoughts outward and reached ahead to where the fogs were taking him. It ran through the skies and surrounded the land twisting around itself like an endless river. A humming sound began to waver along the vaporous thread. The sound became stronger as the fog swallowed the world he knew. The mist flowed higher and Uri followed its path through the clouds. Like a sigh, the hum of the Erda faded and the moon appeared. She was near, nearer than she had ever been before. He could see every feature on her silver face. New stars began to flicker over his head and he realized he stood upon solid ground. He was standing upon a vista that looked down into a dim valley. Silence surrounded him and the thread of smoke was gone.

"What is this place?" he wondered and to his surprise, the thought rippled through the airs around him. "What is this place?" he whispered carefully, and the ripples intensified with the added sound.

The sound of his name formed in his thoughts. Nervously he looked about and his name sounded again.

"What do you want?" he answered and the moonlight grew

disturbed. He waited but no answer came. Looking down into the valley beneath he realized that lights were moving down the mountain. He looked more deeply and found his vision growing increasingly more focused. The lights below were indeed torches, carried by a group traveling on horseback. They walked along the edge of the lower foothills. Uri could not see their faces, their hooded robes blended them into the colors of the night. The rise and fall of their ponies' feet and the occasional gust of wind caused the cloaks to sway and the hilts of their swords gleamed. The troupe seemed vaguely familiar and Uri moved closer to the edge of the ridge.

"Careful Urion." came the unspoken command. Uri gasped as a bright fire leapt up in the air before him. He stumbled backward and sat hard on the ground.

"Do not fear. I am not here to harm you." said the fierce light. "I have come to help you understand child. The riders below are Tristan's people. They are drawing close to their den. Watch!"

Leaching from just beneath the road the riders traveled, Uri watched the dark phantoms flow silently into the evening airs. Black shades, with blades of black metal, lifted like a fume into the night. Without forethought he sent a sharp warning to the riders and noticed that the horses were pulled to an abrupt stop. The lead rider dismounted and went to look over the edge of the steep trail. He did not see as the shadows spilled into the dark below them. The small troupe was hopelessly outnumbered.

"Is there nothing I can do?" he asked the fire.

"Your help would be most appreciated."

Horrified and helpless, he watched the others leap from their ponies brandishing their swords as the Umbra fell upon them. It must have been the silvery light of the Lady Moon that inspired their aim for in seconds the phantoms were cleaved into halves and pieces. Uri could hear their screams as the swords of Druii rent them into parts. Macha had been telling him for weeks that even though the Umbra were without physical form, the body of a phantom is sensible. They can see as well as hear, and when you touch him, they can feel your stroke. She had explained when a shade is cut in half it had the capacity to rejoin itself. Nonetheless, all wraiths dread the point of the sword, for every tear is felt. Over and over again the riders fought, but it was not enough to hinder the Umbra for long. After every strike the shades drew themselves together and returned to fight. Urion saw a warrior fall. The hood fell back and he recognized the face. It was Lorya. She did not move and Uri cried out to the fire as the others drew around her.

"I know nothing about these things, Fire! Tell me now. Tell me so I can help them."

"You hold the same powers as your Elders hold, Urion. The same as your brother Atyn and the same as his forebears. You are Vanyr. All of the elements are at your command."

"But what element can stay the hand of the Umbra? What can hinder this phantom from growing itself again?"

The flaming being did not answer the boy but his fire grew larger and the flames began to roar.

His sound rumbled like a storm coming in from the sea and then the meaning dawned on the boy. "The lighting bolt." he cried, "Atyn has shown me how to wield them. That is the Sword that might splinter these Shades apart."

Urion went to the edge of the rock and began to call the names of the rain and the wind. The wind was the first to answer. Lifting up through leaves, its voice joined the boy's, and together they summoned the rain. Enraged and furious, the thunder rolled. She came to them through the forest as the two merged and Uri prepared himself to set the next bolt to the mark. Again the cold wind and warm rain coupled and Urion released the white fire. The riders fell to the ground covering their ears as the channel of the shadow's escape was forever sealed away. Realizing their hole was destroyed, the Umbra set upon the group with a vicious rage. Quickly Uri collected his energies and sent another burst through the drenching airs. Its terrible power crashed through the forest. The bolt lit the air with a brilliant flash fracturing the phantoms into harmless specks. The wet forest crackled through the rain.

"What fortune has come to us?" questioned the leader rising from the mud, "And Lorya? How does she fare?"

"She still breathes Tristan." answered the soldier who held her. Tristan glanced nervously over the crumbling edge of the mountain. "We must get her back to the Mountain. I will take her on my horse." and as they lifted Lorya up to him the vision of the valley faded and Uri was alone with the intelligent Fire.

"Thank you, Fire. Thank you for helping me."

"You did well, Urion."

Urion made no comment. He moved away from the edge of the cliff feeling the dizziness returning to his limbs.

"Odyn's folk have ever dared to seek the mysteries by force so I must warn you. You work with dangerous elements, Urion. Take care of your thoughts. It is easy to lose your wits under such pressure."

"What is this place, Fire? Where do we stand?" asked the boy, laying down on his belly so he see over the edge without falling.

"There are many names for it, Urion. It is the first point of true realities."

"How come I have never seen it before?"

"The substance here quickens at a faster rate. And the faster it moves the more time is gained."

Urion pondered the riddle for a moment but found he did not have the desire to understand it."

"Do not dwell on this." the Fire replied and Urion could feel it smiling. "The mechanics of these higher realms are not yet your concern, boy. There are more pressing issues at hand. Behold!"

He scooted closer to the edge and a new scene appeared. The peak of Zelimisso gleamed under the light of the moon. Uri realized he watched just above the hidden route that his brother had taken to the Drui. The doorway was clear to him. The glyphs were plain under the starry night and the words to open the door he understood. But as he waited a dread began to crawl over him and from round the edge of the stony gate a blackness began to seep.

"The Umbra seek out the Hold." he cried out to the Fire.

"It has been so for some time now." the Flame corrected him, watching the phantoms shift from one ghastly form to the next as they leaked over the narrow bridge. "They wait the word of their masters. Learn to speak without sound Urion. They are close enough to hear. The peak of Zelmisso is the Gate to the Upper Airs."

"How will I know when they are coming?"

"Vigilance, Urion. It is the only way."

He began to tremble as he watched. The shadows continued to seep from the door. He could hear their muttering laughter filtering to him from below. A swarm of the creatures had gathered about the gate. They moved in and about its edges, forming and reforming themselves and passing the blades of their dark swords along the face of the stone.

"What are they doing?"

"They are unsealing the lock."

Uri's eyes grew wide then, "Will they succeed?"

The Fire answered grimly, "If Odyn's Hold is taken."

"Odyn's Hold will be taken?"

"If it is, then War will be everywhere?" the Fire explained, "And if the Hold is taken, the final battle will be fought where the River meets the Sea."

"The Malkian Isles," Urion whispered watching the moonlight fall. He could hear a voice traveling along its beams but he did not understand what it said. Clouds began to gather around her face and the ground beneath him began to tremble.

"What is lost or gained in this place holds the balance of all the life within all of Erda."

Beneath them the Umbra's gloom now wreathed the mountain peak. Their hideous laughter passed through his gut. The noise made him ill. A painful groan shifted in the lands below them and from the newly open door a flock of Nykertis flowed like a black cloud under the night.

"You must return to your sheath, Urion. They have succeeded in their task. Bring the warning to the Odyn's folk. They have been preparing for this moment."

"But how do I return, Fire? I understand nothing of this work."

"That is the simple part, boy." the Fire replied.

Suddenly the world was tumbling to meet him and like a stone he was drawn back under its force. In an instant the shadowy forest surrounded him but through the dark leaves the little fire glowed. He saw his body beneath him and with a sharp jolt he collapsed into himself. He opened his eyes to find Odyn staring into his face.

"They are coming!" he told him and then he turned on his side to wretch.

CHAPTER XXXI
THE NINTH GATE

Yurah drew the Sword from the whispering sheath. The soft glow of the blade lent its light to Tamil's fumbling hands.

"This is a dangerous place Yurah." Tamil warned softly unlatching the hidden door, "The light of your blade is all we dare risk."

Though he kept pace, she could hear the labored beating of Kiel's heart inside her head. He stumbled as they descended into the depths beneath the third tower and soon Kiel began to fall behind. They rested then and Atyn took him aside and spoke to him gently.

"What troubles you, my friend?"

"We draw near to the source of his powers Atyn." he answered wearily looking into the shadow, "The first gate waits just beyond the bend."

Atyn laid his hand to his chest, reading the misty fog that filtered through his warm blood. "I fear your wounds will betray you, Kiel." he said finally, "You must walk between us. Stay close. Her blade will give comfort."

"What comfort Atyn? To enter even the first of Gates is to leave the sweetest of all gifts behind us. Beyond there is no shelter. Beyond there is no faith. The way is fed with failures. Ildabyth understands what you do not."

The suffocating gloom hissed. In the world outside, despair echoed through the streets. Atyn knew the war had begun. In his mind's eye he could see the Umbra pouring from the Tower above them and echoing within his inner ear, he perceived the chants of the Priests churning the oceans.

"This is as far as you may go, Tamil." said Atyn. "Further in and your life is surely forfeit."

"You can not leave me behind. I have no other purpose but to help you in this work." she answered in disbelief.

"You are needed elsewhere." he explained touching her brow. "The moment is upon us. Blood flows in Basilus. No life is exempt. Your destiny lies with the people of a doomed city."

Tamil shuddered as the events of the streets above filled her mind. She could see Dion, his coat spattered with crimson, moving through the streets, giving orders and offering aid where he could. Nestor was at his side, dutiful and leading a helping hand where he could. She knew her place was with the people of Basilus. Fumbling with the keys she handed them to Atyn.

"I do not think I will need them." Atyn answered closing her hand over them.

"And you, Inrih." he said, turning to face the big man. "This decision is yours, to go to those above or to remain with us. What is the word of your heart?"

"I am no Mage, Atyn. I am a warrior." he answered, placing his hand over the hilt of his sword. "I shall go with the Lady Tamil. They will need a strong hand to protect them if you succeed."

"Then go to your destiny," he answered, "and may the hands of the fates be kind."

Inrih grinned. "The three ladies have always been quite fond of me. I will be waiting when your work is done."

"And I will be counting the moments, my friend." Atyn answered.

They embraced before they parted and the four that remained watched the torchlight fade around the corner.

"The first gate is just ahead." Kiel said distantly.

The tunnel opened out as they turned the bend. A massive pit gaped before them and a series of narrow stairs led straight into a stone wall. A plain gate barred the way. The pointed tips of the bars were dull and the bolt that held it shut was marked with scratches.

"It is made of lead." he told her, lightly touching the grooves. "Stand back a little. It will open easily." Kiel closed his eyes as he spoke the word, reliving the moment he had been at Ildabyth's side. The sound echoed through the endless pit. The hinges creaked and the stone wall dissolved before their eyes.

The next hall was wider and sloped gently down. As they went strange noises began to surround them. Some were throaty, like a group of swine nosing for roots, while others sighed with a sound that had never seen the sun, but most of the noise was a droning echo that rattled with nonsense and demanded to be heard.

Kiel warned them as they approached the Second Gate. The path grew suddenly steep and the dampness made the descent treacherous. Holding to clefts in the wall they went slowly until they reached another ravine. As before, the bridge to the next gate had no railings and every few steps were met by a crumbling stair. At the end, a gate of tin gleamed in the glow of Yurah's blade. Kiel spoke and the word TOAB rang through the hall as the tall and narrow gate melted away and a stench filled their faces. They followed him through the Hall of Neglect and a thin string of slime crawled down Yurah's shoulder. She tried to brush it away but Kiel reached over and cleared it off with the edge of his cloak. She thanked him but he did not answer.

The Third Gate was Brass, filled with filigree and the walls behind it were polished to a mirrored shine. Their reflections smiled as they made their way over the bridge. Yurah put her hand to her face and her reflection began to laugh. Kiel opened the Third Gate with a whisper and gentle wave of his hand. Yurah gasped as the wall of stone faded, for the beauty that lay beyond it was staggering.

"Do not allow your eyes to linger." Kiel spoke softly in her ear. "Nothing is as it seems. If you draw to near the reflections will swallow you. Concentrate upon the dust of your robe, or the stains along your bootstraps, anything but the misty light. It is a perilous walk through Vanity's Hall. Here, take my hand. We must be swift."

Yurah glanced behind her. Istah and Atyn walked together, wary but untouched by the glamour mists, they kept a close pace behind them. She looked down at the hand that held her own. His fingers were graceful and perfect. He kept her close as they walked through the handsome hall though she was well able to walk alone. She wanted to ask him why he held her so near but knew he was in no mood to answer. Certainly it was hopelessness that set him apart from all loving things and she wondered if healing would ever come. After a long time, the hall faded back into the stony corridor. They followed the twisting turns knowing they were moving deeper into the core of the world.

"Why are their no Umbra here, Kiel? I had thought these deeps would be crawling with the shadows of Ildabyth."

He answered with a sad laugh, "Every shade above has walked these halls. Ildabyth created these labyrinths to serve his purposes. The Gates are made of living desires. Most never know they have been ensnared for their prisons are created by their own designs. Hope is forfeit in this place, and every dream is but an idle fancy. All becomes more dangerous with every step further in." he sighed and came to a halt.

The path had led them to a narrow ledge. A dark chasm loomed ahead and the path they had just walked shifted behind them.

"Where do we go from here, Kiel?" Atyn asked looking nervously back at the moving rock.

"This way." he pointed and, to their surprise, a new series of crumbling stairs led into the dark.

"Lead on then." Atyn answered looking at the treacherous path, "We have no other choice."

"It is very dark." Istah replied watching Kiel slip his feet over the edge. "Can we risk the light of the Fire Glass?"

Kiel hesitated, listening to the airs. "His will is bent upon other things." he answered finally, "Do not draw the light from the casing, only open it enough to light our path and only until we reach the next level. Yurah, follow close and keep your hand ready at the Sword."

She opened the casing of the fire glass, allowing a single beam to spread down the narrow crack. The steps were no more than holes that crumbled down the endless crevice. She could not keep her hand to her weapon for she had to use them both to keep to the wall. Her arms began to burn and grains of rock fell into her face. They slipped and caught themselves time after time. Kiel waited, not allowing them to fall too far behind. Yurah began to notice faint streaks along the stones.

"His wounds have opened." she told herself but before she could speak about it, the cavern groaned.

"The lamp is drawing them out from their caves." Kiel warned from ahead, "We can not risk using the light much longer. Believe me, there are worse creatures in these realms than the Umbra. "

They scrabbled down the hole following as swiftly as they could and, much to their relief, the descent did not last much longer. The rocky ladder had led them to another dark pit.

"Cover the lamp." Kiel said before crawling inside. The hole opened quickly opened into a wide theater and just beyond a flight of long stairs lead to the Iron Gate.

He climbed them and without hesitation he cried the word. "IANDO." The Gate sprang apart at the command, revealing the jealous nymphs that waited at the other side. The spites were alive and they laughed and pinched and twisted their skin as they passed by the door, their hateful taunts echoing through the gloom.

"Do not listen. They feed on pain and hurt." he said, pushing himself forward as the mob grew thick around them. Bolder and bolder the creatures became, reaching out their sinister hands to slice their skin. Soon the jealous swarm blocked their way and they could go no further. Yurah drew her sword from the sheath. Atyn and Istah followed suit. The horde backed away at the fierce light. Slowly they inched through the crowd, walking back to back, until they reached the door along the far side.

"Come this way." he said, pulling open the latch and leaving his bloody handprint along the handle.

"Is there any comfort I can give you?" Atyn asked, looking away from the stain.

"There is nothing. This burden is of my own making. Soon we will enter the realm of Betrayal. Trust nothing you see around you and keep to the center path. Draw your swords and follow me. I have been here many times."

Without a wasted step Kiel led them through the dangerous

corridor and with their bright swords drawn, they held wicked things at bay. Arrogance howled as they passed but none of that rancor could touch them. The Copper Gate followed the Iron and the Sixth Hall of Animosity came soon after. Istah pulled the silver door closed behind them and again they entered the world of stone. Yurah found herself in a forgotten nightmare. The airs reeked of sulfur. Her eyes burned and it was painful to breathe. A river of flame flowed through the ravine beneath them. The cascading fire roared between the obsidian walls. Kiel paused, a trickle of blood leaked from his nose. Yurah reached up to wipe it away but he stopped her and turned quickly away.

"He is busy still," he said, toying with the end of his dagger. "War rages above us." and again he wiped the blood from his face, "If the Fates can smile in such a place, I believe that they are doing it. Come quickly. The Seventh Gate marks the beginning of the end."

They walked along of the edge of the fires. The heat was smothering and even Atyn stumbled along the threadlike rim. Yurah struggled with her nightmare memories, settling herself by concentrating on each single step. But it was Kiel who seemed to have the worst of it. The suffocating pressure would drive him to his knees. They would take their turn at his side and the ground shook.

"The Umbra are spreading over the world above." Kiel told her as they waited for the tremors to cease. "Odyn's folk are failing and the Drui are too few in number. Ildabyth waits in his tower watching everything die. He will return to the deeps when the Stars turn toward us. He is saving that moment for her. He will wait to the last instant to take everything she holds dear."

His terror ran like a cold blade through her heart. The scabbard began to stir.

"You have brought us this far, Kiel. Without you we could not have done it. All is not lost, my friend. We are near."

"Very near." he replied to himself, "so near the words I spoke long ago still ring in air. Despair is futile but alas it is all that is left. This curse I have put upon myself."

"The law will hold true, Kiel. If you had the power to draw a thing to yourself, you have the power to end it."

His bitter laugh cut through the suffocating air, "You are to young to understand this." he answered dryly. "Even with all you have lost." then he laughed again, "And even with all you have left to lose. Follow me if you must. The Seventh Gate awaits us."

He led around the next bend and a familiar sight was before her. The river of flame spilled from a crack just ahead. The liquid fire flowed into the deep canyon she had seen in Kiel's dreams. The slender bridge stretched over the chasm. She strained her eyes, wondering if the guardian was waiting at the edge. Kiel knew her thought.

"You will meet him soon enough." he said without turning around. Without an instant of hesitation he walked over the thin bridge to wait impatiently on the other side. A dark hole loomed behind him.

"Do not draw your blade." he commanded, "This walk we must make in the dark."

The sound of the fiery river faded as the way sloped sharply down. She placed her hands along the wall but pulled them away quickly. A sticky slime burned her fingers. They walked after him, following the sound of steps. Sometimes he would call out sharp commands, and sometimes she could hear him muttering curses just ahead. After a while a strange glow lent some light to the tunnel, though it brought no comfort it made sight possible.

The Golden Door arced inward, creating a sheltered cove in the stone path. Yurah recognized the ancient glyphs that ran along its edges. They were the same glyphs that graced the scabbard that hung at her side but now the Senzar was silent. Kiel stood before the gleaming entrance. He began to speak in a steady rhythm. The tones were ugly. Color ran from Atyn's face as he listened and his hands trembled. Yurah had seen the same look upon him the day the Umbra had come for him. Istah placed one hand over Atyn's left ear and the other over his heart. Softly she began to sing into his right ear. Yurah held tight to her sword. Pushing the words away from her mind, she felt the strength of her blade comfort her. Finally his chant ended and when he intoned the final command and the door dissolved. As the golden letters faded into the shadows and a long corridor stretched before them. His face had changed when he turned back to face them. The set of his jaw was cruel and his fingers played nervously along the hilt of his knife.

"Come. They are waiting." and they followed him down the hall.

The arched walls were polished. The shine gleamed, mirroring their images in its crimson black surface as they passed. Candles burned in shallow alcoves along the way. A thick carpet silenced the sound of their boots but ahead the muffled sound of voices could be heard. When the hall opened into the circular room, three sinister statues looked down upon them. Their frozen hands held naked swords notched with jags.

"I have returned, Masters of the Seventh Realm. I have come back to you, begging and humble. Begging for you to grant my sweetest desire for I am an obedient man and I accept graciously that it is only by your hands that I may hold the world of plenty. And it is only through your halls that the thirst of a man can truly be quenched." Kiel said to the still forms.

A low rumble shuddered through the room and the stony eyes of the statues opened. Their eyes were a shining black and the edges of the notched swords glowed crimson.

"What do you dare ask of us, little mage?" the first statue replied.

"I ask for the Path of Power to be held open to me. I seek to possess what I design. Such is the law Masters, for creation does not exist without the created."

"A bold request from one who deserves nothing." the second statue chided, "What do you give in return for this favor?"

"I will give what is innocent and what has been loved best."

The third statue began to laugh, "And does the 'innocent' understand the price to be paid?"

"No. It is hid and will remain so."

"You do not convince me." said the first statue.

"What more do you want to know?"

"Certainly no more of your lies." it replied coyly, "Instead we would prefer to see your Will at play. Behold!" and from the folds of the stone robe a moth appeared. The creature was large as his hand. The pale green wings glowed iridescently in the candle light and from its eyes a peculiar intelligence flowed. It fluttered to him, encircling his head, beating is delicate wings. The sound of its pounding wings echoed through the chamber.

"Kill it." the statue commanded.

Yurah drew a sharp breath and Kiel hesitated.

"It is only a moth. What would it prove?" he asked.

"Very little wizardling. As you have said, 'it is only a moth'." the stone answered sweetly, "You will kill it only because I ask to do it. Such is the nature of the Ildabyth's will."

The moth drew closer. Kiel put out his hand and surrounded the creature. He could feel the fragile life fluttering in his fingers.

"We are losing our patience." said the stone.

"No need to bother." Kiel replied, and he crushed the moth in his hand. Cackling laughter filled the room and the stony beings began to change. Turning first to watery mist and, as the rain began to fall within the chamber, a pool of blood spread slowly over the floor. Behind where they had stood another long hall appeared. Kiel wiped the crushed remains from his hand.

"It is this way." and he did not look back to see if they followed.

The corridor was brilliant with wealth, the walls were etched with silvery designs that moved along with them. She could hear them as they passed. The images were cruel and as they went further in, the reflections became more hideous. Finally she turned to stare. The walls were alive as the battle, taking place above them, played out before her eyes. The skies over Basilus belched gloom. The Umbra seethed through the streets. Wielding the black swords, the shadows fed upon the blood of the living until the last spark of life was captured but this bit they did not use for themselves. This bit was used instead to feed their Master's will. Yurah watched in horror as the fragile fleck of spirit flowed toward the crystal spire. She could see Tamil leaning over a young woman with Inrih on guard at her side. She pushed the long hair aside and gasped at the throat rent wide apart. Tenderly she stroked her brow as the maid pulled her last breath. There was nothing to do. She covered the young face with her bloody shawl. Inrih helped her rise and she moved on to the wounded boy that lay in a nearby alley. Yurah felt a gentle hand at her elbow.

"Come child," said Istah, "It is not wise to linger. These realms take their toll upon us all."

"Indeed." she answered, watching Kiel's silhouette glide down the long hall.

They hurried to catch him and found him standing between two tall columns that reached higher than their eye could follow. The fixed stars glimmered in the dark vault behind him. He was holding a large chalice in his hand.

"Did you know which of the Greater Stars feeds the Yellow Sun of Erda?" he asked Atyn haughtily, never intending to give him time to answer. "Of course you do, my brother, so well you understand the ways of the upper and lower worlds. You are pure. You are perfect, are you not? And how long have you been able to speak with Malkians?" he jeered, "I suppose not long enough to realize what fools they have become. What is Law without questioning its purposes? Fancy, they enjoy doing such a thing."

"What do you mean, Kiel?"

"The Eighth Gate, Atyn. It is the stars of heaven's dome that fill the cup of the Ancient One for as every wise man knows it is power of their force which is bound within all things." he said motioning toward the Gate. "Every desire lies in this abyss. Do you not hunger for it? "

"Kiel. You are not yourself. Your old wounds bleed. We are deep inside Ildabyth's world, the toll it takes upon us all is tremendous. Sit and rest a moment. I can help you. We have come so far to lose ourselves now."

"The way is not far from the Seventh to the Eighth. It is a simple maneuver from one place to the next if you know its secret." he mocked, wiping the blood off his hands. "Is it not Yurah? Come here and stand at my side. Do you know that you are my first true friend in centuries? I have come to love you more than I thought I could ever love a thing. Stand here and I will show you something new. I will show you first because you understand me best." He put his arm around her facing the opening that looked into the sea of stars. "Do you remember when we first met? I was angry then. I was tired and I was filled with old hurts and you did not understand why. But you know me well enough now, do you not? I know you do, every moment I hear you in my thoughts. Do you remember Yurah? Do you remember the way we met? I believe it was there." and he pointed to the fixed star. "That is Rempha's Star, is it not? You know it is. I know you do. You are quite wise, Lady. Born wise, I will say. But the Seventh Daughter of a Seventh Son could be no less than this. I have watched you gazing upon the starry paths and I can tell you hear their voices. Your father's star, my father's star, the Rivers that run through them, and all those wide spaces between, how well you know them all. But did you know that a moment comes when those stars will align to touch the Yellow Sun of Erda? Possibly you did, quite possibly indeed. But there is a thing you might not know. Do you know that I am not angry anymore, Yurah. Did your telepathy suffice to reveal that?" he asked softly, bending close to her, he pressed his lips hard against her mouth and kissed her. "Understanding of these realms is really quite pointed." he whispered in her ear and without warning he pulled his dagger from his belt and cut a deep slash into the palm of her hand. The blood trickled into the cup, "Do not fear me, Yurah." he smiled grimly, "I need but a little." and then he threw the chalice into the gloomy hole and spat through the opening. A dark shadow formed just before them, creating a twisting ladder of utter black. The dark helix crawled through the alabaster columns.

"There. That wasn't so hard now was it?" he smirked. "Come little sister. The last door awaits you." and he climbed down the ladder into the gloom. In disbelief she watched him go, her blood still spilling from the cut.

Istah tore off a piece of her robe and bound the hand tightly. "Can you do this child?" Yurah nodded and climbed after him.

They descended through heaven's door. The ladder of silvery light quickly became more solid beneath their feet until the rungs became a stair of stone, and then changed again into a stair of wood. She could hear Kiel laughing wildly below them. Her heart trembled as she felt his mind leaving him. The sound of water met her then, and around her the walls turned to mortar and stone. A shrill wind blew past her ears. The cold air stunk. Finally they touched the stone floor. Specks of starlight glittered above and just ahead waited the mouth of a large cave. The way was barred by a circle of reddish flame and just beyond a vast catacomb spread out in all directions. Kiel was waiting, pacing along the edge of the fiery ring.

"Behold my trusty companions. My promise has been kept." Kiel said, pacing nearer to the ring of flame. It hissed and the fingers of fire reached toward, "You know what you have come to do," he muttered to himself, choking upon a laugh, "but to do it you must seal the Eight Gates above you for all of eternity. Never will you return to what you have loved best. Never again will you see your sisters, of your brothers, and your father's fair faces. The choice is yours. The choice of leaving everything behind you, it is the only way to reach her. Is it not desire that drives you forth? You are obsessed with it, are you not? Believe me, I know the feel of it. Go to her then, if you must," he sneered, "From here you can only imagine how she suffers under his hand. And she will suffer still more. How tenderly he will hold her when he sucks the last bit of life she has kept hid within her. She waits for you Yurah, just beyond the fiery door. Call to her if the notion stirs you to it. Perhaps she will answer. Perhaps she will not. Either way, the end will not be changed." His eyes grew wilder as he spoke. Blood seeped from under his blouse and wisps of dark filtered through his skin. Her heart was breaking as she watched him suffer.

"We have come this far. You have led us without faltering." said Atyn softly, trying to calm him. "Just as always, you see yourself in too a harsh a light. All may still be put right again. The battle is not lost, Kiel."

"This battle was lost before it began." he told him bleakly, "It is a fool's errand. You must find the way without me." and with no more explanation, Kiel turned away from the Ninth Gate leaving his companions to complete the desperate work as they watched him fade into the shadows.

CHAPTER XXXII
THE FOUR RIVERS

Doxomedon waited for an answer to come. The deserted lands of Mundi appeared in the crystal globe. He pressed his hands against the glass. Like a wind, the old mage raced with the Four Rivers that spilled into the Rempha's land. Climbing upon their shoulders he flew over the stewarding trees, passed above the cool oasis, and moved through the rings of the spiraling city until he reached the center point. It was atop the City of Mundi where he found him. The child was waiting in the garden.

"It has been a long time, Father." he said to the boy.

"Not so long, Doxomedon," Rempha laughed, "but as always, much has changed. The time of blending is close now. "

"I am ready for it." The wizard answered, acutely aware of being several places at the same time. Still he could feel his hands resting upon his crystal in his scrying chamber. Still he could hear the rushing of the waters running through the desert heat and the silent cold of the heavens. He could taste the clear bright air in Rempha's garden. The boy's eyes gleamed as he looked upward toward the sky.

"And the Pleiades?" he asked gazing upon heaven's dark.

"Tirelessly they watch the stars. This moment has been long anticipated."

"Of course it has. Raldaban leads his daughters true. I would have expected no less. Soon the light of Mundi will join the Seven Sisters and, when the Great Bear aligns with these efforts, new hope will come to the forgotten realm."

"Ahh, the Bear. Such an enigma those lamps are." Doxomedon mused, "It is one of those seven lamps that drew my only son away from his home. It is the starry lights of the Greater Bear that holds him captive."

"The Bear hold the essence to the riddle. It is the mystery that lies at the heart of all Erda's troubles. It appears as balance, ever the labor of the forgotten realm."

"And will balance be made this time, Rempha?"

"It is not my place to determine the outcome of any struggle. The Little Kingdom is a free land, designed to be at be at odds with itself. My duty lies in service to the greater cycles. Mundi is dedicated to the battle. As the lights of the constellations converge, she will move through the Lion to touch Saturn's children. There is much hope in this, Doxomedon"

"So much has changed since the last War. Ildabyth's power has grown and so many of Mqttro's ranks have fallen in the fight. Now the Great Tree falters. It falters because of what he has taken. What was not his right to hold."

"You are speaking of Sro's fall." Rempha said gently, "Sro was the first to sacrifice for the long forgotten people. She is Annyd and she understands the Law of Correspondence. Her actions have brought great possibilities."

"And Kiel?"

"Kiel's dilemma called her to that greater duty. All that has been made wrong will have its chance to be put right. Sro returned the Little Kingdom of her own accord. The will of the Annyd can not be dictated, only hindered under the rule of Time. Ildabyth can not steal what has been given freely."

"Ildabyth understands the Laws of the Cycles just as well as you and I." Doxomedon answered, "He is patient and he knows that within the Lady's heart there lies a greater strength. He will linger at her deathbed waiting to swallow the fluttering essence as it begins its ascent toward home. If he succeeds her long years of suffering will have been in vain."

"Sro is aware of the cost. She holds herself in his thoughts, ever-mindful of his efforts." Rempha answered solemnly, "I believe she understands the daemon better than he understands himself. She can perceive his every action before it is done. His plans are no secret to any. Through these long years, Ildabyth has concerned himself with building his armies. It was the Seraphs who held him in exile to the outer dark. Loathing drives him to the fight the Malkians. He knows they keep the secret to all form-life upon their islands. But rivalry is not all that darkens his mind. Ildabyth's jealousy of the Drui is unparalleled. These folk hold a unique bond to the ancient substance of Erda. They have the ability to mold themselves into its many forms. His desire to control the substance of the Little Kingdom has consumed him since the Yellow Sun first burst into life. It drives him to destroy all remnants of that race. Over the millennia he has hunted them deliberately. Their numbers now lie far short of the need. It was a wise choice they made to join the Alfyr but this leaves Ildabyth with even more reason to trouble over Odyn and his people. They are made warriors. They are learned and they are daring but I fear that the Dark Swords of Umbra will deal them many bitter blows. The Alfyr are bound to the realm by their lineage and are subject to its faults. There is only one race that walks within the Little Kingdom without flaw."

"You speak of the Vanyr. Often I have seen their leader in my scrying glass speaking to the Malkians." answered Doxomedon.

"He is the eldest of Jupiter's children. He serves between the Air and the Waters of the Little Kingdom. His kin know him as Atyn Stormbringer. The Seven Satellites did not wander when the greater spirits went to play at other games. Those watchers remained near, allowing their little sister her time to grow. Allowing her people time to understand."

"And as the Mystic, who conceals himself behind the Moon, aligns with the powers of Mercury, Jupiter will touch his eldest son. In that moment the Stormbringer will funnel the triple-force onward."

"Ildabyth hates bitterly. He will be ready for this."

"Ildabyth has yet to learn there is a greater side of truth. He is deluded by his conceit and, while he has busied himself robbing the land, behind the Lady Moon our work has gone on in secret. The three trines will bring the aid that is needed." Rempha told him, pointing to the sky, "Look there, Doxomedon. The Rivers are gathering. Though Ildabyth will seek to use the moment to achieve his end, he does not see all things. The Sword has returned to the Little Kingdom and he has not yet singled out the one who bears the talisman. It is her innocence which protects her from his roving eye."

"Yurah." he said.

"Yes Doxomedon. Sro's child is bound to the fate of the Erda just as she is bound by the dangerous light of the Bear."

"Just as Kiel is bound." he replied softly.

"It is so. The lives of Kiel and Yurah, share the fate of what was not made perfect." he said softly, watching the funneling clouds gather over the night sky.

"The battle is beginning." Rempha said, "Look now, all choices are being made."

Doxomedon pulled his attention back into the scrying chamber. The glass was dark as the growing storm centered itself over Mundi. The Cosmic Rivers were pulling together into a single force and he could hear Iao's voice from across the waters.

"Kiel! Oh fair son of Taygeth!" he heard Iao cry, "Alas, my brother's child. You have lost yourself once more."

"Can he not see he is not safe alone? Can he not know they will come for him?" cried Lyli in disbelief.

"The tale is just as before, Ildabyth will destroy him." gasped Tyla, watching Kiel stumble blindly through the caverns.

"He has lost his mind." replied Sothis sadly. "The damage within was too great. He is blind too what comes for him. Alas, for the Little Kingdom. Alas for our little sister. It is a dreadful turn."

"Now she must stand without him." said Iao bleakly staring into the Anath's mirroring pool. "This is the battle I hoped would never come. Indeed, the Fates have dealt us a bitter strike."

"She has made no error throughout this labor, father." Raeyn replied cautiously, watching Yurah gather her resolve as Kiel disappeared into the darkness, "She has not wasted a whispered word in despair. Her will is firm, though the road is dangerous. She has seen into Kiel's heart and has understood what tortures him. Through he has faltered she remains true. She will remember when the moment comes. She will remember even though the world has gone awry."

"Then she will become just as her mother was." he answered softly, "The single point in the midst of Chaos." Iao stretched out his hand and held it over the mirror. "What a glorious moment it was as she emerged from the Deep." His face filled with concern as the surface of the glass began to waver. He saw the dread of the small company as they backed away from the Ninth Gate. The fiery ring was stretching its blazing fingers toward them trying to clutch their garments to draw them inside the circle. A treacherous laughter began to swell out into the chamber. "The wait is over." Iao told his daughters grimly. "Ildabyth is coming."

Doxomedon held to glass and cried out to Rempha over the sea of dark space.

"What aid does heaven offer, Rempha? A untried maid to stand before such a vile host. Surely she is not meant to face him alone."

"She is not alone." his answer came. "The Jove stands with her."

"The child of Jupiter can not hold him back. Yurah and Kiel are the seed of Elder Stars. Only they can stand against Ildabyth in this wicked realm. Where are the Malkians? Can they not come to her aid?" he asked pulling himself through the havens to stand again at Rempha's side.

"Even the Malkians dare not venture so deep." Rempha replied, "The time has not yet arrived. For the moment the child must bear this burden alone."

"That will not be necessary." a great watery voice boomed over the garden. "I will go to her." A fierce wind blew into their faces as the Riverman rose up from the stormy skies and stood before them.

"Yotru" Rempha replied with the low bow. "I can not say I am surprised you have arrived at my door."

"I have come, Aeon. The Four Fathers have drawn me to them and I am ready to serve that call. The little daughter is special to me."

"She is special to many, though many will never understand it." answered Doxomedon gazing though the storm toward the place the

Great Bear would hold in the heavens.

Rempha followed his stare and after a long moment he answered the elemental.

"Do you realize the nature of this undertaking? Nothing is as it seems in the lower worlds. The need may come for all force to be utilized." Rempha replied to the Riverman.

"I have understood since the day Sro abandon the Sword in my wake, Aeon. The Lady left me with no doubt of her need."

Rempha looked over the sky that loomed over Mundi. The tense clouds churned over the dark night and he finally answered. "Go to her, but forget not the purposes of your Four Fathers. Urdar is failing and the root is starved. Answer your calling, Yotru." he commanded, addressing the River by his birthing name. "A greater destiny awaits you."

His ancient eyes glowed at Rempha's command. Rising through the funneling waters, he pulled his watery robes together and climbing upon the shoulders of the bitter storm, the Riverman raced toward the Little Kingdom.

CHAPTER XXXIII
THE SWORD OF SRO

Deafening laughter blared through the cave. The fiery gate roared in response. They pressed against the rock trying to shield themselves from the fierce heat. Beyond the gate a large domed room materialized and in its center a group of robed men encircled a long alter. The rise and fall of their chanting joined with the hideous laughter.

"What are they saying?" Yurah asked.

"Nothing that is worth repeating," assured Atyn. "They are excited. Their Master is near. We must wait."

After a time a sickly glow appeared in the center of the chamber and the chanting diminished. The oppressive light brought fear with it. Yurah found it difficult to breathe.

"Quid times, viator?" came the soft question spoken in the elder tongue. "What do you fear, wanderer?" the voice repeated and an old man appeared, leaning against a polished staff, appeared just on the other side of the Ninth Gate.

Atyn stepped forward to reply but the ancient being just lightly waved his hand and Atyn was lifted off his feet.

"The question was not yours to answer." came the acrid response. "I wish to hear the voice of the child."

Atyn eyes grew wide for the daemon could not hide his intention. "Do not speak!" he struggled to tell her but the old man laughed and flung him against wall. A smear of blood streaked the rock behind him and he collapsed into a crumpled heap. Istah lay her hand upon Yurah's shoulder telling her to be still. The gray-eyed lady stepped up and stood before the Daemon.

"She is only a child Ildabyth, and children fear many things."

A cruel smile spread over the wrinkled face. "Only a child?" he replied sarcastically. "Certainly Istah, you of all folk should know better than to tease. Have you failed to notice what has happened to your sweet companion? I am sorry dear, I doubt he will ever rise again." the daemon chuckled, looking admiringly at his withered hand. "And it took so little. Still I surprise myself with my power. But oh my, now with just ladies to entertain, I must not forget all my manners. Please come in." he grinned and the flames flickered gently at the edge of the circle. "We have so much to talk about. The world is in such an awful state. Don't you agree? So let us get to the point, shall we. Family affairs are always a good place to start. You know so little about a person until you understand where they came from." and he winked and Yurah felt her belly lurch. "Certainly, I would like to get to know you better little one. Tell me something of you father, child. How has he faired over the years?" the old man smirked. "It must be lonely without her?"

"Where is she, Ildabyth? Where do you keep the Wanderer, Lethe?"

"Lethe? Is that the name you know her by? What nonsense has Mqttro been spouting to your star-crossed seer?" he said glancing maliciously toward Atyn. His violence flared and with a flick of his hand, Atyn was flung face down against the stone. Yurah ran to his side and gently wiped the blood from his face. Istah did not turn to look but kept her eye fixed to the old man.

"Do not tease Ildabyth. Odyn gave us the Lady's name. Lethe awaits the turning of the Great Wheel. And when she perceives it, she will break free from her prison destroying you and your armies. "

"Odyn! Odyn told you that! Well I will say to you, Odyn is a fool! The Lady Lethe. Ha! Obviously his bargain with the Memhir did not profit him much. It is a sad thing to have given an eye and still remain so ignorant. But alas, alas, that is the nature of women's games," the old man winked, "And I am far too wise than to play at them. Knowledge is a dangerous pursuit my dear and I see you are in great need of some. If you would like I could offer you a true hint to her predicament. But first you must agree to the rules and second you must give me something in return. What do you say?"

"What do you want, Ildabyth?"

"Be patient, Istah. That is my surprise. Do you agree to the rules?"

"I do not agree. Nothing true has ever escaped your lips."

"Assurance? Is that what you desire? Look around you, dear. What more assurance do you need?"

"It is plain you offer only despair."

"Oh Istah." he chuckled scornfully, "It is tragic thing that one so beautiful has been raised upon the milk of fools. But listen to my proposal and I can change all of that. I can offer you the world."

"You spend too much time in your dungeons, Ildabyth. You are not aware of what goes on in the realms of above."

"What happens above is what happens below." he countered, "I am just a pawn of greater desires. It is the way of things."

Yurah paid no heed to the game of words going on between them, grateful only that Istah was keeping the Daemon entertained. Her attention was bent upon Atyn. His wounds were familiar. Tristan had suffered a similar hurt. She prepared herself for the transfer of energy, waiting for his pain to fill her, but no pain did come. Touching his face she realized his breath had left him. He was gone and only the shell remained in her arms. The pressure of the choking realm crushed her. The world grew dark and she felt herself falling through the gloom. The fiery gate loomed beneath as the whole of her life rushed by. Streams of luminous globes were flowing through her fingers. The shining orbs were carrying every thought that had ever passed through her mind. The flames leapt up to meet her just as a rush of watery cold swept over her. A familiar voice spoke inside the waking dream.

"I am the one who never sleeps." the old voice said, "I am the journey ever outward. I am the way of return."

"Riverman!" she cried in recognition, "How did you know? How did you find me?

"It is I who ever serves your need, little one. You are the pilgrim. I am the means."

The ancient elemental surrounded her then, and in a rush of clear water she was taken from the center of the hopeless world. Her skin was made clean, all the black and the sooty grease that clung to her was washed away. She rode upon his shoulders, tears running down her cheeks, remembering the moments that had just passed her by. They raced through the realms of Erda and did not rest until they reached the edge where the sky met the stars. The Seraph was waiting for them.

"Greetings Yurah." he said graciously. "Greetings Riverman."

"Greetings Mqttro." she answered, trying to keep her voice from trembling.

"Why do you despair, child?" he questioned

"It is Atyn, Lord. He was passed from the world below. He is gone. Ildabyth murdered him. "

The Seraph bright wings flamed higher when he heard the news. "It is I who keep guard over that Gate. Believe me when I say to you, seventh daughter, the child of Jupiter has not passed through that door."

"But he is gone, Mqttro. I held him and no life flowed in his veins."

"Ildabyth's realm is filled with illusions. What seems real there is not real in the upper worlds."

"What do you mean?"

"Behold, little daughter," he answered gesturing to the valley below. "You must have realized by now is possible to be at more than one place at more than one time."

Yurah looked over the edge of the canyon. As far as her eye could see spread the restless ocean. The Riverman gently touched her hand and they began to move across the churning waters. In an instant the city of Basilus rose from the waves and in another she was struggling through the dark maze of Ildabyth's Gates. She saw herself holding Atyn's motionless body. All around her the noise of battle filled the night air. The clash of swords and the screams of war surrounded her. Fierce women on horses made of fire rode into unworldy dark. The cries of the Umbra crawled under her skin but the Riverman pulled her on. He carried her across the wind and over the mountains until they finally descended over a small lake. Two people were kneeling over a still form. The body did not appear to be solid. It wavered like water under the gentle candlelight.

"You are doing well Urion." whispered an old woman. "You have sealed the breach. The wound is beginning to close." Yurah recognized the voice. It was Macha.

"Why does he not open his eyes?"

"It is not the physical body that lies here. Ildabyth's damage was directed toward the primary form. The vital body is made of finer stuff. The Daemon meant to destroy his visualizing eye. It is what Ildabyth finds most dangerous to his plans. He did not wish for your brother to blend with Mqttro in the upper airs. The time is close. Soon Jupiter will reverse his path in the sky." she said looking into the stars. "Indeed it is the moment the old goat has been waiting for. Hurry now Urion, we must take your brother to the peak of Zelmisso. It is the best we can do for him now."

"But how will we carry him, Macha?" Uri asked, looking about nervously. The flash of the Valkyries blades blazed in the northern sky. The howling of the wind and the cries of the wounded rattled through the leaves. "The Umbra are all around us. Odyn can not be spared from the fight. It is just the two of us, Macha. How shall we break through?"

"Do not worry boy. The vital body is all but weightless. It can be lifted upon a breath of wind. Come now, hurry up. I have a plan." and Macha blew out the lamps.

"He is not dead." Yurah whispered as the vision faded. Nothing but ocean remained and she found herself riding once more upon the broad shoulders of the Riverman.

"No child, he is not dead. Atyn fate now lies in the hands of the younger son." the elemental answered, "but your fate lies at the Ninth Gate. No one else can take your place there."

"But all has gone wrong. Kiel should be with me and he is lost."

"Kiel understood the odds from the start. His fate is not made worse by the efforts he has made. Understand, little daughter, the outcome of this fight could never lie with Kiel. The finish has always rested in your hand."

The whispering sheath responded to the Riverman's words. Its murmuring song spilled over the waters.

"Do you know what the scabbard tells you, child?"

"No Riverman. Though often it has brought me comfort, its whispers have always been foreign to me."

"The Senzar is a precious gift, Yurah. It speaks of the riddles that plague of this sorrowful realm. The same riddles the Annyd sought to unravel as they first began to shape the Little Kingdom. When Kiel returned to draw her back to this forgotten place, Sro finally understood its answer. It is why she left with no word or warning. Ildabyth desires this knowledge over all else" and the Riverman paused to smell the air. "And this is why Little Daughter, Sro left the Sword under Raldabon's guard until the moment of need was dire. You carry the talisman that can turn this battle when all other hope must be abandoned."

The jewel upon the hilt of her sword caught a bit of starlight but as she looked up to the heaven, the clouds came and swallowed the view.

"The word you seek goes by many sounds, but only one sound will reveal the mystery of the final door. Remember that, Yurah. It is important." The roar of the ocean had faded as her feet came to rest upon cliff. She was alone. Slowly she walked to the edge of the canyon. Looking over its edge she could see nothing but smoke and storm but after a moment she felt a heavy weight against her. She had returned to her body. The heat and smell of the dreadful catacomb burned her eyes. She leaned close to Atyn's mouth and felt the warmth of his breath against her cheek. Over her shoulder Istah still debated with the Daemon.

"This world has ever been a place of tears. I will play my part and you shall play yours." she heard Ildabyth say, "Why fight it Istah? Pain is often made into pleasure. It only awaits your consent."

"You have yet to answer my question, Ildabyth. What do you want from me?"

"Well firstly, I would like you to join me in my chamber." he clucked. "It is such a small favor to ask. The Lady in my keeping has not been herself. It seems my little war has taken a heavy toll upon her and she has little left to return to a man. I seek a new consort, Istah." and again he glanced to Atyn, his eyes filled with a dangerous gleam, "and it seems you do as well."

Istah eyes narrowed, knowing the Daemon pressed her into a trap and there was no other place to go. "Perhaps I might consider it Ildabyth, if I could have a moment with the Lady Lethe? A moment alone."

His awful laugh roared through stony walls. The ground began to shake and Istah covered her ears.

"I am growing weary of your lies, Istah." he frowned, "The Lady 'Lethe', as you call her, is the very reason you have sought out my humble domain. I am not blind to desire. I understand the nature of such things better than any. You can hide none of it from me."

"Desire is not my motive."

"All right, call it something else if you wish. Why does your kind insist upon fooling itself with these beneficent delusions? You serve yourself even if you pretend to protect those of lesser fortune. And who are protecting? Is it Kiel? Well, if that is the case then you are far too late. Kiel's fate has been set for centuries. But no. You are a woman, not a fool. It must be something else." he smacked his thin lips. "It must be the child. Children have ever been the imbalance of the female nature. I am beginning to understand you Istah. This motherless child breaks your pathetic heart. You seek reunion for the girl and her name-giver. And yet you fear to speak her mother's name aloud. That is clever enough I suppose, clever enough but it did suffice. But I well tell you now what an unfortunate choice of traveling companions you have made. I have known of your plans to join these two ever since you passed through these walls. Kiel has been my eyes and ears. I have only had to wait until he ran off to attend to this work myself. He has always been such a great help to me. I must say, few things have ever satisfied me more than how he hates himself for it." and the daemon sniggered noisily. "But my, oh my, Kiel must have told you the rules of this game. To pass the Ninth Gate is to seal the others shut forever. Those are the rules. There is no changing them. So why despair? You will lack for nothing. You will never perish and everything the Little Kingdom has to offer will be yours for eternity. I do not understand the problems some have with that."

"I do not choose that way."

"I do not choose that way." he mimicked, "Do not fool yourself my dear. Those are the rules and there is no changing them."

Istah hesitated. The ground was shaking and her mind raced, trying desperately to find a way to buy just a few more moments.

"It seems to me Ildabyth, Kiel has also misunderstood the rules of your little game. You have deceived him before, so how simple could it be to deceive him again? But I know there is another turn to your perversions. Why do you seek to deceive me? I am wiser than he."

"Deception is necessary. Part of the rules, of course and there is no changing that either. No reason even to try it."

"Just answer this, Ildabyth. It is true, what Kiel told us, and the Lady is beyond this door," Istah said reaching her hand up to feel the heat of the flames that barred her way. "But she never sealed the Gates above. How did Lethe pass through these doors? What 'rule' have you failed to share with me, Ildabyth?"

The cavern groaned and a large crack raced about the edge of the cavern. Bits of rock crumbled in the shifting the corridor. The noise seemed to incite the Daemon. His anger flared. Yurah adjusted Atyn's cloak around him, trying protecting him from the falling grit. His hand was warm to the touch.

"I gave you choice, my dear. You have no other to blame but yourself for this." and with a wave of his hand, he crushed her against the wall. Yurah heard the crack of bone echoing down the hall. In stunned horror she watched her friend crumble to the floor.

"And now child." he said to her calmly, "Leave the dead. They cannot help you now. Leave them and come to me. I what a better look at you. Stand up. Stand up so I can see you better."

Cautiously she rose from Atyn's side. Remembering Atyn's words of warning, she did not speak when she turned to face him and kept her eyes cast down.

"Indeed you are a pretty thing." he gloated, "but still so young. Often it is difficult for children to understand the life I offer. Do not let it worry you dearie, I can help you to understand. Just like I helped your mother to understand." and as he began to cackle the fire flamed up around the door. "You are much like her. I see it in the way you carry yourself. Strong and beautiful. Stubborn though, very stubborn."

Yurah glanced up catching the Daemon's eye and a peculiar smiled crawled over his face. "Are you concerned about your companions, dear? Well, you should be. The streets are filled with blood today and no amount of good intentions will staunch it. You have come with to little, too late dear. Too little, too late." his eyes glowed a dim red, still she had not spoken a word to him. The daemon knew a secret was standing before him, but silent it remained.

"Would you like to see her child?" he hissed, "Do not let her appearance mislead you. She never looks very well these days."

And silently the scabbard began to murmur. Its voice rang into the center of her mind. The memory of the ancient language of Stars returned. The Senzar pushed into her thoughts and vision poured into her. The first of the trines had formed. The Yellow Sun of Erda was now contained by the gathering the Greater Lamps. A white fire ignited in the core of her being as Doxomedon stood, wreathed in flame. The mage stood deep within the inner chambers and as the Fates of Taygeth encircled him and his words formed in her mind.

"I am the Watcher that will not speak.
Waiting for choice to be revealed.

Eternal hand of Chaos deep.
A Greater Light unsealed."

The moment had come. Rempha was in the garden, holding the burning globe in his steady hand. Inside the crystal glass, she could see her sisters gathered round the scrying pool. They were calling her name. The invisible hands of Fate held her close. She was no longer afraid.

"Speak!" the Daemon screamed. "Speak to me now or her blood is on your hands."

She did not answer the demand. She drew the Sword from its whispering sheath and a starry light from worlds faraway began to fill the chamber. Then, without a sound and without a restless thought, nor a wasted motion, Yurah thrust her shining blade through the Ninth Gate.

A brilliant light blinded her with its heat as the cavern roared in response. The walls trembled and the ground shook. Yurah fell to her knees as around her the flames of the Ninth Gate shattered like glass. The old man wailed at the intrusion. The Daemon's essence had kept the circle in its place and as the fire exploded into a glittering dust, Ildabyth was scattered into bits. His form burst into a million parts and flew against the dungeon walls. The ashes of what he had once had been burned like acidic embers upon her skin. She choked on the smothering filth as she wrapped her clock around. The final Gate was destroyed, so bowing her head, Yurah ran through the doomed opening to search out her mother's prison bed.

Through the fog she walked alone. A labyrinth stretched before her and she allowed her instincts to pull her onward. Through the winding maze she went and though, dim red eyes watched her from the corners, they dared not approach. Holding the sword before her and she went without faltering and, at length, she found what she sought. A cell, narrow and dark, loomed before her. What was once its door had become no more than a pile of ash. Silently she stepped over the threshold and studied the dismal prison. A dark ceiling towered above her. There was no real light from above, only a dull brown lamp glowed dimly in its arching peak. Ebony chains were embedded into the gray walls and metal tools of torment were spread carelessly over the floor. The stench of filth and refuse reeked from uneven tiles. In the corner there lay an ebony slab. She walked to it and kneeled upon the stone floor. Carefully she touched the lightless straps that would have once bound a body and, as she did, an eerie mist began to form over the bed. Awkwardly, Yurah touched the fog and it swirled through her fingers like smoke. She called her mother's name and a faint light began to shimmer where the heart should have been.

Quickly Yurah took the Sword and held it over the fragile ethers. The etchings along the scabbard began to writhe and the Senzar began to chant. In layered order a new rhythm poured into her mind. She joined in the calling and soon visions of the night sky filled her thoughts. The Yellow Sun was fading as she was rushed through a field of light and dark. She was being pulled through the cold, spaces of the heavens and she raced upon an unseen wind. All around her music ebbed and flowed and soon the dark once more took shape and a mountain appeared. A bright moon was hanging over its icy peak and as the music continued snowy crystals spun into deep drifts along its stony shoulders. Someone was singing, another was laughing and the sounds of rushing water pulled her on. Beneath her a frozen meadow twisted its way through the rugged hillsides and in its center ran a herd of deer. Gracefully they raced through the ice and stone. One of the creatures pulled away from the group, and turned to stare at the cold moonlight that scattered through the leafless trees. The green eyes met her own, "Fear not little sister." the white doe said, "We are ready." And then the vision was gone.

Again she was on her knees in Ildabyth's dungeons. The Fire Glass was in her hands, pouring its healing light into the room. The sword pulsed and its magnetic force began to pull the frail body together. A fragile shell now lay in her arms and in its center a heart glowed brightly. The scabbard was still whispering as a thread of light spread through the form, connecting all parts to the other. In an instant she found herself looking into the forgotten face. Her mother's clear eyes twinkled with the faraway light of Raldaban.

"He is gone." Yurah whispered gently wrapping in her fragile body in her own blue cape as the sound of churning water filled the cavern. She felt his presence behind her as his watery voice spoke.

"I have come for you all." the Riverman spoke, gathering Sro into in his arms. "The end is upon us."

The belly of the world churned violently. Crashing sound exploded from every direction. The Eight Gates were crumbling. From above to below, the realms of Ildabyth were being pulled apart. Erda had been set free from his bondage and her heat burst upward from the central core. The Riverman set them atop his broad shoulders and upon the Ancient Water they rush ahead of the Fire, outrunning the flames.

Atyn opened his eyes to find himself face to face with a strange company, questions pouring through his mind. Yurah now stood with a frail woman at her side. Her skin was pale as rice paper and her eyes as bright as any lamp. Istah lay still in the Riverman's arms.

"What has happened to her?" he gasped, rising up on one arm.

"It was Ildabyth." Yurah answered sadly,   "But do not worry, he is gone."

"Gone?" he replied as the walls began to shake and stones tumbled from ceiling.

"Yes Atyn. He is gone. I will explain later. We must hurry now. The Riverman will take us back to the others."

Atyn gazed up at the colossal nereid. He was like nothing he had ever seen before.

"Would you like some assistance?" Yotru rumbled.

"Yes." Atyn answered simply for was all he could think to say.

"Oh Father. My heart feels as if it may burst. Sro is saved and they are together at last." whispered Lyli.

"It is the sweetest gift of all." answered her sister.

"Hold still daughters." replied Iao. "Be aware. This fight, it is not over. Nothing in the lands of Erda is as it seems. "

CHAPTER XXXIV
THE FINAL DAY

Mqtrro's battle for the upper airs had been going badly. At his feet the maimed bodies of his brothers and sisters lay motionless and now, under their still forms, the land groaned with regret. Doom was everywhere. In the far distance the sparks began to fly from the mouth of Zelmisso.

"It is over." Mqttro cried out, "The Gates of Ildabyth have broken. Back! Back! All and everyone! Back to the islands! Time is over! Back to the Islands of Urdar!"

In the belly of the world the deep rock trembled. In the skies above Zelmisso, Odyn's warriors were fighting ferociously. Riding upon their fiery blue steeds, the Valkyries battled the Umbra but Ildabyth's forces were holding strong. The killing sound of their fell weapons spared none. The dark swords cut the Alfyr from their horses and the brave soldiers fell into the sharp summits below. In the midst of the battle the Seraph appeared. The Umbra wavered in their killing rage. Mqttro swooped down and gently lifted Atyn's airy form from Urion's arms.

"To Yotru!" Mqttro commanded the fiery beast and slapping his flank the horse disappeared into the storm.

Urion raised his arms to greet the seraph. Mqttro's fiery body wavered between the worlds as he spoke to the boy. "The tree falters and my people are falling. Hold yourself ready Urion. Call your brother, the wind. Call your sister, the rain. And when they join, bring forth the Electric Heat from their warm, wet breath. The Umbra must not take the door between earth and air. Be aware! The Shadows are upon you." And then the Malki set his eye toward the Sacred Isles and faded into the clouds. Urion looked down the summit. Beneath his feet the churning dark moaned. The Umbra were once more gathering into a single shadow. The moment had come and with all the strength, and wit and force, he held within him, Urion called upon the wind and rain. Amidst the sparks and ash of Zelmisso, thunderbolts began to spill from the mountaintop. The wails of the Umbra filled the skies as the brilliant strikes rent them into pieces. The Valkeyries rallied round the peak for another strike. Dark smoke rumbled from the gut of Erda and fountains of flame sent their bright tongues high into the air. The phantoms found their pieces and rejoined for another attack. The shadows drew a line between land and air, leaving Urion to stand alone against them. Their killing sound struck him again and again but the bold Valkeyries would not be held back. Odyn led the charge, hacking his way through the murky skins until he carved a path through the shadow. Macha followed, wielding her staff and tearing the phantoms into bits of light. When the old mage finally reached the peak, the old woman raced past him and lifted the boy into her arms. Wiping the blood from his face, she spoke his name aloud but Urion did not heed the lesser call. They had come too late.

"Such irony Macha, that his first battle would be his last." Odyn said softly, watching the fluttering light escape, "But let us not despair for him, mother. In other worlds, he has triumphed. Urion is the grandchild of better realms. Look there now. He is going home." and in the night, the storm clouds parted and the starry lamps twinkled, showing their son the way.

Zelmisso growled and the ground where they stood began to tremble. "The mountain will not wait," he said looking at the fire that spewed from the peak. "Call the Riders, Macha. I am sure we can find something else to do."

Rising through the catacombs of Ildabyth's dark caverns, the Riverman lifted them into the streets of Basilus. As they rose upon his watery back, the histories of Little Kingdom mirrored themselves in the blade of Sro's Sword and Yurah learned of the years that had passed upon the painful world. A silent beauty, a steadfast ritual, never waving, never complaining, there was no beginning nor end to her goal. She was the heart of the world. In death or in life, Sro would not falter in her task and when she saw that her daughter understood, Sro smiled all over the world the clouds began to break apart.

Mqttro drew a deep breath as the rays of the Yellow Sun touched him once again. A new hope had filled his mighty heart. Far below, within a restive sea, the Isles of Urdar still churned in darkness. The Malkian knew the time of cleansing had finally come. He took up his blade and, as he descended into the fray, a massive circle of spinning fire was all the enemy could see.

Odyn led the way and the Valkyries followed. Battle lust was upon them and shadows were cleaved apart upon Zelmisso's peak. Odyn fought as he had never fought before and none of the Ildabyth's shades could stand before him. Far above in the cold heaven, Urion could hear the call toward home as the Bear's light twinkled unseen behind the Yellow Sun but far below, the sounds of war were everywhere and the boy lingered in the Middle Place. Shadows were pouring through the three towers as Tristan's folk battled in the streets of Basilus. Wyverns fought in the skies above the Druii, attacking the phantoms with their fiery breath and the Centaurs, stronger than oxen and quicker than snakes, tore the shadows apart with their deadly blades. The Umbra's screams joined the clang of swords and the smell of burned skin was everywhere.

"What should we do?" Yurah cried through the deafening fray.

Atyn looked about, taking the lifeless Istah into his arms. The war fell like rain about his shoulders. "Find Inrih." he answered.

"I can help with that." shouted a familiar voice. A carriage pulled to a halt beside them. Volos smiled as he jumped from the seat to hold the horses steady. Nestor was shouting from the back. "Hurry! Hurry! Get in! They are coming!"

"I beg your leave, Lady Sro. Change is fast upon us." The Riverman said as they climbed upon the wagon. "Mqttro has need of me. The Elders have set the Cosmic Rivers free. The River of Urdar must soon join with them. It is an errand meant for me alone."

"Go Yotru. Already the sky chokes upon the ashes of the lower worlds." Atyn answered him thoughtfully, "We shall see to the keeping of Basilus."

"I will return." he answered with a low bow and, in a whirl of wind and of water, the Riverman pulled himself up through the smoke and disappeared into the battlefield.

Volos despaired when he heard the news of Kiel and helping lay Istah into the carriage bed he asked. "Is there any hope for them, Atyn. Either of them, any hope at all?"

Atyn nodded, "More than you might imagine, Volos. Take us first to Inrih and a quiet place where we might work."

"Very well, but you must hold tight. The ride may prove to be a bit rough." and in an instant they were off. Deftly the horses made their way through the battleground as Volos carefully skirted the trail of dead that lay scattered in the streets.

"Beware," warned Nestor as they stared upon the ruin. Yurah leaned over to him and wiped the quiet tears from his face, "There is something not right about them," the boy sighed. "something not right at all."

"Look closely Atyn. There are strange marks upon the dead. Not even Dion knows what they are. And he has seen more of this dirty business than most." Volos added.

The oddly bent bodies lie frozen along the cobble streets, their glazed eyes still wide apart.

"Where are they, Volos? Dion and the others." shuddered Yurah.

"They have set up an infirmary in a tavern alongside the piers. Inrih and Tamil are with him helping as they can. But the Umbra's swords destroy everything they touch. Ordinary folk have no chance against them."

"Look up there! Look up!" cried Nestor, pointing the roofs above. "Something marvelous, well I think it is marvelous, anyway. It is a strange band that has come from the hill country. Really, they are much like you, Master Atyn, excepting their ears are most peculiar. They arrived along with the most extraordinary creatures. Soldiers that are both man and horse but the strangest thing of all is a dragon of sorts."

"The wyverns?" asked Atyn.

"Yes, the wyverns. It is true but strange." agreed Volos, "The wyvern and centaur are not inclined to get along. They are far too much alike. Both are ill-tempered and greedy. But today is different. Today their ill natures have served us. The wyverns are hasty with their fiery tongues but the centaurs are brutally strong. They understand a bit of the cruel magic themselves and the phantoms have not taken well to them at all. The fight has turned since they have arrived. Hold on tight, now. It is just down this alleyway."

Volos pulled the carriage to a sharp stop at the end of a narrow lane. A large wooden door hung askew from its hinges.

"Indeed Lady, you are no more solid than the wind" he said, helping the fragile Sro from the cart. "You are barely real at all," he said staring into her endless eyes. "And yet you seem so familiar",

Sro smiled, "You must be thinking of my daughter, Volos. We are much alike."

Volos grinned up at Yurah and agreed. "Indeed you are, Lady. Indeed you are."

The broken door swung open with loud creak. Inrih was there, holding the entryway wide apart.

"There is a place for her down here," Inrih said leading them down a long corridor. "What happened?" he asked looking down at her ashen face.

"Ildabyth dealt her this blow."

"Ildabyth!"

"It was his last act," he said grimly, "Just before he met his end."

"His end? What do you mean?"

"The daemon is no more." replied Atyn, glancing to her. "It appears when Yurah shattered the Ninth Gate, Ildabyth was cast into bits and parts and the lower realms began to collapse from the inside out."

"He is destroyed then?" Inrih said, laying Istah gently upon a palette.

"No it is not over." Sro whispered softly to the great man, "The body Ildabyth created still moves in the world. His priests still chant in their towers and his shadows still serve his will. Now, more than ever, we must hold steady to the task."

"I am ready, mother." Yurah said kneeling over Istah and pulling the crystal glass from under folds of her cloak.

"Then let us begin." said Sro, taking her place at the feet.

Istah opened her eyes just as Tamil and Dion arrived. Both were weary and stained with the weight of a suffering world and the fear of the dying. Dion knelt down beside her,

"It seems you have fared better than most, Lady Istah. But you have always had friends in high places." he said smiling at Yurah. "Do not rise if you value my judgment at all. You have much healing left to do. There is food and drink in the tavern upstairs. Nestor will be bringing it when he comes. Take what you will for there is no lack. I fear most of the folk I have seen this long night have no further need for refreshment."

"Thank you, Dion" she replied. "Help has come from high places and it has made me different than I was before. My ears can now hear what they could not hear before. I can hear as the Shadows suck the life from Erda and I can hear the war as it spreads like a disease over the airs of Urdar. But from over it all I can hear a voice. He is standing upon the mountain. Atyn, it is Urion who beckons."

Atyn was startled, almost dropping the censor he held in his hand. "It is Odyn's folk. The Shadows must be upon the peak of Zelmisso. Urion is with them. Why did I not hear before?"

"This fight has given us little time to listen. Go and do what you must. Your brother does not have to stand alone." said Istah.

"I will go. Please Inrih, stay with her." and he went to heed the call.

Atyn raced up the basement stairs to piers above. Leaping over the wall, he walked on the sands until he found a hidden place among the pilings. Sitting down in the protected dunes and he concentrated upon the sound of his brother's voice. Soon the ashen skies parted and the sun filtered through the smoky mists. Atyn allowed himself to leave his body, he rose through the clouds to fing himself again at the middle point. Beneath him, the skies were on fire. Flames spewed from the peak of Zelmisso and the molten rock flowed down the rocky summit.

"It is magnificent isn't it?" said a voice he knew well. Urion was there, watching the boiling wrath flowed from the summit. When he turned to face him, his eyes were black as the starless heavens, "I have been waiting for you, Atyn. It is almost time."

"What do you mean, little brother? Time for what?"

"A new world has been set into motion. Already the Cosmic Waters return to meet at the base of the tree. Ildabyth has not succeeded in his plan to steal what is best."

"Then Odyn has won the battle?" he asked and Urion laughed.

"The thunderbolts of our father have aided him by chasing the Umbra from the door." he answered modestly, "The final Battle is fought upon the Islands of Urdar and, as waters of Urdar joins with the Four Rivers, the Tree of Life will be revived. Truly, Atyn it will be great moment. It is too bad I must miss it."

"Miss it. What are you talking about Uri? Where are you going?"

"I have other work, it seems." he shrugged, "He who hides behind the Moon has spoken to our Father. There is a place for me, waiting at the heel of Raldaban."

"And what will you be doing there, little brother?"

"Watching over the Seven Maids as the Seven Maids watch over the Little Kingdom." he winked, "But the tale of my fortune must wait for now. I bring a message to you, and a warning. The shift will be upon the world very soon. Go to the others. Return with the Drui to Odyn's Hold. You will be safe there. But you must hurry. The alignments have begun. Nothing will stop it now."

"Where will I find Odyn?"

"He, and his folk, still battle for Zelmisso. If they are able they will join you in the Hold." he answered feeling the unsettling of the skies "When the Waters of the Havens meet Waters of Erda, the poles will alter. That end will be a beginning." he said sadly looking down and the swirling ash and the bleeding hills. "Alas for a little world so fragile. You must hurry, Atyn. There is much to do and time is short. I will be watching when the stars fall back into time."

And for all Atyn understood about life and death, still it was hard to watch him go.

"Our time here has been far too short."

"So it would seem. But know I will not be far, brother." the boy grinned. "The cold winter sky is where you will find me and though I will fade as the Scorpion begins to rise know I will return, bright and able to the East. Just up there Atyn, keeping an eye on you all." and then he disappeared.

The airs above cleared and in the far distance a new speck of light was born. Atyn's gaze lingered upon new-born star until the sounds of battle begin to swell beneath him. The view of the mountain was gone. The valley had changed into a vast ocean. In the ash-filled horizon, flashes of blue and umber lights lit the clouds. Slowly the Islands of Urdar began to take shape. The battle was raging in the airs above the land and sea. Waves of magic poured from the Malkian's gleaming swords but the legions of Umbra matched their every blow.

"Where are you Riverman?" Atyn asked watching the churning swell. He turned his gaze to the Garden, the place where the Tree of Life grew and saw that Mqttro's archers had gathered there. The Umbra were coming to meet them. The phantoms had tripled in size and carried with them the dark scimitars. Mqttro stood at the fore of the line, his eyes fixed to the wraiths. Over the din, his voice boomed and the Umbra hesitated in their assault.

"This place is forbidden to the profane."

The Shades began to laugh. "Out of the way, Son of Ormuzd. Your pitiful flame can not stand against us. Move on now. Scurry back to the wayward Master. Maybe he will throw a crumb. Perhaps even remember your name." and the sinister horde roared with delight.

"Back! Back!" they began to chant, "Back! Back! Waifs and strays, orphans and drifters. Back! Back! Back to the dirt and ooze of Erda." the shades cackled, "Back to the root! Back to the tree! Back to the dust and reek that makes you." and the noise grew louder as the shadows pressed closer. The archers held firm as they came near, holding taut their shining bows and at Mqttro's sign, the arrows flew. The gloom was split apart by the golden flames. A hiss of pain quivered through the dark but it took only a moment before the shadows were one again. The archers drew their bows to hit their mark once more. Their aim was true and the shrieks of the Umbra rattled the mountain. The tattered shades writhed in the release of light but even this seemed to hinder them but a little. The phantoms drew themselves tightly together and their cries had changed from taunts to summons. The language they uttered was cruel, searing the air with its spiteful intentions. The Umbra charged. Their scimitars slashing through to the mountains top. The summoning was potent, drawing upon the depths and the dark weapons carried a poisonous sound. The Seraphs reeled at the dark power that fell upon them.

The Malkians collapsed under the blows, plunging to the ground beneath the dull sky. Frozen yet full aware of every shattering wound, they lay still, unable to save themselves as the Umbra tormented them from the airs above.

"You are losing this war Mqttro!" the Umbra cried in a single voice, "You can not stand against us. This battle was won long ago, but you were a fool and did not want to believe it. Behold Mqttro! Behold the sea! We call to the depths of salty womb. Behold now, your doom is sealed."

A black smoke now poured from the skies, staining the ground and withering all that was green and good. The ocean chocked upon their words and the sea was churned in a fitful wrath. From over the waters the shadows poured. A monster was rising from the deep. A crushing wind filled the airs as the beast stood to blot out the sun. His broad shoulders met Mqttro where he stood before the Great Tree. A featureless face cursed the Seraph and reached out its ruinous hand.

"Rahab! Rahab!" the Malkians cried out in despair.

"Yotru! Rise!" called Mqttro lifting his bright sword into to choking air. "The moment is upon us. Bring Urdar! Call the waters of life. Bring the Water to meet the Sky!"

"Riverman!" Atyn cried to tempest. "The time is now or all shall be lost forever."

"You must return to your body, Atyn." A thundering voice boomed over the battlefield and in an instant the huge form of the Riverman hovered above him.

"If you stay here you will perish." Yotru explained in his cold watery voice, "It is your brother who is destined to play the part as the second of three trines formed. Through your grief, you must remember Stormbringer, Time's Gate is without flaw, and my Four Fathers shall wait until the last configuration graces the havens. Purification is the goal to Mqttro and his soldiers. They have anticipated this moment for thousands of years. But to the folk of Erda, survival now is the aim. Return to Basilus and take all you find to the Portal that lies in her highest tower. This was the moment Ildabyth was waiting to gain from. He is intending to use the alignments of the Trinities for his own designs. We have the power to put an end to those plans but not to the consequences that must be reckoned with. When my Four Fathers reach the River Urdar, the Tree will be renewed but Erda must adjust to the shift. To those upon the surface the presence of their Starry Light will seem more likened to wind than water. The land and waters will cleanse the breach Ildabyth has created. It is a moment of great danger and great opportunity. For a moment, all portals will be laid wide open. Return to beach! Hurry to your cousins and your kinsmen. Guide them to the Portal in the Tower of Priests, take all who will come you. The change will be violent. While the Erda shifts, the winds will drag the water and the air with her. The airs will move in great circles. The crests of the ocean will rise, swallowing all in their path. Your brother told you what to do. You must return to Odyn's Hold. Go now to the portal of the Basilian's priests and find the gateway the southern mountains. Soon the misdeeds of Ildabyth will be undone. But alas Atyn, all that was once good here, will once more be forgotten."

Atyn was stunned by Yotru's words. Doom was everywhere, the wind bellowed and the head of the watery monster stood ready to strike Mqttro where he stood but a seraph's sword can not be stayed. The screams of Ildabyth's shadows and the cries of the Malkians echoed through the shattering gale.

"Do not linger! There is work to do." Yotur cried. The darkness spun, taking its power from the waves and the Riverman drew himself into a whirling torrent of water and wind he went to greet the Four Rivers.

Anath lay under the stars. The sounds of the streamlet rushing through the canyon filled the night. Garan gazed upon the lights that rested peacefully in the clean, crisp air. Their alignments were clear to their experienced eyes.

"The Riverman has reached the Garden." Anath noticed, "The Four Rivers follow swiftly."

"Rempha's eye rests upon the Bear." Garan replied, "Mizar and the pale light, Alcor await the moment."

"It is a dangerous thing we must do. I do not know if the Little Kingdom can bear such a force."

"The Riverman knows his work." he answered, "When the lights settle into final arrangement, he will greet them."

"And the cleansing will begin."

The garret of Iao's house began to flicker with candlelight.

"They are gathering in the upper rooms." Anath said glancing over her shoulder at her father's house, "Will you be coming?"

"No, my love." he said, "I will return to the deep meadows to meet the others. There the Amadryads will join you in spirit as the House of Iao works to bind them. Together we are strong."

"It is a delicate thread we seek to bind within the forgotten realm."

"It is no longer a forgotten world. The Four Rivers will unite with that world. Their tide will change her fate." he said, placing his hand upon her shoulder, "And Yurah will prove true to her destiny."

A faint glow began to spread over the dark lawn. Raeyn was standing upon the portico, holding a lantern in her hand.

"She is waits for you." he smiled.

"Yes," Anath answered, waving up at her sister. "It is time."

"I will return at first light." he told her, "Meet me at the River."

"I will." she said as Garan began to change and she watched the raven glide across the trees.

"I am coming, Raeyn."she called up to her sister.

Yurah looked after him wishing she had followed. There were answers in the places where Atyn could travel. She held him in her thoughts as she kept pace after Tamil and Dion. She helped were she could and the night dragged on. In the streets above the war went on, the dead collected in corners of the basement infirmary until finally Tristan came.

"The Priests of Ildabyth will speak no more." he told them taking a long swig from the flask Inrih offered him. "It has been a bitter fight. Too many of our own have been lost. But not all the news I bring is grim. With the aid of the wyvern, Rudra and Atyn have overtaken the Third Tower. It seems the Priests worked a portal in the upper room. That unworldly door is what made it possible for them to draw the shadows from the deeps of Ildabyth's labyrinth. Quite certainly, it is this secret that his Dowerymen sought to keep from us. A portal is powerful tool."

"A portal? Here in Basilus? I should have known it earlier," exclaimed Inrih, "I should have known it when we met the nykertis in the Straits of Sudra. Only a portal would have allowed the shadows rise from the waters of the secret caves. Ildabyth's conjuring was behind it all along."

"Yes but that night he tried and he failed. Ildabyth's servants did not reach the top of Zelmisso. We pushed them back, back to their Master's Lairs." said Istah. "And any portal, be it Basilian or Malkian could useful to us now."

"Already it has. Since we have claimed the spot, the Umbra have fled." nodded Tristan, "and though Basilus is in shambles, even stranger things are afoot. The sky rains ash. It is only the wyvern that are not bothered by it. The Centaurians are now working to bring survivors here, though I must tell you; above us there is not much left to save." he said, moving aside to allow a Centaur to pass. Upon his broad shoulders, the limp bodies of a young mother and her children rode. They were stained under their throats and along their hands with odd designs.

"What are these marks?" asked Istah holding the pale arm under the lamp.

"I believe it is a binding spell." answered Tristan. "But I have not been able to recognize the script. It must be very old."

"It is ancient as the days of the first beginning." answered Sro, studying the signs. "Ildabyth has planned well, just in case."

"In case of what, Lady?" asked Tristan.

"In case his first plan failed." she answered grimly looking over the battered bodies, "But these few will not have to suffer. There are ways to remedy every evil. Come Yurah, bring out the Fire Glass and unsheathe the blade. It is not too late. Though we can not give them back their lives, we can still give them peace."

Yurah worked with her mother to set free the souls Ildabyth had sought to bind. She felt the breath of light that escaped hurry on to the upper airs. Watching it flutter she worried over Kiel.

"He is on my mind as well," said Sro, lightly touching her arm. "He has always been."

"You know him better than I. You spoke to him often. He told us that you saved him by giving yourself in return."

Sro smiled sadly, "I understood his dilemma, my dear." she explained, "but our bond was never as he perceived it. In truth, no word was ever exchanged between us. Ildabyth was far too vigilant for that."

"No words? What do you mean mother? He knew where you were. We could have never found you without him."

"It was only in dreams that Kiel ever perceived my silent thoughts. Since the moment I entered the Little Kingdom, I dared not uttered a sound. It was far too dangerous. Silence has been my only shield."

"So that is why we did not know where you were. It is why it took so long to find you."

"Yes my dear. Voice is the key to all things. Ildabyth has always known it. Since Time began, here in the Little Kingdom, Ildabyth has sought that secret sound. But the true Word; the pure and perfect tone of creation is kept safely hid. The Daemon spent his years trying to deceive any and all to reveal it. He held me prisoner, but I held my silence." Her slim body wavered like a mist but voice remained clear and she said. "Alas for Doxomedon's son. The Muses of Taygeth endowed him with gift of Voice and when his song flowed over the Cosmic Sea, Ildabyth perceived it. Kiel did not realize the degree of his treachery and became a pawn of his jealous desires. I helped him as I could but I dared not reveal to him the Word that would set him free. That was not my purpose, Kiel's destiny is his own to shape. Such is the Law." she said. "The stuff that makes the world responds to the essence of the spoken word. It is a common knowledge, though most are not aware of the depth of it. It took the Sword and the silent sound to shatter the Ninth Gate. It was left in the care of Ralbadan by plan not accident. Ildabyth's powers had grown far too strong. Bringing the Sword to the realms of Erda held much danger. You returned to the Little Kingdom with the talisman of the Annyd in your innocent hand. When the Secret Word moved into her deepest realms, Ildabyth's creation began to unravel. A new beginning lies ahead. Though much that was lovely will pass from this place, Erda is being remade. A new world where hope still lives."

"Hope, mother."

"Yes, there is always been hope in the Little Kingdom."

"Even for Kiel? Even as pain and betrayal have consumed the mind?"

"Even so my dear." she said. "Even there hope remains."

"Then I must go to him." she answered. "I fear he will not find his way alone."

"Kiel is the lost son of a faraway star. Though he does not know it, he waits for you. Go to him and do what you can but take care, my daughter. Basilus is still a dangerous place."

Kiel stumbled in pouring doom, but no one noticed. He was but another unfortunate trying to outrun a ruined world. With bleak efficiency the Umbra had left the streets of Basilus strewn with bodies and parts. The noise of war had faded and the distant weeping and the groans of the wounded seemed an eerie calm. He ran without faith and without purpose. He did not stop until he came to the edge of the ocean wall. He sat at its edge and began to sing aloud, waiting for the morning. He paid no mind to his rasping voice, and he paid no mind to his forgotten rhymes. Placing his song upon the waves, the sad sweet cries drifted over the waters. The song wandered and he forgot himself wandering with it in the waters of oblivion. The birds came to him and walked along the piers calling to the sun. But the sun would not rise. Clinging to a statue that looked over the dismal dawn, he wiped the gray ash from the balustrade.

"What is this?" he muttered, smearing the slippery paste between his fingers. "Has our star fallen from the sky?"

"It has not fallen, Kiel." a soft voice answered, "Somewhere beyond this gray storm, she still shines."

His eyes widened when he saw her there, alive and warm next to him. Questions flooded into his mind but no words could he utter to ask them. If only an apology he could find the strength to offer but Yurah had no need for such a thing.

"I heard you singing." she whispered, gently taking his hand. "Come back with me, now. The others are waiting."

They walked slowly through the city. Foreboding filled her as she helped him through the rubble. She knew from his stumbling that under the blood-stained cloak his wounds had reopened. Still he followed obediently glancing over the broken buildings and stained streets with a glazed indifference.

"We can slow down a little. Rest a moment, if you like. The worst is over for now."

He looked up at her then and found the words he meant to say. Touching her face tenderly with his tattered hands he whispered. "Do not fool yourself into believing we are safe, my dearest friend. We are not safe, Yurah. Ildabyth lingers in this falling ash." and he closed his eyes and sniffed the air. "Morning will never come," she heard him murmur and then the street grew dark as midnight. An enormous shadow blocked their way. A spark of life gleamed in Kiel's eyes as the Umbra drew near. Picking up a fallen brick, Kiel placed himself between Yurah and the phantom's dark sword. The Umbra growled, and with barely a motion the shadow lashed out and struck him to the ground. Dirt crushed into his mouth as he slid over the street. He stood, spitting the grime into his sleeve wondering where all the pain had gone. He picked up a rock for each hand. He shouted a command to the Shadow using words the Shade could not ignore. The Umbra turned to face him, and began to laugh.

"What do you think you are doing, fool? The Master will not take kindly to such use of his language."

"It was your Master that taught me." Kiel replied. "And all creatures, be they light or dark, know the laws must be obeyed."

For instant the phantom wondered at the ragged, wounded man.

"I do not trifle with such hopeless rabble." he answered finally, "There is other work to attend too" and he cast a leering eye at Yurah. Kiel repeated the command and the Shadow hesitated.

"I could not understand you." he sneered, "Your pronunciation is quite pathetic. Stand back fool, and maybe you might learn something. I will show you the proper way the Word is brought into the world." and the shade threw back his cape and howled into the gloom. A creeping cold wind began to hiss around their shoulders and a shuffling sound echoed from between the piers and fish-houses. The dead were rising to the shadow's call. All through the ravaged streets of Basilus, hollowed eyes and the broken bodies made answer to the sound. Steady they came, moved by the madness within them, they set their eye upon him. The phantom laughed and drew the black weapon to face the girl.

The dead had risen and while Yurah fought the Shade, the unthinking mob fell upon Kiel. There was little she could do but listen as they tore him into bits. Breaking the Umbra with a final strike of her Sword she rushed to where she had last seen him. His blood spattered the stones, bits of skin and parts of a tattered cloak were all that remained. Though her battle was brief, the mob had taken Kiel and strewn his parts through the war-torn streets of Basilus. She took the worn, bloody rag and held it close. Looking into the ash filled skies, Kiel's hopeless words filled in her mind. There was nothing left for her to do. She rose from the stained cobbled stone and began to make her way back along the dock. It was not long before she saw a boy coming to meet her. It was Nestor.

"You saw him, didn't you?" he cried as he began to run.

"I did, Nestor but only for a little while." she answered sadly, "A Shadow came between us and Kiel was taken away."

"Where Yurah? Tell me where and I will follow."

She did not have the heart to tell the boy what had happened. She laid her hand upon his shoulder, "I must speak to the others before we go."

CHAPTER XXXV
THE TIDE TURNS

"He has taken the dead and made them live again. Now they serve him where the Umbra have failed." whispered Tyla to her twin.

"Ildabyth will be fooled by his schemes once more." said Lyli. "This will stop nothing from going forward. We will call when the Four Rivers touch the Isles of Urdar. The Portals will be wide opened then and they may find safe haven in Odyn's Hold."

"But the Rivers are potent, if she does not remember, the shift will go too far and there will be nothing left to save. Even the harbor of the Alfyr will be swallowed up by the waves." answered Tyla.

"She will remember the ancient law."

"She will be the first to arrive. The moment is crucial."

"She will have the Sword and the Sensar at her side. She will remember."

"But what of Ildabyth? He is not dead."

"He is in bits."

"Still the battle is unsettled."

Sothis paused from her work, holding the lighted candles in her hand. "Stop this debate. The time for talk has past. Our work awaits us. Quiet now, I think I hear the others coming."

Hathor raced into the room, with Raeyn and Anath just behind him. Tyla swooped down and pulled a single hair from his tail. The cat turned and spat at her.

"There are candles burning all around. Be still or you will wait outside!" she scolded the cat. Hathor whipped his insulted tail and went to sulk in the window.

"We are almost ready." Sothis said as they walked into the room. Lyli agreed and uncorked a small bottle she held in her hand. Pouring the substance around the edge of the scrying pool, Tyla bent down laid a candle to the shining liquid. The flames were low and burned a golden white.

"It is so lovely when it is set afire." Lyli smiled, stepping back from the water. "The nitre burns evenly tonight. Azoth brings light without shadow. It is a fortunate sign."

"Driin brought us the batch." replied Sothis, "Tonight exactness is crucial."

"Will they be with us?"

"Yes, they will stand in Oiolosse's halls and aid us from the mountain." replied Iao looking back through the dark glass, "All of

Taygeth awaits the moment as well. The Muses and the Fates are ready, as Doxomedon and Derdekea steady the crystal. It is Rempha who shall open the door to the moment but it is Yurah who must close it."

"She will be alone, father. Kiel will not stand with her. This is not as we planned it."

"His decision was not unexpected; only un-hoped for. She will understand when her moment comes."

"And we shall help her." replied the twins, stirring twisting symbols into the living fire.

"Delirium is often speckled with bits of truth." Sro answered when she heard the tale, "It is true what Kiel said. His ash returns to the dust of Erda."

"What does it mean mother? What will come of this unsettled score?"

"It is not won, Yurah but all is not lost. The turning of the world has not ceased, hope remains in this imperfect place."

"I can not see any hope here." Tamil said, looking over the piles of dead. "His presence lingers in the stone. The Waters are coming to swallow her. Under the salty deeps these works will fade from memory and a new world will begin."

"But what of Kiel?"

"The Druii have gone to him." answered Atyn. "They have taken the shape of Eagles and, just as they had done before, they have bore his scattered parts away to their healers. They wait our word in the grottoes of Tristan's mountain. When the portals open they will travel with us from the portals within those Crystal Halls."

"We will meet them in Odyn's Hold." added Inrih, "The horses are almost ready." he shouted but his voice was lost to the storm. A door had blown wide open and the howling wind whipped through the room. "It is time to go." he signaled.

The wind poured ash. The air was choking. The survivors gathered under the long porch. A handful of Basilians, Volos and his apprentices, and what horses they manage to save from the stables were making ready to move on to the towers. Dion's companions helped along the walking wounded while the Druii gathered the rest to ride upon their ponies. The centaurs huddled with them under the protecting roof. The wyvern looked down upon the group from the eaves of the fish huts.

"It will be a long walk." said Inrih, staring up through the smoke.

"The portal will be the swiftest way to safety."

Erda groaned. Balls of hot ash fell all around them and fires began to spring from the forgotten wagons that lie broken along the piers.

"I will not allow my folk to pass again through these wicked streets." said the Centaur, "Our work here is finished. It is time we return to our homes."

"The world will not be as it was." Atyn told the creature, "Your homelands will not be safe when the change comes."

"But it is our home. We have fought for it too long to leave it now." the centaur answered sharply.

"I have seen what will come. The waters will rise and swallow the land. There is no time to delay in debate."

The Centaur laughed, "I will not trust the destiny of my folks to the warnings of any beast that walks on but two legs." and the other centaurs that stood with him, nodded their agreement. "We will return to the lands we have fought for." he said casting a wary eye toward the group of wyvern. "We know no fear, Master Atyn. We will return to our homeland. Our god gave it to us and we will protect it."

"Do not let these years of war fog your reason. A new beginning waits for you. If you do not choose to take it all your folk may be lost forever."

"Save your breath. I have heard too many lies to believe another. But do not think of us as ingrates. We thank you for your help in removing the Umbra from the world. Ildabyth's shadows have plagued our borders for many years. Who can say, Master Atyn, chance may bring us together once more. Farewell. Our wives and children await our return. May luck be with you on your way back to the wilderness." and the Centaurs turned their backs upon them and galloped away through the streets of Basilus.

The Wyvern watched them go. Their glowing eyes narrowed. They shifted nervously about, smoke leaked from their long snouts. They turned to face Tristan and the others, viewing them now with new suspicions.

"We will not come with you, Lords of Erda. The Centaurians seek to take our lands and we will not allow it. We must follow them. We have too much to lose."

Atyn shook his head, "There will be nothing left to lose. The world will shift, and the waters will come. Your faithlessness blinds you to the truth."

"It is not faithlessness, it is reason that guides us. Reason and logic are the Wyverns only friends. Trust me sir when I say the stars above have no interest in our affairs. It is by our wits alone that we have survived in the forgotten world. The Centaurians know it too and now seek advantage. We will not allow them to plunder what is rightfully ours. Do not fear for our safety. The Wyverns have always fared best alone."

And for a few moments more, they tried to reason with the dragons but as the dust from the Centaurian hooves rose from the path the wyvern horde refused all arguments. Collecting their numbers into a tight formation they began their journey toward the northern shores of Basilus.

"We said all we could." Tristan remarked watching them fade into the sky.

"They must make their own way now." added Atyn. They gathered themselves together, helping the wounded and managing the horses and they began to make their way through the streets.

When they reached the upper tier they found the gates had been pried from their hinges and the gardens were destroyed. Cautiously they made their way through the scattered waste and falling ash until they reached the center tower. The surface of the tower was smooth. The clear stone captured the reflection of the burning city below. Inrih began to walk around, trying to find the door.

"There is no need for that." said Dion carefully feeling his way along the smooth wall. In a moment he stopped. His fingers had found the seamless opening. Pulling a small key from his jacked, he placed it an unseen latch. The gate opened without a sound.

"The Dowerymen believe themselves to be better than all else. But really they are just as other folk," he replied to their unspoken surprise, "and will lose their good sense in drinking games just a quick as any. In other words, I won it in a bet. I thought the day might come when it could be handy." he grinned stepping aside to let them enter.

The stairs spiraled gracefully up the sides of the tower. Nestor and Volos helped the injured from the horses. The stable boys gently coaxed the beasts upward. They climbed easily for a while but soon they come across the sealed door.

"Do you have a key for this one, Dion?" Inrih asked.

"No. This is another thing entirely." he replied with a frown. "I do not know what to do. But maybe you do Lady."

Yurah placed her hand upon the hilt of the ancient Sword and whispering of the Scabbard made quick answer to her need. She drew the Blade and laid it gently against the lock, repeating the rhythms the senzar had spoken. The door sprang apart with a sharp crack.

"Nice work!" Dion exclaimed, leaping over the threshold to hold the door ajar. "I thought you might know its secret." and he winked as she passed.

The next stairwell was smeared with soot and reeked of sulfur. Yurah recalled the smell from a dream long ago. Sro spoke to her softly.

"A portal is more than a door. It can be better imagined as the connecting points of spidery web. When the Cosmic Waters blend evenly into the River Urdar, that web will be enlivened. The lines of force from Mundi and Raldaban's daughters have already joined with the Bear, leaving each of those configurations to create another. The turning point will come as Jupiter, the hidden Neptune, and the messenger of the yellow sun form the last triangle. It is then that Mercury's voice will be heard. Listen to him, little daughter, and you will know what to do." she paused for a moment leaning against the wall to catch her breath.

"What is the matter, mother?" Yurah asked.

"It is not the first time I have walked these stairs daughter. I fear I recall it all to well." she sighed. "But times change and now I walk up them under different circumstance. Today the Sword of the Ancients is destined for your hand. It is that binding thread that will give her the time she needs."

"Who mother? Give who time?"

"Erda. This little world needs time. Time to heal and time to change. The Elder Stars gave her that name. In the old language it means, the Virgin who holds the Babe." she answered, stumbling along the stairs.

Dion was suddenly at her elbow, "You have over-spent yourself, Lady. Let me help you." he said wrapping his arm about her shoulders. He was surprised how frail she seemed. "You are all such strange folk, Lady. Please tell me now, are you made of flesh at all?"

"I am bone and blood but the years have changed me. I am not of the stuff I once was."

"Well lean against me. It is not too much further now. I remember there is another door just beyond that curve. And do not worry, you are no burden at all."

"You have been here before Dion?"

"I knew things about them most did not." he shrugged, "I suppose this kept me in their favor. I was brought here several times at their order. But you must believe me, it was enough to keep from wanting to return ever again."

When they turned the corner they found the door was gone. The smell of burned skin hung like a cloud. The chamber was destroyed, the upper roof was shattered and its walls scorched.

"It looks as if the Wyvern had their work cut out for them." remarked Dion looking over the wreck. Yurah walked to the center of the tower room peering down into smoldering pit."

"It is the door he used to burrow into the core of Erda." Sro said.

"From here he called to the deeps to form the Umbra. Then he called to the world to draw bodies that would house them."

"The Umbra are not alive and are not dead." he shuddered.

"In the beginning they were his hands, and later they became his armies" Sro told them, "Now Ildabyth has set his phantoms loose across the whole of the world. The largest prize is upon the Isle of Urdar. There they will battle for the Tree. He has sought the Secret of the Tree almost more than any other."

"Any other than you, Lady." Dion answered astutely. "It seems to me Ildabyth held quite an interest in what benefits you could bring to him."

Sro did not have time to answer. The hole began to gurgle and the tower swayed. "I do not think we have much time." he replied, glancing down the stairs and too his relief, Atyn and Inrih were turning the corner.

"The building will not hold up under this much longer." Atyn cried.

"This is the first time I have ever seen a portal open." said Inrih approaching the dank opening. "It is smaller than I expected. No more than two or three at a time will be able enter."

"A portal is a volatile thing. There will be no room for error." Sro replied staring down the hole. "You will enter first, Yurah. You will become the grounding point of the Pleiades. You are the one that must hold the final balancing point between Mundi and the Bear."

"The Web will be unfastened then. It is a dangerous moment." replied Atyn.

Sro nodded. "There are places in every world which connect the forces from the upper realms. One is the Isle of Urdar, the point where the Malkians steward the Tree. Another is the Refuge of the Drui. Tristan's stone caverns Erda's secrets will be kept safe through this change." she explained. "But all the forces of the endless havens will not suffice unless someone holds true to the Upper Gate, the place at the top of the world. This is the place where the grounding rod of the Annyd will enter Erda. The Sword must be there to meet them when they come. It is the Sword you carry, Yurah. The blade is the eye of the needle the Elders seek. It is the only thing that will settle her again. It is the only point which will able her to redo, and realign."

The others were quickly gathering outside the hall. The heat and stench were oppressive. Inrih looked out the shattered casement. The sky was raining bits of fire and the streets were burning.

"Nothing will survive this." Dion said quietly as the land groaned

"The gates are opening" Atyn shouted over the din, "Yurah, it is time!"

She looked at the hole that Ildabyth had made but all had changed. A beam of radiance now spilled from what had been only spit and fume. The light was filled with a multitude of reflections, some she understood and some she did not. The shinning mirrors were doors to everywhere. She could see her father's house and her sister's faces. The streets of Mundi shone in the dazzling light. Atyn was standing at the portal. Then the sounds of war consumed her thoughts and she felt herself falling through the hole.

"Behind you, Mqttro!" his Captain bellowed, severing the arm of phantom. Its black sword plummeted helplessly to the ground and the thing screamed as it raced to retrieve it.

"We can not last much longer." the warrior cried, hacking the head off another, "The attack comes from the sky and from sea. There are not enough of us to face two fronts."

"Help will come Rama." Mqttro replied, "It will come when Rempha calls it. We must hold them off until the sign is given."

"Then I beg the fates that it comes soon." he answered, reeling his horse about and chopping through a tentacle that reached from the thrashing waves. "This ocean beast is killing us, and the Umbra refuse to die."

Mqttro hacked through another phantom but over the din he could hear a new sound. The Riverman was above him, his arms joining with the tumultuous clouds and his feet steady in the garden before the Tree. The clouds began to clear and in a moment dome of heaven was alive with the twinkling lights. All around the glittering bits of watery radiance began to fall.

"He has done it." cried Mqttro, "He has joined the Four Waters with the River Urdar. Brace yourself Rama. The shift is upon us."

The wind began to scream as Rama answered. "The Waters of the Heavens shall bury the Shadows into the sea. But we are not safe. We must rise higher."

"Urdar will take us to the place between sunshine and sky." cried Mqttro above the fray. "Back to the garden! This fight is over!"

The sparkling waters spilled over them as they rose, clearing a way through the filth of war. The Riverman of Raldaban joined the River Urdar to his Four Fathers and the Malkain Isles began to ascend over the sea. Ever climbing higher into the sky they rose, passing through the dust and pain of the world as the Tree of Life was lifted from the Battlefield of Erda. For an instant, Mqttro could see the Riverman, standing upon the highest ground but then the whole of the world lurched. The powers of Mundi had finally shifted her from her resting place and the cries of the Umbra wailed in the lower airs.

"The Waters will guide her. Time is short Stormbringer! Your Father awaits, Mercury is calling." the Riverman cried out as Atyn joined his voice with Messenger. The three stood at the centering point and Erda rumbled at the word. Mqttro looked up as it began to rain and Isles of Urdar became the place between sunshine and shade, and the Little Kingdom began to spin out of control.

Odyn stood with the Valkyeries, bewildered by the brutal force that had gathered around the peak of Zelmisso. Then he looked behind him and stared back into the lands of Erda. The waves rose like mountains and the wild water swallowed the villages and towns upon the land. "Memhir!" he cried in despair, "What have we done?' and the stars fell backward above him.

"I can see her!" cried Lyli, "She stands before him. All alone."

"She is not alone. We are with her." said Iao. "Listen now daughters. Listen to the stars. They have joined with the Four Fathers of Yotru. They are opening the doors. Their song moves her into a new beginning."

"Into cataclysm! This battle is not yet won!"

"The battle is not yet lost."

"He shall overwhelm her. His evil is older than the dust of the world and Yurah, she is only a child."

"Yurah is a child of the Annyd. She will remember."

"Yurah is precisely where she is meant to be." said Sothis, gazing into the watery scene. "The realm of the Odyn rules the Upper Point of the Three. It was the first sign the Rune foretold."

"And into the Erda, strength and potential will pour the second sign told us." Replied Lyli,

"The Watery realm will awaken her. Justice will stand as Time's door turns." said Tyla.

"And Time's door is laid wide apart but alas, it is a long contest. The trials of illusion and pain will lead to suffering, terrible. The Eater of the Dead makes is so." explained Anath, perceiving the Amydrades aligning with the will of the stars.

"The eternal creation endures at the point of the Fire and Frost." Sothis said, "The Seraph have risen. It is the fortunate sign."

"And the Gift will be won through great toil." Iao added softly. "She holds key. Whisper daughters, whisper now and she will understand."

The Daughters of Iao looked down upon their little sister and over the ocean of time and the waters of space their voices carried to the

Little Kingdom.

The blade bore a subtle light all its own. Like a shattering mirror, its living radiance poured into the unsettling airs, realities blended from every direction. Around her the wind rushed upward. The faces of her sisters flooded past her, the pool, the candlelight and the eyes of Hathor, ever quiet and calm. Tasting the stench of the Umbra and hearing the cries of despair upon the Isles of Urdar. The battlefield raged in the unworldly light, in the streets of Basilus the rain poured, the hands of the Drui, stained dark with blood of wounded, had made their way back to their crystal caves. The injured and the dying were being tended by the firelight, and the sounds of their harps filled her ears. The pale moon, clung to the Oiolosse's hall and the starry light of Raldabon pierced the waters of the Tristan's lake. Plain, the single line rang between the two points and she heard Eide calling her name. Suddenly, the green of a mountain forest appeared through the rushing wave and her feet touched the soil of Erda. The ground shook and a shadow loomed over her.

"So we meet again, child." the terrible voice boomed, "Just at heavens perfect moment."

The Scabbard began to murmur and through the wind and rain she could hear voices calling.

"Step aside now, little daughter. Do not think you can stop this." the voice continued, "Heaven's Gate is mine. The change is mine. Erda is mine. And your life, well that will be mine as well."

Gathering her senses, Yurah realized it was Ildabyth's voice that roared over the wind. No longer did he stand as an old man, his body had been undone. He had become a formless thing and what appeared before her now was a sucking void. It hissed as it spoke.

"I must admit you had me fooled." the darkness said. "I did not expect the Elders to send a child to save their blundering plans." The thing leaned over her, its stinking breath was like ice. "But now I say I will not be fooled a second time."

Yurah did not quail under the Void, a strange light had caught her eye. The Sword's glow rested in two worlds. She could see Rempha there, holding open the door of Time. In her hand she perceived the power of the starry trines pouring their force through the Blade. The Sword she carried was the needles eye.

"A child with a grown-up toy," Ildabyth chuckled, "But then the Annyd were never able to recognize proper warriors." the darkness paused for an instant, seemingly waiting for her to answer and when she did not he continued.

"Still it is a useful device." he mused playfully, "Indeed, I believe

I fancy it quite a lot. That Sword child, you will no longer be needing it. Give it over. "

Remembering her mother's words, she was careful to hold her tongue. Silence was her ally. Keeping her thoughts focused, she listened. In the distance she could hear the cries of the fallen warriors. The ash rained down upon the land and Erda groaned as the powers of the distant Suns pulled her to face them. The land was sliding over itself, cascading into the sea, the sky fell backward and the world was breaking into ruin.

"What do you think you are doing, child? Playing your mother's games? Such a foolish thing to do." The land quivered as he spoke. She did not answer and the darkness swelled around her. "I know you fear me, child. I can see it in your face. Speak now!" She kept her silence allowing the will of the Sword to fill her. His fury waved over the mountaintops but he softened his voice and drew dangerously near. "It makes no difference child. The Stars will do my work for me. The Life will perish as Erda spins out of control. I will swallow it all before it returns to the source. All of it will be mine." his hideous laughter rattled the airs. "What fools, they know how to begin a thing but not how to finish it. I know you feel her screaming my dear. And their work, all of it dear, in vain, in vain, indeed." he smacked, delighting in his vicious insights. "But you do not understand everything child. It matters not to me. I am patient. Let the world turn into oblivion. Let it be unmade. I will take what I wish when I wish it." the voice jeered, "I have all the time of the world in my hands. So hold your tongue if that pleases you." Ildabyth cackled through the hold. "And think not that your Sword is safe in your hand for it is nothing close. Humor me, child before the world crashes into oblivion. What other precious things do you keep?" as the wind began to shape itself into a hideous face. The Summoning Stone had caught his eye. She touched the jewel with her soft fingers and the forest behind her began to stir.

"The roots of Oliban can not defeat me." Ildabyth jeered. His laughter rattled the ground and in an instant the trees were sucked down into the dirt.

"And what else do we have," he mocked, "Hmm, a little book. You have much to learn child. But all the knowledge of the world is not strong enough to quell my desires. Nothing of the world is more than dust, ever changing and ever failing." and the dark tore the book from her hand and it was swallowed by the void. Ildabyth belched and giggled.

"And that annoying glass! Hand it here." the heavy pouch was torn from her shoulder, the glass fell upon the ground. "All light will fail at my will." and wilting stench smothered the glass.

Fear swept her as she was left alone in the dark. The world quaked and the wind blew like a torrent. The Daemon was laughing. He had taken everything with just a subtle wave of force. The Sword, trembled in her hand. Ildabyth tasted his victory.

The Scabbard began to chant. The message came first as shapes. The ground slipped and the clouds raced against the wind. The Void of Ildabyth swelled into the skies as she understood the Senzar's meaning,

"It is not by holding to the things of the world that life is kept. Creating what is perfect is done by setting the life within free. Behold little daughter, the hand crafts by following the heart." and in her mind, shapes appeared. It began with a single point and, from that point the trine appeared, and on to the cube and, so on and so, until all of creation was made. New worlds sprung out before her eyes and surrounding them all were multitudes of shimmering beings.

"Cuimnech, O traod annrach, Cuimench. Cuimnech an" the Senzar whispered and she looked more closely into the multitude. She knew their faces and she knew their names. Rempha was there, with Taygeth and Achernar; Mirfak and Raldabon. The starry lights had become the past and the future was splintered in all directions. A Voice rang out over the storm. She could hear herself calling out to the sky. The Sword gleamed like a sun in her innocent hand and to the above the Cosmic Waters flowed to met her, giving her purpose she had never known before. Yurah drew herself upright and with strength of land and sky, she cast the heirloom into the storm. The sky exploded as the blade was joined with a Thunderbolt and the Winds of Time and Waters of the Deeps carried it upward into the tempest. The Three Trines joined into one and within that Needle's Eye, the Starry Light seized Sro's sword and plunged it into the summit of Zelmisso. The ancient blade was driven deep into the heart of the mountain and, as it found its mark, the backwards turning of world shuddered to a halt.

Ildabyth wailed as the prize was cast away for he could not follow what had been returned in perfect faith. The moment he had long awaited had not come. The talisman of the Annyd was again lost to him. The Darkness that made him began to spin, drawing its force into a funnel, pulling the shadows and pain he had created into a single point. His screams filled the skies as the ground waved back and forth, trying to stabilize back to a center. Yurah collapsed to her knees. Threads of pain and evil poured into the void that once was Ildabyth. His curses rattled the mountain but the work had been done and the Erda held firm. The wind pulled into the point of dark he had become. Debris flew wildly all around her and then, just as suddenly as he was there, Ildabyth was gone. The foul voice had been silenced and Yurah found herself alone. Trembling she stood before the Portal. The mountain fumed. Looking about at the broken trees she stumbled through the stones to gather the remains of her tattered cloak. Wrapping it around her she looked up to the heavens.

The clouds were clearing swiftly. Flashes of silent lighting lit the distant sky. The night opened up above her and the Queen of Heaven twinkled in the vault above. At her side stood the Virgin child, and the Lady began to speak.

"Behold the crown of stars, seventh daughter." she said in the language of silence. "Do not despair over what has been lost. The Virgin holds the spindle in her innocent hand. Behold child, the Isles of Urdar have not perished in the fight. Between the sun and shade they now stand, between the point of Fire and Frost the Tree will thrive. The Malkains have ever been the messengers of this realm. Every sound that is uttered in the Little Kingdom is borne to us upon their wings. Listen child for all around you rings the voice of the Oldest One." and the Lady faded back into the distant night the song of the stars rang through upon the gray stones. The war was over and the sky lightened, seeing her birthing day gifts scattered upon the stones she went to gather them as the strange music played. Finally she sat upon the soiled ground and pulling her own flute from its soft pouch she too joined the song. The melodies flowed into the ever-changing night and Yurah played on, watching the thunderbolts dance about the mouth of Zelmisso. Waiting for the boom to follow, Yurah looked closer to see it was not lighting at all but Odyn and the Valkyries responding to the call. The sound to the flute was drawing them from the battlefield of the Malkians to the Gate.

Odyn and his warriors gently touched the soil of Erda and then the survivors of Basilus and the Drui began to emerge through the Portal. Weary and war-torn, they drew close to each other, sharing grief and joys until the clouds once more began to close over them. Heavy drops of rain washed over the bruised faces.

Atyn looked upward into the unsettled sky, "We will meet again Mqttro," he told the clouds. "at the place where Sun and Shade meet."

Odyn was near. With his seeing eye he looked out and over the long vista and watched as the oceans rose to cover the lands. The rain dripped over the edge of his broad hat,

"Do not despair, Lord of Wodyn." he heard the Menhir murmur from the skirt of heaven. "The tears of Jupiter will clear away the taint." Odyn sighed as the sweet sound of her voice faded into the winds. He pointed to the muddy trail. "Come everyone. Let's go home."

CHAPTER XXXVI
THE NEW BEGINNING

"It could be said that all existence is like a reflection in a mirror, without substance, without time, only a phantom of the mind." Odyn mused, his head wreathed in a cloud of smoke. "The Menhir has told me the world exists for us to perceive it. If there were no intelligent beings to observe the world, nothing would exist at all." He continued as he passed the pipe on to Macha. The old woman pulled in a deep draw and released a ring of smoke into the air.

"The Menhir has told you many things you have yet to understand." she replied bluntly.

Yurah listened to them from over her cup, watching the tea leaves as they settled into a pattern at its bottom and wondering of Kiel. She felt a gentle touch on her arm.

"He is calling for you." a soft voice said. Rising from her chair Yurah followed her mother from Odyn's Hall to place where he rested. The Drui had found his mutilated body. Carefully they had gathered his every part and with power the joining stars brought to the Little Kingdom, the Drui had made him whole once more.

Rudra waited for them at the door. "Do not let his mood frighten you." he told them gesturing to the still form, "I have given him something to help him sleep. There is much healing left to do."

She went to him. Sitting next to bed she called his name. He opened his eyes. Still they were as restless as a sea storm.

"I did not think I would see you again," he said distantly, "not with ruin of the world all around us."

"But the world is still turning." she answered softly. "A new beginning has come. Be at peace. All will be made right by Rempha's reckonings."

"Rempha," he answered softly, "I can remember now. The Drui placed me in the Lake and then the stars came to me. They gathered me together and put into one piece again. Rempha was with them. He is not a child you know. Actually he is much older than he looks."

"I imagined as much," she smiled cautiously.

"He took me to see my father." he continued thoughtfully, "It had been a long time. I had quite forgotten what he looked like."

"Your father?"

"Yes, Doxomedon was his name. It seems I had forgotten that as well. Anyway, my father is quite old." he added sadly, taking a ringlet of her hair and twisting in his fingers.

"Did you speak with him?" she asked, wondering at his peculiar mood.

"There was nothing to say." he answered letting the ringlet slip from his fingers, "So much has happened. It was difficult. I was very tired and there were so many others around."

"It has been a long time. Our homes are far from this little world."

"Home? So far away, too far I suppose. You know I had quite forgotten the feel of the place. In the beginning I was just a wanderer, rambling my way among the stars. Then time grew heavy and I became a beggar and then it seemed my burdens grew heavier still. I am not exactly sure when it happened, but in the end I became the fool. Whatever you choose to call me, Yurah in truth I left my home behind me very long ago and can not return."

"It is not so Kiel. They wait for you. They have waited for thousands and thousands of years."

"I have been away too long, Yurah." he laughed unhappily, "There is too much I do not understand."

"What don't you understand Kiel?" she asked him gently.

He cast his eyes away from her then, "I do not understand why the Druii restored me once again," he said softly, "I suppose you could not know how often I have wished for death. This life was not what I wanted. Still I return. Again and again, I return and all along all I really only wanted to sleep, Yurah. Just to sleep."

"Give yourself some time. Odyn's Halls are fair. You will heal here."

"Here? Where I lie, burdening all who know me," he answered sharply, looking toward the window at the endless rain. "Wallowing like a sloth as the Sea swallows the land beneath us. Here where day will never come."

"Day will come again and you will be ready. Soon we will return." she said, "You will join us. We will all go home."

"I will not return home. I am ruined. Just as the world beneath us is ruined, I am as broken and dull as a Basilian slave. I will not go home. I can not stand to look in his eyes again. That is why I needed to speak with you Yurah." he said, taking her hand. "There is something I must say before you go. You have done what I dared not do. The Gates of the Ildabyth's world could not hold you. I want you to know when you return to your Father's house and when you look across the heavens, I will be looking back. Ever will I search for you at the heels of Raldaban and I want you to understand that I shall sorely miss your company. But more than this, more than anything else, I want you to know that I will not forget you. Though the door of time stands between us, I will not forget."

"I will not forget either Kiel." she told him softly. The gray eyes

softened then and the storm within seemed to ease. Kiel closed his
eyes to sleep.

The rain poured for weeks. Days were gray, nights were black,
and not a star could be seen through the thick clouds. Still the warmth
of Odyn's hall brought cheer. The Drui tended to the creatures of the
forest and the Valkeryies kept the flames burning in the Odyn's hearth.
Atyn spent his time with the healers. The survivors of Basilus learned
not to mourn their past but instead how to rebuild their future. Inrih
and Tamil studied Odyn's maps and made plans to build a great ship
when the new lands rose from the sea they would take any who would
go with them and inhabit the world once more.

Kiel spent most of his days in a thoughtful silence. Sometimes he
would take brief comfort in Yurah's company. They would walk the
cliffs beyond the Hold and talk of the unseen stars above. Then there
where the nights when Dion would play the lute and Kiel would sing.
His melodies were lovely and all who listened would taste the sadness
of Erda as the skies cried above. But more often he would wander
alone and watch the water rise to swallow the lesser hills below
Zelmisso. Nestor would find him, huddled and lost, brooding over his
past and weeping in the cold rains. The boy would help him back to
the Hold, caring for him like an adoring brother.

"Will he ever heal, mother?" Yurah asked, watching them return
to the warming fires once more.

"In time my dear."

"He seems to know no hope at all." she sighed watching his
ragged steps as Nestor helped him through the door.

"There is always hope child. And if Kiel holds none for himself
then we must hold it for him."

She pondered the words and looked up into the rain.

"One day this sky will cease to fall and we will return home. But
even that thought leaves my heart with no peace. Kiel and I are bound
to one another, how can I go when he believes he must stay behind?"

"Only he shall be able to mend his flaw. Such is the natural way
of things. The Little Kingdom is a mournful place, and yet." she
paused. A cool wind moved through their cloaks and above them the
dark softened. The branches of the trees stirred and the lightening
clouds rushed over the palest of blues. "And yet morning still comes."
Yurah answered, watching in wonder as the faint sky was being reborn.
Rudra was walking the gentle air carrying a flask of wine.

Sro laughed, "A gift Rudra?"

"I have you to thank for it Lady."

"But wine is your specialty Rudra, not mine."

"It is not the wine, Lady." he smiled, "That is a simple to do. It is the gift of the new day that I thank you for." he answered. "The worst is over. Soon we will begin again."

"Yes, it will be soon." she answered closing her eyes but in the moment before the first light of dawn, Yurah understood she meant more than she had said. Sro felt her know it.

"I will not hide my thoughts from you," she said sadly, "though I am sure by now you have already guessed, I can not return to Raldabon Yurah. Not now, not just yet."

Yurah looked into her mother's face in disbelief.

"The work of the Annyd is not finished. I will remain here in Odyn's Hold only until the waters subside. Then I will return to the warm core of Erda. I will help her in healing the damage that Ildabyth has done. I will help her grow new lands. I will tend to her cycles of water and air. I will wait until the healing is done."

"I can not leave you. You have bound yourself to the Little Kingdom for so long and Kiel. His mind is shattered. How can I leave what I have come to love so deeply?"

"I understand your sufferings child. The Little Kingdom is a fragile place. Erda will need time to mend. Here the days seem long, but in truth each rising sun is but an instant in a greater day. Return to your father. Tell him what has happened and tell him I will be home soon."

Tears ran down her face. The misty rain was filled with sun, across the summit of the grand Zelmisso a glorious rainbow climbed over the sky.

"Morning has come child." Sro spoke softly into her ear. "Soon the rains will fade and the waters will recede. When night falls and the heavens become bright and the clear, Rempha will open the Gates of Heaven. Then you will be able to return to the far side of the heavens. It is but a moment away."

"A moment and then an eternity."

"The moment is an ever-changing thing. It can not be held too. Truth fades and realities ebb, as day passes into night and the night again become the day. The realm of Erda is not the place where the essence of spirit dwells. That place is only known in the realms beyond Time's Door. Hold true to the moment and listen. The Secret Word is not passed in scripture. It is kept hid through letters and myth. Silence is the means by which the greater light turns the lesser wheels. The Law moves from the above to the below. Look past the Yellow Sun and you will hear his silent calling." and at her word, the light burst over the peak of the mountain.

She sat at his side as the twilight crept between the trees. Zelmisso was a gleaming beacon against the setting sun. The aroma of the damp forest mingled with the new warmth left by the sunny afternoon. Silently they waited while lavender skies deepened into gray.

"What will you do, Kiel?" she asked as the last rays faded under the mountain shadows.

"Inrih and Tamil plan to take all the survivors of Basilus upon their boat. They will find new lands and build new lives. They have asked me to come along. Dion wants me to teach him about the stars." he smiled, "He said it is only proper since I shall always have my eye set to them."

"I do not know if I can bear to say good-bye."

"Do not despair." he answered. Then he chuckled. It was real laugh. The first one she had heard in weeks. "Fancy me saying that. But the sun has risen over the world again. Time will not forget. In truth it never has. It never will. Come on now, Yurah. We will walk together yet another time. Nestor tells me they are preparing a feast."

When they arrived, they found the door to Odyn's hall filled with candlelight. The children were hauling baskets of bread and copper plates to the tables. Dion was playing his lute, matching every note of Theo's harp with a counterpoint while the tap of Macha cane kept time behind them. Sro and Istah leaned over a table with a small lamp. They were reading a map that Atyn had spread out before them. Odyn rested near the fire, smoking his pipe and drinking a tall cup of Rudra's wine. He stood up when he saw them enter.

"Hail Daughter of Raldabon!" he proclaimed, "Hail Kiel of Taygeth! We have been waiting for you." and at the wave of his hand the room was filled with children carrying platters of meat and fruit. Soon every plate was filled and the glasses set to the rim with a cool sweet wine. Odyn held up his glass and declared.

"The hand of Ildabyth has failed to claim her. The rains have stopped and a new world cries out to be remade. We have lost much to the dark but we have not lost all. We will rebuild. In starting anew much that has been made wrong will be made again by a better plan. The Sword of the Annyd bore the end of the storm. Join me in salute to the Starry Queen. She has given us the gift of another day." and he lifted the goblet to his lips and all drank with him.

They ate their meal, talking and laughing freely with one another. Yurah ate quietly, just as she had always done, listening to the conversation around her. Kiel said little, and spun his food idly over his plate. The time was coming soon for good-byes.

At length Odyn rose from his chair, "The night has fallen and day will follow. We will gather under the lovely Moon and say our farewells."

Standing under the brilliant night, the folk of Odyn's Hold gathered round. The Seer cast the protecting circle and the children heralded the rise of the moon with their silver trumpets.

Sro was at her right side and all the others stood to her left.

Yurah unhooked the Scabbard from her belt and handed in to her mother.

"The Sword remains here in the stone of Erda. It is the ancient talisman and this sheath is its haven. The time may arise when you have need of it."

"No child. The whispering Sensar was your father's gift. He intended it for the purpose that it did serve. The Sword of the Annyd will remain in the heart of Erda until such cycles are again to close. Things such as this are permanent and will not be undone. Take the scabbard home. When I return to Raldaban we will forge a new sword in the heart fires of Oiolosse's mountain. And do not fear. It is a promise I intend to keep."

"But you must have something I carry." Yurah sighed. "It is the giving that returns us to our true selves. You know this mother, you know it better than I."

Sro smiled then and said "Then lend me the magic mirror, child. Then I will be able to see you and your sisters. And even from here I will speak once more to your father."

Yurah laid the scrying mirror into Sro's fragile hand and their tears fell into its middle.

"There is so much more I need to say." she said

"And I will not be so far away that I can not hear it." Sro whispered over the reflection.

Yurah gave Istah the Fire Glass. "It will be helpful in healing of the new race of men."

"Aye, Lady. It will be helpful indeed." Istah answered softly, taking the crystal in hand. "I will always use it as I remember this day. Thank you." and the tall gray-eyed woman kissed the child upon the brow.

Lorya was given the Summoning Stone. "It is a precious thing," she whispered, "The forests of all the world shall be remade by its power." and the warrior bowed low in honor.

She turned then to Odyn and when she handed him the Book of Secrets he smiled so large she thought his face might break.

"So finally, you have run out of words old man." chuckled Macha when he did not speak. Odyn did not answer he could only shake his head and sigh.

"He means he is eternally grateful." grinned the old woman, taping her cane sharply against his boot. Yurah smiled and Rudra laughed aloud.

She turned to Kiel then offering him her silver flute but he put up his hand and refused the gift. "When Taygeth rises over the water and Riverman lingers near, play it for me then." he said, "Though it is far away but I will know the sound. It will be carried by orbs of morning that flow past the riverbed. That is where all things of the Old One live their lives. Find me there. I will be waiting and I will answer. I will not forget."

"I will find you there." she told him kissing him lightly on the brow as he placed the soft pouch over her shoulder.

"Listen now, I hear your sister's calling. Rempha has opened the Gates." Sro whispered as the light began to shine.

Kiel bent down, gently kissing her cheek he whispered, "I will be looking upward to the heavens. I will not forget."

"The Riverman is waiting Yurah." said Atyn. "Yotru has come to take you home."

The Riverman was waiting at the airs above. Stirring like the ocean tides, he was restless. Unsettled and dangerous he seemed but Yurah no longer feared him. She went to his side and turned to face the others. Atyn stood with her to the left and the Mqttro at her right. The Riverman lifted them and swiftly the ground became a speck beneath them. They reached the vista and they lingered, looking down into the Valley of the Little Kingdom.

"What fate will the years bring to Erda?" she asked the Malkian.

"The opportunity to begin once more."

"And what of Ildabyth?"

"He too will begin again, but the years will pass and the people of this world will have grown wiser."

"So the war will come again."

"It will come."

"And will the end be certain?"

"Only the turning of Rempha's Door is certain, child."

For long while they were silent, each entertaining the possibilities their destinies held.

"And do you know your fate, Atyn?"

"I will visit my brother. The light of the Bear is his duty now and afterward I will join this world again, to aid the Malkians in their labors."

"It is such a sad little realm." she said, "but I have come to love it deeply."

"As have we all," answered Atyn as the Malki's wings blazed brightly.

"It is time child." the Riverman said softly, "Open the Winds of Raldabon so we may fly home."

"I will return." she whispered to the life in the valley below "I will not forget you." and then Riverman joined with the Wind of Raldabon and together they flowed into the milky lights to make their way across the stars.

Legend holds that the Seventh Sister still visits the Isles of Urdar where the sun and shade collide. She is the ever faithful Light, and those who walk in the Valley of Erda bear witness to her as the centuries pass, and she brings the messages of hope from the Pleiades. The Sisters patiently wait for their lost kin to return to Raldabon with hearts sad and true. They wait for Erda to heal from the hurts Ildabyth had dealt her. From her hidden star, the Lost Pleiade ever whispers words of comfort, not only to her wandering companion but to all the wanderers that have found their way in the lower vales of the Little Kingdom.

www.ingramcontent.com/pod-product-compliance
Lightning Source LLC
Chambersburg PA
CBHW070219260626
47160CB00002B/597